A Land in

Shadow

Book 1 of:
The World She Silenced

Daniel Whitman

First paperback edition May 2019
Second paperback edition October 2025

Book cover design by ebooklaunch.com

ISBN 9798993447308 (paperback)

To David, Parker, Wells, Dudeck, Nick, and Brandon, the original party that made the adventure happen.

Contents

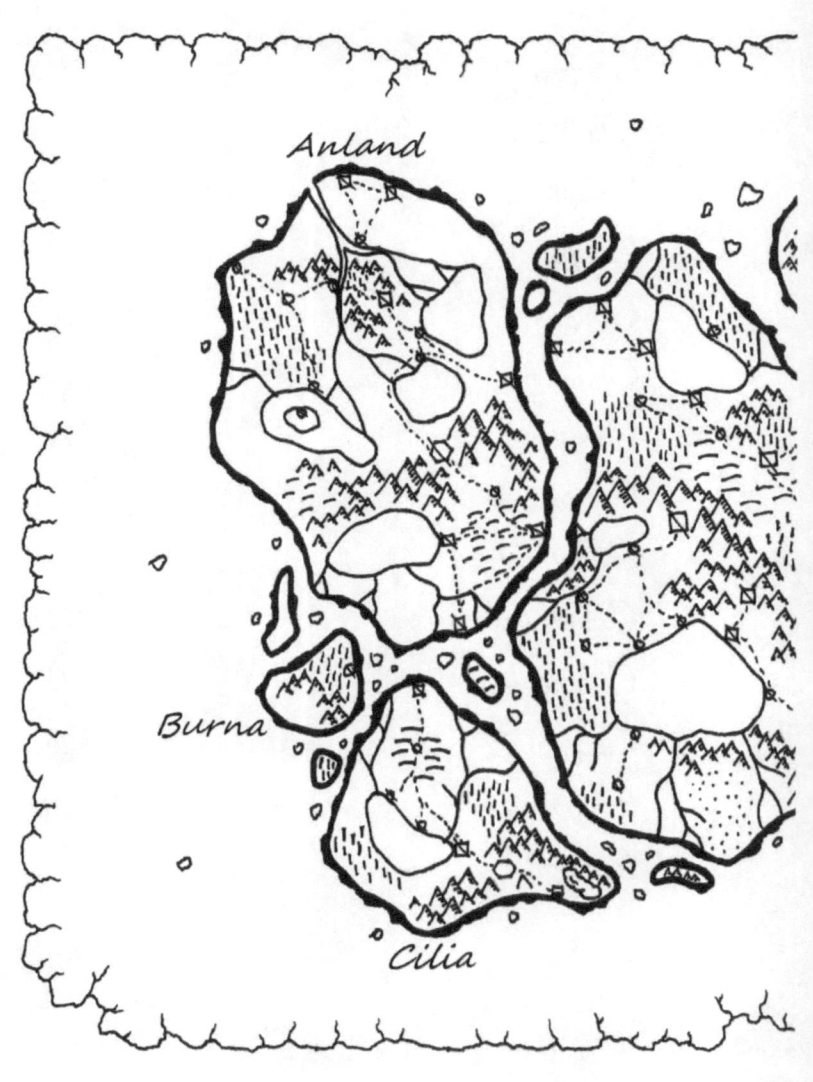

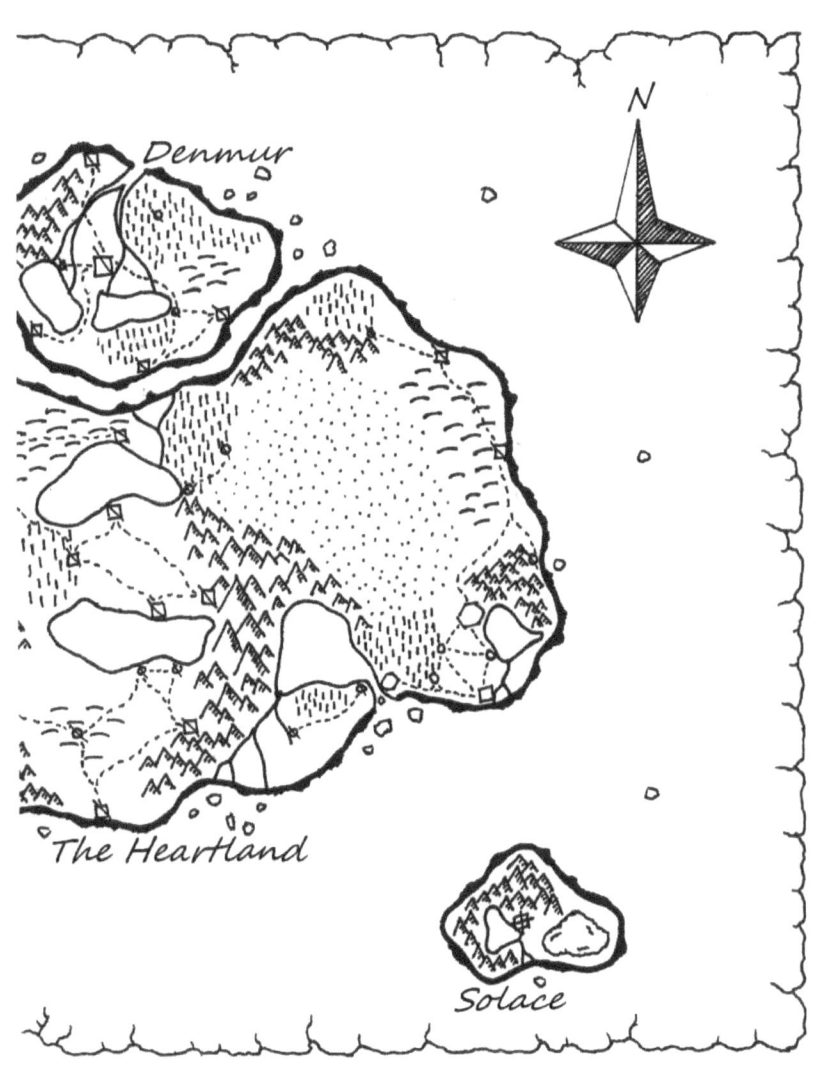

From the Sun and the Moon
To the sea of the stars

The one that was lost
To the depth of the scars

Shall descend from on high
To the truth of the lie

The one will be found
To the war of the night

From the past and the dark
To be the Beacon of Light

Prologue

The woman walked down the dimly lit castle corridor. The passageway was made of aged stone bricks with cracks running along their faces like veins. On the walls hung ancient tapestries of various colors depicting legends long forgotten. Flickering torches dotted the passage, their eerie light sending shadows dancing around the corridor. Ash blackened the aged stone around the torches, and cobwebs hung lifelessly from the worn ceiling. Along the stone floor lay a beautiful red carpet flowing down the length of the passage. Golden tassels adorned its edges, and marvelous swirling patterns ran along its length in a river of golden thread.

The woman hardly noticed; she had walked this passage before. She was an elegant woman of unparalleled beauty. Two, piercing emerald eyes shone from her soft face, and long, silky black hair cascaded over her shoulders in a marvelous braid. A long, gorgeous black skirt flowed out behind her, with splashes of orange and yellow flaring out at the ends of her skirt like flames in the folds of the cloth. A seductive slit ran up the side of the skirt, revealing a perfect, pale leg that seemed to shine in the flickering light. She wore a simple black top that revealed much of her slim, seductive form. Spectacular pauldrons of gold curved around her shoulders in the pattern of dragon scales, giving her an indomitable majesty, and a beautiful, golden diadem studded with glimmering green gems crowned her head. In her left hand she held an intricate sword of the most elegant design. Golden chains and emeralds ran along the length of the copper scabbard, and the hilt seemed to grow out of the blade like the trunk of a tree, creating a natural and comfortable grip to any who wielded it.

At the far end of the corridor was an aged wooden door banded with iron reinforcements. Upon reaching the door, the woman placed a hand against it and effortlessly pushed it inwards. Closing the door behind her, she entered the room, and scanned her shining eyes across the chamber, smiling. Everything was still as it should be.

The room was a small, plain stone chamber brightly illuminated by torches on three of the walls. The floor was made of plain wooden planks, all scuffed and worn with the passage of time. On the far side sat a large wooden desk covered in books and papers. Hunched over in a wooden chair sat a gorgeous woman, pondering the words of one of the texts.

The woman had fiery red hair that fell over her back in a wave of flame. She had an angular face and fierce, orange eyes. Her smooth, olive skin was marred only by a gruesome scar that cut across her left cheek and ran up to meet her eye. A luxurious red and gold dress flowed around her, quite out of place in the archaic room. Her wrists were clamped by large shackles, tethering her to the wall with long, iron chains. She looked up as the woman entered the room, her eyes shadowed by confusion.

"Ashyla," the fiery woman said hesitantly, a questioning look plastered over her face. "It makes no sense. Why would you do that? You saved them."

Ashyla smiled. She walked toward the desk, a glimmer of mischief shining in her eyes. "My dear Mariah," she replied, placing her hands upon the desk. "Did I? Did I truly save them? You should know more than anyone — not everything is always as it seems."

Mariah had no answer. She studied Ashyla in an attempt to read her motives, but with little success. Frustrated, Mariah turned back to the book, a scowl shadowing her face.

A harmonious laugh escaped Ashyla's lips, and she glanced down at the book. "Oh," she said, reaching for the tome. "What do we have here?" Her eyes locked onto Mariah, and she held the book out in front of her, a sly smile twisting her gentle face. "The History of the First Night. A truly heartbreaking tale, would you not say?"

A green fire lit in Ashyla's eyes, and the book began to morph and wilt in her hand. Two graceful wings erupted from the cover, and delicate legs sprouted from the bottom. Ashyla smiled. In her hand was a black butterfly. Its wings were two tapestries of shadow, and its legs needles of night. With a sudden flap of its wings, the butterfly shot into the air and disappeared into the flickering shadows.

Mariah narrowed her eyes at Ashyla, a flash of anger crossing her face. "Why are you here, to mock me?" she asked, her voice sharp like a razor.

"Why Mariah, how hurtful! When have I ever come just to mock you?" Ashyla laughed. "No, there is so much more to this that even you fail to realize. It is true that I saved them — your dear Beacon and his group of companions."

Mariah studied Ashyla quizzically. "But why? What would you have to gain from that?" she asked, standing up from the desk. "When I uttered the prophecy, I saw great hope in this desolate land of Shadow. I saw the coming of the Beacon who will bring about the end of this darkness you inflicted. I saw the Beacon emerge like a beam of fire. I saw the Shadow fall. I saw the Light return. Yet I thought it was always nothing but a dream. But now, since you saved them … You saved the Beacon. You saved the one destined to strike you down."

Ashyla laughed tauntingly and stepped back from the desk

with her hands raised in the air. "You and this precious little prophecy," she said, her voice growing softer. "Do you truly believe that destiny is fixed? Do you truly believe you saw the future?"

Mariah studied Ashyla, a wary look in her gaze. "I know what I saw."

Ashyla only smiled. "And who am I to doubt you," she teased, her eyes sparkling. "Now, as for the Beacon, it is quite simple, really, as to why I let him live. I like to think of myself as … generous. I cannot just sit idly by and watch innocent people die."

Mariah settled back, doubtful. "Generous. Is that so?" she said while shaking her head, a hard edge cutting into her words.

"Would you not agree?"

"And innocent people!? Do you know how many innocents were slaughtered because of you?" Mariah exploded, a furious flame in her gaze. "Countless! Don't pity me with your generosity."

"And what of the innocents that were slaughtered because of *you*?" Ashyla screeched, taking a threatening step forward. "You stood by and did *nothing*."

Mariah glared, and she opened her mouth, but Ashyla cut her off with a harsh slap. Immediately Ashyla's gaze grew soft, and she composed herself with a deep breath.

"And as for my generosity," Ashyla continued, "you are still alive, are you not?" Ashyla stroked the side of Mariah's face where she had just struck, like a mother coddling an infant. "My dear Mariah, I could never kill you. You will always have a safe place in my heart."

Disgusted, Mariah slapped Ashyla's hand away. "Is that what you told the others before you killed them?" She cast an accusing glare at Ashyla, her eyes two orange flames of fury. "Before you cast the Shadow across the land? There could have been peace, yet you were too corrupted by your vengeance! If …"

Ashyla's face turned hard, and she cut off Mariah with a ferocious glare. "Child …" She paused, and shook her head, her cool mask returning and a mischievous twinkle appearing in her eyes.

"Oh Mariah, always so feisty," Ashyla teased. "I do enjoy that about you. As for the Shadow, what is done is done; there is no changing the past. Not even I could reverse what happened. But" — Ashyla winked at Mariah — "perhaps your precious Beacon can."

Mariah sighed in exasperation. "And so, it brings me back to my question," she said, studying Ashyla. "Why? Why did you save them?"

Ashyla ran her braid through her hand, and she seemed to ponder for a moment. She began to pace the room, but then her lips curled into a sly smirk. After a long silence, she glanced up at Mariah. "Entertainment."

Mariah turned a questioning eye to Ashyla.

"Entertainment?" Unable to contain herself, Mariah burst out into a charming laugh. "Entertainment, you say? First generosity, and now this? Don't play me for a fool."

A defiant look in her eyes, Mariah began to strut over to Ashyla, her chains scraping against the ground behind her.

"My dear Ashyla," she taunted. "I haven't just sat idly by for these years. No, I've watched you, and if there's one thing I've learned, it's that you don't do things for mere entertainment."

Ashyla raised an eyebrow, a cheeky smirk appearing on her delicate face. "Oh, is that so?"

Mariah stopped, staring down at Ashyla like a lioness over its prey. "Never have you done something for such a meaningless reason as entertainment. There is always some end goal you have buried deep within your pointless lies."

Ashyla stepped back, holding her arms out to the side as a teasing laugh escaped her lips. "Then pray tell, my dear Mariah, what other reason would I have to save the Beacon, if not entertainment? Why else would I go through the trouble of saving the one destined to strike me down — if not to sit back and see how fate takes its course? Perhaps I have changed, or perhaps I am just having some fun."

Mariah paused; her momentum halted as surely as if it had

hit an iron wall. She stepped back; her face clouded by uncertainty.

"I don't know," she sighed, her eyes scanning the ground. "As I said before, none of it makes sense."

Ashyla laughed, and she turned away from Mariah, her skirt flowing about like the graceful wing of a butterfly. "What did I say?" she called over her shoulder. "This is most entertaining." A triumphant gleam in her eyes, Ashyla glanced down to her sword, its golden chains twinkling in the flickering torchlight.

"Wait."

Ashyla paused, and she glanced back at Mariah. "Yes?"

Mariah glanced up and smirked. "No, it's never been entertainment; you can't fool me with that. But it has been other pointless reasons such as revenge."

Ashyla's mischievous gaze turned into a glare.

Mariah studied at the marvelous sword in Ashyla's hand. "You can't defeat him," she said, her voice growing stronger with every word. "The seal they placed —"

"My dear Mariah …" Ashyla interrupted; her fist clenched about her sword.

"That seal binds you," Mariah continued triumphantly. "You cannot hope to break it; your true power was lost long ago. All you have now *is* lies."

Ashyla stepped back, her eyes shooting daggers of ice. "I would be very considerate of your next words."

Mariah's eyes gleamed with arrogance, and an insolent smile beamed on her face. "Or what? Are you going to turn me into a butterfly?"

"Child," Ashyla hissed, any hint of friendliness erased from her once gentle face.

"Ever since Sergarious and the heroes —" Mariah was cut off as Ashyla darted forward, her arm cocked behind her. With startling strength and speed, Ashyla thrust her palm into Mariah's chest with a sickly *thud*. Mariah let out a sharp cry of pain as she was sent careening backwards, crashing through the wooden desk and into the far stone wall, sending splinters of shattered wood soaring through the air. The chains attached to Mariah's wrists suddenly tightened, dragging her up and leaving her splayed tightly against the stone in a sacrificial crucifix.

Ashyla stalked forward to the suspended woman as a wolf would to a sheep, a merciless inferno burning in her relentless gaze.

"I am not the only one who is bound, child," she spat at Mariah, a furious look twisting her face. Reaching down, Ashyla unsheathed her sword and placed the razor edge against Mariah's neck. "You think you know the workings of the world. Hah! You claim to even know the workings of me! I can assure you that you do not."

Without as much as a blink, Ashyla moved her sword away from Mariah's neck, then deliberately jabbed the sword into the stone by Mariah's head. It pierced through the stone as if the wall wasn't even there. It didn't even make a sound. Mariah paled, and she glanced sideways at the sword, fear plastered across her soft face.

A venomous smile twisting her lips, Ashyla reached up and grabbed Mariah's face, pulling it down and locking her with an icy glare. "Remember, child, before me you are nothing. Yes, I am bound, thanks to your miserable pets, yet still here you are, cowering before me."

"Only because of your corrupted lackeys," Mariah spat.

Ashyla studied Mariah for a moment, before shaking her head. Slowly, she removed her sword from the wall and re-sheathed it by her side. A vile, mocking laugh escaped her lips, and she ran her thumb across Mariah's scar. "What a shame, to mar such a beautiful face." Ashyla moved her thumb up along the gruesome scar and placed it atop Mariah's eye.

Mariah tried to struggle free, but she was frozen in place, locked by the infernal chains in the wall. "No," she whimpered in a desperate attempt to reason with insane warden in front of her.

Ashyla steadily pressed with her thumb, threatening to

gouge out Mariah's eye. "I would hate to scar it even more ..." she whispered menacingly, continuing to apply ever more pressure. Mariah tried to tear herself away, but she was trapped. She felt the pressure, felt her eye swelling inside her skull, threatening to burst. A silent scream escaped Mariah's lips, and tears began to stream from her eyes.

With a final, menacing laugh, Ashyla released Mariah. Ashyla took a step back, her visage returning to the calm, collected expression from before with all signs of mania disappearing.

"You see, my dear Mariah, it is quite simple," she said softly. "I do not enjoy having to do this, especially not to someone as wonderful as you. As I said, you will always have a safe place in my heart." Ashyla shot her a beaming smile and turned to exit the chamber.

Trembling, Mariah raised her head, and watched Ashyla gracefully strode away, silent.

Suddenly, Ashyla stopped, and she turned back to Mariah. "Oh, I almost forgot."

She raised her hand, and a black butterfly flew out of the flickering shadows and landed upon her palm. With a satisfied smile, Ashyla closed her hand upon the butterfly, and when she reopened it, a large iron key rested on her palm. Striding over to Mariah, Ashyla placed the key into the lock on Mariah's shackles, and with a twist, the binding restraints fell loose. As soon as they landed on the floor, they vanished into dust.

Mariah collapsed, landing heavily on her hands and knees. She glanced up, a look of bewilderment apparent on her face.

"What? You freed me? How is this possible?" she asked, perplexed. "Why?"

Ashyla smiled, and she glanced at the iron key in her hand. Her eyes gleamed, and the key morphed back into an inky butterfly, which flew away into the surrounding shadows.

"Did I?"

Laughing, Ashyla strode away from Mariah, her elegant

braid bobbing behind her. "There is nothing to fear anymore. Do not let her shackles close upon you."

Mariah frowned, and she held out her hand. Her orange eyes sparkled, and suddenly a bright flame appeared in her hand, basking the area in a warm glow. Mariah smiled, reveling in the ecstasy of her freedom. After years of being suppressed by her own fear, her power could once again flow rampant throughout her. Closing her hand, she extinguished the flame and glanced back up at Ashyla. "But why? First you save the Beacon, and now me?"

Ashyla turned around, laughing. "Always 'why', 'why', 'why'. My dear Mariah, did we not just discuss this? I am most generous."

Mariah's expression shadowed, and she reached up to massage her left eye. "I would hardly say generous ..."

"No?" Ashyla replied, seemingly taken aback. "Hm, perhaps not. I apologize, I ..." Her voice trailed off, and then she let out a gentle laugh. "Now stand, that is enough groveling on the floor."

Mariah stood up reluctantly, brushing off the dust from her clothes. She stretched her wrists, flexing muscles long trapped in the unforgiving clutches of iron. Warily, she looked at Ashyla. "What are you trying to do? You released me; I can strike you down."

Ashyla smiled. "You are always free to try. But, as much as I would love a little dance, remember, I cannot stop the Shadow. But ..." A mischievous gleam shot across Ashyla's eyes, and she brushed her braid through her hand. "There are others who would like to see you."

Mariah studied Ashyla for a moment, torn. Slowly, she shook her head. "I don't understand," she mumbled.

"You do not have to."

Mariah locked her gaze on Ashyla. "This isn't some deception?" she asked, doubtful.

Ashyla shook her head, feigning hurt in her expression.

"Still, you do not trust me? Go, while the haunting is gone.

Go to the Flame or go to the Beacon; they are quite lost without you. Guide them, show them the way, for they will soon be overwhelmed in this wretched land of Shadow."

Mariah hesitated, still unsure. She flexed her fingers, and with sudden grandeur, billowing flames burst to life in her hands. Turning, she gave one last, cautious glance at Ashyla.

Ashyla smiled. "Go to them. Go to your prophesied Beacon."

Nodding, Mariah gestured towards the ceiling. A column of fire shot up from the ground, enveloping her in a glorious dance of flames. The blaze shot out, basking the area in warmth and light. Then, as quickly as they came, they were gone. As the flames cleared up, the room stood empty, with no trace of Mariah.

Ashyla laughed. Turning, she walked over to what remained of the wooden desk. A book was sitting in the wreckage. Glancing down, Ashyla read the title and smiled. A History of the First Night.

Letting out a sigh, Ashyla sat down in the wooden chair, crossing her legs and brushing her hand across her elegant braid. She held out her sword in front of her, studying it, and gazing across the golden chains and shimmering emeralds.

Mariah was always the feisty one. But soon —

Ashyla's thoughts were interrupted by a knocking on the door. "Ah, you have finally arrived," she said, still studying her sword. "Please, come in. Make yourself comfortable."

The door opened, and a tall woman strode into the room. Long, flowing black hair fell over the left side of her head. A delicate face with smooth, pale skin created a sharp yet alluring contrast. Her eyes shone like sapphires and her lips were a rosy embrace. She wore a long, black cloak accented by scarlet coloring at the edges, and high, silver boots that covered much of her legs, yet still revealed the tops of her thighs. Sheathed at her side was a black longsword crafted with a dazzling hilt of silver. Two gems sparkled out from the crossguard like a pair of watchful eyes.

Entering the room, the woman looked around in surprise.

The wooden desk lay shattered against the wall and Ashyla now sat coyly in the wooden chair. Mariah was gone.

"She is free," she said slowly, still studying the room. Then she narrowed her eyes and pinned Ashyla with a surprised glare. "Calitha let you release her?" she asked, her voice growing stronger.

"My dear Saber, ever the observant one," Ashyla teased, standing up from the chair. "Calitha did not permit anything, I merely showed Mariah that there is nothing to be afraid of."

"But why?" Saber blurted, a hard edge in her voice. "Why keep her trapped for ten long years only to 'show her' that on a whim?"

Ashyla smiled, ignoring the question. "Worry not about Mariah," she said. "She is well under control. As for you, I did not call you here to talk about this. No, there is another matter we must discuss."

Saber narrowed her eyes in annoyance, and entered the room, closing the door behind her. "I'm listening."

Ashyla strode over to Saber. "Of course, you know of the prophecy."

"Obviously."

"As told in the prophecy, a Beacon is said to come forth and save Ansalon from the Shadow," Ashyla continued, ignoring Saber's reply. "Well, as it is — and skipping a few minor details — after many long years of searching, the Beacon has finally been found."

Saber looked up in surprise, but Ashyla continued before she could say anything. "Yes, yes. In a small village in the southeast of the Heartland, a new Beacon appeared. Only this time, it truly *was* him. And so, the Mistresses dispatched a legion to crush the Beacon and end all hope for the Light. But of course, I could not let such a fine opportunity pass through my fingers. So, naturally, I ventured out to the village and saved the Beacon —"

"Wait, you what?" Saber cried out, anger twisting her gentle face. Her eyes became two piercing flames of blue, and she locked

Ashyla with a fiery glare.

Ashyla shot Saber with a sly smile. "I am certain I did not stutter. I saved him," she said, mischief glimmering in her eyes. "For how could I let the mighty Beacon fall to the Shadow? That would be most tragic."

Saber grunted in annoyance, and began to pace back and forth, her black cloak flowing out behind her. "Why would you do something so reckless?" Saber fumed. "Just when we were about to claim victory, just when any hope of the Light returning was about to be crushed, you *saved* him? Why? What the fuck were you thinking?"

"My dear Saber," Ashyla said, laughing. "I am not asking you to understand. I am asking you to listen."

Saber stopped pacing, and she turned to Ashyla, fury twisting her face into a scowl. "Why?" she spat. "This isn't why I spent ten years behind the Flame. This isn't why I spent ten years deceiving and seducing to gain a foothold. I joined you to watch them squirm under my power." Saber paused for a moment; her fists clenched at her side. "And yet, here we are now, siding with those wretches."

"Are you not the talkative one today?" Ashyla said coolly, striding up to Saber. Reaching up, Ashyla brushed Saber's hair away from her face. "Listen to me."

At Ashyla's touch, Saber tensed, her eyes burning in a furious glare, but she didn't pull away.

Smiling, Ashyla turned away from Saber, satisfied she would listen. "I have a task for you. Go to Anland, there you will find the Beacon and his companions. Contact the Mistresses."

Saber snorted.

Ashyla paused, and she cast a mischievous wink at Saber. "Just make sure that the hordes of brainless undead do not devour all my hard work and effort. Is that understood?"

Saber stood silent. She studied Ashyla for a long moment, trying to grasp some reasoning, to no avail. Slowly, Saber shook her head. "Siding with those wretches … Why?" she mumbled to herself. Then she fixed Ashyla with a defiant gaze.

Ashyla sighed, a bored expression on her face. She ran her hand through her braid. She had heard enough of that infuriating question for one day.

"Shall I pretend to be nice and say please so that you stop being a child about it?"

"You want me to protect them, *'please'*?" Saber said, spitting at Ashyla's feet. "Why? Why do I even listen to you? I know you have no power."

"It seems that everyone is trying to test me today," Ashyla said softly, a dangerous undertone in her voice. Reaching out, she grabbed the back of Saber's head, pulling her close. Whispering now, she leaned. "I will always have power. Remember that child. As I told you, go find that sister of yours. Or would you like to share her fate?" Ashyla asked, her lips brushing against Saber's ear and sending a shiver running down the woman's body. "That would be most … unpleasant for you. I, however, would rather enjoy it."

Saber's face paled, and she tried to pull away, but the Goddess's grasp bound her in place. Suddenly, a shadowy butterfly flapped into view, fluttering just before Saber's face. The two black wings were endless curtains of darkness, drawing the victim into their murky abysses. As Saber watched, the butterfly's head morphed into a long needle, its razor-sharp point shining in the flickering light. With a sudden flap of its wings, the butterfly lunged at Saber, its needle aimed right at her eye.

Saber screamed and fell back, stumbling in her panic, and landing hard on the floor. Gasping for breath, she looked up at Ashyla standing above her, the calm and collected expression having returned to the Goddess's face. There was no black butterfly, no sharp needle. There was only Ashyla.

Ashyla smiled. "My dear Saber, what seems to be the matter?" she taunted. She held out her hand to help Saber to her feet, but after a moment of consideration, pulled it back.

Saber studied Ashyla; her arrogance humbled at the mention of her sister. Regaining her composure, Saber rose to her feet and brushed the dust from her flowing coat. She tried to say something, but another black butterfly appeared just behind Ashyla's head before vanishing just as quickly as it arrived. Saber glared.

Ashyla laughed.

With an irritated grunt, Saber quickly turned around. Gathering her cloak and her wits about her, she stormed out of the chamber, her high boots clicking on the stone floor.

Smiling, Ashyla sat back in the chair, and once again raised her sword up before her eyes.

Yes, the Beacon — such a pointless title. It was so kind of them to finally return. Now, with Mariah by their side, that miserable wretch will have no choice but to reveal himself. Of course, Saber will be there too, protecting them from the Shadow while they performed their little hunt. She may be ever the fighter, but she knew her place. And, if not, well …

Shaking her head, Ashyla stood up from the chair and gave one final glance at the empty room.

Soon, once that deplorable killer emerged, once she found the demon hiding in the weeds, the damage that was caused would finally be repaired.

Giving one last glance at her sword, Ashyla brushed her hand over her beautiful braid before gracefully approaching the aged door. Without looking back, she exited the room, closing the door gently behind her. Silent, she walked down the decrepit corridor and into the darkness.

That damage would finally be repaired. What was done would finally be undone. The seal would be broken. Her children … they would finally have their peace.

She would have her retribution.

Chapter 1

Ro looked around at the dark, gloomy prison, his keen eyes having little difficulty seeing in the dim light. It was always the same, every day.

He was a draconian, a dragonborn, of sorts. Shining, gray scales covered his muscular frame like a mail of steel. His silver eyes watched the world with a knowing wisdom — at least he thought it was a "knowing wisdom". He kept his head high, his shoulders proud, and vowed to never let the dreary world drive him to the ground.

The surrounding prison was nothing more than a small, plain stone building with a handful of cages arranged around the area. Torches dotted the walls, faintly illuminating the surrounding area. Years of weathering had worn down the building, and spiders and rats ran rampant around the place. Cobwebs and dust blanketed the area, and a sickly odor hung like an unwelcome guest. The cells were formed from thick iron bars forged together in an impenetrable cage, but long years of neglect had allowed rust to grow and weaken the metal. Each of the prisoners' ankles were clamped tight by a pair of magical, iron shackles, enchanted to prevent the prisoners from casting any spells and escaping. None knew where the shackles had come from, or how the prison had come by such powerful relics. It was as if the shackles were placed there through the will of the heavens. Try as the prisoners might, there was no escaping the binding enchantments.

Ro was not the only one trapped in the cramped, unpleasant dungeon. There were five others imprisoned alongside him. There were two gnomes, SmibSmob and Nalgene, who claimed to be brothers of some sort. SmibSmob was a thin, frail gnome with shining blue eyes. He was warm, and seemed comfortable in the shadows, as if he were a part of their wispy darkness. Nalgene was an unusually robust gnome who insisted on interjecting in the happenings of the others. His blue eyes matched his brothers, but their similarities ended there. While SmibSmob was reserved, Nalgene was arrogant and stubborn, only listening to what his brother had to say. Ro thought Nalgene was surely a dwarf, but the gnome claimed otherwise.

There was also Andromeda, a tantalizing feline woman with immense strength in her delicate and agile frame. She clung to the shadows of her cell, and at times it was difficult for even Ro's sharp eyes to spot her. Whenever Ro looked upon her, his silver stare was matched by her fierce gaze, and he felt a sense that he was just a mouse for her to play with.

Then there was Fasto, a dim-witted orc who seemed to ponder a lot about cracks in the floor and rattle on about how he longed for the touch of the forest. Two dull, red eyes shone above his jutting jaw. Often, in the dead of night, he could be found staring blankly at the others, his eyes glazed over with thought — or perhaps without thought.

Finally, there was Margaret, an attractive female orc with tangled shoulder-length hair. She seemed apathetic about her situation, choosing to remain absorbed in her own dark thoughts. She had a curious right arm, bulky and black, as if some vile demon had possessed it long ago. Whenever it was mentioned, she seemed to retreat away and sit shivering in the corner of her cage, haunted by its unsettling presence.

It was strange how they were all thrown into the ghastly prison at the same time those short two years ago. Not only that, but none of them seem to remember the reason why they were even there, or what happened before. It is as if the memories of those moments were torn from their minds —

Ro's thoughts were interrupted by the soft voice of SmibSmob.

"I reckon it has to be past noon," the gnome said. "Where is that guard? He's not usually late."

"Indeed," Ro agreed. The guard had always brought their food promptly at noon, and the fact that he was late unsettled Ro. Something was wrong. The thought persisted at the back of his mind, casting a hint of doubt into his voice. "I'm sure he'll be here any moment."

"I hope," SmibSmob replied. "Our meager breakfast didn't do much for me. I don't mean to be the obvious one, but our meals have been shrinking as of late." It was true, their meals had been losing their wholesomeness. Cooked strips of meat had been reduced to bland soup, and portions of vegetables had been replaced by stale bread. "What I would do to escape this dreary prison —"

"Ah, quit yer whinin', me brother," Nalgene snorted, obviously irritated by the fellow gnome. "Ye ain't gonna be escapin' anytime soon, so there's no use in cryin' about it. We all be hungry here, and some o' us more than others."

Margaret let out a quiet laugh from her cage. "Oh, you silly gnomes," she teased. "You think *you're* hungry. What about me? I'm much bigger than you."

Andromeda chuckled in agreement, her eyes shining out from her cage like two apparitions. She licked her lips, and turned her gaze to the door, eagerly awaiting her next meal.

"Eh, what do ye be tryin' to say, ye damn orc?" Nalgene

fired back at Margaret. "It takes a lot o' energy to power these fine noggins. Why do ye think that dolt Fasto don't be needin' any food?"

Margaret laughed, and she shot Nalgene a playful wink. "'Fine' is not the word I would use."

Ro let out an amused sigh and turned away from the others. It was always the same, every day. It was amusing how the few years together brought them so close — at least Ro felt that they had.

Suddenly, he heard the rattling of keys, and the door to the prison creaked open, sending a ray of blinding light into the room. Eager to be fed, the companions turned their gazes onto the door, their quarreling silenced by the promise of food.

The guard entered the room, bearing a food tray. He was a good fellow, a stout man with short, shaggy hair and a rough beard. He looked around, letting his eyes adjust to the dimly lit building. After a quick scan confirming that all the prisoners were still present, he traveled around and doled out their portions. Satisfied that everything was still as it should be, he exited the prison, locking the door behind him.

Ro looked down at the food that was placed in his cell. It was a small bowl of soup, or what he assumed was soup. Chunks of white and yellow bobbed around the brown liquid. After a long, uncertain stare, he gave the soup a quick taste. A bland mixture of broth and strange chunks washed over his tongue. He nearly choked on it. It wasn't the worst thing he'd had in the prison, and it beat stale bread. Even so, he'd prefer a good strip of meat. Or some honey-glazed ham.

But his complaints were silenced by the clawing hunger in his stomach. He glanced around and, seeing most of the others seemingly enjoying the soup, he turned back to his own meal. Giving one last look at the brown liquid, he quickly downed it in one gulp, emptying the bowl.

"Agh, tastes like a dwarf's hairy arse," Nalgene groaned, letting out a vile belch. "Yer right, me brother, these meals are bloody awful. If I be havin' to eat one more piece o' stale bread or drink one more bowl o' damn soup, this prison won't be hearin' the end o' it. Bloody awful."

Ro gave a silent chuckle. "Pray, my good friend. It wasn't *that* bad."

"Ah, shut it ye damn dragon," Nalgene fumed. "Ye always be tryin' to find the good in this damn place, but let me tell ye, there ain't be no good in that awful soup."

"For once I have to agree with the annoying gnome," Margaret chimed in. She stood in her cage, pacing back and forth like a ravenous wolf, her eyes gleaming with hunger. "This food is hardly what I'd call edible."

All around the other companions nodded in agreement, except for Fasto, who was frantically searching the floor for something. Ro studied the others, his draconian eyes having little trouble seeing them in the gloomy light. He shook his head slowly, a faint smile on his face.

Always the same, every day.

Clearing his throat, SmibSmob looked up at his brother, a look of excitement beaming on his face. "You know brother, I reckon if we were able to get these magical shackles off, you'd be able to fix this food."

"Bloody hell, by what, waterin' the damn thing?" Nalgene snorted at SmibSmob. "Sometimes I be thinkin' that ye got a mighty fine noggin on yer head, but other times, this be all that comes out o' it."

SmibSmob stammered for a moment, at a loss. An injured expression darkened his face, and his usual bright attitude crumbled away.

"As if you should be the one talking about 'fine noggins,'" Margaret jabbed at Nalgene, an irritated scowl twisting her face. "Did we not just discuss this?" Nalgene's face turned red, and he turned to the orc, an insult ready on his sharp tongue.

Ro shook his head, blocking out the rest of his friends' banter. This was their usual routine: bickering and laughing. Still, what could the gnome mean by watering it?

He could only guess.

Suddenly, Ro heard a high-pitched squeal from the other end of the room. Whipping his head around, he saw Fasto gripping a plump rat tightly in his hand.

"Now friend, drink soup," Fasto said while dunking the struggling rat into his soup, sending the brown broth splashing all over the cold cell floor. "Fasto want to help friend. Now drink, be full."

"Aye now, ye bloody dolt, what in the bloody hell are ye doin'?" Nalgene growled at the orc. He grumbled something else under his breath, but Ro could not catch the words. Shaking his head, Nalgene cleared his throat. "We've talked about this. The rats be plenty fine on their own without ye drowning them in soup."

Fasto looked up at the gruff gnome, his eyes wide with injury, and splashes of soup running down his face. "But they my friends. And Fasto help his friends," he whined, before continuing to shove the traumatized rat into his empty soup bowl.

"Ah, but it seems you've lost all your soup," SmibSmob said, disappointed. He shook his head and sat down on the hard ground. "Not that it was much of a loss."

"And how in the bloody hell did ye even catch that damn thing?" Nalgene grumbled. "Ye might as well be a brick, for all the talent ye got."

"But," Fasto whimpered, not quite able to understand the insult, "they my friends."

"Alright, leave the orc alone," Ro said, a hint of amusement clear in his voice. "Let the poor rat go, Fasto, and drink up whatever is left of your soup."

"Oh no, don't you dare let that rat go," Andromeda said, her soft voice flowing out from her cage like a siren's song. A murderous gleam shot across her eyes, and she licked her lips in hunger. "I'd much rather you toss it over to me so I can enjoy a decent meal."

Fasto let out a terrified shriek and fell back against his cage, unknowingly releasing the rat in his lapse of terror. "No! Fasto must protect Harry. Fasto must protect friend!"

"Bwahahahahaha!" Nalgene bawled. "Ye named the damn thing, now did ye? What in the bloody hell is wrong with ye, ye dolt? It's a bloody rat, not some —" Nalgene was interrupted by a thunderous explosion from outside, sending dust and debris cascading from the crumbling ceiling. Stumbling back in his cage, he let out a cry of alarm: "Agh, what in the bloody hell is goin' on?"

The companions stood in a stunned silence, anxiously listening for the source of the blast. Nothing. Ro glanced around at the others, and an urge to protect them rushed through his body. What was that?

He had no answer.

Another explosion rocked the building, sending the companions scrambling back in alarm. Shouts could be heard from outside, and the clash of weapons echoed through the stone walls. Suddenly, the guard burst through the door, blood dripping down the side of his face. His breath came in short gasps, and he let out strained grunts of pain. An arrow shaft protruded from his thigh, causing him to limp. Fumbling around in his pocket, he pulled out a large iron key. Stumbling towards Ro's cage, he rattled the key in the lock, his hands unsteady.

"Listen, I don't know what you did or why you are all trapped in here," he gasped, "but on my good will, and as a proud member of the Flame, I can't let any living perish to the Shadow. No matter how devious, or how vile a man is, I believe there is always a chance for redemption."

The lock clicked and the heavy iron door swung slowly outwards. The iron key fell out of his trembling, injured hands, but he seemed not to notice.

"This is your chance for that redemption. Free the others," he implored. "Join the Flame. We need your help out there. I know you don't see why you should help us, but as one of the living, please

— just please — help us defeat this endless Shadow."

Giving one last nod to Ro, the guard turned away. A gleam of fire lit in the man's eyes, and a smile curled on his lips. Raising his bloodied longsword in a final salute, he charged out the door, shouting, "For Ansalon! For the Flame burning bright! The Beacon shall come and bring back the Light!" The door closed behind him, leaving them alone in the dim prison.

Ro stood stunned and unsure what to make of the guard's valiant speech. As one of the living? Fight back against the Shadow? What was the man saying? And the Flame? The Beacon? He didn't understand, what could it all mean?

"Aye, ye damn dragon, quit yer gawkin' and get us out o' these bloody cages," Nalgene said, impatience seeping into his voice. "We ain't got all day, and I'd rather not be here for the next explosion, or this bloody Shadow thing."

Snapping out of his thoughts, Ro looked down at the large key lying on the dusty floor. Reaching down, he picked it up in his clawed hands and turned it in front of his eyes. Glancing back down, he studied the magical shackles binding his ankles.

Perhaps …

Reaching down, he fit the key into one of the locks on the shackles. Giving it a twist, the shackle popped open with a sharp *click*. Relieved, he hastily freed himself from the other. As the shackles fell to the floor, a surge of power bubbled up from deep within, overwhelming him after years of suppression. Energy crackled through him, filling every scale with exhilarating vitality. A mighty roar escaped his lips, and a bolt of lightning shot out of his mouth, crashing into the ceiling with a brilliant shower of sparks.

He was finally free! He felt so … alive, so —

His thoughts were interrupted by the shouting of his companions.

"Aye, ye damn dragon, ye be tryin' to bring the bloody ceiling down on our heads?" Nalgene cried in alarm, frantically trying to protect his head. "Just unlock these bloody cages, ye beardless dwarf, ye don't be needin' to kill us all in the process!"

Margaret chuckled softly to herself. "Yet again I actually agree with the annoying little gnome."

"Indeed," SmibSmob said, anxiously rubbing his hands together. His gaze seemed distant, however, as if his mind were lost elsewhere. "So, the key? I don't mean to be the obvious one, but I'd rather not be in this dreary place when whatever it is outside finds its way in."

"That's what I be sayin'!" Nalgene grunted, not noticing SmibSmob's hesitation. "Ye and yer fine noggin, me brother."

Shaking his head, Ro strode over to the cage that held Andromeda and slid the key into the lock.

"Alright, let's get you out of here," he said.

The lock clicked, and the cage door swung steadily outward. Reaching down, he fit the key into her shackles. With a twist, the shackles fell to the floor, freeing her from their silencing imprisonment. Andromeda's eyes gleamed with joy, and for a moment she seemed to fade into the darkness, vanishing even from Ro's watchful gaze.

"Mmmm, much appreciated," she purred as she exited the cage, brushing him with her tail as she passed. "Let's free the others, shall we?"

Shaking his head, Ro released the others from their cages and shackles. He freed SmibSmob next, who graciously thanked him with an exaggerated bow and a distant, "thanks." As the gnome passed by, Ro felt a sense of unease, and something darker, viler, emanating from the gnome. Shrugging, he brushed it aside. He was probably imagining things.

After SmibSmob, Ro released Fasto, who had completely forgotten about the rat. As the shackles fell, Fasto thanked Ro by giving him an awkward embrace and a much-too-wordy speech about how "Fasto grateful" and "Fasto must repay friend."

After managing to detach Fasto from himself, Ro then freed Margaret, who smiled and gave him a playful wink. As she passed, an icy chill washed over Ro, and an unearthly chill pierced into his flesh. Frost radiated from her demonic arm, as if some mysterious power had just been unleashed from within.

Finally, Ro released Nalgene. He was met by an infuriated gnome stamping his feet and shouting, "Is that how it is, ye damn dragon! Ye be freein' me last, eh?"

Chuckling, Ro unlocked the shackles.

As soon as Nalgene's shackles fell loose, the gnome called back his long-suppressed powers and conjured up a magical ball of water and lobbed it in Ro's face. A surge of frigid water crashed into Ro, pummeling the breath from his shocked body. Suddenly, he knew all too well what Nalgene had meant by "watering the food." Grumbling to himself, Nalgene trudged past Ro, leaving him stunned in the entrance of the cell.

Regaining his composure, Ro shook the water from his scales and fixed his gaze on Nalgene. The thoughts of his companions awakened powers rushed through his mind.

Just who *were* they?

Some long-abandoned memory itched at the back of his mind, as if he knew about their powers from long ago. But it shied away whenever he reached for it.

"Alright," Ro said, irritated. "Now that we're all free from our bonds, let's get out of this forsaken place."

"Mmmm, I like the sound of that," Andromeda purred, her tail twitching. "Let's make haste, I wouldn't want to be caught in the next explosion."

"Right," Margaret added. "No need to stay here any longer than needed."

Nodding, Ro started for the door, the key ready in his hand. This was it: their first real view of the outside world in two years. Or was it? Why couldn't he remember?

"Be ready," he said defensively. "There's still a battle raging outside." As he reached the door, he heard shouts coming from outside, and the sounds of scuffling just beyond the door.

Cautiously, he placed the key in the lock, preparing to open the worn portal. Behind him, the others watched with great interest, eager to escape the dreadful prison.

Suddenly, there was a great explosion at the door, sending Ro flying backward. He slammed into the far stone wall and fell to the cold floor in a daze. His vision blurry, he glanced up at the scene in front of him, barely able to make out the figures of his companions. Where the door once stood, a great hole of scorching flames took its place. A tremendous heat radiated out from the fire, basking the room in an unholy inferno. Squinting up at the flames, Ro could make out the shapes of humanoid figures rushing through the fiery wall, charging at his shocked companions. He blinked, and his vision regained a sense of clarity. Shambling corpses and vile skeletons flooded through the blazing gateway. Rotting flesh hung loosely about their decaying frames, and yellow bones protruded from their ashy skin at unnatural angles. Their wide maws hung open, displaying vicious fangs, and their hollow eyes shone thirsty for blood. Living blood.

The companions' blood.

Ro's eyes opened in shock. Undead? How was that possible?

Charging through the flames, the undead horde surged into the room like a great wave of death. Shaking his head, Ro rose to his feet, and a sense of fear settled over him.

It couldn't be.

Hazily, he looked back over at his companions, locked in mortal combat with the legion of undead. Immediately his clarity returned. Adrenaline coursed through his veins, and a boiling rage filled his mind. His draconian power unleashed inside of him, crashing through him with a terrifying fury. A roar escaped his lips, and a blinding bolt of lightning shot out of his mouth at the nearest skeleton, blasting it into shards of chard bone.

Letting out another terrifying roar, Ro charged into the fray. He rushed over to Fasto, who was struggling against a zombie. Ro tore the zombie away and slammed it into the hard floor. His eyes flared, and he crushed the zombie's head underfoot with a sickening *crunch.*

Whirling around, he faced down the rest of the undead. Snarling, he dashed to-and-fro, tearing zombies apart with his talons and blasting skeletons away with devastating bolts of lightning. His eyes shot across the room, observing how his companions were faring. Andromeda was fending off a pair of zombies with her razor claws and crushing maw. SmibSmob and Nalgene fought side-by-side, casting devastating spells of water and shadow, decimating the hordes of undead. Margaret rushed around, crushing skeletons with devastating punches from her demonic arm.

Suddenly, the raging wall of flame subsided, leaving a smoldering hole in the side of the building. Dark, cloaked figures entered the prison, studying at the surrounding carnage.

Not hesitating to see who the cloaked figures were, Ro leaped at the nearest one, tearing at it with his talons. His claws cut through flesh, letting out a mist of blood. The figure fell back, crying out in pain. Moving in to land the finishing blow, Ro felt a searing stabbing pain in his back. His vision wavered, and he fell to his knees.

No, not like this. He couldn't die like this.

He looked back and saw one of the cloaked figures standing over him, a gleam of triumph in its eyes. The damned bastard had gotten him with a dagger.

Suddenly, Andromeda appeared, leaping at the figure looming over Ro. With a furious roar, she tore the cloaked figure off his back and crashed onto the floor in a mess of blood and gore.

Struggling to his feet, Ro looked around, his sense of fury redoubled. Whirling around, he charged at the nearest cloaked figure, ripping at it with his claws. A bolt of lightning shot from his mouth, blasting the figure in the face, and sending it soaring backwards, dead. He bellowed an enraged roar and let the lust of battle overcome him, enveloping him in its fiery embrace.

Ro felt himself fall away, relying purely on battle instincts to keep him alive. He lost track of how many he tore with his vicious claws, or how many he blasted away with his bolts of lightning. Sometime during the fight, he found himself reunited with Fasto, who had retrieved a flanged mace from one of the cloaked cultists. Together they pushed back against the horde of enemies. At one-point Andromeda rushed in front of him, only disappear again into the shadows, a bloody cultist locked in her jaw. Another time he spotted Margaret, the haze of bloodlust twisting her face, and an inner flame of rage gleaming in her eyes. She was straddled on top of a zombie, beating its head into a pulp, sending pieces of gore flying in all directions.

But the horde just kept advancing. No matter how many undead the companions slaughtered, or how many cultists they struck down, there was always another to take its place. Ro's fury had already worn off, replaced by a feeling of exhaustion that weighed on his weary muscles. Wounds covered his body, leaving him battered and sore all over. His back pulsed like a radiating drum, and a fiery pain had settled in, dulling his senses. He glanced over at Fasto, who was no better off. The orc was panting heavily, and blood oozed from slashes and bruises all over.

They needed to get out of there.

Turning, he saw the others, all but SmibSmob battered and bloodied. Andromeda looked over at him, her dark fur matted with black blood. She looked like a feral beast from a nightmare. She nodded, and then quickly turned around and ripped apart another zombie, splattering more blood across her delicate form, before disappearing into the surrounding shadows.

One last, thunderous roar bursting from his maw, Ro leaped back into the fray in one final, desperate stand against the endless legions of undead. But before he could strike down another decaying foe, an icy chill crashed over him, and his very life-force seemed to be trying to escape his very body. His mind dazed, he glanced up and was immediately filled with a sense of pure terror.

A massive, hulking figure stood menacingly in the gaping hole in the wall. The gargantuan being was donned from head to toe in fearsome black plate mail adorned with skulls and markings of death. Piercing spikes jutted out from the armor, and a thick, black cape flowed out behind it like a waterfall of shadow. In its hand, the creature held a mighty greatsword of pure black, an icy frost emanating from its razor edge. A shadowy aura seemed to swirl around the diabolical being, casting the place in a void of darkness. But it was the eyes that held Ro's attention. Two chasms of icy blue flames, drawing his soul into their murky depth, and leaving him with a sense of inescapable terror.

The being's eyes captivated Ro, gripping him like an icy vice, and paralyzing him in place. He couldn't move.

He tried to resist, but his horror overwhelmed him. Petrified, he watched as the dreadknight slowly stalked towards the gnome brothers. He tried to call out, but his voice stuck in his throat. Panicking, the two gnomes cast everything they had at it. Nalgene rained down torrents of huge water bolts, and SmibSmob cast swirling beams of shadow and death. The towering creature hardly noticed. The dreadknight pushed on, its deliberate march of doom not the least hindered by the mighty spells. The gnomes' eyes filled with terror, and they fell back, meekly attempting to retreat. The dreadknight raised its massive, black blade, and with a sudden, frosty slash, cut them both down.

Ro watched on, unable to act. His senses blurred in anguish, and he let out a cry of despair. How could this be happening? How? It couldn't be real!

He heard a scream and saw Margaret charge the fearsome being, a storm of ice swirling around her demonic arm. With a cry of fury, she slammed her fist into the dreadknight, unleashing all her power with the devastating blow. The massive dreadknight staggered backward, but only a step. Then, with surprising speed, the creature shot forward and grabbed Margaret by the throat, lifting her effortlessly into the air. She cried out in agony, struggling to free herself from the iron grip. With a flick of its wrist, the dreadknight launched Margaret, sending her crashing into the far wall with a shriek of pain. Limply, she fell to the hard floor, motionless.

Ro let out a cry, his mind numb. No, no, no, no! It couldn't be happening! It couldn't be real!

Turning, the dreadknight strode toward him and Fasto. Ro tried to retreat, but his mind was too overcome with terror for him to move. Tears started streaming down his face. Beside him, Fasto stood up, his face a mask of courage. The orc was just too damn dim-witted to realize what he was up against. Ro wished the fool would run.

Fasto's mouth snarled with rage, and he rushed the mighty dreadknight, swinging his bloody mace out in front of him. The dreadknight's black greatsword flashed, and Fasto fell to the ground, an icy frost forming over a fatal slash across his chest.

"NOOOO!" Ro cried as he fell backward, sobbing uncontrollably. He couldn't save them — any of them. He let them down. He failed.

Barely conscious of his surroundings, he felt a crushing hand grip his throat. The image of the dreadknight's icy blue eyes filled his mind, and suddenly he was soaring through the air. With an anguished cry of pain, he crashed into one of the cells, bending the thick, iron bars in the impact. A sharp pain shot up his spine like a blazing dagger, and his legs became numb.

He failed them all.

He tumbled to the ground; tears streaming down his face.

A streak of black darted from the shadows, and Andromeda leaped at the fiendish dreadknight, her fangs bared for a deadly strike. She landed on the black pauldron of the vile creature, biting down at the dreadknight's neck and tearing at its armor with her razor claws. It hardly noticed. With terrifying power, the dreadknight reached up and tore Andromeda off, throwing her down to the unforgiving ground with a sickening *crack* of bones. She let out a wail and rolled on the ground in agony. The dreadknight's eyes flared, and it raised its dark greatsword above its head, ready to deliver the final blow.

Suddenly, a great light filled Ro's vision, and he fell back, covering his eyes. The light dimmed, and he looked across the room, bewildered. Standing in front of the dreadknight, shining sword in hand, was a beautiful woman, the likes of whom he'd never seen. A long, black braid cascaded over her shoulders, and chains of gold and emeralds glimmered against her alluring figure. A long black skirt with orange streaks flowed out behind her like the graceful wing of a butterfly. An aura of brilliant light shone about her, overwhelming the dreadknight's dark shadow.

With a swing of her sword, the woman sent out a beam of purifying light, disintegrating all the cultists and undead in a dazzling flash of radiance. The woman turned to the hulking dreadknight, and she raised her sword up high to match the black greatsword of the abomination. The dreadknight shot forward, its shadowy sword cutting through the air. With a graceful tuck, the woman dodged the devastating slice, landing gently upon her feet. Without hesitation, she leaped up at the armored terror, swinging her radiant sword of light.

Two emerald eyes formed in Ro's mind, and a delicate yet commanding voice entered his thoughts, driving away all anguish and despair.

Now is not the time for you to die, my Beacon! Go forth and embrace your salvation, go forth and fulfill your destiny! Drive back the legions of Shadow, find the missing God, bring back the long-forgotten Light, and bring peace to the realm! Now go, save the lands of Ansalon!

Ro's mind muddled, and his body grew weary. He felt himself being lifted into the air, his pain ebbing away. Renewed energy coursed through his veins, as if he had just awoken from a long, restful slumber. As his eyes slid shut, the brilliant scene around him, from the prison to the dreadknight to the beautiful woman, seemed to break apart into millions of black butterflies.

A *Land in Shadow*

Was this what it was like to die?

Then came a blinding flash of light, and everything went black.

Chapter 2

The cold ground pressed into Andromeda's back. Her eyes were shut, and her mind raged against hazy thoughts. What happened?

She remembered the explosion that rocked the stone prison, and the frantic, bleeding soldier that rushed into the building, entrusting the iron key to Ro. She remembered the soldier shouting about the Flame and the Shadow before rushing outside into the onslaught. But what else? The solider had said something else. What was it?

The memories started flying back to her, as if she was unlocking new doors within her mind. The fiery explosion, the horde of undead, it all came soaring back. She remembered. The musical crunching of bones, the whistling slash of her claws. She remembered. The wall of flame dying down, the cloaked cultists rushing in, overwhelming Ro and the others. She remembered pouncing at the dark cultist, dragging him off Ro's back. The sweet taste of blood filling her mouth. She remembered.

But there was more …

Suddenly she saw the two icy-blue chasms of fiery death flicker to life within her mind. The memory came crashing over her like a surging tsunami, washing her away with a wave of terror. No! What was that ... monster? She couldn't fight it. She wasn't powerful enough.

The two dreadful blue eyes grew within her mind, filling her thoughts with a deathly chill.

She remembered.

Leaping at the hulking, armored figure. Futilely raking her claws across the impenetrable armor.

She remembered.

The searing agony of her arm as it shattered against the ground, and the imminent sense of oblivion as the black greatsword descended upon her.

A sharp cry of despair escaped Andromeda's lips, and the memories of the battle against the undead abomination haunted her thoughts. She clutched at her arm and felt ... nothing. No searing pain, no crippling anguish sending her into a daze. Nothing. It was as if some divine power had mended her broken body.

The final memory returned with a burst of clarity. The blinding flash of light. The dazzling woman standing among the shadows, a dark braid cascading down her back. She remembered the woman's shimmering sword, its razor edge shining with a bloodthirsty light. The woman dashing through the prison, mercilessly slaughtering any who stood before her. The woman casting a mighty ball of swirling energy at the dreadknight, before leaping upon the terror and slicing it apart with devastating slashes of her sword. She remembered two piercing eyes boring into her. The delicate voice filling her mind with a soothing determination. The shattering of the world into countless black butterflies.

She remembered.

The Light.

The Shadow.

The Beacon.

With a gasp of breath, Andromeda sat up, her eyes shooting open. Who was that woman? Such delicate beauty, yet such immense ... power.

Her eyes gleamed dangerously.

If only...

Shaking her head, she cleared herself of the thoughts and tried to gauge where she was.

Concentrating, Andromeda glanced around, taking in her surroundings. She was sitting inside the small clearing of a forest. However, the forest was dark and sinister, full of haunting shadows and unseen terrors of the night. Tall, black trees loomed all around her, their bare, twisting branches reaching up to claw the sky down. The sky was dim and shadowed, as if light had long ago forsaken its heavenly boughs. Her mind flashed back to the bloody soldier's speech about the Shadow. There was no doubt where she was.

The other companions lay scattered about the clearing — Andromeda's feline eyes had little trouble making out their dark forms laying in the shadows. As with Andromeda, all signs of injuries or battle had been erased from their bodies. Nalgene and SmibSmob no longer had the fatal gash across their chests. Margaret lay strewn across the ground peacefully, and Fasto lay beside her, an innocent smile spread wide across his face. Lastly, there was Ro, lost in a peaceful slumber. Andromeda sighed with relief.

But how did they get here?

Andromeda's thoughts were interrupted by a deep growling from the dark woods, the thunderous grumbling of awakened beast. Cautiously, she stood up, her ears twitching. The guttural growling came again, closer. Andromeda whirled about, her eyes scanning across the trees. Nothing. All was silent. Suddenly, a shadow flickered through the trees, and Andromeda rushed around to meet it, her eyes opened wide.

Shambling towards her from the edge of the clearing was the nightmarish, twisted form of a bear. Two beady, black eyes shone out from its marred face. Tendons and rotten tissue hung from its figure in vile strips, and chunks of flesh were missing throughout its body. With one final growl the undead bear charged toward Andromeda, its dead eyes shining for blood.

Horrified, Andromeda quickly retreated into the surrounding darkness, her body vanishing into the night, becoming nothing more than a passing shadow. Not even Ro's sharp eyes would be able to detect her. She slithered across the ground like a lethal specter of death, silent as she approached the horrendous creature. A gentle breeze blew against her back, but she thought nothing of it. She had her target. As Andromeda prepared to pounce, her target's head snapped over to her, its rotting nose twitching in the cool breeze. It could still smell. With a disturbing growl, it lunged at her.

Andromeda leaped back in alarm, barely dodging the razor-sharp claws of the beast.

Her stealth faded as she landed firmly on her hind legs, but with an explosion of strength, she sprung back at the target, her claws raking across its unholy face. Blood and pus spattered as Andromeda tore her target's eye out. The dreadful creature hardly noticed. Its claws flashed, and the bear's paw came crashing down upon Andromeda, who just managed to get her arm up and block the mighty attack. Her arm burned with pain, and she staggered back under the weight of the blow, her mind reeling with alarm. How was it still standing? She tore its face off!

Hissing with rage, Andromeda pounced back at the undead bear, her jaws wide in a vicious snarl. With a *thud*, she landed on the creature's back, sinking her fangs deep into the beast. Bitter, tainted blood filled her mouth, choking her. Whirling around, the bear swatted her off, sending her crashing to the ground like a rag doll. The air rushed from her lungs as she slammed into the cold earth, and she struggled for breath in a desperate attempt to regain her composure.

Andromeda tried to get up, but the creature loomed over her, its remaining eye gleaming. She had to fade away, had to get away from the beast, but before she could escape, it slammed a paw down upon her chest, pinning her in place with its claws. Hissing with fury, Andromeda raked the rotting underside of the bear with her claws, tearing its black flesh.

She might as well have been trying to pet the beast, for all the good it did.

Burning pain jabbed into her chest as the bear's claws dug deeper. Her vision grew blurry, and her thoughts turned back to the alluring woman and her tremendous power.

Suddenly, the bear was blasted off her, a jet of water sending it staggering back. Gasping for breath, Andromeda glanced up to see Nalgene standing in the clearing, his hard face boiling with rage.

"Aye now, ye beastie, I don't be knowin' what ye are but listen up ye no-good-beardless-dwarf," he growled. "Nobody hurts me pretty kitty like that, ye hear! Nobody!"

With a teasing smile Nalgene glanced down at Andromeda, and he tossed her what passed for a playful wink. "Ah I'm just pulling yer whiskers, ye damn cat. Ye ain't me pretty kitty, that'd be bloody messed up, don't ye think? Bwahahaha," he roared with laughter.

Andromeda could only stare. Maybe that slash did some damage to his head.

After an awkward moment of silence, Nalgene grunted and hurried over to help Andromeda back to her feet.

"Much appreciated," she said uneasily, standing up. "But take care, this … thing —"

She was interrupted by the bear's growling, and the thundering charge of the undead beast. Frantic, Andromeda tackled Nalgene to the ground, pulling him away from the slashing claws.

"Aye now, what do ye think yer doin'?" Nalgene cried, his eyes wide with alarm. He tried to say something else, but it was lost as he crashed to the ground.

Ignoring Nalgene, Andromeda leaped back up, tensing her

muscles and readying for a pounce.

This was her kill.

With a thrust of her legs, she darted to her target's side, raking her claws along its flank and sending blood shooting out in a dark fountain. Undeterred, the bear whirled about, its bulky arm already swinging for her delicate face.

An explosion of pain erupted as the rotting paw smashed into Andromeda's face, sending her careening back, blood trickling down her mouth. Tearing her claws into the ground to regain her balance, she managed to stay on her feet. Her head pounding, and her chest burning, Andromeda licked her lips, letting the sweet taste of her own blood fill her mouth. Growling, she crouched, readying her muscles for another pounce, and faded into the shadows.

Before she could pounce, a brilliant lightning bolt streaked across the clearing, slamming into the side of the undead bear with a shining shower of sparks. A second one followed, and the vile creature was sent skidding backwards. Then a third, a fourth, and a fifth bolt of lightning crashed into the dreadful beast. Unable to resist the brilliant barrage, the bear went soaring back, only to crash into one of the black trees. Letting out one final growl, the undead bear fell to the ground, limp.

Andromeda's eyes shot over and saw Ro standing unsteadily in the clearing, his eyes ablaze with horror and confusion.

"Ah, well at least someone else besides this damn cat is up, eh?" Nalgene said, as he rose from the ground. "I was hoping for me brother, but ye'll do just fine. Speaking of which, where is the damn cat? Probably turned tail and ran, eh?"

Looking around, a weak smile appeared on Ro's face. "What was that … thing? And where are we? We were just in the prison, but now …" He trailed off and glanced around at the others still laying on the ground. "Well, at least everyone is safe, I suppose," he sighed, his voice growing quiet and weak. "Some Beacon I would have been."

Andromeda's ears twitched with intrigue. Some Beacon?

Interesting. Did that mean he heard the voice too?

"Bwahahahaha," Nalgene laughed, interrupting her thoughts. "Don't ye be gettin' too soft on me now, ye damn dragon. Yeah, we all be fine here. Just be takin' a little nap, be my guess. As for what that lil' beastie was, well, I'd say ask the damn cat. But of course, bloody whiskers don't seem to be —"

"Indeed, we are all fine," Andromeda said dryly as she stepped out of the shadows, her tail twitching irritably. "As far as I can tell, the creature was some kind of undead bear. Seems there are more undead than just the ones we faced in prison."

But where are all the undead coming from? So many questions, and no answers. It was like trying to hunt invisible prey.

Not for the last time, Andromeda found herself thinking back to the alluring woman with the flowing braid and shining sword. Shaking her head to clear the thought, she turned back to her companions.

"Come here, ye damn cat," Nalgene said, walking toward Andromeda. Tendrils of water began weaving through his plump fingers.

Andromeda's eyes widened with alarm, but before she could do anything, Nalgene was next to her, his hands resting gently over her battered arm. A surge of icy water rushed over her, and her breath was blasted from her lungs from the sudden shock. Yet she did not struggle. Her fiery pain was washed away with the soothing water, and a jolt of energy filled her worn muscles. The bleeding holes in her chest closed, and her damaged arm mended itself. It was as if she had never been injured.

Nodding, Nalgene stepped back, satisfied.

Surprised, she fixed her gaze on the gnome. She flexed her mended arm, testing the muscles. There was no soreness, no stiffness. It was healed. "Much appreciated," she said, giving Nalgene a grateful nod. Turning away, she glanced back at the rest of the companions, who still lay unconscious.

"Let's wake the others, shall we? I'm interested to see what they think."

Nodding his head in agreement, Ro woke Margaret, gently shaking her out of her slumber. Nalgene rushed over to SmibSmob, an unusual anxiety shadowing his face. He placed his hands across SmibSmob's chest, and a swirling rush of water surged from his hands, covering his brother in a cool blanket. As soon as the crystalline water covered SmibSmob, the gnome's eyes opened, and he let out a soft cough.

Andromeda stalked over to Fasto, who was still smiling gleefully. Putting her hand on his shoulder, she shook him to his senses. Fasto's eyes shot open, terror swirling in their depths. The orc tried to run, tried to escape, but Andromeda pinned him firmly to the ground. Fasto's mouth opened to scream, but Andromeda clamped her hand across his mouth, silencing the horrified orc.

"Shhhh," Andromeda whispered dangerously. "Be quiet, or I'll be sure to make you quiet. It's just me."

Immediately Fasto's clarity returned, and he relaxed. His eyes shone with some new knowledge, and he seemed a different orc than in the prison. Comfort enveloped him; he was at home in the dark forest.

Fasto's darted over to the corpse of the bear, then locked on Andromeda. When he spoke, his voice rang clear as a bell. "What happened? Are my friends safe? I — Fasto — should've been awake to help."

Andromeda's mouth dropped. He was almost coherent. Something wasn't right.

"Ah, yes, thank you," she stammered. Something most certainly wasn't right.

Shaking her head, Andromeda turned to the others and let Fasto to his feet, where he studied the looming forest with sharp eyes. Everyone else was finally awake. Margaret stood by Ro, fear darkening her eyes.

"What happened?" Margaret said softly. "I remember a blinding light, and a deathly wave of ice that covered the prison.

There were a weird woman and a commanding voice in my head. Then …" Margaret's voice trailed off, and she glanced up to Ro. "I don't know."

Andromeda studied the orc, her eyes narrowing. Ice? No, there was no ice. That must have been the armored terror's sword, right?

Noticing Andromeda's gaze, Margaret stepped away from Ro, her voice growing stronger. "But I'm safe now, and that's all that matters."

Troubled, Andromeda turned to Nalgene, who was helping his brother to his feet. SmibSmob studied the shadowy forest around them, his face pale.

"I don't mean to be the obvious one," the thin gnome said, "but I don't think we're in the prison anymore."

Nalgene snorted in amusement. "Ye said it, me brother. What a fine noggin ye must have." His voice rose to a shout, consumed by fits of laughter. "O' course we ain't in the bloody prison anymore! We be in a shittin' spooky forest! How in the bloody hell —"

Nalgene was interrupted by a sharp growl from Ro. "Don't you have any sense of caution?" the draconian hissed, his eyes studying the trees in alarm. "You saw what attacked us. Do you want to bring more of them?"

Andromeda ignored the rest. She did not care for their pointless bickering. She had other, more productive things to worry about. An image of the woman searing into her mind, Andromeda stalked over to SmibSmob.

She had to know.

"What do you remember?" she purred, trying not to sound overly curious. "Anything?"

SmibSmob scratched his head, his brow furrowed in thought. "Well, I remember that hulking, armored demon. Then there was a blinding light, and a shining woman. Two spooky green eyes appeared, and a soothing voice began speaking in my head,"

SmibSmob said. "Before I knew it, abyssal tentacles shot from the shadows and pummeled the undead. Two mighty tentacles collapsed upon the armored demon and ripped it down into a fiery inferno. After that ... black butterflies?"

Andromeda studied the gnome. That certainly was *not* what had happened. Apparently, it seems they all saw the woman and heard the voice. But shadowy tentacles? Hardly. And what of the black butterflies?

Andromeda had no answers. Frustration mounting within her, she turned away from SmibSmob, leaving him to his thoughts.

"Ah, come to think o' it," Nalgene said, approaching his brother. "I saw the damn woman too. What did she say? Somethin' about a Shadow and some kind o' signal light?"

Nalgene scratched his head, trying to remember.

"But there ain't be no tentacles. Just a lot o' bloody water. I be thinkin' I was gonna drown, but before I could, some damn butterflies appeared, and then I was here. I dunno. Spooky stuff, I be thinkin'."

Andromeda studied Nalgene for a moment, her tail twitching irritably. How did they all manage to see something different? Shaking her head, Andromeda turned to see Fasto approaching her with Margaret and Ro trailing close behind.

"Fasto — I saw a hail of arrows raining down from above," the orc said, as calmly and fluently as ever. "Somehow, they didn't strike us. They protected friends."

"Eh? Who are you and what did ye do with that bumblin' dolt of an orc?" Nalgene exclaimed, wheeling about to face the orc. "And don't ye be throwin' around that big 'f' word o' y —"

Before he could finish, Nalgene was interrupted as a small flame burst to life under his feet.

"Bah! Fire! What in the bloody hell!?" he shouted, stumbling away from the mysterious flame.

Before their eyes the small fire grew into a massive inferno, basking the area in a warm light. The companions rushed away from the raging flames, while Andromeda quickly vanished into the darkness.

As quickly as it came, the swirling inferno vanished, leaving a smoldering patch of dirt in its wake. Standing where the flame monolith disappeared was a gorgeous woman with fiery-red hair that cascaded over her back in an orange waterfall. Fierce, orange eyes shone in contrast with her smooth, olive skin. A gruesome scar cut across her left cheek and up to her bloodshot left eye, but it didn't hinder her beauty. She was ragged, and fatigue weighed heavily on her shoulders. But when she glanced up at them, a beaming smile appeared on her face. It was elation.

"Good! At last, I have found you!" she exclaimed in a most melodious voice. Turning, her eyes locked onto Andromeda, and she waved her over. "Come, come, there's no need to hide in the shadows."

Andromeda froze. She should be invisible.

Unsettled, Andromeda emerged from her hiding place. The other companions studied the woman with uneasy expressions.

Nalgene took a step forward, his fists raised menacingly. "Alright there, pretty. Ye best be havin' a good reason to be interruptin' our merry gatherin' with yer damn fires and stuff," he fumed, water forming in his gnarled hands. "Now, unless ye be wantin' some of me water in yer face ye better —"

Nalgene was interrupted as the woman erupted into laughter.

"Oh, Nalgene! I see you're as impatient as ever."

Nalgene returned a suspicious stare.

"Aye, that'd be me name," he said after a moment, breaking the silence. "And me patience do be runnin' thin. Who ye be? And how in the bloody hell do ye be knowin' me name?"

The woman quickly grew somber as a harsh realization set in.

"I see. Then I suppose I should introduce myself. My name is Mariah," she said, her voice growing softer as she studied the companions. "And I know all of you, my good gnome. But it is quite troubling that you don't know me."

"It would be hard to forget someone like you," SmibSmob chimed in an effort to lighten the heavy mood.

"My thoughts exactly," Mariah replied, her gaze shadowed by doubt.

"How did you find us?" Ro asked, a hint of distrust clear in his voice.

Mariah sighed. "I have been searching for you ever since you were freed from the prison. Of course, she chose the middle of the forest."

"So, you know what happened?" Ro asked. "And where we are?"

"Yes, I know what happened," Mariah continued. Gathering up her red and golden dress, she sat on the ground, unconcerned that she might dirty the luxurious cloth. "Come, gather around. It seems we have much to discuss."

Cautiously, the companions formed a semi-circle around Mariah — all except Margaret, who was pretending to ignore the fiery woman. Thoughts raced through Andromeda's mind as she took a seat. How did the woman know them? And why would they know her? If only she could remember …

"Currently, we are in the north of Anland," Mariah started, her voice soft.

"Anland, ye say? How in the bloody hell did we get here? Weren't we just in the Heartland?" Nalgene asked.

"Indeed, you were," Mariah said. "But you were transported here by means of your … great magic."

She paused, and her crystal gaze darted around the clearing, as if seeing haunting specters. A hint of panic appeared. The fear began to claw back to the surface. Calitha was hunting for her. Calitha wanted her back. She was not as free as Ashyla had claimed.

"Listen closely, for I have not much time," she continued. "This isn't the same Anland you might've known before. A great

A Land in Shadow

Shadow has been cast over the realm. The land around you has fallen, becoming nothing more than a vile and dead place, full of unearthly horrors of the night. Dreadful gates of the Shadow have opened across the lands, drawing in the very land's life force and twisting it to darkness. The Shadow has but one purpose. To destroy. What truly terrifies me is those who wish to use the Shadow for their own gains. For over two centuries the Light has been fighting against the horrid legions of the Shadow, and I fear the worst is still yet to come. But worry not, for there is still hope."

Mariah stood up, and gestured behind the companions, a flame rising from her palm. Andromeda whirled around, only to face a billowing flame. But the inferno was not hot. Instead, it enveloped her body in a comforting warmth. From behind her, Mariah spoke in a strong, commanding voice. "I give to each of you the means to survive in this twisted land. From within my flames, you shall find your weapons once used to battle against the evil of this world. Let them taste the darkness once again." The warm fires vanished, leaving a smoldering arc on the ground. From within the ashes, objects began to rise and form like the birth of a phoenix.

Materializing before Andromeda was a mighty halberd; a shining axe-head perched upon a strong wooden shaft. Alongside the weapon was wondrous leather armor, made of the finest materials and blackened like the darkness of night. Some memory pricked at the back of Andromeda's mind, but it was buried in her amazement.

Eying her companions, Andromeda saw that they were similarly amazed and were holding various weapons and armor.

"Take back your weapons, strike back against the Shadow, and bring hope back to the Light," Mariah beseeched the group. "Travel east, there you will reunite with the Flame. Now go. Save the lands of Ansalon! Remember, I will be there, always, watching over you, my Beacon."

As Mariah finished, she began to smolder away, as if she were a burning sheet of paper.

"Wait!" Andromeda cried. "Where are you going?"

Mariah glanced up, her eyes shining bright. "There is another I must find. Now go!"

With those words, Mariah fell into ashes, blowing away into the dark forest.

Andromeda could only stare, her thoughts a surging storm. Beacon ... that was what the other woman had said.

An image of the beautiful woman from the prison and the enchanting emerald gaze once again appeared in her mind.

If only ...

Shaking the image away, Andromeda turned to her companions, each now brandishing their equipment to face the Shadow. Ro donned shining plate mail. In his hand was a mighty greatsword and strapped across his back was a sturdy shield and fierce longsword. Noticing Andromeda's gaze, Ro nodded to her, a new fire of determination burning within his eyes. Fasto wore tough leather armor, and in his hands, he held a longbow of splendid, white wood. Hanging at his side was a golden quiver of arrows. Margaret equipped a marvelous plate mail, similar to what Ro was wearing except that it seemed to shimmer like a crystal sheet of ice. Lastly, there were the two brothers. Each now wore a flowing robe of smooth silk; Nalgene's was a light blue while SmibSmob's was a dark purple. In Nalgene's hands was a glass bottle full of shimmering water, and atop SmibSmob's head sat a massive, pointed hat that drooped over the small gnome's eyes.

Turning away from her companions, Andromeda narrowed her eyes, her thoughts rushing back to what Mariah had said. The Shadow has been covering the land for over two centuries? How could they not have known about it? Why couldn't she remember before the prison? Clearly, Mariah knew more than what she was telling them.

Twitching her tail irritably, she shot back around to face the others, who were all watching her with concern. Once again, she found herself thinking of the beautiful woman at the prison.

If only … no, it wasn't important. She had to focus on the hunt at hand.

Andromeda's eyes gleamed with a devilish light.

"To the east, shall we?" she said.

Nodding, Ro started off to the east, a wary look on his face. He swapped his greatsword for his longsword and shield. Mustering themselves, the rest of the companions followed behind him, caution marking their steps.

"Take care now," Ro muttered. "We are surrounded by danger."

"Ah, get over it, ye damn dragon, it just be a bunch of spooky trees, that's all," Nalgene jabbed, a triumphant smile spread wide across his face.

"We can't underestimate anything," Fasto said. "Even the trees."

"Bah! Nothin' to be scared o' …"

Not caring what else Nalgene said, not even caring if the others followed, Andromeda stalked into the black, twisted forest, her newfound halberd clutched tightly in her hand.

The companions trekked east through the forsaken forest, slowly making their way between the interwoven limbs of the crooked, ancient trees. Ro took the lead and was hacking a path through the twisted branches with his sharp longsword. The others were similarly on edge, slashing at the dark trees whenever they found a chance. As they marched onward, they began to hear unnatural sounds echoing among the blackened trunks like a mournful river of despair. Shadows flickered in and out of existence at the corners of their vision, and the sounds of unearthly groans and snarls crept ever closer.

"Undead are near," Fasto said, studying the surrounding forest. "Numerous. I — Fasto knows."

SmibSmob nodded in agreement. "I don't mean to be the obvious one," he said, a quiver in his voice. "But I reckon we're being followed."

"Probably just more zombies," Margaret replied nonchalantly. "Nothing that we haven't handled before."

Andromeda analyzed the dark forest around her, having little trouble seeing the undead shambling around in the dim light.

"No, we're not being not followed," she started.

"We're being surrounded," Ro finished for her, his eyes darting around, similarly watching the undead move about in the shadows. Sheathing his longsword, he pulled out his mighty greatsword. Planting his feet firmly on the ground, he raised his sword up into a steady guard. "Ready," he hissed, still vigilantly eyeing the shadows.

Let them come.

Without hesitation, Andromeda faded back into the darkness of the woods, letting the shadows of the night embrace her. Gripping her halberd steadily in her right hand, she placed her left hand on the ground, tensing her muscles to pounce on the nearest enemy. Her eyes gleamed with delight.

Let them come.

The hordes of undead rushed at the companions, zombies and skeletons alike boring in to drown them in a sea of death. But the companions were ready.

With a raging battle-cry, Ro hurled himself into the mob of undead, his greatsword cleaving back-and-forth, splintering the looming trees and decimating the vile ranks of the unholy creatures. Nalgene and SmibSmob once again fought side-by-side, raining down their terrifying spells in a vortex of water and shadow. Their cloaks flowed around them in a furious grace, blue and purple flowing together against the black of darkness. At one point, SmibSmob reached into his massive, pointed hat, only to pull out from within a black, steel mace, which he used to smash any undead that wandered too nearby. Margaret dashed among the trees, crushing undead into oblivion with decimating punches from her demonic arm, and sending devastating waves of frost showering out from her fist, laying waste to the foul horde. Fasto stood between the inky trunks of two massive trees and was hailing a seemingly endless supply of streaking arrows down upon the undead with remarkable accuracy, striking down any who ventured too close to his friends. A snarl twisted his face into a terrifying mask of rage.

Andromeda dashed among the shadows, pouncing at an unsuspecting target and tearing it down into the darkness. She felt more powerful than before. Having capable weapons is always a good confidence booster.

She thought back to the elegant woman from the prison, and her eyes burned ever more brightly.

She wanted to embrace the power she had witnessed …

Leaping into the throng of enemies, Andromeda heaved her halberd around effortlessly, splitting skulls and spilling the dark, oozing blood of her enemies. Invigorated, she leaped atop the nearest one, sinking her deadly fangs deep into its throat. With a hiss of delight, she ripped the unfortunate creature's throat out, releasing a spray of black blood, and matting down her black fur with streaks of oozing gore.

Ignoring the foul taste of the rotten blood in her mouth, Andromeda scanned for another target. Fading back into the darkness, she stalked between the dusky trees, her eyes locked on her next prey: a zombie about to pounce on an unsuspecting Fasto.

A roar escaping her mouth, Andromeda lunged at the target, hauling it into the shadows and away from the vulnerable back of Fasto. Plunging her halberd deep into the creature's chest, she finished it with a sickening *crunch* of bones and rotting flesh. Whirling around, she tore the halberd out from her fallen prey, her eyes already searching for her next target.

Flexing her powerful hind legs, she sprung over the growling form of Fasto, landing among the trees next to an enraged Margaret, who was gleefully pummeling one of the vile creatures into a shower of gore. Warily glancing at her vicious companion, Andromeda noticed a small cut shining out on the orc's delicate face. Shaking her head, Andromeda faded back into the shadows, her halberd ready to embrace another target.

Andromeda's focus was interrupted by a shout from Ro, who had made his way over to the gnomes. Lightning shot from his maw, illuminating the dim woods in a blinding flash.

"Follow me!" he cried. "The way is cleared, let's escape this forest!" Gesturing his mighty greatsword to the east, he charged through the trees, leveling any that dared stand in his way.

Glancing toward Ro, Nalgene smiled. "Now yer talkin' some sense, ye damn dragon. C'mon, me brother, let's get outta this bloody forest."

Nodding his head in agreement, SmibSmob placed the black mace back in his hat, and with an exuberant gesture, flipped the hat up into the air to land upon his head.

"Fasto, Margaret — follow us!" SmibSmob called back to his companions.

Smiling with delight, Andromeda bounded off to catch the others while Fasto dragged a bloodthirsty Margaret along after her.

The companions pushed along through the twisting branches of the forest, the haunting sounds of the undead trailing close behind. Andromeda remained at the back of the party, alongside Fasto, and dispatched any undead that followed too closely.

As they ran, a faint shimmer of a dim light began to shine through the shadows of the forest. With a renewed sense of hope, the companions redoubled their efforts, crashing through the woods with a growing sense of determination. As the pale light of freedom grew closer, the pursuing hordes of undead fell farther behind, disappearing into the shadows of the gloomy trees. With one final surge of resolve, the companions burst through the black, twisting trees, escaping into the fading light of the open lands. As the companions glanced up to observe the land, their sparks of hope were smothered by the brutal landscape before them.

The very earth around them seemed empty, devoid of its

very life-force. The grass was gray and wilted, and any bushes or shrubs that dotted the land were twisted mockeries of their previous selves. To the north and distant south loomed great mountain ranges, watching over them like dark guardians of the night. To the east the sun was rising over the horizon, but it was dim and bleak, as if some terrible shadow had devoured all its light.

"What do ye make of that?" Nalgene grunted, taken aback by the withering sight of the land.

"Mariah was right," SmibSmob gasped, his eyes filled with horror. "The land is … has been … decimated."

Andromeda glanced back to the forest, wishing she could escape. Somberly, she gazed into the murky depths of the woods. A shadow flickered. Before Andromeda could move, two billowing purple eyes came to life in the thick shadows like two fiery chasms of death. Andromeda froze, a terrible sense of doom washing over her. But as quickly as they came, the two demonic eyes vanished, leaving nothing but the empty forest.

Andromeda shook her head, unwilling to admit to her lapse of terror. "It was nothing," she mumbled to herself, regaining her composure. Her mind started to drift once more to the beautiful woman, but her thoughts were interrupted by the annoying voice of Nalgene.

"Woah, now what do ye make of that, eh?" the gnome repeated. Sometimes he just wouldn't quit talking.

Turning to Nalgene, Andromeda found he was pointing at something to the east. Intrigued, she glanced at the far distance and saw a great, orange ball of flame hurling through the sky like a fallen star reaching up to the heavens. Andromeda stared in wonder, the memory of the cloaked figure disappearing from her mind.

"Wow, Fasto wonders. Fasto thinks go there," Fasto declared, entranced, with drool leaking from his agape mouth. "Fasto go there now."

The orc's sudden change was startling. Something absolutely wasn't right. Maybe they should just leave him behind to wander among the trees.

"You're right, Fasto," SmibSmob whispered, his blue eyes wide with amazement. It seemed he did not share her thoughts. "We need to head east, to reunite with the Flame."

"Brilliant," Margaret remarked, examining the others with a disapproving look. "A ball of fire shooting up into the sky. Sure, let's head straight for it. What could go wrong? I'm sure it'll all work out for us."

"Yer damn right it will," Nalgene laughed, skipping after Fasto, who was already heading toward the flame. "C'mon, me brother, let's go find us that bloody Flame." Nodding eagerly, SmibSmob was more than happy to oblige.

Margaret shot Nalgene with a dirty look, but after a moment, followed him with a disgruntled sigh.

Andromeda glanced over at Ro, who seemed hesitant to follow the others. Noticing her gaze on him, Ro gave her a weak smile. His breath was ragged — wearing heavy armor in battle was exhausting. Andromeda walked over to him, a mischievous glimmer in her eyes. She brushed his back with her tail.

"Let's go, shall we?" she purred to him softly, before bounding forward to catch up with the others, leaving him alone behind.

She didn't look back.

The companions trekked east along the barren wasteland, following behind Fasto to where the heavenly ball of flame hurled itself into the sky. As they marched along, the dim, distant sun rose steadily into the sky, but it provided little warmth, and less light. Far in the distance, the ruined carcass of a once great city rose up over the horizon. Determined, Fasto pushed them along, eager to reach the city before nightfall.

As the cold, muted sun passed its zenith, the ragged companions found themselves upon an old, dusty road, as desolate as the rest of the unholy land. Following along the grim trail, they reached the fallen front gate of the devastated city just as the dull sun was sinking to the west. They were not alone. Calmly sitting atop a gray boulder on the edge of the dusty road was a lightly armored man, sharpening a shining greatsword with a worn whetstone.

The man was fairly built, and of average height. He had short, black hair that was matted with sweat, and a dark, ragged beard like a shadow over his face. His eyes were fierce and showed wisdom well beyond his age.

Andromeda watched the strange man warily, her tail slowly flicking back and forth. Cautiously, she approached him, her halberd appearing in her hand.

Noticing her approach, the man ran the whetstone across his greatsword one, final time, showering the ground in a hail of red sparks. He looked up, his brown eyes piercing her with a scrutinizing stare.

"Good to see a fellow Spark still burning bright," he hailed in a deep, weary voice.

"Eh, what're ye rabblin' about?" Nalgene said, moving up to stand behind Andromeda. "I ain't no Spark or whatever ye be callin' me."

The man paused, his eyes narrowing. "Oh, is that so?" the man said, a dangerous undertone seeping into his voice. "Then you must be the … Shadowfriends I've been looking for. I was told I'd find your ilk wandering around these parts. It seems she wasn't lying after all."

Slowly, he stood up, raising his greatsword out in front of him. With a raging roar the mighty sword burst into flames, billowing into an orange weapon of fury. Looking out from behind his sword, the man glared at the companions, his sharp eyes shooting daggers of ice. However, behind the man's dangerous facade, Andromeda noticed uncertainty and doubt swirling in the man's eyes. Before she could ponder, it disappeared.

"Traitors of the Light don't deserve to live," he hissed, matching her scrutinizing stare.

Andromeda planted her feet, holding her halberd out in a steady guard. Shaking away any distractions, her eyes targeted the prey.

Her tail slashed back and forth, and she prepared to fade into the growing darkness, her eyes gleaming with a demonic light. The other companions rushed up to support her, but she ignored them. She was already locked on the target.

Time to embrace the power.

Suddenly, before she had time to react, before she even had time to breathe, her challenger took a step. There was a *pop* beneath his feet, then he was *there*, holding his fiery greatsword up to her throat.

The immense heat from the flaming weapon washed over her, blasting her out of her shadowy stealth. Andromeda tried to flee, tried to retreat and embrace the darkness, but she could not move. The man's dark eyes held her like an iron vice, their accusing stare locking her in place. Her companions were shouting and raising their weapons in a panic against the man. But in her shock, Andromeda did not hear them. She did not even hear the faint hesitation in the man's voice. All she heard was a deep growling sealing her fate in a soft promise of vengeance.

"Prepare to die."

Chapter 3

"Wait!" SmibSmob cried at Andromeda. She did not hear him. SmibSmob's dark power began to prod at the back of his mind like a persistent itch, begging to burst free. Time seemed to move in slow motion, each moment passing by like a trickling river, every heartbeat seeming to last an eternity. He saw Nalgene come up behind Andromeda and speak to the man. He saw the ragged man stand up ever so calmly. Then he saw the man's fierce greatsword ignite like the flames of a thousand suns.

They were supposed to be reunited with the Flame, not destroyed by it!

He saw Andromeda plant her clawed feet, her deceivingly delicate frame fading away into the black of night. Her halberd was raised out in front of her, and her sharp, feline eyes shone like two shimmering beacons. Then, suddenly, there was a *pop* of flame, and the man was there, his fiery greatsword raging against Andromeda's neck.

The darkness within SmibSmob crashed against the walls in his mind in a frenzy. He hated his distasteful power: its constant shadow present at the edges of his mind, its vile taint that left him with a dreadful feeling of disgust, and most of all its corrupting influence that twisted his very being into one of darkness and despair. But without it, he felt so … empty, devoid of any meaning. And Andromeda needed help, needed his help.

So be it.

Pushing past his doubts, SmibSmob tore down the barriers set strong within his mind and allowed the darkness to overcome him like a raging torrent.

The dark power rumbled through SmibSmob's body, filling him with a new and twisted energy. Life coursed through him, and he felt as if he could conquer all of Ansalon. His senses were heightened, expanding his mind into the neighboring lands. He could see the smallest detail in the world around him. He could hear even the faint sound of his companions' beating hearts. He could feel the weakest breeze blowing across the forsaken ground. The shadow within flowed through his blood, sending black, crackling power arcing across his fingertips. His mellow, blue eyes now glowed with an unearthly, purple light. A thin smile slowly spread across his lips.

So be it.

Glancing back at Andromeda, SmibSmob saw her lying on the ground, a look of shock and surprise on her face. The man with the incendiary greatsword had turned to Nalgene, an icy glare shooting from his eyes. Behind him, the other companions were rushing to Andromeda's aid, but he ignored them. He had more important matters at hand. Raising his hand, SmibSmob conjured a great ball of darkness that swirled around like a vortex of shadow.

With an evil chuckle, he hurled the magical globe at the man and braced himself to receive the influx of revitalizing energy. Alarmed, the enraged man's eyes shot up. The man's face twisted into an annoyed frown, and his greatsword lowered to the ground. There was another *pop* of fire beneath his feet, and then he vanished. SmibSmob felt the faint disturbance in the air and heard the faint scuffing on the ground as the man propelled himself forward. Suddenly, he appeared at SmibSmob's side, his greatsword descending upon the gnome with staggering precision. A searing pain exploded into SmibSmob's side as the sword struck, and a wave of heat rolled over him. Before he could even hope to dodge, he was sent stumbling back by the immense weight of the blow. Coughing up blood, SmibSmob glared at his attacker, his dark rage boiling deep within.

How dare the man strike him?

Crawling back to his feet, SmibSmob raised his hands once more, preparing to unleash a devastating wave of shadow down upon the miserable offender. But the transgressor had already disappeared.

Before SmibSmob could react, Nalgene rushed over to him, a look of concern twisting his hardened face with worry. "Are ye alright, me brother?" Nalgene said, his voice shaking. "Fer some reason he only hit ye with the flat o' his sword ..."

Nodding curtly, and not really caring what Nalgene had to say, SmibSmob glanced around, trying to find where his pathetic sinner had scurried off to. His brother was always worrying. Such a nuisance.

Finding the offender clashing with Ro, SmibSmob raised his hands, ready to deliver justice. Next to him, Nalgene was doing the same, but SmibSmob ignored him. He had more important matters at hand. Writhing tendrils of shadow rose from his hands, and billowing darkness oozed out of him in a sickening aura.

Now the man must die.

A wicked smile wide on his face, SmibSmob launched two devastating beams of shadow from his hands, crackling black energy swirling about the beams in a twisting web of destruction. With a burst of darkness, the twin beams rammed into the side of the pitiful transgressor, sending him sliding back across the barren ground.

Rejuvenating energy surged through SmibSmob in a

tingling wave of euphoria. The pain in his side lessened, and the blistering burn marks from the fiery greatsword faded away, leaving not even the faintest hint of their existence.

Staggering back, the wretched sinner glared up at SmibSmob, his eyes filled with a burning rage. Cackling maliciously, SmibSmob raised his hands, ready to rain down more vile beams of darkness on his offender. But the sinner was not there. SmibSmob felt the ignition of the fire, the faint murmur in the air, and heard the quiet rustle of the dead grass. Prepared this time, he whirled about, his purple cloak fanning around him like a dark orchid of death. Black energy arced forth from his hands, ready to obliterate his pathetic transgressor in a swirling void of shadow. But he was not fast enough. With a sickening *crack* the man slammed the pommel of his fearsome greatsword into SmibSmob's face, shattering his nose and sending him stumbling to the earth in anguish. The man glared at SmibSmob before disappearing once more.

SmibSmob landed hard on the ground, his breath blasted from his frail body. His eyes blurred, and tears started streaming down his face. He did not notice. All he felt was his foul, twisted power retreating from his mind, leaving him panting on the cold ground. He was nothing more than an exhausted husk. His senses dulled, and the void of emptiness clawed itself back open inside him. He was empty and broken without his power's tantalizing touch, yet still purer than when he indulged in its corrupting grasp.

Nalgene bolted over to SmibSmob, and crouched protectively above him, his face a mixture of rage and despair. "Me brother! Are ye alright?" Nalgene cried while placing his hands atop SmibSmob's chest.

A trickling ripple of water surged from Nalgene's hand to spread over SmibSmob's body, basking him a cool, silky embrace. Immediately, energy returned to SmibSmob like an explosion of life. The searing pain from his face began to ebb away, and his fractured nose reformed itself under the cooling water.

Coughing, SmibSmob slowly sat up, his entire body aching with the effort. "Yes, I'm alright, just a little sore, that's all."

Oh, what would he do without Nalgene …? His brother was always there for him, worrying about his well-being. Even through their arguments, he was always there.

Smiling with joy, Nalgene stood up with a lone tear trickling down his face. "Atta boy! What a mighty fine beatin' ye took just then," he snorted, a faint chuckle hidden under his breath. "Ain't no man ever gonna beat up us gnomes, eh?"

Wiping the solitary tear from his face, Nalgene turned to face the rest of the companions, who were still locked in combat against the fearsome man. With a grunt, he charged over to aid them in the clash, swirling orbs of water rising from his gnarled hands.

With a weak smile, SmibSmob stood up, turning to see how the rest of his companions were faring. He knew he would not be able to call upon his power for some time, as he had overexerted himself. Even so, thanks to Mariah, he could still help them.

Reaching up, he pulled the large, pointed hat from atop his head and stuck his arm inside.

Praying for something helpful, he felt around the inside of the hat, his stubby fingers exploring around the expansive folds of the cloth. The hat, one of his gifts from Mariah, was still an enigma to him. It certainly seemed a regular hat, but when he put his hand inside, he felt a spark, and then there would be something inside, as if he willed it into existence. He did not understand how he knew the hat would produce an item. He just knew, as if some long-lost memory had awoken within his mind. Earlier, he was able to pull out an exquisitely crafted mace of the finest black steel and used it to bash any undead that had wandered too close in the dreadful forest. But he did not choose to summon a mace then, it just … happened.

Suddenly, SmibSmob's fingers brushed against something, and with a burst of excitement, he hastily pulled it out to examine his find. As he studied the object, a disappointed frown spread across his face. Clutched in his frail hand was a fresh, steaming loaf of bread. What was he supposed to do with that, throw it at the man?

Sighing, SmibSmob tossed the bread behind him.

His disappointment was only heightened as he gazed at his companions, who were still clashing with the mighty man. Fasto and Margaret lay on the ground, covered in various painful — yet surprisingly not fatal — injuries. Nalgene crouched over Margaret, who had severe burn marks across her chest. Water flowed from the gnome's hands, washing over Margaret in its healing embrace. Fasto lay next to her, similar burn marks marring the side of his face. Ro and Andromeda fought side-by-side against the man, their animal figures twirling around each other in a devastating dance of death. Ro donned his longsword and shield, and Andromeda her halberd, and together they were driving the man back. But there was hesitation in Andromeda's swings, and confusion shadowed her face.

Another flare beneath his feet, and the man vanished once more, immediately reappearing behind Andromeda, his raging greatsword homing in on her delicate back. This time SmibSmob felt no disturbance in the air, and heard no scuffling on the barren, dead ground. With a fiery slash, the man cut across Andromeda's back, sending her body crashing forward into the dusty earth.

With a furious, thundering roar, Ro whirled around to face the man, his longsword already slicing across, ready to deliver the final blow. The man was not ready. He did not see it coming and there was no way he would be able to dodge it. The longsword arced in, its aim true upon the man's exposed throat.

But the man didn't move. A brief fire flickered across his neck.

With a *thud* the sword crashed into the man's neck but stopped as if striking against an impenetrable shield. A small patch of what looked like iron had seemingly grown on the man's skin! Smirking, the man glanced down at the shining longsword, and then up to a bewildered Ro.

Swinging his fearsome greatsword, the man parried away Ro's longsword, launching it from the draconian's clawed grasp. Shooting forward, his eyes gleaming with a murderous light, the man slammed the octagonal pommel into Ro's chest. With a grunt of pain, Ro staggered back under the blow. Twirling around, the man swept out Ro's legs, sending him crashing down to the cold, desolate ground like a fallen giant. The man's eyes shot up, their accusing glare fixating on SmibSmob. Letting out a weak cry, SmibSmob tried to retreat, tried to get away from the penetrating gaze. He reached into his hat again, his fingers frantically searching for something, anything that might help him against the terrifying monster before him. He found nothing. The man took a step forward, his flaming greatsword rising like a beacon of doom.

"Ho, Captain Osann, is it? Hold yourself for a moment," a charming, sing-song voice said from the ruined city. "Now, what seems to be the problem?"

SmibSmob froze, his mind writhing in thought. Captain? That explained a lot, he supposed. The man was no amateur.

Captain Osann paused, and his mighty greatsword extinguished its billowing flames. Turning, he locked his eyes on the newcomer, and he gave a respectful nod of his head. "Good to see a fellow Spark still —"

"Oh, spare me the formalities Osann," the newcomer interrupted, striding out to stand in front of the Captain. The man was a short, frail man with a thin, pale face showing out from under a draping hood. A flowing, crimson cloak flowed about him in a scarlet wave. Various pouches and trinkets hung loosely at his waist, and a deck of shimmering, metal cards riffled through his nimble hands. Stopping in front of the Captain, he gave a mischievous, crooked smile, and with a flourishing gesture, the shining cards vanished. Captain Osann stiffened and opened his mouth as if to protest.

"Yes, yes, whatever," the cloaked man snickered, giving an exaggerated bow. "May your light pierce the Shadow."

As the man was rising from his bow, SmibSmob heard a feral growl, and he whipped his head around, only to see Nalgene glaring at the newcomer, a mighty orb of water raised high above his head. Behind him stood Margaret, her vicious, demon arm swirling with a vortex of ice, and Fasto, with a piercing arrow drawn and nocked in his marvelous bow, ready to release at a moment's notice.

"And who do ye be? Name yerself," Nalgene commanded in a gruff voice, the swirling water twirling above his head in a tantalizing threat of doom.

Chuckling to himself, the cloaked figure turned to the companions, and scrutinized them with his shallow, green eyes. His eyebrow rose and he mumbled something quietly to himself. Looking about deliberately, he let his hard gaze fall upon each of the companions, studying them with a knowing eye. SmibSmob swore that the strange man had rested his gaze upon him a heartbeat more than the others, but he shook away the thought. With a soft chuckle, the man turned back to face Nalgene.

"Well, I suppose a proper introduction wouldn't hurt," he said, clearing his throat. "Name's Kraalek." Giving a cheeky smirk, he bent down in another exaggerated bow. "Or General Kraalek Cardmaster, for the sake of our good man Osann's formalities."

SmibSmob gaped at Kraalek, his mind racing in a whirlwind of thoughts and emotions. General? If Osann was only a Captain …

He did not want to finish the thought.

His knees grew weak, and his hands felt sweaty and dull. Shakily, he returned his large, pointed hat to his head, and began to slowly make his way over to Nalgene and the others.

"Kraalek, eh?" Nalgene growled mockingly. "Funky name, ye got there. Ye best hope people be rememberin' it when yer —"

"Wait Nalgene!" SmibSmob cried, a clear tone of desperation in his voice. Fighting them would be suicide. "Don't … just wait!"

Kraalek laughed. "Yes, Nalgene, is it? Do listen to the little fellow." He raised an eyebrow, and a faint, dangerous shimmer burned deep within his eyes. "Unless, perhaps, you're feeling a little lucky today."

With that, Kraalek gracefully leaped into the air, and turned away from the others, his crimson robe flowing about like a scarlet flower. The shining deck of metallic cards appeared in his hands again, and he started to skip off to the great, ruined city.

"Night is falling, so Osann will lead all of you to his camp in the city," he called back to them in his charming voice. "There, we can talk further." He paused and turned his head to glance at the stunned Captain. "Oh, and Osann, I can assure you that they're not Shadowfriends. Isn't that right?"

Giving the Captain a crooked smirk, he turned back around, and continued skipping towards the fallen city, chuckling to himself softly.

SmibSmob stared, a mask of confusion upon his face. Just what was with this guy, this Kraalek? Definitely no amateur. He was up to something. SmibSmob smelled it.

Nalgene stood dumbfounded, his tantalizing vortex of water disappearing in the air. Behind him Fasto continued to stand ready, the razor arrow still nocked in his smooth, white bow. Margaret snorted in amusement, and the icy storm vanished. Captain Osann turned to them, just as bewildered as the rest. Clearing his throat, he thrust his sword into the cold ground and slowly walked over to help Ro back to his feet.

Nalgene jumped, breaking free from shock's iron grasp. "Eh, wha'd'ye think yer doin', Osann?" he snarled, his hands raising once more.

The Captain paused, his hand reaching out to lift Ro to his feet.

"General's orders," he said dryly before hauling Ro up with tremendous strength and lending him his shoulder to rest on.

Ro's eyes blinked open slowly, a filmy haze settling over them.

"Ah, what in the bloody dwarf's hairy arse is goin' on," Nalgene grunted to himself, throwing his hands down in anger. Frustrated, he stomped over to the dazed Ro, and placed his rough hands upon the draconian's chest, releasing a shimmering pool of warm water over Ro's battered form. "Damn dragon," he grumbled.

Shaking himself back to his senses, SmibSmob rushed over to Andromeda, who was still lying unconscious on the ground. Frantically, with the memories of Captain Osann's sword slashing wildly across her back still fresh in the gnome's mind, he turned her over to gaze upon the wound, a well of despair rising in his mind. Looking upon the alluring feline's delicate back, he fell back in surprise. There was nothing. No fatal slash, only a large, blistering scorch mark was visible where the sword's fearsome flames caressed her back in their molten embrace.

Vaguely, he thought he remembered Nalgene saying something about the flat of the mighty greatsword, but he discarded the thought as soon as it came.

Quite puzzled, SmibSmob glanced up to find his brother. He always seemed to know what to do. Nalgene stormed towards him, followed closely by Ro, who had concern darkening his face in a shadow, and Captain Osann, whose eyes churned with an inner turmoil. Bending over Andromeda, Nalgene muttered a stream of curses, and cast his warm, healing water upon the injured woman.

Andromeda's eyes shot open, and a quick gasp escaped her lips. Scrambling to her feet, her gaze sliced across the companions, and her face surged with a boiling rage. Her tail lashed back and forth, and she let out a menacing growl before starting to fade away into the coming shadows of the night.

"Wait, Andromeda!" Ro gently called out to her, his voice dripping with anxiety.

Andromeda paused, her eyes darting about wildly. Captain Osann cautiously moved next to Ro; his hands raised in a sign of peace. Andromeda whipped her head around to face him, snarling fiercely. Their eyes locked; Andromeda's sharp, feline fires, and the Captain's deep, brown wells. A flash of confusion, and something else, something deeper, tore across Andromeda's gaze, breaking her from her frenzy. She reappeared, returning to them from out of the enclosing darkness. Giving the Captain a faint nod, she turned to Nalgene.

"Much appreciated," she purred to the gnome, before striding over to stand by Ro.

SmibSmob glanced around at the others, lost in the winding trail of events. Nalgene, still muttering to himself, now also stood by Ro, and they were both throwing threatening glares at Captain Osann, each for their own reason. Behind SmibSmob, Fasto and Margaret approached, their footsteps making soft thuds on the ground. They too moved to stand about Ro, with Margaret gazing blankly at the others, and Fasto staring awkwardly at the Captain.

The sun had long since disappeared, and the black shade of night was casting its dark reach across the sky.

"So, to the camp?" SmibSmob stammered, clearing his throat. "It seems to be getting quite dark, and I'd rather not be out here all night."

Nodding, Captain Osann slowly walked over to retrieve his greatsword, which was still thrust into the desolate ground. With barely an effort, he unsheathed the mighty weapon from the clutches of the earth and let it rest on his burly shoulder. Turning to the others, his eyes shone with a renewed light, and he spoke in his deep, knowing voice.

"The gnome's right. Night is casting its black shadow upon the land," he said. "You may not trust me, but you would do well to follow me into the safety of the fallen city."

"Eh, no way I'm followin' yer bloody arse, Osann!" Nalgene fumed, crossing his arms and stomping his foot in protest. "Ye helped us after that damn Kraalek and all, but that don't be changin' the fact ye still tried to kill us! Claimin' we be

Shadowfriends or somethin', yer bloody mad in the head!"

Margaret snickered to herself in amusement. "Oh yes, this is going just splendidly. Heading to the great ball of fire, what an idea."

Captain Osann seemed taken aback by Nalgene's outburst, and a hurt expression washed over his once stoic face. "You don't understand," he murmured quietly, his eyes swelling with raw, powerful emotion. "My family ..."

"I don't give a dwarf's hairy arse about yer bloody family!" Nalgene shouted, streams of water starting to swirl around his body in a terrifying dance. "That don't be changin' the fact that ye —"

"Nalgene!" Ro roared, stepping forward and clasping the infuriated gnome's shoulder in an iron grasp. "That's enough. None of us like it, but we have to trust him. Just this once."

"But ..."

"Nalgene, my brother, please just listen to me," SmibSmob jumped in, walking up to stand beside Nalgene. Ro was right, for once. There was no hope if they started fighting again.

"Remember the prison, we can't fight the undead, this so-called Shadow," he continued. "Mariah told us to get help, and Captain Osann might just be our help." Glancing around, he saw the rest of his companions nodding in agreement, except Margaret and Andromeda, who stood in the background, silent.

"Yes, Fasto listen to flame-woman," Fasto piped in. "She pretty, and friend, gave Fasto bow and arrow. So Fasto follow her lead."

The Captain looked up, intrigue flickering over his face. "Mariah, you say," he muttered. "Could it be possible?"

His rage subdued, Nalgene turned to look at SmibSmob, shame shadowing over his face. "Yer right, me brother. Ye and yer fine noggin'," he mumbled. Turning back to Captain Osann, his voice strengthened. "Yeah, we saw Mariah, even talked to her, if ye'd believe it. Told us to find some Flame 'er somethin'."

"It's true," Ro added, brandishing his shining greatsword

out in his scaled hands. "She gave us these wondrous gifts."

SmibSmob nodded, and behind him, Fasto was eagerly doing the same.

Captain Osann gave the companions a long, scrutinizing stare. "Is it so? Has Mariah really returned?" he wondered. "Then perhaps, there is still hope. The Beacon can still arrive and defeat this eternal abyss that's covering the land."

With a sudden start, he thrust his mighty greatsword back into the ground and bent low onto his knee, his hand crossed over the center of his chest. With renewed energy, he spoke in a deep, powerful voice.

"Then I, Captain Kirk Osann of the Flame of Ansalon, do pledge myself and swear unto you that I will deliver you safely to the warming hands of the Flame. May the Beacon one day burn bright."

SmibSmob thought he saw the Captain giving an uncertain, sideways glance as he made his pledge, but he could not be sure. After a moment's pause, Captain Osann rose to his feet, a triumphant smile beaming upon his face. Tearing his sword from the dark ground, he laid it back to rest upon his sturdy shoulder.

"Now, follow me," he commanded, "into the great Ruins of Calinad."

◆   ◆   ◆

Captain Osann led the companions through the winding streets of the ravaged city, the torch in his hand illuminating the desolation around them. The surrounding city lay in ruins, rubble and debris scattered about the deserted roadways. Rows of shattered buildings flanked the sides of the streets, looming over the companions like a parade of fallen angels. Dust blanketed the once-grand city like a dim sheet of snow, leaving the companions with a sense of loss. SmibSmob gazed around in horror, his thoughts racing. Could the Shadow really have caused this much wanton destruction?

The others shared similar emotions of despair at the fallen city around them — except for Margaret, who appeared disinterested in the destruction around her.

SmibSmob gazed up to the heavens in an attempt to forget about unsolicited death surrounding him. There were no stars, only an empty blackness. Something else seemed off about the looming night sky, but SmibSmob could not place it.

The companions continued their grim trek through the devastated city, following Captain Osann's single torch shining out like a lone warrior against the overbearing clutches of the night. After some time of wandering through the labyrinth of streets they eventually found themselves in a sprawling, open square of the city. Piles of rubble dotted the clearing, and long-dead corpses of fallen trees littered the roadways — burnt and twisted into a horrific parody of life. A massive cathedral lay in ruins at the end of the square. Rising in front of the cathedral's fallen gates like a defiant soldier stood an elegant, surging fountain forged from the whitest of marble. Pure, blue water still flowed free, falling in cascading waterfalls from the fountain's graceful boughs. Laying in front of the majestic fountain was a camp consisting of a great number of bedrolls, supplies, and a burning fire.

Atop the white lip of the fountain sat Kraalek, effortlessly riffling his metallic cards through his nimble fingers. Noticing the companions' arrival, the General glanced up and gave them a crooked smile.

"So, what do you think?" he said exuberantly, throwing his arms out wide and gesturing to the destruction around them. "Ah, it's a pity, really. Anyway, I'm sure you tied up any loose ends with Osann, isn't that right?"

Not waiting for their response, he jumped off the edge of the flowing fountain, landing softly on his feet. "Come, gather around, for we have much to discuss."

"Eh, do we now?" Nalgene started, an agitated tone in his gruff voice. "Do ye think ye can just pull us around like —"

"Nalgene!" Ro interrupted, his voice harsh.

Kraalek laughed.

"Oh, you do so intrigue me. Come," he said, throwing them a mischievous wink. "Trust me."

Extinguishing his torch, Captain Osann strode toward his camp, laying his sword down by the supplies. The companions followed him, scattering themselves around the burning fire. SmibSmob sat by Nalgene, hoping that his rash brother would not have another outburst. Ro, Fasto, and Margaret all sat together, although Margaret seemed not to notice the other two, her gaze lost in the dancing flames. Andromeda sat alone, studying those around her. Kraalek returned to his perch on the fountain, while Captain Osann stood attentively nearby, uncomfortable at the situation.

"Now," Ro started, warily. "What did you want to discuss?"

"Yes, isn't that what we're all wondering," Margaret shot in, her voice cold and dry.

SmibSmob observed quietly, his thoughts whirling in a violent storm. What would a General want to do with them? He was a tricky one, that was for sure.

"General Kraalek," Captain Osann said, his voice distant. "They claim to have seen Mariah."

The General perked up at this. "Oh, is that so?" He glanced around at the companions, his knowing eyes resting on each of them for a moment. "Pray tell?"

"Well, Fasto was in spooky forest," Fasto piped in, his eyes gleaming. "Then pretty fire lady appear and give Fasto bow and arrow. Pretty lady tell Fasto to go east, and tell Fasto to go to fire, so Fasto go there. Now Fasto here, by fire, getting warm."

The General gave the orc a long, blank stare. Shaking his head, he chuckled softly to himself. "Indeed. Anyone else?"

"Well," SmibSmob started, uncertain what to say. Kraalek's eyes bored into him with a surprising pressure, and the General raised a thin, intrigued eyebrow. Clearing his throat, SmibSmob continued. "Well ... uh ... she saved us from an attack from a ... er ... some undead."

Andromeda flinched at this, but SmibSmob pushed on, his voice growing steadier.

"She then brought us to a forest, where she told us about the Shadow, the Light, and the war they have been waging against each other. Then she gave us our mighty gifts, equipping us with the weapons and armor we would need to survive, before disappearing. We traveled out of that forest and ... well, now we're here."

Breathing a faint sigh of relief, he anxiously looked around at his companions. He was uncomfortable and did not want to give too much information to the shady General. His eyes locked with Ro's, and the draconian gave him a slight, approving nod.

Kraalek studied SmibSmob, a thoughtful look on his face. Reaching into one of the pouches hanging from his waist, Kraalek pulled out a small, brown die. Rolling it in his frail hand, the General shook his head, giving a soft chuckle, before replacing it back into its respective pouch.

"And pray tell, my little gnome, what exactly did she tell you?" he asked.

SmibSmob stuttered, unsure of what to say. The man was testing him. The man was good.

Sweat started beading on his forehead, and his small hands grew clammy. Suddenly, in the back of his mind, he felt the persistent itch urging to break free. His power came flooding back into his being, crashing against the standing barriers in his mind with a renewed violence. Caught off guard, SmibSmob's words caught in his throat, unwilling to escape.

"She told us of how the Shadow has been casting the land in a darkness," Ro jumped in, noticing SmibSmob's obvious discomfort. "She told us of how it has been spreading over this once-great land for over two centuries, and how it has been opening horrible chasms across the land, spreading destruction. She told us of how the Flame ... er, the Light ... has been fighting back against its overwhelming darkness. And how the Flame, well, that we had to reunite with it and save Ansalon."

Kraalek burst into a mocking laugh. "Oh, is that so? Now, answer me this, if the Shadow has been covering the land for over two centuries, why would Mariah have had to tell you of it? You should've already known of it, isn't that right?"

The draconian had no answer.

Kraalek gave another, mocking chuckle. "And you're going to save Ansalon? Right. And I'm going to fly away on a fiery dragon. Pray tell, have you ever heard of the Beacon?"

SmibSmob stiffened, and his heart thundered in his chest. His mind was thrown back to the fateful day in the prison. The dreadknight, the mortal slash freezing over his chest. He remembered the tantalizing woman, her revealing dress fanning out like the flaming wing of a butterfly, and her soft, alluring voice coursing like a river through his mind, telling him of how he was the Beacon, and how he had to drive back the black legions of Shadow. The other companions were similarly taken aback by the question, even Margaret. Captain Osann gave the General a dangerous, uncomfortable look, but said nothing.

Kraalek shook his head, a crooked smirk forming on his lips.

"Interesting," he started slyly, the fire beneath him giving his face an eerie glow in the darkness of night. "Listen and listen closely. Why you do not already know this, I may never know. You were correct, the Shadow has been holding Ansalon in its dark clutches for over two centuries. Stories say that it began after a group of heroes fighting side-by-side with Mariah and the legendary Sergarious challenged the Goddess. While it is not known what happened during that battle, the aftermath was certain. Sergarious, along with the mighty companions, vanished. Enraged, the Goddess cast the Shadow over the land, sending a wave of darkness and despair crashing over Ansalon. We can only imagine why the Goddess did such a thing, as ancient histories hint that these lands were her source of pride and joy, but nevertheless, countless were slaughtered in the darkness. Mariah, who had escaped from the fateful battle, rallied the remaining living from across the lands under the banner of the Flame, and pushed back against the Shadow. But it was to no use — the Shadow swept us away. We … I … lost so much …"

Kraalek trailed off, his gaze lost in the dancing fire beneath him.

After a long moment, SmibSmob broke the silence. "General?" he asked. His voice sounded hollow in the overbearing darkness.

"Ah, right," Kraalek said, snapping out of his trance. Clearing his throat, he continued his story. "Some fifty years ago, after the Fall of the Moon, Mariah uttered the prophecy, and renewed hope within the Flame. She told of a Beacon that would rise, defeat the Shadow, and bring the Light back to the lands of Ansalon. And how we rallied. We all thought we would see the end of the Shadow. But it wasn't enough. Ten years ago, Mariah vanished, alongside the supposed Beacon. The Flame collapsed. Even with the expert guidance of Saber, it has been hopeless. Many have abandoned the cause of the Flame, turning themselves to the Shadow. Others refused to fight, while others … others took their own lives."

The General's voice softened, and he gazed upon the companions, his eyes raging with a simmering fire deep within. "But, if what you say is true, and Mariah has returned, then perhaps there is still hope."

The companions sat quietly for a long moment, their eyes glimmering in the hypnotic dance of the fire, and their thoughts slowly absorbing the General's words. SmibSmob was dumbfounded, and even Nalgene seemed to forget his hostility.

Fasto stared at Kraalek with wide eyes, saliva falling from his open mouth in slobbery drops. Andromeda's eyes gleamed with thought, and Ro's face darkened, his expression unreadable. Margaret was staring at the General with a surprising look of interest, all previous signs of apathy erased from sight.

But something did not make sense. Something was nagging at SmibSmob's mind, clawing open a chasm of intrigue. In a soft, meek voice, he broke the grim silence. "Why are you telling us this?"

Kraalek chuckled softly.

"Oh, pray tell," he said mysteriously, reaching into the pouch bulging at his side. "Why indeed? It's curious, isn't it? You should already know what I've said, but from the look on your faces, I can tell that you have no idea. Now, tell me, little fellow, are you feeling lucky today?"

Kraalek held out his frail hand to SmibSmob, the brown, wooden die resting snugly in the General's palm. Not waiting for the gnome's response, Kraalek cast the die away, letting it fall to the ground and ricochet across the cold stone streets of the square to land at the gnome's feet.

Glancing down, SmibSmob studied the strange die, his mind muddled by confusion. There weren't any marks on the die — just blank, polished faces, shining with an orange glow from the nearby fire. He looked back up at Kraalek, his face a mask of wonder.

"I don't understand."

The General shrugged his shoulders and gave the gnome an apologetic look. Chuckling, he leaped off the edge of the marble fountain, landing softly on his nimble feet. Stalking over to SmibSmob, he reached down, his pale hand snatching up the wooden die.

"Sorry," he whispered, while giving the gnome a sly glance. "You lost, isn't that right?"

Whirling around, his crimson robe flowing around him in a

scarlet swirl, Kraalek skipped away from the bewildered SmibSmob. Chuckling, the General called back over his shoulder. "Alas, I must be on my way," he said. "Osann will lead you to the Flame and guide you through this black Shadow. There, perhaps, we shall meet again. Until then ..."

Reaching into another of his many pouches, Kraalek pulled out a shining, orange gem that sparkled like a miniature star in the dim light of the burning fire. Suddenly, a swirling vortex of flame shot out of the small gem, embracing the General in a billowing fire. As quickly as it came, the blazing maelstrom disappeared, leaving not a trace of the sly General. SmibSmob shook his head, still dumbfounded by the earlier exchange.

Beside SmibSmob, Nalgene muttered to himself in a gruff voice. "Eh, pullin' us like puppets, I'll be damned ..."

The companions sat in silence for a moment longer, the edges of night creeping in as the fire slowly smoldered. Looking around, SmibSmob found his companions lost in their own thoughts. Andromeda still lay alone, her gaze locked onto Captain Osann. Ro sat quietly next to Margaret, a frown apparent on his draconian face. The female orc was once again lost in the alluring dance of the flames. Fasto kneeled on the ground, his eyes wide with a newfound wonder, as if he were praising the now-gone General.

Clearing his throat, the Captain broke the overbearing silence with his deep, knowing voice. "Get some rest. It seems that there is a bedroll already set for each of you. I'll keep watch."

Shaking his head, Captain Osann grabbed his mighty greatsword and stalked over to the edge of the fire's dim light. He sat down, alone in his grim vigil, with his back turned to the companions.

The companions slowly got up, each claiming their own respective bedroll. As SmibSmob lay on the cold, hard streets of the fallen Calinad, his mind swirled in torment, thoughts of their journey crashing through his mind. The prison. Mariah. Captain Osann. His mind rocked about as if caught in a violent storm.

Mariah. Nalgene. The others. The woman. Kraalek. Black butterflies. The Beacon. And overwhelming it all, his dark power clawed and ripped at his mind more ferociously than he could ever remember, trying to corrupt his being and twist him into madness.

Sighing in frustration, SmibSmob closed his eyes, letting the cool, soothing embrace of exhaustion fall across him.

Daniel Whitman

Chapter 4

Nalgene awoke to the soft drumming of rain falling in the cool, morning air. He felt refreshed, reinvigorated from yesterday's troubles, as if the comforting rain was washing away all his sorrows. Even though his blue cloak sagged with dampness, his eyes sparkled with renewed vigor. Aye, this was what he needed. He hadn't felt the rain on his skin for over two years, ever since … since what?

He could not remember. Like the others, his memories from before the prison had fallen from the recesses of his mind. Shaking his head, Nalgene arose from the hard ground, throwing his bedroll to the side. His gaze wandered across the carcass of the city, absorbing its broken grandeur in the pale, morning light. Cold rays of sunlight were just starting to shine through the cracks of the ruined buildings, basking the clearing in an eerie glow.

Looking around, Nalgene found his companions still wallowing deep within the trenches of slumber. Ro and Margaret lay side-by-side, their breath even and steady. Fasto lay peacefully nearby, yet his mouth ran rampant, telling a silent tale of forgotten dreams. Andromeda rolled about furiously, her tail slashing back and forth in frustration. And finally, there was SmibSmob, his brother, who lay still upon the hard ground. Ah, his brother … He knew of the dark power that burned deep within him, and he feared what it would do to him.

Not wanting to press the thought, Nalgene tore his eyes away from his brother, only to find them resting upon the smooth, marble fountain standing strong before the fallen cathedral.

The fountain's elegant beauty seemed misplaced in such wanton destruction, yet still, it seemed right to the gnome. Its pure, blue water cascading over its white lip, only to land splashing in a shimmering pool of harmony. Something tugged at the back of Nalgene's mind, some thought, some memory, but he could not place it. It was as if he had seen the marvelous fountain before in a long-forgotten life. He studied the fountain for a moment longer, trying to unravel its forgotten mysteries, but to no avail.

Blasted fountain.

Turning away, Nalgene cast another glance around the camp. The once billowing fire had been reduced to charred ashes, beaten down by the constant pounding of the rain. He smiled. He knew the power of the rain.

Once more, he glanced at his slumbering companions. It was so peaceful. There was Ro, Andromeda, Margaret, Fasto, and of course, his dear SmibSmob. But then it hit him.

One person was missing. Where was that sneaky Osann? So much for keeping watch.

Straightening himself, Nalgene studied the city square. Nothing seemed out of place, yet an uneasy sense of dread was slowly boiling inside of him. Taking one, final look around the area, Nalgene narrowed his eyes in trepidation. Where did he be? He'd bet a dwarf's hairy ass that the bloody Osann was off with the Shadow.

He didn't care what the shifty General said, or what Ro said. The Captain meant no good. Grunting to himself, he shuffled out of the square, trying to be as quiet as possible. Unfortunately, stealth was never one of his exceptional skills.

Nalgene crept through the cobble streets, looking for any sign of the missing Captain. He looked in ruined buildings, down thin alleys, and even under fallen stones. Scouting wasn't one of his exceptional skills, either.

After some time of very perceptive and competent searching, he found himself looking down another nondescript street. It was remarkable how similar everything looks when it is all decrepit. But as he stepped forward, he heard a faint sound. Straining his ears, the gnome was just able to make out the deep, rumbling voice of Captain Osann drifting through the air.

Aha! He knew it!

Stomping his feet in triumph, forgetting all prospects of stealth, Nalgene marched toward the source of the Captain's voice.

As he neared, he began to hear another voice — not a deep, knowing voice like Captain Osann's, but a softer, more dangerous voice, a voice that cut deep into Nalgene's very being and filled him with a harrowing sense of fear. Suppressing his anxiety, Nalgene pressed forward with a distinct lack of caution. Thankfully, the rain masked his footsteps, drowning him out with its constant drumming. The voices steadily grew louder and clearer, and he began to piece together the wispy strands of sentences.

"You don't … couldn't …"

"… is that so?"

Just who in the bloody hell was that bastard Osann talking to, and what about?

As Nalgene made his way about the fallen buildings, his eyes darted down every street. With every turn he expected to come face-to-face with the Captain, but the gnome had no such luck. By now, the square was far behind, and he was alone. He was not ignorant of the danger.

"Listen! … I know."

"… Oh, I don't think you do …"

"Trust me … received my orders."

Where in the blasted city were they?

The pale sun started to cast its bleak rays of light over top the buildings. The voices grew louder, and a rage began to simmer deep within him. But just as fast as it grew the cool rain pattered down and extinguished it.

"No ... anything but that."

"Then you better remember ..."

"Yes, but I promised them. I took an oath!"

"Break it."

Nalgene turned a final corner and stumbled upon what he sought. The Captain was at the far end of the street, his head bowed and his once strong form sagging like a broken man. But that's not what caught Nalgene's eye. Standing over the defeated Captain like a shadowy tyrant was a dark, cloaked figure. Patterns of skulls and other markings of death swirled around the inky robe. At the being's side hung a ghastly, black dagger, sharpened to razor perfection. The being's face was masked by a draping cowl. And shining out where the being's eyes should have been were two, billowing purple flames of despair, penetrating even the heartiest of person's resolve.

Nalgene froze. All thoughts of Captain Osann and the conversation he was having with the shadowy figure vanished from his mind. His simmering sense of dread and rage boiled over in an explosive fury. Unconsciously, he brought his hands out in front of him, a vortex of water already forming in their midst. This was it. He knew that Captain Osann could not be trusted, and this was all the proof he needed. Growling, he focused on the cloaked figure, preparing to send it to oblivion. His power seemed stronger somehow, as if it were being enhanced and redoubled by his fury.

And still the rain came down.

But before Nalgene could unleash his devastating blast of water, the shadowy figure's raging eyes shot over to him, pinning him in place with their accusing, damning stare. The two purple chasms flared with anger, and the being raised its hand, casting a shadowy bolt of energy to obliterate the stunned gnome. Alarmed,

Nalgene fell back in fear, his mind racing with terror. Blood hell! He was daft — no better than a beardless dwarf!

Without hesitation, without even looking back, Nalgene rushed down the winding streets, back toward the square.

The shells of buildings flew past Nalgene in a wild blur, but he dared not slow. His lungs burned with the effort, and his small legs strained in exhaustion, yet he did not feel tired. He only felt the rain beating upon his rough face, and it pushed him ever onward. He rushed left, and then right, and then left again, his mind whirling about in fury.

Osann! That shitty and bloody awful excuse for a good man!

Nalgene tore into the square, his breath coming in short gasps. Reaching his companions, he froze in shock. He found Captain Osann already there, waking the others from their slumber. Noticing Nalgene's abrupt arrival, the Captain gave him a curt nod in greeting, before collecting up his bedroll as if nothing was amiss.

Captain Osann did not meet Nalgene's eyes.

Nalgene's rage burned hot, and the gnome felt as if he were about to erupt into violence. His eyes shot blades of ice at the Captain, and his mind whirled about in a frenzy. How dare Captain Osann lie to him. He gave his oath and yet he's throwing it all away to some dark, cloaked figure. And for what? Bloody hell, how dare the Captain lie to him? He made his promise, told them that he would guide them and protect them, and yet he was deceiving them while their backs were turned.

Swirling water formed within Nalgene's fists, and a growl escaped his lips. How dare Osann lie to him. But as much as he wanted to unleash on the pathetic traitor, the soft rain quenched his brash emotions.

He knew he couldn't be a dolt. He knew he shouldn't make a scene. The unbearable dragon would never listen. So, he would just watch Osann and make sure he didn't do anything. Especially around his brother. One wrong move and he was gone. He'd be sure of it.

Shaking his thoughts away, Nalgene stalked over to his belongings and picked up the glass bottle that Mariah had bestowed upon him. He turned it over in his rough hands, admiring its elegant beauty and the shimmering water trapped within the crystal cage. He shot another icy glare at the Captain before turning his gaze back to the miraculous bottle.

Not this time …

Chuckling softly to himself, he tucked the sparkling bottle away, and stood there helplessly, trying to fend off against the overwhelming tide of events.

The other companions had since awoken and were busy preparing to venture out of the ruined city. Margaret made a snide remark about the unpleasant weather, but none cared to listen, not even the great and chivalrous Ro. Noticing his brother's distress, SmibSmob warily made his way over to Nalgene, worry shadowing his face.

"You alright there, brother?" SmibSmob started. "I don't mean to alarm you, but you're not looking too good."

"Well," Nalgene said, his voice low. "That bloody Osann's a traitor, I saw it with me own two eyes."

SmibSmob's mouth opened in shock, and he shot a quick glance at the Captain. "A traitor?" he asked. "Are you sure? What did you see?"

"Well, I was walkin' through the streets, when I be stumblin' into that bloody Osann," Nalgene growled. "He was talkin' with some cloaked freak, but when I —"

"When you what?" Captain Osann interrupted, appearing by Nalgene's side. He loomed over the gnome like a giant.

Nalgene jumped in alarm and whirled about to face the traitor. "Bah," he spat at the Captain. "Ye be knowin' what happened."

He raised his hands, and two menacing orbs of water formed over his fists. His rage boiled over once more, and he charged at the

Captain, his fists swinging wildly. How dare Osann lie to him. He gave his oath.

"Nalgene!" SmibSmob shouted, rushing forward to stop his brother. Fighting would not solve anything. Even if the Captain was a traitor, they needed him, at least for now. But once they were free … that would be a different matter entirely.

Immediately Nalgene skidded to a halt, and his fists lowered to his side, the swirling water disappearing. He glared at the traitor, and he opened his mouth, but the rain silenced his words and quenched his burning fury.

Captain Osann had not moved — or even reacted to Nalgene's charge. It was as if he wanted to be beaten for his sins. Frowning, he stared at Nalgene, his face a mask of disappointment. "Pack your stuff," he grumbled. "We leave at once." Shaking his head, he walked away without saying another word.

Nalgene turned to SmibSmob. "Why did ye stop me, me brother?" he asked, desperately wanting to obliterate the Captain. If only it was not raining.

SmibSmob stared at him for a long moment, trying to find his words. "We need him," he finally said. "I don't know what you saw, but we can't rush around trying to kill our only guide."

"Yer right," Nalgene grumbled, quite ashamed. He could not meet SmibSmob's piercing eyes. Shaking his head, Nalgene turned away, doubt clouding his mind.

Bloody rain. Bloody Osann.

As the companions finished gathering their varied belongings, Nalgene found himself gazing upon the marvelous fountain. Once again, he felt a prick at the back of his mind, as if something were attempting to break through an impenetrable barrier.

What were its mysteries?

His dark eyes pored over the fountain, reevaluating even the smallest of details. The pure, white marble, not a single scratch upon its ethereal surface, and the graceful, flowing water, oblivious to the desolation surrounding it.

Nalgene felt the rain fall upon his open face.

Stupid bloody hunk of rock. What was it hiding?

The prick gnawing at the back of his mind grew into a deadly spear, jabbing into his every thought. That damned fountain. Why was he so drawn to it?

He let out a feral growl, and his rough hands curled into iron fists.

The masterful engravings etched into the roots of the stone, and the sculpted figures of enchanting white holding up the fragile foundations.

His mind screamed, urging the glorified stone to tell him its secrets.

Nalgene felt the rain weave down his body, and the mighty spear in his mind rose into a roaring inferno, crashing down with a terrible power. His vision grew blurry, and he grew unsteady on his feet.

"YE BLOODY ROCK!" he growled.

The rain enveloped his mind, washing over him with a cool embrace, and his vision went black.

The barrier cracked.

◆　　◆　　◆

The gnome paraded through the cheering crowd, elevated atop a swirling platform of the purest of water. To his right was his brother, the mighty Gnome of the Shadow, who brought peace and tranquility to warring kingdoms across the lands. To his left was his dear friend, the chivalrous Dragon of Hope. Flowing out behind the gnome, his blue cloak shone bright in the brilliant morning light, leading a procession of battle-worn soldiers from the forsaken battlefield. The gnome waved to the surrounding crowd, casting cheerful showers raining down upon the sea of citizens, and bringing about an ever-louder roar of excitement. This was his, and only his, moment of glory.

The city around them rose up to meet the very heavens, the buildings brushing against the sky like colossal obelisks of power. Rows of marvelous buildings lined the sides of the winding street, and dancing flames billowed about the area, basking the crowd in a warm embrace. An aura of exhilaration filled the air with a tangible fire, but a suppressed undertone of hardship cut deep. Newfound widows and orphans lined the streets, hoping for a glimpse of the ones they knew had not returned. Yet no one noticed, or cared to notice, for the heroes had arrived, marking the end of the terrible war.

The gnome led the triumphant procession through the winding streets of the grand city. As the shining sun crested its peak, they came upon a massive square opening in the heart of the city. Four, twisting spires rose up from the corners, each holding aloft the weight of the heavens. Standing strong at the back of the square was a mighty granite cathedral shaped to withstand the biting test of time. Rising proudly in front of the great cathedral doors was an enchanting fountain, forged from the purest of marble from another time. Magnificent figures and etchings adorned the crystalline surface, yet the fountain ran empty, its water lost to the brutal ages.

The crowd grew ever denser near the fountain, and an excess of various wagons and stands dotted the area, all filled with hopeful merchants eager to sell their exotic goods. Pushing past the bustling crowd, the gnome had only one goal — one, final challenge to overcome. Upon arriving at the beautiful fountain, he reached into the billowing folds of his cloak, pulling out a shimmering bottle, sparkling with the mesmerizing dance of the water within. He held it out in front of him, holding it high as if it were a sacred offering. To his right, his brother's eyes sparkled, and he gave the gnome an assuring nod. To his left, his dear friend smiled with approval, urging the gnome to finish the task. The gnome turned to face the *cheering crowd. This was it. The pinnacle of his triumph. Ushering from his lips poured out a grand speech, the words of which have long since been forgotten. Time seemed a blur for the gnome. Was he talking for a minute or an hour? He knew not. His only focus was the crystalline bottle he held in his rough hands, the white fountain rising behind him, and the glory it would bring him. Completing his speech, the crowd sang exuberantly. He turned back to the fountain, and after one final glance at his brother, he opened the glass bottle.*

A rush of ecstasy and power washed over the gnome. Rising from the narrow opening was the shimmering water, swaying in a tantalizing dance. He poured his very lifeblood — and others' — into this water, sacrificing their combined Inner Fire to create an unbreakable bond with the liquid. It was a grim process, but it brought him glory.

Raising his hands, the water poured out in a seemingly endless supply, forming a swirling orb above the gnome's head. The orb pulsed with the promise of life, and the crowd fell to an eerie silence, lost in the miraculous display. The gnome did not notice. Fully enveloped in the true potential of his power, the gnome cast the mighty orb down upon the fragile fountain.

But it stood strong.

As the water crashed down upon the marble fountain, it rushed into the inner workings, sending not a single splash over the lip. The crowd gazed on with uncertainty, unsure how to react. But then, as if born from some heavenly miracle, the fountain came back to life. Shimmering, pure water flowed over its surface, cascading in myriad waterfalls to land gently in the basin below. The crowd cheered with a new respect, rushing forward to embrace their savior.

The gnome fell back, exhaustion falling across his body. He did it. This is how they would remember him — the monuments he left throughout the land. He turned, casting his eyes upon the dense crowd, a smile beaming on his gnarled face. This was his glory. He did it.

A Land in Shadow

Suddenly, a man standing in the back of the crowd caught his attention. Narrowing his eyes, he gazed upon the strange man. He had long, shaggy hair colored to an inky black, and a bushy mustache that curled across his gentle face. A flowing, blue cape waved out behind him, a stark contrast to the man's otherwise ordinary clothes. The man gave the gnome a smile, his teeth sparkling with the purest of white. He offered the gnome a wave, raising an armored hand in greeting. But in that hand, he held a mysterious hammer, of the likes the gnome had never seen. It twisted in gold and silver, catching the sun in a brilliant light. The gnome smiled back at the man, and turned, gesturing to his brother and friend to follow him down into the crowd. It was time to leave. It was time to gather the others and prepare for the end — for the final battle. As he took a step forward, a dark haze fell over his vision. His mind grew muddled, and his legs grew weary. He saw the strange man. He saw the marvelous hammer ...

◆   ◆   ◆

Nalgene fell back, the vivid memories already fading from his mind. Gasping for breath, he looked around, his eyes darting wildly.

"What in the bloody hell?"

Not a heartbeat had since passed, yet to Nalgene it had felt like an eternity. The rain still solemnly drummed on the stone streets. The others had finished rummaging through their little belongings and had their newly acquired bedrolls packed and ready for travel. Nalgene turned back to the fountain, but he felt nothing. No persistent itch at the back of his mind, no piercing spear penetrating his thoughts. Something seemed missing — something vital, some key piece of history, but Nalgene could not place it. He tried to grasp the fading strands of the tangible memory, but to no avail. It was gone, not even a fragment of the past remaining in the gnome's mind.

Regaining his composure, Nalgene slowly shook his head, turning away from the white fountain, turning away from the forgotten memories of the past.

Stupid fountain.

Rejoining the others, Nalgene still felt a jarring hatred for Captain Osann, but now it was more controlled, more a deep, simmering rage than a fiery outburst of emotions. He was watching him — that bloody traitor.

The sun had just crested above the fallen buildings, basking the camp in a pale light. The Captain beckoned the companions to gather around, his face a hard mask of steel.

"It is time," he said stoically. "The sun is past its quarter. We should be off. I would like to reach the southern crossroads with all haste."

Ro nodded in agreement, eager to leave the ruined city.

"Lead the way," SmibSmob said, shooting a sideways glance at his brother.

Nalgene only growled, fixing the Captain with an icy glare.

The Captain led the companions through the winding streets, leading them to where the mighty southern gate had once proudly stood. They proceeded with caution, constantly monitoring the area around them, watching for any signs of the Shadow. Nalgene thought it to be a bluff, a false front from the Captain, yet still he watched, his deep eyes studying every flickering shadow. As they trekked through the grand city, the rain began to lighten up to a drizzle.

When the companions finally arrived at the once-mighty southern gate, they found it had been reduced to a pile of rubble and debris. No one dared break the grim silence. As they passed through the devastation, Nalgene saw a dark form flutter at the edges of his vision. Whipping his head around, his gaze locked onto the blazing purple eyes of a black cloaked figure. He was not the only one to notice the shadowy stalker. The cloaked form let out a silent chuckle, raising its hand, before disappearing into the surrounding shadows. Before Nalgene could react, before he could unleash a devastating torrent of boiling water, an arrow streaked past his face, just missing a fatal blow.

Nalgene fell back, letting out an alarmed cry. Rising out from among the rubble and debris of the gate was a legion of undead, their soulless eyes eager to kill. Mobs of deathly zombies trudged forward from the shadows. Ranks of armored skeletons poured out from the ruins, armed with razor-sharp swords and axes, pointed spears and reinforced shields, and powerful longbows nocked with arrows. Behind Nalgene, the others scrambled into position, raising their arms against their nightmarish foes. SmibSmob rushed up to his brother's side, ready to devastate the undead horde in a torrent of water and shadow.

"We have no hope of outrunning them," Ro observed, trying to take control of the dire situation. "They have bows. They'll shoot us down as we turn."

"Oh, isn't that just perfect," Margaret sighed, frustration weighing her voice down.

"No worry, friend," Fasto jumped in. "Fasto has white bow. Fasto shoot other bow. Fasto protect friend."

"Don't call me that," Margaret growled, her black, demonic arm swirling with a vortex of ice. "Just shoot them."

"Ready!" Ro shouted, his shining longsword held at his side defensively, and his iron shield held out like an impenetrable wall.

Captain Osann said nothing as he raised his now flaming greatsword in front of him. Searing heat radiated from the mighty weapon in a sharp wave, basking the companions in warmth.

Nalgene let out a vicious growl, throwing one final glare at the masked traitor. He had a simmering rage to quench.

Suddenly, a massive zombie burst forward from the rest of the horde. Rippling muscles roped across its rotting flesh, and a wide mouth hung open, displaying rows of razor teeth. The unearthly creature propelled itself forward, every pulse of its bulging legs sending it soaring toward its target. A guttural scream thundered out from its maw, and it locked its empty eyes upon Nalgene.

Andromeda leaped out of the shadows, tearing into the mighty zombie with a terrifying ferocity. Her eyes glowed with a devilish light, and she severed chunks of flesh from the undead abomination. Her claws sunk into the creature's burly shoulders, and with a surprising surge of strength, she tore the zombie's head off, its skull locked firmly in her deadly jaws. She whipped around, leaping off the gruesome carcass, her mighty halberd appearing in her hand. As suddenly as she came, she was lost in the shadows, no doubt seeking her next target.

Nalgene shook his head in wonder. A lone raindrop splashed across his face, and he let out a silent chuckle.

The remaining horde surged forward, oblivious to the dreadful fate of the first zombie. Roaring, the companions rushed forward to meet them. Nalgene raised his hands, unleashing a barrage of devastating orbs of water upon the back lines. Beside him, SmibSmob had already succumbed to his dark power, and his demonic eyes shone eager for blood. Blasts of shadow crashed into the ranks of undead, only to be followed up by a hail of water.

He wished SmibSmob didn't have to use it.

Turning away from his brother, Nalgene focused on the oncoming storm of undead, a wild growl escaping his lips. He raised his hands, sending a deadly stream of water piercing into a zombie that had wandered too close.

Rushing forward, he called forth a massive wave of water, sending it pummeling down upon the undead legion. Arrows streaked past him, both from Fasto and the skeleton archers, but he ignored them. His mind was too far invested in his boiling rage. Swirling orbs of water shot forth from his rough hands, smashing the undead with frightening force. From the corner of his eye, he saw Ro locked in combat with a host of undead, a pile of rotting bodies already forming about the fearsome draconian. Noticing a zombie charging for the draconian's exposed back, Nalgene blasted it down with a piercing stream of water, before turning away, not waiting for the draconian's thanks. A massive pillar of fire shot forth from the ground, disintegrating many undead in a searing rush of flame. Nalgene ignored it. He felt the soft touch of the rain fall across him. His eyes darted about wildly, and he sent forth a mighty orb of swirling water at any undead he saw.

Suddenly, a crushing pain exploded in Nalgene's side, and he was sent staggering back, crashing into the muddy ground. His breath was blasted from his lungs, and he curled up on the ground, trying to clear his hazy vision. Damn zombie or something must have got him.

Coughing, he pushed himself up to stand shakily on his feet. Another explosion of pain surged through his body, and he went soaring back, landing upon the wet ground. A massive zombie threw itself on top of him, blasting away whatever composure he still had. The stench of rotting flesh overwhelmed the gnome and he felt razor teeth tear into his shoulder, ripping across the bone with unbearable pain.

His vision grew black.

He tried to conjure up a vortex of water, tried to summon up anything that would free himself from the hulking abomination tearing into him. All he got was a pitiful squirt of water. With another explosion of wrenching pain, the putrid teeth sank back into him, crushing his ribs under their immense power. Nalgene felt his ribs fracture under the pressure, felt his small lung collapse under the weight of the monstrous teeth. He tried to reach for the crystalline bottle, but it was beyond his grasp. His mind started to fade. Images of Captain Osann, the traitor, and SmibSmob, his dear brother, filled his black vision.

Fucking Osann.

He saw the cloaked figure mocking him in his mind, taunting him with its glowing purple eyes. A red haze started to seep over the edge of the gnome's mind. He saw his brother, twisted by his dark power, decimating all that they held dear. He saw the others, even Ro, being overwhelmed in an endless tide of undead, all while Osann stood laughing in the background. The burning red haze filled his mind.

One, final raindrop fell upon him, washing over his fragile form.

A roaring geyser burst from beneath the gnome, blasting apart the hulking being tearing into the gnome's flesh. The gnome placed his hand upon his chest, releasing a rush of soothing water over his broken body. The torn flesh wove itself back together, the punctured lung breathed with a new life, and the shattered bones reformed themselves with a newfound strength. The gnome shot to his feet. Raising his rough hands, a swirling tide of water rose up to meet him, conjuring into a mighty vortex beneath his feet. Throwing his hands to the boiling sky, he rose up into the air upon his new perch. His blue cloak flapped about wildly, even though the wind stood calm. His eyes glowed a fiery blue.

With a thunderous crash, the gnome ripped his hands down, bringing down the very might of the heavens. Lightning streaked across the sky, crashing into the surrounding horde with terrifying precision. Torrents of rain unleashed from the heavens, covering the area in a torrential downpour. Arrows shot up at the elevated gnome, but he paid them no heed, for he was beyond such trivial nuisances. Tendrils of water shot forward to meet the oncoming hail of arrows, tearing them out of the sky. The gnome smiled.

Gazing around, he saw the forms of others battling against the horde. There was a she-orc, obliterating undead with ruthless brutality. Sharp fragments of ice covered the area about her, and a dozen frozen bodies lay scattered at her feet. Then there was the feline, assassinating undead with a shadowy grace. She now fought against a host of shielded skeletons and desperately sought to bypass their iron defenses. Next was another orc, raining down an endless volley of arrows upon the unearthly creatures. A broken shaft protruded from the orc's arm, but he growled it off, as he was focused more on the others than his own well-being. There was also a draconian, who cleaved through the undead with mythical strength, and blasted them down with his breath of lightning. Blood oozed down his armor, although whether it was his or the enemies, the gnome could not tell. Finally, there was another gnome. A purple cloak flowed about him, and devastating spells of shadow shot forth from his hands, ripping the surrounding undeads' very life force for his own use. A wide smile twisted the shadowy gnome's face into a crazed mask of glee.

The red haze faltered.

His brother …

Shaking his head, the gnome quickly turned away from the others. He knew there should have been another fighting against the vile legion, but he brushed the thought away. He had an unholy legion to destroy. Raising his hands, a swirling vortex of water enveloped the gnome, creating a mighty pillar of destruction in his wake. He clenched his gnarled fists, and the surrounding water swirled about ever faster, gaining power from the torrential downpour, expanding out into an unstoppable wave of death. Lightning streaked across the sky with ever more fury. The others stared up at him in wonder, then cried out in alarm. He saw the others turn away in panic, desperation clear in their eyes. The orcs, the feline, the draconian, all but the shadowy gnome fleeing in terror before his presence.

The gnome smiled, and he opened his hands, unleashing the surging wave of devastation.

◆   ◆   ◆

Nalgene awoke to the scaled face of Ro hovering over him. The draconian was vigorously shaking him, and a look of desperation twisted his face. Nalgene's whole body ached, and his mind was muddled and cloudy. What in the bloody hell happened?

He could not remember. Ro was speaking to him, but the gnome did not register it. Shrugging the draconian off, he slowly rose to his feet, his legs shaking with effort. He gazed around, absorbing the surrounding carnage with horror.

Mountains of rotting bodies littered the area, and the earth was shattered, the very ground torn and tossed about. A heavy dampness hung about in the air, and pools of water shimmered across the area. Looking closer, Nalgene saw a purple, cloaked form upon the muddy ground.

No! It couldn't be!

Frantic, Nalgene rushed over to his brother, tears beginning to form in the corners of his eyes.

Nalgene reached his brother, tearing him out of the thick mud to lay on his back. SmibSmob lay lifeless, his face pale and taut. Blood seeped from the side of the frail gnome's head, and one arm twisted at an unnatural angle. Clutched within the gnome's hands was his pointed hat, which now hung limp, dripping wet.

Nalgene fell back, anguish overwhelming his torn mind. What had he done?

His thoughts whirled in a furious storm. Ro rushed up to stand next to him, but the gnome did not notice. His thoughts were only for his brother. The draconian tried to shake him to his senses. Nalgene thought he heard Ro shouting in his ear, shouting how he could still save him, but he brushed it away, for he was too absorbed in his despair. Andromeda appeared from out of the shadows, her delicate face twisted with distress. She stalked over to the gnome, placing her tail upon his shoulder in an attempt to comfort him. She tried to tell him SmibSmob was not lost, but Nalgene ignored her. He had failed. Margaret and Fasto made their way over to the others. Fasto wore a look of concern, and he ran over to Nalgene, mumbling about "friend" and "help." Margaret merely stood in the background, shaking her head in disappointment.

Then Nalgene saw another figure rising out from among the piles of twisted bodies. Captain Osann staggered forward, his mighty sword dragging through the ground behind him. Nalgene's mind snapped. Everything came rushing back like a raging tsunami, ripping away his despair. He remembered the traitor. He remembered the black stalker with the purple eyes. A wild growl escaped his lips. Sound crashed into his ears, and Ro's voice broke through the haze:

"Save your brother."

Nalgene placed his hands upon his fallen brother's chest, unleashing a furious torrent of water, enveloping SmibSmob in a seething vortex. SmibSmob's eyes shot open, all signs of weariness erased from his face. Coughing, he rose to his feet, wrapping Nalgene in a loving embrace.

Tears streamed from Nalgene's eyes, but they were cut short as he gazed upon the Captain, who stood silently to the side, studying the exchange.

Nalgene released his brother, his eyes locked on the traitor. The boiling rage burst to life within him, and he stormed over to the Captain, his face twisted in fury. He thought back to the conversation he had overheard, back to the agent of Shadow with whom the Captain had spoken. Ro tried to hold Nalgene back, but the gnome brushed him off, continuing his march to the traitor. The rage burned hotter, and this time there was no rain to dampen the flame.

"Ye bloody traitor!" Nalgene exploded, an orb of water forming in his clenched fist. "I saw ye. I saw ye talkin' with the Shadow, talkin' with that purple-eyed freak!"

Behind him Andromeda flinched.

"All o' that horse shit about oaths and protectin' us and gettin' us to the Flame, well go shove it up yer hairy arse, ye scum! Ye may want to hurt all o' us, but let me tell ye, I won't be lettin' that happen!" Nalgene planted his feet into the mud, his face burning a bright red. He panted heavily, and he raised his fist up in front of his face in a clear threat.

Captain Osann stood quietly. For a moment, Nalgene felt a sense of pity for the broken man but quickly tossed the feeling into the billowing inferno of his fury.

"Nalgene, my dear friend," Ro said quietly, moving up to stand next to the gnome. "What are you saying? He gave us his oath." The draconian's voice wavered with uncertainty.

Nalgene snorted. Oaths are nothing more than words. "Well? Should I tell 'em?" he snarled. "Or are ye gonna tell 'em, eh, Osann?"

The Captain looked up at the companions, his normally stoic face torn with emotions. "You don't understand," he whispered, his eyes wavering.

"Eh, what was that?" Nalgene screamed.

"You don't understand," Captain Osann repeated, his voice growing steadier. "I did what I had to do. We all have our choices to make, and for me — my family …"

The Captain's voice broke, and his strong shoulders sagged under his great burden. Ro gazed upon him in sympathy.

"Yer bloody family, eh!" Nalgene relentlessly shouted back. "And ye don't be thinkin' that some of us be havin' families too?"

Thoughts of his brother filled his mind, thoughts of Osann tearing him apart with his flaming greatsword, thoughts of the traitor killing his brother in the darkness of night. His fury overwhelmed his mind, and Nalgene took a step forward, the once tame orb of water growing into a massive globe of destruction. Ro shouted at him, but he ignored it. Andromeda rushed in front of the Captain, her expression torn with an inner conflict. Nalgene snarled at her.

Sacrifices could be made.

Fasto rushed beside him, a pleading look on his face. The orc tried to say something, but Nalgene shut it out. The traitor had to die. No one else saw what he had seen and no one else knew of the Captain's deception. This was his burden to bear. He heard himself shouting out, heard himself accusing the Captain. He took a final step forward, raising the swirling orb up like a billowing beacon of death. The Captain just stood, his eyes upon the ground, broken. It had to be done.

Suddenly, a frail hand pressed upon Nalgene's shoulder. SmibSmob had to understand … He saw him. He was just trying to warn them …

The furious torrent of water disappeared, and Nalgene turned to face his brother. SmibSmob stood behind him calmly, an understanding look upon his face. SmibSmob shook his head, locking eyes with his brother.

"Nalgene, we need him," he said. "We've already been over this. He gave us his promise."

"But ye don't understand," Nalgene replied. "I saw him talkin' with the Shadow."

"Even if he were with the Shadow," SmibSmob replied, "he can still guide us to the Flame. We can't do this alone."

"SmibSmob's right," Ro jumped in, moving up to stand beside Nalgene. "We need to trust him. We need to trust Mariah."

Nalgene's mind whirled. He knew the Captain was a traitor. He knew he meant to break his oath, yet the others — even his dear brother — refused to believe him.

He stammered, at a loss for words. Why don't they see it?

He turned back to the Captain, his rage bursting to life whenever he laid his eyes upon the traitor.

Bloody hell, even the damned dragon didn't believe it.

Andromeda stood next to the Captain, her face steeled and unreadable. Captain Osann locked eyes with Nalgene, a desperate look upon his face. The Captain moved his mouth, silently pleading with the furious gnome.

"Captain friend," Fasto piped in, rushing up and embracing Captain Osann. "Fasto trust friend."

Nalgene shook his head, turning back to his brother. SmibSmob took a step back, his pointed hat once again resting upon his head. The gnome's blue eyes pierced Nalgene, pinning him in place with their knowing stare.

"Nalgene," SmibSmob said.

Nalgene turned back to the Captain, pointing an accusing finger at him. "A'ight, ye damn scum," he said threateningly. "Me brother says to trust ye, so I'll be trustin' ye. But I'll be trustin' me own two eyes as well. I know what I saw, even if the others don't believe it. One wrong move from yer hairy arse and yer gone."

Captain Osann let out a silent sigh of relief, lifting his shoulders high and proud. The Captain's renewed vigor cast a doubt upon the gnome's thoughts. Maybe the man really was here to help.

But he discarded the thought. He knew what he saw, and he had to stand strong by it.

Captain Osann raised his mighty sword up onto his strong shoulder. He gazed upon the companions with a tangible aura of determination. His deep voice rang out clear: "Come, follow me. I gave you my oath, and I intend to keep it. Even ..." He cleared his throat and glanced at Nalgene, giving him a slight nod.

Nalgene only growled in return.

"Now, follow me, towards the Light and the Flame," Captain Osann beckoned.

The Captain led them south upon the dusty road. The land around them grew ever bleaker and more devoid of life. There were no trees and no shrubs, just vast emptiness. It was a desolate plain, gray smear on the canvas of the world. An aura of despair hung about the air, and the companions looked on, spirits low. The sun still shone with a cold, pale light, and the nights were lonely and dark, the moonless sky bearing in on them like an oppressive shadow. The companions stood ever alert, constantly watching for any sign of undead, but there was none. The land was empty, barren of even the vile minions of the Shadow. Nalgene had the sense that they were being watched, and his mind thought back to the cloaked figure of black, and the blazing, purple eyes, but he saw nothing. As the days passed, Captain Osann lost his vigor, and his eyes started to gaze across the dreadful land, as if searching for something. His confidence grew weary, yet still he pushed them southward with an iron determination.

As the third night began reaching its black grasp across the land, the companions found themselves at a fork in the road, one side branching east while the other continued south. Far to the west lay the edges of the mountain range, the wispy peaks just visible in the coming darkness. What lay to the south, they knew not.

The Captain bid them rest their weary feet for the night. He seemed unsure, and his eyes kept glancing to the west. "Let us rest the night here," Captain Osann told the companions. "Take care for what shadows may attack from the darkness. We will continue south at the first light of dawn."

The weary companions eagerly agreed.

Satisfied, the Captain turned to the east, his gaze staring off into the starless night. He muttered something to himself and set off into the enveloping darkness.

Nalgene watched the Captain leave, his mind whirling in suspicion. "And where do ye think yer goin', eh, Osann?" Nalgene asked.

The Captain turned back to him, but he did not meet the gnome's eyes. "To scout ahead," he said, his voice as deep and stoic as ever. "Stay at the fork, I shall return before morn."

With that, he turned away, disappearing into the shadows.

Nalgene snorted. No shot in shit he was staying here.

His mind rushed back to the cloaked figure, and he clenched his fists, his knuckles turning white. He knew where the traitor was going: right back to the Shadow where he belonged. He'd bet a dwarf's hairy ass on it.

He felt an inner fury starting to simmer within, but he kept it down. After waiting a moment, he turned back to the others, who were content with resting for the everlasting night. Nalgene chuckled softly to himself.

They all had a family they wanted to protect. It was just a

matter of how they wanted to do it. And clearly Osann was going about it the wrong way. What a shame. He could rot in oblivion for all Nalgene cared.

"A'ight, listen up. Damn Osann left us, and I be thinkin' it's about bloody time we left him."

Chapter 5

"Great. Another brilliant idea," Margaret jabbed at Nalgene. "Let's leave the only person who has any idea where we are because you *think* we should?"

Margaret shook her head. Why was she still following these idiots?

She let out a tormented sigh. She wanted to just let it all go, to run across the open lands. More than anything, she wanted freedom. She knew the unforgiving clutches of slavery. She knew the hopeless horror of being alone. She knows the feeling of being trapped by your very own self. And yet, here she was, as much a prisoner as ever, her demonic arm pulsing with its inner life. She resented it, hated what it signified: she was a monster. But there was no escape. Still, it pulsed, as much a part of her as it was its own, twisted being. The haunting memories of her early childhood began to boil up from the forgotten depths of her mind, but she cast them away, banishing them from her thoughts.

Glancing around, Margaret was just able to make out her companions in the darkness. None of them seemed to notice, or care for, her back-handed remark, as they were all too focused on Ro's argument with Nalgene. She chuckled silently to herself. Ro was so willing to become a leader, to become the so-called Beacon, yet he wouldn't find any followers here. Why would they follow such an idiot? They all heard the voice.

Shaking her head in amusement, Margaret glanced back down to her demonic arm, studying its twisting muscles. She grunted in frustration. Her shoulder ached with a shallow pain, no doubt from idiot gnome's little outburst from earlier, but she was too proud to admit to it. She did not understand Nalgene, did not care to understand Nalgene. One moment he's drooling over his brother, and the other, he's calling down lightning and casting titanic waves of destruction across his wake, nearly killing his frail brother in the process.

He was also an idiot.

Sighing, Margaret walked over to where the others were gathered.

"I'm tellin' ye," Nalgene growled at Ro. "Damn Osann is off talkin' with the Shadow. 'Scouting ahead,' me hairy arse."

"Listen," Ro shot back. "We can't be having this pointless argument every time Captain Osann does something."

Margaret shook her head in amusement. Ro was still trying to control the annoying little gnome. What a fool. Even so, she could not help but feel as if Nalgene were right. Even though she was repulsed by the very thought, she knew the gnome would not lie, especially if SmibSmob were there.

Gazing around, Margaret was just able to make out the forms of SmibSmob and Fasto in the background. SmibSmob stood next to Nalgene, while Fasto sided with Ro.

Andromeda was nowhere to be seen.

Margaret was quite fond of the elusive feline. She felt a sort of kinship for her, as if they had shared some fated part of their past. No matter the situation, Andromeda had always seemed steadfast and sure, pushing forward regardless of what the others thought. But recently Andromeda was distant and closed off. Ever since she had first encountered the Captain, she had hidden away with herself, rarely speaking or interacting with the others. She just moved aimlessly about, waiting for the next horde of undead to strike so she could eagerly rush into the bloody fray. Margaret shook her head.

It was a shame. She just wished she didn't feel the same way.

Margaret's thoughts were interrupted by a bright flare shining up in the night. She whipped her head about and saw the slender and attractive form of Andromeda, who now held a torch. The feline stalked forward to Ro, gently brushing him with her slender tail.

"Perhaps this will help," Andromeda purred. "No use standing in the darkness."

Handing the torch over to Ro, Andromeda briefly locked her eyes with Margaret's. The feline's eyes narrowed, sparkling in the orange glow of the torch. After a heartbeat, Andromeda looked away, and stalked over to the edge of the light, her expression unreadable.

Margaret's arm burst to life, pulsing wildly and emanating an icy chill from its twisted, corded muscles. There was something dark buried in the feline, but Margaret did not care to pry. Everyone had their monster.

By the light of the torch, Margaret was able to make out her companions more clearly. Nalgene stood steadfast, his feet planted firmly into the cold ground and his arms crossed over his chest. A snarl covered his face in a mask of rage. Beside him, SmibSmob stood calmly, his brow furrowed in thought. Ro tried to appear calm and in control, but Margaret could see the subtle twitching of his scaled hands, and the slight frown of his clenched maw. Margaret did not know what to think of Fasto. He stood next to Ro, as dumb an expression upon his face as ever, and he stared blankly at the empty sky, drool dripping from the corner of his open mouth.

What an idiot.

Focusing back on the argument, she noticed Ro faltering. The draconian knew that Nalgene was right. He just did not want to admit it.

What a leader.

"Ye damn dragon," Nalgene fumed. "I couldn't give a dwarf's hairy arse about the dark. Nothin' spooky about some night. We got a torch now, too. I be sayin' it's about bloody time we leave, and head east, away from the bloody traitor."

"No, we wait," Ro replied, his voice wavering. "He gave us his oath."

"And the bloody bastard's gonna break it, ye dolt!" Nalgene roared.

Fasto blinked, as if he had some grand epiphany. His face beamed with excitement, and he turned to Nalgene, a wild look on his face. "Fasto think —"

"Ah, shut it, ye bloody rat!" Nalgene shouted at the orc. Fasto gasped, and an injured look appeared on his face. Nalgene raised his fist, shaking it threateningly. "Now, ye listen here, ye damn dragon, I be sayin' we go east, so we be goin' east!"

"But," Ro started, raising his fist up to match the gnome's, "we have no idea where we're going. We don't know where we are! Captain Osann does. He can guide us."

"I don't be givin' a shit where we be goin', as long as it's away from that bloody traitor!"

"I don't mean to be the obvious one," SmibSmob jumped in. "But it's the middle of the night. If we're going to head east, we had better do it now. But if not, I would like to get some sleep."

"Ah, ye see?" Nalgene shouted triumphantly. "Me brother thinks we should head east … eh, wait what'd ye say?"

Margaret snickered. "That's the first intelligent thing I've heard in this whole argument." She shook her head, pretending not to care about what the others thought of her remark. But deep down, she knew she did. How frustrating. She could only growl.

"Exactly!" Nalgene exclaimed, giving Margaret a nod of approval. "Even the damn orc be thinkin' that we should be headin' east!"

Margaret rolled her eyes.

Ro started to reply, but his vain attempt at an argument was cut off by a dangerous purr from Andromeda, who was moving up to join the others. Her tail lashed back and forth violently, and her eyes gleamed with a murderous light. Even in the glowing light from the torch, she seemed a moving shadow, as if she were some otherworldly specter, her body fading in and out of the darkness. Margaret suddenly found the argument incredibly interesting.

"I have to agree with the gnome," Andromeda said softly, moving up to stand in front of Ro. She placed a gentle hand upon the draconian's chest, and gazed up at him with wide, open eyes. Margaret twitched. The feline ran her hand down the draconian's strong chest, a soothing purr of affection emitting from her.

"We can't trust the Captain, but we can trust Nalgene, and I'd much appreciate it if we were to leave the Captain behind," she declared, turning to face the others. "So, to the east, shall we?"

With that, Andromeda strode away, making not a sound as she crossed the cold, hard ground. Her figure slowly faded away into the dark clutches of the night, like some wavering mirage in the hot desert sun. Her halberd appeared in her hand, and she gave them one last encouraging nod before disappearing from the flickering light.

The companions stood silently for a moment, each one measuring Andromeda's words. Ro was silent. Margaret gazed at the place where Andromeda had disappeared, still feeling quite vexed.

The grim silence was broken by the obnoxious laughing of Nalgene.

"Bwahahaha," he boomed. "Damn cat's got the right idea. To the east."

After a brief pause, Ro relented, giving Nalgene a nod of agreement.

"To the east," he echoed softly. His shoulders hung limp, and his eyes studied the ground, defeated. He clenched his fists in frustration, but he knew he had lost. He had to accept the reality of it.

Margaret could not help but let out another silent chuckle. What a leader, indeed.

After the companions gathered their wits and their belongings, they set off eastward, fighting past their mounting exhaustion. The companions followed Ro silently down the abandoned road, not even Nalgene daring to break the looming silence. The barren plains stretched out for eternity, offering no escape from their grim fate. Above them, the starless sky gazed down at them in its empty life, devoid of any light. As they followed the fork east, the unnatural growls and sounds of the undead began to drift through. But whether it was their imagination or reality, they knew not.

Andromeda had reunited with them, appearing out of the hazy shadows to stalk at the back of the tightly huddled group. Her eyes darted around, and her ears twitched nervously. Margaret tried not to notice her. Nalgene and SmibSmob hovered behind the draconian, enjoying each other's promise of protection. Even Nalgene dared not travel alone in such forsaken lands. Fasto wandered about near Margaret, aimlessly following the torch in front of him. He kept giving her sideways glances, and would try to tell her of their friendship, but Margaret coldly ignored him.

As the night dragged on, there was no sign of Captain Osann — only the howl of the mournful wind and the ghastly growls from the shadows. The companions' resolve grew weary, and the blanket of exhaustion loomed over them. Margaret's vision grew hazy, and her feet dragged in the dirt behind her. But there were grumbling growls off in the darkness, and that was enough to keep her awake. She glanced around at her companions, who were similarly stumbling around, only to be reminded of the ever-present danger of the Shadow.

Suddenly, a sharp cry howled from Fasto. Immediately, Margaret's clarity returned, her blood pounding through her veins. The demonic arm at her side burst forth with a new life, and an icy chill surged from its black depths. Whipping her head around, she saw Fasto fall to the ground, a dark shape tearing into his flesh.

The creature was a nightmarish parody of a wolf. Its wide jaws hung open, displaying rows of yellow teeth. Rotting flesh hung loose from its body, and bones stuck out at unnatural angles. Sharp claws jutted out from its paws, tearing into the orc, drawing crimson lines of blood.

With the scent of blood filling the air, the undead wolf's empty eyes flared with an unholy fire. Raising its head, it released a bone-chilling howl from its maw. The high-pitched howl was twisted and unnatural, cutting through the air with an awful shriek, and cutting deep into Margaret's ears, driving her back in pain.

Nearby, another dreadful howl answered, and then another. Howls cried out from the shadows until the screeching of undead wolves echoed from every angle. Margaret whirled about, trying to find the nearby creatures, but her eyes could not pierce the impenetrable blackness. The others tried to enter some formation against the oncoming pack. Nalgene had blasted the wolf off Fasto and was busy washing away the injuries. SmibSmob looked around, and a crooked smile appeared on his face. He raised his hands, summoning up mighty orbs of shadow, the swirling void in their depths matching the surrounding darkness. Ro drew his longsword, its shining edge flickering in the torchlight. Andromeda was nowhere to be seen.

Suddenly, one of the howls was cut short, its screeching call ending with an abrupt yelp followed by silence. Andromeda rushed out of the shadows, black blood covering her snarling jaws. With a hiss, she lunged back into the darkness, her halberd appearing in her delicate hand. Ro let out a cry of alarm, and before Margaret could react, the pack was upon them.

Dozens of bloodthirsty undead wolves charged into the

light, eager for a feast. Margaret whirled about, her demonic arm pulsing with renewed determination. Without thinking, she swung her arm around, connecting with the jaws of an undead wolf. With a destructive blast of ice, the pitiful creature was sent sprawling, its head a shattered mass of gore and ice. Margaret knew there was no controlling her arm, knew there was no trying to hold it back. Growling, she embraced the blood lust, leaping into the oncoming wave of twisted wolves.

A vortex of ice formed about her, piercing any creature that dared wander too close with razor shards of chilling ice. Margaret locked her eyes on a wolf, her gentle face curled back in a snarl. Letting out a roar, she rushed over to the wolf, raising her arms up. She felt the satisfying crunch as her fist crushed the wolf's rotting skull, felt the oozing embrace as the creature's lifeblood splattered across her face, giving her a frenzied appearance. Half a dozen wolves surrounded her, eager to avenge their fallen member, but she did not care. She smiled and licked her lips, letting the vile taste of the wolf's blood wash over her tongue.

She loved it. More enemies, more fun, right?

With an incomprehensible battle-cry, she charged at the surrounding wolves. A massive spike of ice formed in her black fist, and with terrifying force, she launched it at the first wolf, sending it flying back with a pathetic squeal. Margaret's eyes gleamed murderously.

One down. Five to go.

The other undead wolves dashed about her, trying to get around her destructive fist of ice. They darted in and out, trying to sink their rotting claws into her soft flesh. One crashed into her back, but she shrugged it off, her shining plate mail shielding her from injury. Another lunged for her side, but with surprising speed, she drove her fist down upon the wolf's skull, crushing the creature's head into the ground. A wave of black blood and oozing pus splattered out, covering the surrounding area in gore. Margaret almost laughed in delight.

Two down. Four to go.

The other wolves snarled at her, and she snarled right back. Lifting her demonic fist to her mouth, she licked off the thick, tainted blood. A rush of energy crashed over her as the blood flowed down her throat. A wild laugh escaped her lips, and her face twisted with crazed pleasure.

She needed more!

She danced with the wolves, deflecting their attacks with a wave of her fist. Shards of ice pierced the rotting hides of the wolves, but they did not seem to notice. They only had one focus. Her. One of the wolves pounced, its open jaw targeted on her exposed neck. Undeterred, Margaret raised her black fist into the air, calling forth a mighty spear of ice from the earth. The freezing stake shot into the wolf's skull, holding it in place above the ground, suspended by its shattered jaw. The wolf tried to escape, tried to dislodge itself from the icy spike piercing its head, but Margaret abruptly ended its whimpering, crushing its life with a swing of her black fist.

Three down. Only three more.

Margaret let out a maniacal cackle, and her ruby eyes gleamed like those of some monstrous devil. An icy chill surged from her body, casting frost upon the surrounding ground.

The companions were driving the nightmarish pack back. Nalgene and SmibSmob made short work of the twisted creatures, damning them into the unforgiving clutches of oblivion with a tantalizing dance of water and shadow. Nalgene kept himself under control, but SmibSmob next to him cared little for the others' well-being, unleashing mighty orbs of darkness wherever he pleased. Fasto and Ro fought together, the draconian holding up the torch like a flickering beacon and slashing at any wolves that ventured too near with his shining longsword. Blood stained the once-pure blade. Fasto rained down a hail of arrows, piercing the undead creatures with an accuracy matched only by his titanic stupidity. Andromeda faded in and out of the shadows, bringing a score of undead wolves to silence from within their comfort of night. She was silent. She was deadly. And she was a killer.

Margaret snarled, charging at the remaining three abominations in her wake. She brought her demonic arm to bear in front of her. Another deadly shard of ice shot forth from her fist, but the wolves darted to the side, avoiding a fatal blow. The three undead wolves surrounded her. With a guttural growl, they pounced. Margaret whipped around, trying to deflect the attacking wolves. Her fist connected with one, sending it crashing out of the air. Another landed upon her back, futilely trying to rip through her mighty plate mail with its vicious claws. With a growl, she reached behind her, clutching the wolf's maw and whipping it down to the ground in front of her.

The third leaped for her side, but she twisted out of the way, only to lunge out and grab the undead wolf with her black fist while it was still pouncing through the air. With a diabolical laugh, Margaret clenched her fist, and dozens of shards of ice rushed into the wolf, piercing it with needles of death. Still laughing, she brought the wolf up to her mouth, tearing off a chunk of its rotting flesh with her sharp teeth. Dark blood oozed down her face, matched only by the color of her shining eyes. She felt alive. Tossing aside the carcass, Margaret turned back to the other undead wolves.

Four down. Only two remain.

Wispy strands of frost began to emanate from her body, giving her the appearance of a shimmering specter. Her gaze darted around in a frantic search for blood. Licking her lips, she charged at the undead creatures.

The remaining two wolves danced around her, desperately trying to land a single blow. Their claws slid off her impenetrable plate mail with a piercing screech, and their open maws were met by devastating fists of ice. One of the wolves darted for her legs, trying to tear apart her tendons. Margaret kicked it away, sending it sprawling into the nearby ground with a sickening *crunch* of bones. The other leaped for her face, its jaw hung wide. Margaret saw its empty eyes, saw its rotting tongue flail from the side of its mouth. She gave a crooked smile. Shooting forward, she clamped the undead wolf's maw shut with her black fist. Locking onto its eyes, she slowly began to emit a deathly chill from her fist, steadily freezing the abomination. She wanted to see it struggle, wanted to see its last moments of despair as the icy touch of frost overcame its body.

With a bloodthirsty roar, she smashed the frozen wolf into the ground, sending tiny shards of the fractured being raining down upon the battlefield. She let out a cry of ecstasy, her mind rushing with delight.

Five down. Only one left.

The aura of frost about her burst out from her with a violent nova of ice. Around her, the very earth was succumbing to her icy presence, the air biting with a murderous chill. She felt alive. Her eyes flared to life with an icy flame. The darkness from her demonic arm started to spread across her body, its black tendrils reaching out to corrupt her. She let out another diabolical laugh, turning to face the remaining wolf.

The remaining wolf was back on its feet, oblivious to the shattered ribs that now hung from its rotting flank. It growled, and Margaret matched it, raising her devilish fist to finish the fight. Suddenly, a white arrow whistled past her ear, sinking into the shoulder of the creature. Caught off guard, Margaret glanced to the side in surprise. Realizing her mistake, she whipped her head back around, her black fist rising in front of her as a mighty ice spear formed within her iron grasp. But it was too late. The undead wolf landed upon her chest, its twisted maw hot by her face. Margaret felt the wretched claws dig into her neck, felt her blood flow from the wound.

Her mind fell apart. All thoughts of her demonic arm, her icy shard, and the other companions crumbled away into oblivion. She felt the claws piercing her flesh, felt the hot blood ooze out of her neck. A furious haze grew over the edges of her mind, and her eyes grew cold and distant. She felt the rotting claws rend across her flesh, felt her blood flow across her body. Her face twisted into a ferocious snarl, and a wild growl erupted from deep within. She felt the wolf tearing its claws into her flesh. The building vortex of ice disappeared around her. Everything fell away, she had only one focus:

The wolf.

Letting out a terrifying roar, she tore the creature off her, whipping it down into the ground.

The wolf.

She leaped atop the wolf, unleashing a barrage of punches onto its skull.

The wolf.

The wolf's bones shattered under the furious assault, releasing a spray of thick blood upon Margaret, but she did not relent. Raising her black fist, she smashed it down upon the wolf with a devastating shock wave of ice.

The wolf.

Berserk, she pummeled where the wolf once was, sending massive shards of ice crashing into the hard ground. There was shouting behind her, but she ignored it. It was not important.

The wolf.

Her body grew weary, yet still she pounded upon the bloody pulp of bile and gore that was once the wolf. Her hands shattered upon the unforgiving ground, but that only reinforced her frenzy.

The wolf.

Blood covered her form, masking her in a coat of thick gore. She felt hands upon her, trying to pull her away from the unrecognizable carcass, but she shrugged them off. She only had one focus.

The wolf.

Suddenly, a surge of cooling water washed over her. Immediately her clarity returned, and she fell back, exhausted. The thick blood washed away, the torn flesh of her neck wove itself back together, and her shattered knuckles reformed with an iron strength. The haze faded, and her thoughts came rushing back in a torrent. Her black arm pulsed, but it was slower, more controlled than before. Glancing up, she saw Nalgene hovering over her, his rough hands planted firmly on her chest. The others stood behind him, looking down upon her with unease. Ro was trying to speak to her, but she ignored him.

Fucking idiots.

Still tasting the delight, Margaret leaped to her feet and shook herself off. The monster would have to wait.

Around her, the night still loomed in, a black wall of darkness that they dared not pass. Corpses of the fallen wolves littered the area, their putrid blood spilling across the land. Below Margaret lay a battered pulp, its original form unrecognizable. Tiny shards of bone and bits of rotting flesh dotted the area like the gruesome petals of flowers. Margaret thought it looked quite beautiful.

Turning away from the carnage, she met Ro's eyes, only able to offer him an evasive smile.

"Are you alright?" Ro said chivalrously, his face dripping with concern. He glanced at the bloody pulp behind her, and then warily met her eyes once again. "Ah, you ... I'm glad you're alright."

Margaret chuckled silently to herself. What a leader.

The companions resumed their journey east, their weariness creeping back upon them after the rush of battle. As the night dragged on, the torch's light slowly faded, and the menacing tendrils of shadow slowly clawed their way back to haunt the companions. Yet still they marched on, the unknown landscape moving past them in the thick darkness. Margaret no longer cared for the lingering dread hovering about them. All she wanted was to rest, to embrace the cool touch of slumber. And the intensity of the fight against the pack of undead wolves weighed heavily upon her slim shoulders, dragging her feet down into the cold ground.

There was no sign of Captain Osann.

As the night wore on, and the torch grew dim, the companions found themselves among the ruins of a small village along the dusty road. Fallen buildings and desecrated structures littered the area, looking over the companions from the edge of the flickering torchlight in a silent vigil, mourning the loss of life. Eerie shadows darted among the rubble, but the weary companions cared not. Exhausted, they collapsed to the ground and let the rushing tide of sleep wash over them, praying that the creatures of the Shadow would not happen upon them in the darkness.

As the others lay down to rest, Margaret found herself gazing up at the moonless night sky, lost in thought. She brought her twisted arm out in front of her and studied its winding black muscles. She felt its relentless pulsing, and her mind was thrown back across the days. She thought of the prison, and the long two years they spent locked away there, the long two years without the dreadful pulsing. And how free she had felt without her demonic companion. But that was no more, and now here she was, lost in the great abyss of the Shadow. She thought of her companions, who she insisted on not caring for, however empty that promise was.

Idiots. Why was she still here? She could leave them and finally pursue her freedom. But ... she couldn't. Why not? They wouldn't even notice that she was gone, right?

She had no answers. Margaret tried to think back to before the prison, but all she found was a hazy mist, taunting her with lost memories. She remembered her childhood, her slavery, and her ... best not to think about it. But from there it was forgotten, stolen by the clutches of time. Her brow furrowed, and a feral growl escaped her lips.

She remembered her twisted childhood, her monster, her escape from slavery, and her exile into the vast world. She remembered a strange man with a billowing blue cape, approaching her with a marvelous hammer raised high ...

She tried to push past the mist, tried to break through the

restrictive barrier, but it threw her away, forever guarding its secrets. Those were mysteries to be kept until another night.

♦   ♦   ♦

Margaret awoke to the pale light of the shallow sun. Her back ached from sleeping on the hard ground, but she paid it no mind. Opening her eyes, she sat up, observing the surrounding area. The broken skeletons of fallen buildings jutted up into the air, casting jagged shadows in the cold sunlight. To the east of the ruined village was a great lake, spanning the horizon with dazzling splendor. An old dock sat in disrepair along the coast. The lonely road that the companions had taken continued to the heart of the village, where it diverged, forking to the south and south-east.

Around her, most of the other companions had already awakened from their slumber and were cautiously studying the area. Ro glanced about the ruins aimlessly, his eyes troubled and unfocused. He kept glancing back along the road, perhaps hoping that the missing Captain would appear. Nalgene stomped around, grumbling to himself. He too kept glancing down the abandoned road and would shoot a knowing glare at Ro whenever the draconian was not looking. Fasto was sitting on the hard ground, furiously scratching something into the earth. Margaret thought it might have been some vain attempt at a map, but it was too nonsensical to make out. SmibSmob still rested, his breath steady and even, and his pointed hat tucked firmly under his frail arm. As for Andromeda, there was no sign, but Margaret knew she would not be far.

Margaret stood up, shaking away any lingering exhaustion. She made her way over to Ro, who was gazing down the west road. Noticing her approach, Ro glanced up, a weak smile appearing on his weary face.

"Up at last, I see," he said to her, his voice soft. "Ah, are you alright? After the battle … I don't know, you seemed …"

"Shhhhhh," Margaret replied, cutting off his pathetic stammering. She didn't have the stamina to deal with worthless sympathy right now. "I'm perfectly fine. Just a little skirmish, that's all. No big deal."

With that, she turned away from Ro, a sly smirk on her lips. Idiot.

Yet as much as she would deny it, she felt her devilish arm pulse with a renewed life at the mention of the fight against the wolves, as if it were revitalized by the thought of blood. Was it just a little skirmish?

She could not be sure.

Her thoughts were interrupted by the obnoxious voice of Nalgene behind her.

"A'ight, that's enough o' yer standin' around. I be thinkin' it's about time we get movin' outta this bloody town," the gnome said, stomping over and crossing his burly arms over his chest. "Ye hear that, ye damn dragon? I be thinkin' we should keep headin' to the east. Gotta be an end to this bloody Shadow somewhere."

"Oh, what brilliant insight you have," Margaret muttered, but no one noticed.

Ro turned to the gnome, his expression fierce. But instead of arguing against Nalgene, Ro merely nodded, conforming to the gnome's wishes.

Surprised, Nalgene nodded back to the draconian, before moving off to wake his brother, once again grumbling to himself. Margaret, quite amused by Ro's leadership, watched him go, his blue cloak billowing out behind him like the ebb and flow of the crashing tides.

Andromeda appeared out of the streaking shadows, her visage calm and unreadable. She seemed to flow across the ground, as if she were a ghastly reaper, promising one's untimely demise. Andromeda locked eyes with Margaret, holding the orc in an iron grip, before looking away and striding over to Ro. She brushed the draconian with her tail and gave him a passing purr. Margaret couldn't fathom what game the feline was playing. Like all cats, this one was full of mischief. Deadly, cunning mischief, no doubt. She just hoped she wasn't the mouse.

Yet still Margaret found herself trusting Andromeda. Everyone had their monster. And monsters formed packs.

But her black, twisted arm pulsed ever more persistently.

The companions gathered their belongings and prepared to continue their determined journey across the barren lands. Now headed by the gnome brothers, they ventured forth on the forlorn road, heading southeast out of the fallen village. Margaret trailed the others, her mind a hurricane of flying thoughts. She brought her demonic arm up, examining its muscles. She hated it. Hated all that it signified — her years of abuse and slavery.

Her transformation into what she had become.

She had to believe that. Yet as much as she resented her demonic powers, they had proven quite useful over the past few days. Obliterating undead with mighty pillars of ice was indeed satisfying. And the more she thought, the more doubtful she grew in her resolve.

"Aye, ye damn orc, are ye comin'?" Nalgene shouted, interrupting her thoughts.

Margaret dropped her arm, placing it out of sight and out of mind, or so she hoped. No matter how much she tried to hide it, it still pulsed. She hated it, right?

She glanced up at the gnome and threw him a shallow nod. Satisfied, Nalgene turned and resumed his vigilant march out of the village.

As the companions traveled along the forsaken road, Margaret could not help glance back at the desecrated village, back at the winding shadows, back to another missed opportunity. Shrugging, she marched forward, trying to forget about the unwelcome thoughts. Yet her arm still pulsed, and she shuddered — although not from any cold.

The companions followed the abandoned road as it turned east, winding around the sprawling lake that now lay to the north. As the days passed by, another lake appeared to the south, looming over the horizon in sparkling splendor. Short, pale days weighed heavily on their shoulders, and long, unforgiving nights dashed away their hope. The lifeless lands about them expanded out in the distance, offering little reassurance that the Shadow would soon end. Doubts began to cloud the companions' minds — doubts of abandoning the Captain, doubts that they should turn back — but they never acted upon them. They merely growled and dug their feet into the ground, pushing forward with unshakable determination.

However, as they continued their venture east, a black, unwavering darkness appeared over the horizon ahead, looming in the far distance. This was not just the inescapable black of the night, it was somehow darker still, hovering in the distance like an ominous void, devouring any light that dared wander too closely.

As the third morning's sun was rising into the cold sky, the forlorn road the companions were traveling upon collided with another from the west, merging into a single, dreary road and steadily winding its way forevermore east. A wispy fog had settled over the area, covering the land in a haunting haze where flickering shadows danced just out of reach. Growling, the companions pushed forward, trudging wearily to the east.

As the pale sun fell past its zenith, the fog grew ever stronger, hovering over the land in a dense blanket. Suddenly, a billowing orb of flame, identical to the one that had brought them to Captain Osann, streaked up to the sky from the near distance, piercing the gloomy fog like a holy beacon from the heavens. Margaret's eyes shot up, and she watched the fiery majesty trek across the sky before disappearing into the cold air.

"Ahhh. See, what did I tell ye?" Nalgene started enthusiastically, his wide eyes gazing toward the area where the soaring inferno had disappeared. "There be an end to the Shadow out here. Just gotta follow the Flame, right?"

The others, besides Margaret, were quick to agree, their spirits lifted at the first sign of escape from the forsaken lands of darkness. Margaret shook her head.

"Oh great, another stroke of brilliance," Margaret shot at Nalgene, her voice fierce. "Because following the blazing orb worked out so well for us last time."

Nalgene shot her a hard glare, but she merely gave him a dry smile in return. The last blazing orb had led them to the Captain who had so graciously left them at the brink of death.

Yet protest as she might, the others were set, as unwavering as a mountain of iron. Ro gazed down the path, his shoulders high with a newfound hope. Fasto stared up in wonder, muttering something about "pretty fire" and "Fasto go." Even SmibSmob seemed eager to find the source of the conflagration, and he urged the others on with a steady determination.

Morons.

Only Andromeda seemed doubtful. But she said nothing, only narrowing her eyes and gliding across the beaten path. Sighing, Margaret followed the others into the menacing fog.

Soon after the companions resumed their journey, Margaret's arm burst to life, pulsing wildly at her side. Glancing around warily, she knew they were being followed. Eyeing her companions, she found that they too were on edge and were glancing at the fog in alarm. Suddenly, Nalgene let out a cry and rushed over to the side of the dusty road. Margaret dashed over to him, clenching her fist to ease the pulsing. It did not work.

Laying prone upon the hard ground was a man, bloodied and torn, with not the faintest hint breath escaping his still lungs. Turning the body over, Margaret let out a gasp of shock.

The man was fairly built, and of average height. He had short, black hair that was matted with blood and sweat, and a short, ragged beard like a shadow over his face. Clasped firmly in his cold hands was a strange token, shaped like a cross with a billowing flame erupting from its top. But that was not what sent a wave of horror rushing through her body. Across the man's face, like some ghastly brand from the touch of oblivion, was a thin, blistered handprint. But before she could react, before she could hope to grasp what horror had done such a gruesome deed, another sharp cry from Nalgene erupted next to her.

She heard the crashing of the hooves, the thunderous cadence of death. Suddenly, a mighty undead stallion burst forth from the thick fog, a skeleton warrior brandishing a longsword perched atop it. The stallion was vile and nightmarish, its cold, empty eyes glaring at the companions with an undying hatred. Mighty, iron hooves tore at the earth with abandon, and rippling muscles shone across the rotting body.

Margaret rushed to her feet, already raising her demonic arm. Around her, the other companions were scrambling desperately to try and regain their composure. She ignored them. Andromeda leaped from the shadows, crashing into the flank of the undead stallion. She tore at the tendons with her razor claws, sinking her teeth into the beast's neck. The skeleton tried to swing at her, tried to slash her down with its longsword, but the feline was too agile. Before the sword had even begun its descent, Andromeda had launched herself off the stallion, gracefully turning in the air. Her halberd appeared in her hand, and with terrifying strength, she cleaved the skeleton's head clean off, sending it crashing into the dense fog. Before the head touched the ground, she faded away into the black embrace of darkness.

Margaret smiled. Even she had to applaud the feline's prowess. But her celebration was cut short. More undead stallions thundered out of the fog, descending upon the companions, the skeletons upon their backs slashing wildly, their sword whistling through the damp air. Ro rushed up to meet them, his greatsword sweeping across, sending a spray of black blood spilling over the lands. SmibSmob and Nalgene rushed to follow suit, deadly spells of water and shadow already pouring forth from their hands. Fasto rained a hail of shining arrows down upon the unearthly horde, his face twisted in rage. Margaret felt her arm pulse.

Without hesitation she charged into the fray, a wild battle cry bellowing from her lips. A lone undead stallion stood before her; its skeleton rider already cut down by a white arrow. Growling, she embraced her blood lust, damning herself to the will of her demons.

An icy vortex rushed about her. A massive shard of ice formed in her hand, and she launched it at the undead stallion, burying it in the rotting hide. Her mouth opened wide, her sharp teeth gleaming for blood, she charged at the stallion. Her demonic arm crashed into the beast's chest, shattering bone and sending a spray of dark blood raining over her. The abomination raised its mighty hooves, kicking forward with terrifying power. As the iron hooves cut through the air, Margaret darted to the side. Whipping around, her black arm rammed into the flank of the stallion, sending it staggering back from the weight of the blow. Reaching out, she buried her hand into the rotting hide of the beast, and with a feral roar, she unleashed a wave of piercing cold that froze the side of the stallion in a sheet of crystalline ice.

The stallion's head whipped over to her, its empty eyes locking upon her twisted arm. Margaret smiled. With a devilish chuckle, she tightened her muscles, exploding forward with destructive force, shattering the frozen flesh of the stallion and sending a shower of shining shards and oozing blood out like a gruesome nova of death.

Her eyes gleaming wildly, she once again punched through the stallion's chest, tearing out the abomination's blackened heart. She felt her teeth bury into its dead muscle, felt the river of thick blood rush down her throat in a delightful waterfall of ecstasy.

One down.

Two more undead stallions appeared around her, their skeleton riders looming over her. Margaret let out a cry of glee. She raised her demonic fist, a swirling vortex of ice forming around it.

But before she could attack, before she could unleash a destructive torrent of ice upon the nightmarish creatures, a searing pain jolted across the back of her neck. A shrill cry escaped her lips. The pulsing of her black arm stopped, and the swirling ice about her fell crashing to the ground. Her mind grew weary, and a black haze swept over her. As she fell to the ground, she was able to make out the slim figure of a zombie through the foggy haze. A ragged cloak hung torn over its rotting body, giving it a spectral appearance. Its hand was raised, and wispy strands of frost emanated from its pale palm.

Everything went black.

Chapter 6

An agonizing scream penetrated Ro's ears, and his head shot around in a vain attempt to find the source through the dense fog. Even his sharp, draconian eyes had little success in the haze. Shit. What happened?

A rush of adrenaline surged through his veins, and his blood boiled in an urge to protect his friends.

His eyes darted about, searching for his companions. Torrents of water and shadow still rained destructive downpours upon the legion of undead stallions. A white arrow whistled past his ear, thudding into the skull of an approaching skeleton, sending it crumbling to the cold ground. Of Margaret or Andromeda, he saw no sign. His breath caught in his throat, and his noble heart stood silent for a moment.

Where were they?

His mind swirled like the heavy fog about him. Raising his mighty greatsword out in a guard, he tensed his corded muscles, preparing to charge into the unknown beyond the foggy barrier. He did not know from where the scream had come, but it did not matter.

All that mattered was he had to save his companion. Images of a broken Andromeda splayed across the ground darted through his thoughts, only to be matched by horrific images of a fallen Margaret being devoured by the vicious undead. Ro faltered, doubt crashing down upon his burly shoulders and sending his hopes dashed to the ground.

NO! He had to save them!

But before he could regain his composure, before he could cast away the shackles of doubt, an undead stallion rammed him in the side, sending him flying back, his breath blasted from his lungs. As he lay panting on the ground, the decrepit stallion reared up, its iron hooves shining like twin blades of death. He tried to roll away, but he was fatigued, and his armor was heavy. He couldn't avoid it. With a terrifying force, the stallion stomped upon Ro's wrist, the menacing hooves shattering his scaled hand.

A searing pain burned through Ro's broken hand, sending him careening in anguish. A black daze washed over his vision, and he let out a billowing cry. Through his wavering gaze he saw the nightmarish stallion rear once more, its deadly hooves targeted on his head. A skeleton warrior rode upon its back, its empty eyes mocking his helplessness. Ro's hand seared, but it seemed distant.

He couldn't die like this. He still had to save his companions. He still had to save …

A mighty bolt of fiery lightning shot from his maw, slamming into the stallion with a shower of blue sparks. Growling his pain away, Ro stumbled to his feet, his determination burning like a rekindled flame. His pain was nothing to him. Only the pain of his companions mattered. He would withstand the full might of oblivion before he let one of his companions fall into the black clutches of death. His mind swirled with rage. He wished he could take the injuries and exhaustion of the others upon himself, but he knew it to be a hopeless dream. His shattered hand still sent waves of crippling pain washing over him. But it would be nothing to the pain he would feel if one of his companions, nay, his friends, were to succumb to the Shadow.

With his mighty greatsword now rendered useless by his broken hand, Ro let it fall to the ground and unsheathed his shining longsword. Only his instincts, armor, and raging fury could protect him from the reaching claws of doom. Roaring, Ro charged at the stallion, another strike of lighting shooting forth from his open maw, crashing into the stallion and driving it back. The undead stallion reared up in rage, its empty eyes glaring down upon Ro with hatred. He did not care. His thoughts were only for his companions. Whirling around, his longsword darted out, slashing at the mighty chest of the beast. A torrent of black blood sprayed out of the wound, but the creature didn't notice.

Behind Ro, another menacing stallion charged out of the surrounding fog, a skeleton warrior perched upon its rotting back. With a sickening *crack*, the second stallion slammed into Ro, sending him crashing hard to the ground, his breath blasted from his lungs. His shining sword soared from his hand, disappearing into the swirling fog. Ro groveled on the ground, his breath coming into short gasps. A searing pain erupted from his chest with every strained breath. His ribs were fractured. He reached around and grabbed his shield from his back in a desperate attempt to defend himself, but it was kicked from his hand. He had nothing — no sword, no shield and no breath.

Coughing up blood, Ro glanced up to the dark sky. Above him, the two stallions reared, their iron hooves cutting through the air, and their skeleton riders glaring down upon him. Behind the undead beasts, Ro saw his mighty greatsword lying upon the ground, its edge calling out to him, shining like the last flicker of hope. He coughed up another shower of thick blood.

Ro's mind went blank. Instincts took control.

The stallions crashed their hooves to the ground, rending the hard earth and sending clouds of dust billowing into the air. Ro managed to twist to the side, placing his body between the iron hooves. He crawled between their legs as quickly as he could — he knew the next strike would be his end. His chest exploded with renewed fury, sending waves of pain pulsing through him. He ignored them. All that mattered was his companions. He had to help them, to save them — to save her.

The stallions turned above Ro as he stumbled to his feet, his breath heaving. He eyed his greatsword, now covered with a blanket of dust upon the ground behind the two mighty stallions. The undead beasts stared him down, their rotting muscles twisting with power. Digging their menacing hooves into the ground, they charged, ripping through the swirling fog like battle rams of death. Roaring, Ro raised his claws in defiance.

Ro stepped to the side of the stallions, the sharp claws of his good hand tearing through rotting flesh. He felt a *thud* across his back as one of the skeleton riders swung its sword down upon his armored back. Ro stumbled forward from the blow and turned his head to look behind him. He couldn't win. But damn it all he was going to try.

The stallions approached and Ro lunged forward, his claw ripping the face of one of the stallions. His breath burned, and his body hung heavy with exhaustion.

He ignored it — or he tried to.

The mighty stallion reared up, and this time he couldn't avoid it. With a sickening *thud*, the horse crashed down upon his chest, pinning him to the barren earth. His body seared like a fearsome inferno. He could not move, could not breathe, could not escape. The other stallion appeared above him, its hollow eyes boring into him, taunting him. He tried to release a devastating breath of lightning, tried to decimate the undead beast upon him, but could not. His ribs cracked under the tremendous pressure. His vision wavered, growing black. There was no escape now.

Suddenly, two white arrows streaked across Ro's vision, piercing the skulls of the skeleton riders and sending shards of bone soaring through the air. The skeletons fell to the ground. Two more arrows then streaked out of the fog, crashing into the rotting flank of the stallion atop Ro. The stallion reared, its head whipping about to find the mysterious archer. Then another two arrows struck the flank of the other stallion, sending it staggering back in rage. Ro's breath rushed into his lungs, bringing with it a renewed sense of determination.

He knew the two beasts would not be distracted for long. He had to think, had to defeat the two menaces, had to save his companions. He saw his mighty greatsword upon the ground, not four paces away.

Crawling to his feet, ignoring his protesting body, Ro rushed for his greatsword. His hand gripped the handle, and with enormous strength, he heaved it up to his shoulder. He only had one chance, one chance to save his companions. His eyes burned with a frenzied light, and they glared at the two stallions in raging contempt. The undead beasts turned to face him, their rotting muscles rippling with an unholy power. Ro growled. The stallions charged.

As the mighty beasts stormed toward him, it seemed as if time were screeching to a halt. With a roar of denial, ignoring the searing pain crippling his broken body, Ro brought his greatsword down in front of him, its sharp point shining out like a holy spear of light. With a sickening *crack*, the undead stallion rammed into the greatsword, impaling itself upon the razor edge. But it did not stop — did not even seem to notice the greatsword piercing its chest. Another explosion of pain rocked Ro's body as the stallion crashed into him, sending him staggering backward. But he did not fall. He had too much to lose. Planting his feet firmly into the ground, Ro locked his eyes upon his greatsword, which was stuck in the rotting flesh of the stallion. With a rush of breath, he unleashed a devastating blast of lightning upon the sword, sending a crackling surge of energy coursing through the mighty sword. A blinding nova of lightning exploded out from the sword, incinerating the inside of the beast.

After one final attempt at charging Ro, the stallion fell to the ground, lifeless.

But there was little time to celebrate. Undeterred by the loss of its companion, the remaining stallion rushed at Ro, its hooves thundering against the ground with an unearthly fury. Ro tried to move, tried to dodge the oncoming storm, but his body hung still. His mind screamed in protest, but he could do no more.

But it wasn't enough. He had to … save …

Andromeda burst from the swirling fog, landing upon the undead stallion. Her claws ripped into its rotting flesh, and her jaws tore at its hide. With a surge of power, she leaped off the beast, twisting gracefully in the air. Her halberd appeared in her hand, and with a gruesome *thud*, she landed upon the stallion's head, driving her halberd through its thick skull. A feral growl escaped her lips, and she pounced from the fallen beast, tearing her halberd out with her, unleashing a spray of black blood and rotting gore. Whipping about, her halberd disappeared, and she landed silently upon the ground, licking the tainted blood from her lips. The stallion collapsed to the ground behind her.

Andromeda looked up to Ro, her eyes twinkling with delight, and she gave him a soft smile. Letting out a sigh of relief, Ro returned a weak smile before collapsing to the ground. With the rush of battle past, a surge of pain crashed over him, bringing him to his knees. His broken hand burned with a renewed fury, and his crushed ribs groaned with protest at his every breath. His head grew faint, and his vision wavered. His chest heaved, and he let out another cough, splattering the uncaring ground with his lifeblood. A numbing weakness settled over his body, and a wave of exhaustion pummeled his will.

Alarmed, Andromeda rushed over to Ro, her tail waving with worry. Her soft fur pressed against him, and she tried to call to him, tried to breach his wall of pain. Ro noticed nothing. Every heartbeat seemed an agonizing century, dragging him to the ground. Another cough, and more of his blood covered the ground. His mind grew distant.

He tried to fight off the Shadow. But he failed. He failed as the Beacon. Failed as a companion, as a friend.

His mind rushed back to the shrill, pained scream he had heard. His determination started to boil back to life within.

Shakily, he glanced up, his eyes scanning the swirling fog. Beside him, Andromeda jumped with pleasure, overjoyed to see a sign of life from him. The simmering boil had sparked into a steady flame, gaining intensity into a raging inferno. He had to save her, had to save his friend. He had to save Margaret.

Ro pulled himself to his feet, growling with the effort. His muscles pulsed with a rejuvenated life, casting away the pain crippling his body. Only his companions' pain mattered. He had to save her. Andromeda let out a joyous mewl, her tail brushing against his battered body.

"Ro! Are you alright?"

Ro gave no answer, only grumbling a single name. "Margaret," he muttered.

She studied him for a moment, before nodding, her sharp eyes soft with understanding. "Let's go, shall we?"

The two companions pushed into the dense fog, Ro leaning upon Andromeda for support. Around them the battle raged on, the undead horde trying to smother any sign of life. Bolts of water and shadow crashed overhead, washing away the vile creatures in a torrent of death. White arrows streaked across the battlefield, striking undead down from their unholy perches. But the two companions ignored it, trudging onward with iron determination. They had to save her. A pair of skeleton warriors stumbled into their path, but Andromeda made short work of them, fading into the surrounding darkness before shattering their skulls with her mighty halberd and crushing their bones with her terrifying strength.

They had to save her.

As they pushed onward, the fallen form of Margaret appeared through the fog, laying lifeless upon the ground. Growling, Ro rushed over to her, Andromeda close behind.

Margaret lay prone, her body unmoving. Her black arm sat dormant, and not a trace of ice was to be found upon her. But that was not what caught Ro's attention. Branded across the back of her neck was a blistering handprint, withering like a touch from death. Ro collapsed in horror, his mind swirling with grief. What could have done such a thing? What vile minion of the Shadow brought this upon her?

His heart heavy, he turned her over, his eyes gazing upon her gentle face, which lay cold and pale.

Suddenly, Andromeda let out a cry of alarm, and Ro jumped to his feet, his mind burning for vengeance. He had to avenge her. Andromeda leaped next to him, her halberd held out defensively, her body fading away. He did not care what had alarmed Andromeda, did not care what monstrosity would charge out of the swirling fog. He would kill it. He had to avenge Margaret. He had no weapon, had no defense, but it did not matter. His rage billowed ever hotter. He had to avenge her.

Raising his claws before him, Ro studied the fog. Steadily trudging out of the haze was the frail figure of a zombie, a ragged cloak draping over its rotting form. Its hands rested by its side, and wispy strands of frost emanated from its palms. Behind the abomination were three skeleton warriors, their sharp swords raised in front of them. A furious growl escaped Ro's lips. His body screamed with pain, but it was drowned out in his rage. His eyes locked with Andromeda's, and she gave him a gentle nod.

"Go," she whispered to him. "I'll handle the skeletons."

She licked her lips and faded into the everlasting embrace of the shadows. Ro nodded. Turning back to the dreadful zombie, he flexed his legs, and with a burst of power, he charged at the scum.

Ro thundered across the hard ground, his uninjured hand ready at his side, its sharp claws targeted on the zombie's thin throat. Letting out a vicious roar, his claws flashed, tearing at the creature's ragged cloak. But there was no blood, no ripping of flesh. Ro glanced down to his claw, only to find the shreds of the ragged cloak hanging loose in his fingers.

The zombie evaded him?

Snarling, he threw the cloth to the ground and charged once again at the zombie.

His claws slashed once more, this time connecting with the creature's arm. Rotting flesh tore apart, and black blood sprayed out of the wound. The zombie hardly noticed. Its frosty hand whipped across, forcing Ro to collapse to the ground, just managing to avoid the touch of death. His body cried in protest, and his ribs erupted with an even fiercer pain. His rage would not sustain him forever.

Before he could regain his footing, the zombie's hand came crashing down. Ro twisted to the side, his breath coming in short gasps. Eyeing his opponent, he saw the ground grow withered and black under the zombie's touch. An image of the brand across Margaret's neck filled his mind, overwhelming his thoughts. The zombie's hollow eyes mocked him, mocked his despair. Screaming, Ro forced himself to his feet, ignoring the raging pain coursing through him.

He had to avenge her.

His claws flashed.

He had to avenge her.

A bolt of lightning shot out of his maw.

He had to avenge her.

A feral roar filled the air.

He had to avenge her.

Black blood rained down upon him.

He had to avenge her.

He had to …

Soft fur pressed against his skin, freeing him from his fury. Andromeda stood by him, her tail caressing his back, soothing his pain. Ro collapsed to his knees, his breath coming in faint gasps. The wretched zombie lay in shreds at his feet, and its frosty hands hung still. But Ro felt little sense for celebration. No matter how much he tore the zombie's rotting flesh from its bones, no matter how much he cried out in denial, it did not change Margaret's fate. She still lay lifeless, the touch of despair branded across her neck.

Shrugging Andromeda away, Ro crawled over to Margaret, an overwhelming shadow of grief covering his mind. He had avenged her, but it didn't matter. He could not save her. Ro lifted her up into his arms and stared helplessly at her soft face. Tears welled up in his eyes, but he fought them back.

Around Ro the battle grew silent and still. Beside him Andromeda had drug over another fallen body; a man, bloodied and torn. Short, black hair matted with blood and sweat clung to his head, and a short, ragged beard shadowed his face. Across his face was a blistering handprint, identical to the one seared into Margaret's neck. Ro glanced over to him, and a furious rush of emotions crashed over him. No. Not the Captain too!

Ro had failed. He was no leader, no Beacon. He was nothing. He had failed. A simmering rage began to boil to life within, and he wanted to lash out, to cast the blame on another, but he knew he could only blame himself.

The other companions approached behind him, their footsteps sloshing through the bloody ground. Upon noticing Margaret, Fasto let out a whimper, falling to his knees and letting out cries of "Fasto friend" and "Fasto help." SmibSmob moved to stand next to Andromeda, his face pale with exhaustion, while Nalgene bolted over to Margaret, his eyes swimming with fear.

"Damn orc," Nalgene mumbled to himself. "Had to go and get yerself hurt, didn't ye?"

Rushing over, he placed his rough hands upon Margaret's chest, and a swirling cascade of water washed over her body. Margaret did not move. Growling, Nalgene redoubled his efforts, a torrent of water flowing out of his hands. Ro glanced up, his eyes locking upon Nalgene. At the sight of the gnome his thoughts were thrown back to nights before, when the gnome had insisted that they abandon the Captain. A red wall of rage formed within Ro's mind.

It was all his fault.

A Land in Shadow

In his heart he knew it was not true, but he did not care.

It was Nalgene who insisted that they abandon Captain Osann and that they venture on their own into the Shadow. He urged them away from the Flame, away from all that Mariah had bestowed upon them. The gnome claimed the Captain was a traitor, claimed that he was with the Shadow. Nalgene was the traitor. Even after the years they stood beside each other in the prison, this was how he repaid their friendship. He was the traitor. Ro didn't fail. Nalgene did.

Ro exploded forward, shoving Nalgene off Margaret and throwing him to the ground. Ro's face twisted into a mask of rage as a wild growl rumbled from his throat.

"It's your fault!" Ro screamed at the gnome. He stood up, towering over the miserable creature. "You begged us to come this way! You urged us to abandon the Captain! Now look at what you've done! Both Margaret and the Captain are dead! Cast your precious water over them as you will, it won't change their fate! You've killed them! You're a traitor!"

The companions stood stunned around him. Fasto looked up from his whimpering, his eyes wide with fear. SmibSmob stammered, at a loss for words, while Andromeda merely looked away, shaking her head in disappointment. Nalgene stared up at Ro, his face blank with confusion. The gnome glanced at the two bodies on the ground before locking eyes with the enraged draconian, and inner fire burning deep within.

"What did ye say, ye sack o' shit?" Nalgene started, rising to his feet and brushing off the dust. "Ye think this is me fault? Ye think that *I* be a traitor?"

The gnome shook with fury, and his fists clenched in rage, water forming within their grasp. Ro wavered. Suddenly he had the feeling the gnome was towering over *him*, but he did not relent.

"Ye think that because o' me, Margaret and this other dolt are gone?" Nalgene growled. "Open yer bloody eyes, ye bastard! That corpse ain't even yer sacred Captain, and even if it were, I wouldn't give a dwarf's hairy arse if he were dead! As fer the damn orc, it's the bloody Shadow! This ain't yer mum's bloody, fluffed-up children's story, ye bastard! There ain't always gonna be a happy endin'! She knew what she was gettin' into, she coulda stayed with the scum Osann, but she didn't! So, listen here, ye bloody arse, don't be callin' *me* the traitor, cause while ye were here mopin' about how bloody awful ye feel, the rest o' us were keepin' the undead scum off yer scaly arse!"

Ro shrunk before Nalgene. He knew the gnome was right, but he could not admit it.

He glanced down at the bloodied man beneath him. Examining closer, he saw it was indeed not the Captain. He raised his gaze back to the gnome, his resolve crumbling.

He tried to argue with Nalgene, tried to fire back at the traitor, but when his mouth moved only silence escaped.

Nalgene glared up at him, as a billowing flame would rage beneath a dry tree. "Eh, ye damn dragon, wha'd'ye be tryin' to say?" the gnome roared. "C'mon, ye bloody bitch, spit it out!"

Ro had no answer. His words caught in his throat, refusing to give way. The red wall of rage crumbled to ashes in his mind, replaced by a clawing pit of grief.

"Brother," SmibSmob started, his voice soft. But before he could continue, Nalgene cut him off with an icy glare.

"Eh? Nothin', ye bloody dragon?" Nalgene screamed. Ro could only stare. "Don't be callin' me a traitor. Get yer head outta yer bloody arse."

With that, the gnome relaxed, his fury played out. Sighing, he glanced away, exhaustion weighing his burly shoulders down. Ro stood silent, his fists clenching and relaxing rhythmically. He did not know what to think, what to feel. The whole world had come crumbling down around him, and he had no hope of repairing it.

The surrounding land stood quiet, as if eagerly waiting for the tension to snap, and none of the companions dared break the solemn silence. Fasto made his way over to the fallen Margaret, enveloping her in his warm embrace. SmibSmob moved next to his brother and placed a comforting hand across his shoulders. Andromeda studied them, her expression unreadable.

The swirling fog had begun to clear out, allowing the falling sun to pierce through the darkness with its pale light. As the companions eyed the lands about them, a flickering light appeared in the west, growing steadily closer. Ro watched the approaching light, and his sharp draconian eyes made out a humanoid figure brandishing a torch in the distance. The man donned a light mail with crimson cloth and held a mighty greatsword at rest on his shoulder. As the man approached, Ro saw his rough hair and his shadowy beard. He saw his dark eyes, filled with wisdom well past his age.

"It's the Captain," Ro breathed with disbelief.

Ro could only imagine how he had found them. Noticing the Captain's arrival, the other companions turned to regard him, their gazes wary. Nalgene snorted with disgust, and Andromeda seemed to wither away, isolating herself in the safety of her thoughts. But Fasto and SmibSmob were less guarded, even going as far as to give a courteous wave.

"Good to see a fellow Spark still burning bright," he hailed, extinguishing the torch. He was worn and ragged. But protecting his vulnerability was an iron shell of defense that had not been present before. Ro studied the Captain for a moment, and he could hardly believe it was the same man who had been accused of being a traitor. Even Andromeda seemed to gaze upon the man with a new light.

"Well, will ye look at that," Nalgene snarled at Captain Osann, spitting on the ground with contempt. "The bloody traitor has returned. Ye be here to grovel at our feet, cryin' about yer blasted family? Or perhaps ye be here to give us to the bloody Shadow?"

The gnome quieted as the Captain fixed him with a cool stare. No longer did Captain Osann wither under the relentless beating of the gnome. No longer did his resolve crumble at the taunts and accusations cast his way. He stood firm against the oncoming surge. The Captain's eyes swirled with an inner grief, but he remained steadfast.

"My family is dead."

Nalgene flinched, and a gasp escaped Ro's lips.

His mind was thrown back to days past, to when the Captain had pleaded with them for the sake of his family, begging them to understand. But his cries had fallen upon deaf ears. Ro's stomach twisted, and a vile taste filled his mouth.

Glancing around, he saw the others had similar reactions. Tears were welling in Fasto's eyes, and the orc moved to give the Captain a soothing hug, but he froze after the Captain locked his stare upon him. SmibSmob's face was drawn and pale. He had removed his pointed hat from his head, and was meaninglessly studying it, silent. Andromeda studied the Captain, her expression swimming with thought. Even Nalgene seemed taken aback, all previous hatred for the Captain fleeing his thoughts in grief.

"Eh ... well," Nalgene stammered, casting a mournful glance at his brother. SmibSmob did not meet his gaze. His rough voice grew silent. "Damn Osann ..."

"How did you find us?" Andromeda jumped in, her voice soft. She strode over to Captain Osann, her delicate figure seeming to glide across the land, and held him pinned with her gaze. The Captain had no answer, and he did not meet her eyes.

"Mmmm, indeed," she said slowly, and gestured to Margaret. "And what can you tell us of this?"

Captain Osann's eyes widened with shock, and he rushed over to the fallen bodies, mumbling to himself.

"She has a handprint across the back of her neck," Ro said, moving up to stand next to the Captain. "And this man has one splayed across his face."

He shuddered at the sight of the blistering seal, but he kept his gaze locked upon Margaret. He needed to avenge her.

Captain Osann nodded, brushing Margaret's hair away from her neck. After a moment, he set her gently upon the ground and moved to the fallen man. He kneeled upon the ground and placed his hand across the center of his chest.

"May your Spark join the everlasting Light," he mumbled, his eyes closed, "and pierce the ever-longing Shadow."

The Captain opened his eyes, his expression stoic, and he reached into his pouch, pulling out the symbol of the burning cross. Laying it upon his fallen companion's chest, a dull flame burst to life upon the token, flickering for a heartbeat before forever dying away, leaving only a single, orange spark rising into the heavens like a solitary star.

"What in the bloody hell?" Nalgene started, but he trailed off as the Captain rose.

"She has been touched by a Brander," Captain Osann said. "Feared among the Flame, Branders are dreadful creatures with the ability to mark that which they touch, casting their enemy into a death-like stasis." The Captain bent down, and gently picked up Margaret, laying her across his arms. "Worry not, she will wake soon enough."

Ro felt a tide of relief wash over his body. Margaret was alive! With that realization, all his weariness from the battle surged over him. His broken hand raged with agony, and his crushed ribs seared with pain. A black haze settled over his mind, and his body grew weary and weak. He felt himself falling back upon the ground, felt himself crash into the cold earth. He did not care.

She was alive!

A rush of cool water enveloped him, and immediately his clarity returned. His shattered ribs formed back into place, and his broken hand mended itself, restringing tendons and muscle into a devastating claw. A gasp escaped his lips, but as quickly as it came, the soothing flow of water was gone. Ro opened his eyes, only to find the scowling face of Nalgene hovering above it.

"Damn dragon," the gnome growled.

Shaking his head, Ro rose to his feet. The other companions had already prepared themselves to continue their journey. Fasto now carried Margaret with the utmost care, and SmibSmob stood beside him, merrily eating a steaming loaf of bread. Nalgene glared at his brother. A soft brush of fur caressed Ro's back, and he turned to find Andromeda holding his lost weapons. Even after the vile gore of the battle, his two swords and shield still shone bright, unblemished by the taint of the Shadow.

"Thank you," he stammered at Andromeda, but she turned and walked to the Captain. Sighing, Ro studied his weapons for a moment, turning them about in his hands. His greatsword seemed lighter, yet stronger, as if his devastating blast of lightning had tempered it into an invincible steel. Of course, he was probably imagining it. Stress does strange things to the mind, giving it false hope.

"Alright, Osann. Where do ye be takin' us?" Nalgene grunted. His voice was hesitant, and he looked down at his rough hands, refusing to meet anyone's gaze.

The Captain glanced around at them, giving each of them a reassuring nod. "By my oath to the Flame, follow me, my friends."

Captain Osann led the companions back to the west, traveling along the dusty road they had ventured forth on, his flickering torch shining out like a guiding beacon. The swirling fog had disappeared, but the pale sun was quickly descending to the horizon, its cold light already fading from the land. As the reaches of light succumbed to the darkness, the companions found themselves upon the fork in the road and they rested for the night. This time the Captain remained present, keeping watch through the unforgiving night.

The Captain woke them at the first light of dawn, urging them to make haste. He led them steadily west, choosing the southern road at the fork, and pushing onward through the barren lands. There was no sign of life, and still Margaret lay lifeless. As they marched, the two great lakes glittered to the north and south, stretching out far into the horizon. As their second day of travel came to an end the companions wandered into another ruined village on the coast of the southern lake. The small port town lay in shambles, unrecognizable buildings dotting the forsaken grounds. Fallen trees of inky black reached up into the dark sky, threatening to tear the very heavens down. Ro eyed the fallen village in dismay. There were so many deaths ...

What truly frightened him was how unfazed he was by the sight of the ruins. They had become commonplace.

He shuddered at the thought of how far the Shadow's reach had stretched across the withered lands.

The companions settled among the ruins for the night. Ro stared up at the starless sky, his mind wandering through his memories. Something seemed absent from the black void, but he could not place it. Kraalek's voice echoed in the back of his mind:

Fall of the Moon ...

He could only imagine what that meant.

Ro's thoughts were interrupted by a gentle cough, and the cheerful cries of Fasto. Margaret had returned. He rushed to his feet, searching for his awakened companion.

He found her surrounded by Fasto and SmibSmob, each holding a shining torch against the darkness. They leaned in close and bombarded her with a barrage of questions. A smile beaming on his face, Ro sprinted over to join them. Noticing the commotion, Nalgene was quick to follow.

Margaret was weary with exhaustion, yet her eyes sparkled with life. The blistering of the brand across her neck had faded, yet a pale scar remained in its place. Noticing Ro's approach, she gave him a weak smile, but her gaze quickly grew troubled. At what, Ro could only guess.

"What was it like?" SmibSmob questioned, his eyes wide with wonder, and his mouth open with excitement. Margaret ignored him.

"Are you alright?" Ro asked, his voice heavy with worry. "I had thought you —" He was cut off as Margaret silenced him with an upraised hand.

"Yes, I'm just fine," Margaret replied. "Just tired, that's all …" Her voice trailed off, and she stared behind Ro, her eyes narrowing. Turning, Ro found the Captain to be standing beside him, a gentle smile upon his usual stone face.

"Oh, so he's no longer a traitor then. How convenient," Margaret sneered, turning away from the Captain. Nalgene snorted but remained silent.

"Captain friend," Fasto jumped in, a wild expression on his face. "Captain say family dead."

Captain Osann flinched.

"Captain good," Fasto continued.

Margaret gave her fellow orc a blank stare. "Indeed," she said flatly. Before she could continue, Andromeda appeared from the darkness, a genuine smile on her face. She locked eyes with the she-orc and gave her a respecting nod.

"What Fasto says is true," Andromeda purred, pacing through the other companions. "He found us after the battle, claiming that his family was killed by the Shadow." She halted next to the Captain and brushed him with her soft tail. Captain Osann twitched with discomfort, but Andromeda shot him a mischievous smile. "Mmmm, perhaps he could explain better."

Ro shook his head. He had a feeling that she was playing them.

He was not sure if he enjoyed that thought.

Captain Osann cleared his throat, regaining his composure. "Indeed. While I know not the details of the battle, at some point you were marked by a Brander, casting you into a deathly stasis, and placing the mark across your neck. After the undead fiends had been driven off, I arrived to find your companions gathered around you, and I guided them west, which is where we are now."

Andromeda chuckled to herself, but the Captain ignored her.

Margaret gazed at the Captain for a long moment, allowing the silence of the Shadow to creep in. She reached up, running her fingers along the back of her neck. A frown darkened her gentle face. Silently, he pleaded to her. He meant to help them — he hoped. Couldn't she see that?

Nalgene grumbled to himself, a scowl plastered on his face, and both Fasto and SmibSmob eagerly waited for Margaret's response.

"Alright, I'll trust you" Margaret said, nodding to the Captain. Ro let out a sigh of relief, and both Fasto and SmibSmob shone with a beaming smile. Even in the overwhelming darkness of the Shadow, a rekindled hope could be seen flickering to life.

"Perfect," Andromeda purred, striding into the ruins where her delicate figure disappeared into the shadows. She cast one final glance over her shoulder, and her eyes twinkled mischievously in the torchlight. "Let's get some rest, shall we?"

Nodding in agreement, the companions lay to rest upon the ground until the first light of dawn.

As exhaustion seeped into Ro, his final thoughts were of Margaret.

◆   ◆   ◆

Ro was awakened by the Captain, who urged him to make haste. The surrounding ruins seemed mournful in the pale, morning sun, as if grieving for the loss of life. The sky was clear, yet still it appeared cold and unforgiving. About him, the other companions were already prepared to venture forth, and even Margaret seemed eager to continue.

The companions marched out of the ravaged village, heading southwest along the dusty road. The great lake shimmered to the east, following the companions along in the distance. As they traveled across the forsaken lands, they stumbled upon an undead rabbit, its rotting flesh hanging in shambles and its long, pointed ears nothing more than a mockery of their former life. Nalgene seemed strangely intrigued by the vile creature and even sent out a gentle spray of water to comfort the beast. Instead, the water ultimately killed the dreadful abomination. Nalgene wore his familiar scowl for the remainder of the day.

As the cold sun sank to the horizon, the companions came upon a rushing river that cut across the road. Remains of a once strong bridge lay in ruins along the bank, barring the companions from continuing their journey. Irritated by the ruined bridge, Margaret promptly froze a wide stretch across the river, creating a crossing of ice. As she crossed, she scratched at the back of her neck, grumbling to herself. Intrigued, the companions followed her across, warily trekking across the precarious bridge. Just as they reached the opposite bank, Fasto slipped and fell into what he thought were the rushing depths below. Shaking his head, the Captain trudged into the frigid water and pulled Fasto out from the shallow riverbed, throwing him onto the shore. Shivering in terror, Fasto eyed the companions, mumbling nonsense to whoever cared enough to listen. The companions all agreed it would be best to rest for the night.

Upon waking, the companions continued along the forlorn road, their spirits restored after the previous day's mishaps. After two more days of travel, the companions came upon another river, which tore across the lands and came to rest in the shimmering lake to the east. Unlike the first river, there was still a worn bridge running across the length of the river. When they reached the bridge, however, the companions froze in their tracks.

Elegantly sitting upon a rock at the foot of the bridge was a most beautiful woman. Long, silky black hair cascaded over her shoulders in a marvelous braid. A flowing, black skirt fell over her pale legs, and splashes of orange and yellow flared out at the edge of the cloth like billowing flames. Her simple black top left little to the imagination, revealing her shining skin and seductive form. Pauldrons of gold and sparkling jewelry draped across her body in a golden web, and magnificent emeralds accented her unmatched beauty. Held out in front of her was a marvelous sword, which she turned over in her hands.

Ro gasped, his mind thrown back to the prison. He remembered this woman, remembered her holy light piercing the vile legions of undead. He remembered her clash against the titanic dreadknight of shadow, casting an aura of brilliant light over his broken body. He remembered the commanding voice, and the promises that it made. A rush of emotion overwhelmed Ro, leaving him helpless before the beautiful woman.

Noticing their arrival, Ashyla set down her sword and shot them a dazzling smile of the purest white. Her gaze flicked up, locking the companions with an alluring, yet unwavering, stare.

"Ah, my dears," she said in a gentle voice while gracefully gliding off the rock. Her skirt flowed out behind her like the flaming wing of a butterfly, and she strode over to the companions, her soft steps silent against the hard ground. "So nice to finally see you again."

Ro stared in wonder, his mind whirling about in a furious rush of thoughts. What did she mean, again? There was the prison, but beyond that …

Ashyla laughed, interrupting his thoughts, her eyes sparkling like a misty twilight.

"So, you remember not." She paused, and a brief flash of intrigue washed across her face, but it was gone as quickly as it had come. She shot them another smile and continued her steady advance.

"How tragic."

Daniel Whitman

*C*hapter 7

Andromeda stood stunned; her eyes locked on Ashyla. She could not even begin to comprehend Ashyla's words, as she was too captivated by her own thoughts. This woman, this most beautiful woman, who had rescued them from certain death, now stood before them in all her dazzling splendor. Around her, the other companions had similar reactions, gazing upon Ashyla with awe and wonder.

The woman held such power ...

Shaking her head, Andromeda tried to clear herself of such thoughts, but they persisted at the edges of her mind. No matter how much she denied it, how much she tried to cast away her lust, her eyes were drawn to the tantalizing woman in front of her — her silky, pale skin, cascading, black hair, and, most crucially, her overwhelming power ... No! She needed to focus on the hunt at hand.

As Ashyla approached, Andromeda felt a sudden weight fall across her shoulders, binding her in place. She tried to move, tried to call out, but the weight felt too substantial. There was no possible way she could move — or even talk! Or that's how it seemed. She didn't notice the small butterfly that had landed on her back.

Ashyla passed through the companions, her blazing dress flowing out behind her. She stopped in front of Andromeda, and Andromeda had the sense that the woman was gazing into her very soul, undermining her deepest secrets and darkest memories. Ashyla smirked, and raised her slender hand, gently brushing it across Andromeda's face.

As Andromeda watched, a black butterfly flickered into view, landing gently upon Ashyla's arm. It flapped its wings in a mesmerizing dance, slowly approaching the bound feline. Intrigue filled Andromeda's mind, and she studied the strange butterfly, trying to measure the mystical creature. It was just like the ones from the prison. But as quickly as it had come, the butterfly vanished, leaving only an empty, pale arm, which still held Andromeda's face. Ashyla smiled, and locked eyes with Andromeda, giving a satisfactory nod, before turning away.

Unnerved, Andromeda tried to move, but she was still bound in place. All she could hope to do was watch.

Ashyla continued through the companions, brushing past each of them with an alluring smile. She paused in front of SmibSmob, gazing down at him in intrigue. She reached out, cupping his chin, and raised his head. SmibSmob's eyes shot open, shifting from their gentle blue to their unholy light. Chuckling to herself, Ashyla released the gnome and turned away, her black dress whirling about her like a shadowy orchid caught in the wind. SmibSmob stood frozen, helplessly gaping at the beautiful woman.

Finally, Ashyla paused in front of Captain Osann and gave him a knowing stare, her sharp eyes cutting into his very being. She reached out, placing her hand upon the center of his chest. With that singular, gentle touch, the Captain staggered back, letting out a silent cry. His eyes pleaded with Ashyla, but she was relentless, driving him back with her touch. Despair washed over his gaze, and he crumpled to the ground, overwhelmed with sorrow. Ashyla smirked, mocking the Captain's helplessness.

Turning around, Ashyla strode away from the companions, her cascading braid waving behind her. Immediately, the binding pressure lifted from the companions, leaving them gasping for breath. Behind them, butterflies flitted away. Andromeda glanced about at her companions, her eyes wide. What even happened?

SmibSmob stood silent, his face drawn, pale and smothered with self-doubt. Nalgene tried to comfort his brother, but SmibSmob shrugged him off. The Captain dragged himself back to his feet, a mask of denial rejecting all that the Goddess had cast upon him. Fasto and Margaret stood helplessly, unable to comfort the others. Margaret clenched her black fist by her side, while Fasto glared at Ashyla, his eyes as cold as the ice from Margaret's arm. Ro rushed over to Andromeda, trying to calm her with his protective spirit, but her fears held firm, like iron spikes driven into her mind.

Andromeda's gaze shot over to Ashyla, who now leaned upon the rock, apparently uninterested in their company. Andromeda studied the woman, desperately trying to identify some weakness, some crack in the alluring facade.

She found none. The woman appeared perfect.

Next to her, Captain Osann staggered forward, his greatsword held in front of him. His face was twisted with despair, but it burned with an inner fire.

"Name yourself," he ordered Ashyla, his voice steeled. His greatsword flickered, hinting at the raging inferno that could burst to life across its razor edge.

Ashyla glanced up, scorching the Captain with an accusing glare. She moved off the rock, and paced forward to the Captain, her black skirt flowing out behind her.

"Why, my dear Osann. You know not of me?" She paused, throwing a cheeky smile at the Captain. "Such a pity. I figured you the more studious type."

Captain Osann spat at her. He planted his feet, raising his greatsword threateningly. Flickers of flame spiraled about the blade, casting blasts of heat across the cold lands.

"I repeat," he said, his voice harsh. His eyes narrowed dangerously, and he tensed his muscles, ready to pounce upon the arrogant woman. "Name yourself."

Ashyla shot the Captain a teasing smile, flashing her brilliant teeth and reaching up to caress her majestic braid. "Pray tell, my dear Osann, what is it you hope to accomplish?" The Captain snarled, and his greatsword erupted into a blazing inferno. Ashyla laughed.

"All your bravado, all your flaming grandeur and strength. It is all a lie. While you stand mighty and pretend to know not of me, I certainly know you, my dear Osann."

The Captain took a threatening step forward, his eyes cold and unforgiving. "No," he growled through his teeth.

"Brilliant. Strike me down," Ashyla goaded, holding her arms out wide and throwing a sideways glance at the companions. "But please, do try harder than you did against your dear friends."

Andromeda flinched, Ashyla's words striking true. Her mind was thrown back to when they had first met the Captain, where he had vowed to strike them down. Yet still, here they were, by his side as he led them across the forsaken lands. He ruthlessly attacked them, yet not one of them had fallen to his billowing blade. He didn't even strike them with the edge!

"Captain …" Andromeda whispered. Her stomach wretched at his name, but she smothered her disgust. She — they needed him.

Ashyla's eyes fell upon her, their knowing gaze piercing through her wild mind. Andromeda's mind screamed in protest, yet resist as she might, her deepest thoughts were thrown into the open daylight.

Ashyla smiled.

"No!" Andromeda cried, collapsing to her knees in defeat. Her mind tore apart. All her thoughts and secrets, it all come crashing down upon her in a furious storm. Try as she might, she could not hope to resist the surge. A voice, exactly like the one from the prison, entered her mind. A gentle yet commanding voice. Ashyla's voice.

I see. Ever since your childhood ...

The thoughts rushed in, unwelcome.

You tried to save them, tried to protect them.

Andromeda shied from the memories, but still they came.

You failed. You watched them die, watched them get cut down by the marauders, but there was nothing you could do. You were weak, helpless before the harsh reality of this land. As you wept over their torn corpses, you vowed you would never succumb to the weight of the world, that you would pounce forward and dominate any hunt that came upon you. You craved power, lusted it, all for the promise of revenge ...

How selfish.

An image of a strange man with a flowing blue cloak formed in her mind. He had a bushy mustache and an innocent smile. In his hand was an elegant hammer, sparkling in the sunlight ...

And, because of him, you found it.

But the thought was cut off, as if it were locked behind some iron barrier. Ashyla's slim mouth curled into a frown.

The shackles restraining Andromeda's mind released, relieving her from the chaotic turmoil. She tried to grasp at what she saw, tried to make sense of the strange man, but she had no answers.

Andromeda glanced up, studying the enchanting woman in front of her. Her eyes ran across her flowing skirt, her smooth, pale skin, and her golden jewelry before returning to her hypnotic gaze. As her eyes locked with Ashyla's, the stone shackles crashed back upon her mind, binding her to the unwelcome thoughts. The inner voice appeared once more; its thundering clarity redoubled.

You lusted for power, and nothing else mattered before your insatiable hunger! The thoughts of your slaughtered family faded before the might of your desire, leaving nothing but a chasm in your heart. And after the escape from the prison, it grew into a billowing inferno. You pretended to be a friend. But you were just following your own greed.

But that all changed. In your meeting with Osann, you saw the fatal flaw of your lust. You saw the empty shell you were. You saw the heartless void that was your existence. You connected with him. He too had a false shell, he too smothered his emotions behind a masquerade, but unlike you, underneath the twisting lies, he had something to fight for.

Andromeda gasped, and her stomach lurched at the thought. She hated the Captain, despised him … right? He tried to kill her, tried to betray her. But as much as she denied it, the voice rang true. She tried to reject the thoughts, but the voice cut through her feeble defenses, pouncing upon her vulnerability with a brutal savagery.

Deny it as you will, you can never hope to escape the void clawing at your mind! You tried to reject it, tried to promise yourself there was more beneath the murky surface! But every time you looked upon Osann, you were gazing upon a shattered mirror. You were empty, a shallow mockery of life! Deny it as you will, you know the truth! You did not hate him; you hated the image that you saw in his dark eyes! And so, you pounced upon the first thought of abandoning him, you eagerly fled from what you so despised, and for what? To finally do some good? To purify the endless Shadow? Nay, you were selfish, ignorant of the troubles about you. Yet still here you are, hoping at a chance for redemption. You stride about, veiled in the darkness, thinking to use your lust to protect the others.

Pathetic.

Andromeda wanted to scream, to let out a roar of denial. Yet her breath caught in her throat, and she could only gape at the woman in front of her. Her tail thrashed about wildly, and a blaze burned deep within her eyes, searing Ashyla with a scorching rage. Yet still the voice mocked her, taunted her with its twisting deceptions.

She was overwhelmed with its power …

A growl escaped Andromeda's lips, and her mouth curled back into a ferocious snarl.

Ashyla smiled.

You see it before you, my dear Andromeda. Power is a poisoned blade. It can cut down the mightiest of foes, or the holiest of friends. Deny it as you will, you know this. You know the noxious truth.

And, my dear Andromeda, the poison has already spread.

"NO!" Andromeda screamed in denial. Her halberd appeared in her hand, and her body began fading into the darkness. "It's all lies! I see through your deception! You may try to tear me apart with your deceit, but it is nothing more than empty promises!"

The air hung silent about the companions, broken only by the mocking laughter of Ashyla.

"Andromeda," Ro gaped. He moved to comfort Andromeda, but she warded him off with a fiery glare. Pain flashed across his face. He wanted to help, wanted to guide her through the darkness, but this was her hunt, and hers alone.

"What in the bloody hell?" Nalgene grunted. "Damn cat."

Beside him, SmibSmob still stood oblivious to the others, his face taut and pale, and his hands aimlessly searching the expanses of his pointed hat. Fasto was appalled, his jaw hung open in shock. Even Margaret seemed wary. She had felt a sort of kinship with Andromeda, some deeper spark of connection. Yet this was beyond her understanding.

The Captain stood silent.

"You lie," Andromeda spat at Ashyla. The restricting shackles binding her mind had lifted, and a soothing calm settled over her body.

With a flick of her wrist, her halberd disappeared, and she returned from her shadowy stealth. Her tail slashed fiercely, and her sharp eyes shot daggers of ice, but her visage remained calm and collected. Ashyla gave her a quizzical look, her rosy lips curling into a soft smirk.

"You lie," Andromeda repeated. "You lie. Mmmm, you may stand there now, twisting us about as if we were your prey, but

I know your game. Do you think you can play us as some god?"

Ashyla smiled. "God? Why, you must have read your history. Unlike dear Osann."

Andromeda ignored her. "You lie. You cannot control me. You cannot break me."

"What in the bloody hell are ye ramblin' about, ye damn cat?" Nalgene burst in. Confusion clouded his face, and his gaze darted between the two women in a frantic search of the truth. "I dunno what yer screamin' about, but I ain't be likin' it. Sure, this woman be actin' a little weird around me brother, but there ain't be no bloody lies, that's fer sure. She wasn't even talkin'!"

"Well observed, my dear gnome. You truly are insightful," Ashyla applauded Nalgene, shooting him a dazzling smile. "And worry not, for your dear brother is just, ah, exploring his own thoughts."

Nalgene merely growled, and SmibSmob remained silent.

"No, you don't understand," Andromeda spat.

"Andromeda, remember the prison," Ro jumped in. He clenched his longsword by his side, betraying his discomfort. "This woman saved us. When we were cut down by the minions of Shadow, she came down in a flash of light, driving the darkness back. She brought us to the forest, away from our deaths." He paused, and his brow furrowed in thought — an uncomfortable thought.

"But why?"

Andromeda hesitated; her rage played out. Why indeed? She could only wonder.

The other companions glanced at Ro, confusion in their gazes.

"Eh? That ain't be what happened," Nalgene started, turning to Ro. But before he could continue, the Captain jumped in.

"Why indeed?" Captain Osann echoed. His face was pale, yet a resolved strength shone brightly upon his dark features. "They claim you have saved them." He paused, and he turned his gaze to the companions. "No." His voice grew harsh, and he pinned Ro with a threatening glare. "You said it was Mariah who rescued you from the Shadow."

Ro stammered, at a loss for words. SmibSmob flinched.

Ashyla laughed. "Oh, is that so?" She turned her eyes to Andromeda, their shining depths piercing her resolve. "This is most amusing. And you claim that I lie? Look around you, my dear Andromeda, you all lie. How ... selfish."

"No!" Andromeda hissed, a billowing hatred burning inside of her. She will not be controlled. She will not be broken. She will not be pulled around like some lifeless puppet. "You lie."

Ashyla smiled. "And pray tell, my dear Andromeda, when have I not spoken the truth?"

Andromeda paused. She had no answer. She tried to think, tried to call the enchanting woman out on her deception. But she could not. It was the truth.

She could not accept that, could not allow Ashyla to control her. Yet her thoughts rang hollow, empty of resolve. "No," she said in a vain attempt at denial.

Ashyla laughed, her sweet melody washing over Andromeda. "My dear Andromeda, how far have you fallen. You vow to never be broken yet look at you now."

Andromeda growled, and her halberd appeared in her hand. She knew Ashyla was right, but she crushed the thought under the weight of her fury. Her sharp eyes locked onto her target, scanning for a weakness.

Before she could act, the Captain appeared in front of Andromeda, his mighty greatsword held threateningly at her throat. His eyes held little mercy. Flickers of flame erupted from the sword, brushing Andromeda with their searing heat. Andromeda tried to escape, tried to fade away into the shadows, but the Captain's feral gaze locked her in place.

Ashyla laughed, mocking their petty arguments. "Oh my, what a turn," she taunted. Captain Osann shot an icy glare at her, and she raised her hands in feint alarm.

"Silence!" the Captain ordered, his voice harsh and remorseless. Conflict crashed in his eyes, yet his face was as hard as stone.

Ashyla bowed, her black hair brushing against the cold ground. "As you command," she teased. "Else I might accidentally let your secret slip, my dear traitor."

Captain Osann snarled, clenching his greatsword, his knuckles turning white.

"Ye see? What did I tell ye!" Nalgene shouted, his buried anger bursting forth. This time there was no calming rain. This time SmibSmob was not there to soothe his rage. "Bloody traitor! I might not be knowin' what the bloody hell is goin' on, but I be trustin' this woman more than yer sorry arse, Osann!"

He raised his hands, and swirling vortexes of water formed within his grasp. With a furious cry, he launched them at the Captain.

Andromeda could only watch in horror. No! The woman was lying! Why didn't they understand?

In the background, Ashyla looked on with amusement, a sly smirk curled on her smooth face. Andromeda snarled. She wanted to pounce at the woman, pounce at her lies, yet she knew it would be for naught. She denied Ashyla, yet still, she admired her power. Shaking her head, her attention was caught by the two orbs of water streaking towards the Captain. Time seemed to slow, as if hesitating to see the outcome. And still Andromeda could only watch as the destruction unraveled.

Shouting, Ro leaped in front of the Captain, his shining shield held out in front of him in an iron wall. With a frightful splash, the oncoming water crashed into Ro, driving him to the ground. He landed upon the unforgiving earth, his breath blasted from his body, but he was far from out of the fight. Ro looked up, his accusing glare locking onto Nalgene, burning into the gnome with its raging intensity. Coughing, he forced himself to his feet, still holding the shield out before him.

"Ye damn dragon!" Nalgene roared, not backing away from the furious draconian. He raised his hands, and a mighty vortex formed above his head, its swirling water dancing about in a tantalizing display of might. "Ye better move yer sorry arse, or else I be blastin' ye to the stinkin' pits o' oblivion!"

Nalgene took a threatening step forward, his face a mask of fury. SmibSmob still stood silently by, absorbed in his own dark thoughts.

"He gave us his vow!" Ro said, standing firm under the gnome's threat. "He would lead us to the Light, lead us out of these lands of Shadow. He would reunite us with —"

"And I meant to keep that promise," growled the Captain, interrupting Ro. Turning, he removed his sword from Andromeda's neck, and placed it at the base of Ro's neck.

"Yet, you still doubt me a traitor," he snarled, his voice lowering dangerously. "I should think you the traitors. You lied. You lied to me, and my General. Shadowfriends ... I should have killed you when I first got the chance."

"Why don't ye be killin' us now, eh?" Nalgene screeched at the Captain, his face twisted in a furious storm. "Ye be wantin' to fight, eh? I'll take ye on, ye filthy scum, I'll be makin' sure ye never see the bloody Light again!"

Growling, he lowered his hands, and the mighty surge dissipated. He reached into his flowing blue cloak and pulled forth his crystalline bottle. The water inside rang clear and pure, yet under the weight of Nalgene's rage it seemed inky and black.

"Outta the way, ye bloody dragon!"

A very confused Fasto moved up to stand next to the gnome, his white bow raised, and a deadly arrow already nocked, ready to pierce the Captain's skull. The orc was lost in the twisting events around him, yet he seemed determined to strike Captain Osann down. So much for being a friend.

"Then we shall fight," the Captain hissed, raising his mighty greatsword. There was no mercy in his harsh gaze. "I'll be sure to take at least one of you with me before I die." His greatsword erupted into its full splendor, its billowing fires of death lunging at the companions.

And still, Andromeda could only watch in horror. They simply refused to understand.

Her eyes shot over to Ashyla, who stood idly by with an amused look on her face. Noticing Andromeda's glare, Ashyla merely chuckled and shrugged, shooting Andromeda an apologetic smile. Andromeda's mind whirled about in torment.

The woman was lying! Yes, she saved them and rescued them from the prison, but here she stood now, mocking them and pulling them about as if they were her prey. Andromeda wouldn't allow it.

But she knew Ashyla was right, and she didn't care. She had to protect the others. She had to have something to fight for.

Andromeda stared at Margaret, who stood similarly horrified. The orc's eyes shone in desperation, and she gave Andromeda a pleading nod. Andromeda nodded, and her tail slashed violently behind her. She had to have something to fight for.

"No! Stop! Don't you see, she's doing this to us!" Andromeda exclaimed, leaping forward and crashing into Ro, driving him away from the infuriated Captain. Her halberd appeared in her hand, and she held it out at Ashyla, its razor edge shining in the fading light of the pale sun. Her gaze cut across the companions, locking onto the Captain like two iron daggers driving into his chest. She felt alive, the thrill of the hunt coursing through her boiling blood. She had to have something to fight for.

"It's her," she snarled, her fangs gleaming. "She's pulling us about like her prey, turning us against each other for her own amusement! She may have saved us, but ..."

Andromeda trailed off. But what? But the power — No!

"Listen to Andromeda," SmibSmob piped in, shaking out of his despairing thoughts. He looked up with a newfound life, his blue eyes shining like beacons in the dark. Reaching up, he returned his pointed hat to his head, and his purple cloak billowed in the still air. "Listen to yourselves. She's playing us."

The companions stood in a shocked silence. The air about them sparked with anticipation, waiting for tension to snap. The Captain's face was an emotionless mountain. He would still fight. Ro studied Andromeda, frowning. Nalgene and Fasto remained still, although their aim remained targeted on the traitorous Captain.

"Please," SmibSmob pleaded. "Don't do this."

Nalgene glanced over to the fellow gnome, and all hostility fled from him. "Me brother," Nalgene sighed, returning his crystalline flask into the folds of his blue cloak. "Ye and yer fine noggin. Yer right. Bloody hell, yer right. It's this damn woman, she's bloody usin' us. Just like that bastard Kraalek. Pullin' us like puppets."

Reaching up, he patted Fasto's arm, and the orc lowered his bow, confusion saturating his expression. Fasto was hopelessly lost in the twisting webs.

Rushing over to Ro, Margaret helped him to his feet and pulled him back to the others. As she passed, she gave Andromeda a satisfactory nod. But her black fist was held clenched at her side, and its unforgiving cold cast a deathly chill in the still air.

The Captain seemed unconvinced. He glared at Andromeda, his flaming greatsword still held out in a guard. Please. He had to understand … The pow — NO!

Her thought was interrupted by her lust for power, but she buried the urge, smothering it behind a wall of hatred and denial. Her eyes locked with the Captain's, pleading with him. He had to understand. It was the woman, the alluring and powerful — NO! She needed to focus on the hunt!

Andromeda's halberd disappeared, and she visibly relaxed, holding her empty hands up to the Captain in a display of peace.

"Please," she begged, her voice soft. Her tail reached around, brushing against the Captain's side. He flinched. "Please," she echoed, her voice gaining strength.

The Captain broke, a twisting tide of anguish washed over his face. He nodded, and as quickly as it had come, the maelstrom of torment was concealed by his stoic mask. Turning around, he raised his flaming greatsword above his head, then lowered it down in line with Ashyla. The Captain's eyes were frigid spears of fury.

"What say you?" Captain Osann said, his voice low and steady. He planted his feet, readying to spring at the arrogant woman.

Ashyla smiled, a most dazzling smile of the purest white. "My dear Osann," Ashyla started, her voice gentle and soft, as if she were soothing a lost babe. She raised her hands to the side, displaying them openly in a sign of surrender.

"Be reasonable," she teased, throwing a sly wink the Captain's way.

He ignored her. His gaze hardened, and the inferno about his greatsword burst forth with ever more rage.

"What say you?" the Captain repeated, his voice shallow and dangerous, and a cutting-edge seeping into his words. Ro stepped forward next to the Captain, his greatsword held firmly in his hands. The draconian fixed Ashyla with an iron glare yet doubt flickered behind the harsh barrier. Fasto soon followed, raising his bow and nocking an arrow, ready to strike Ashyla down. Even the two gnomes readied themselves against the Goddess, Nalgene standing protectively by his brother's side, his face a jagged boulder.

Andromeda watched on with distress. She kept telling herself she hated the woman, yet, even still, she could not watch her die. Not yet.

Was it because of the alluring power? No. That was not the reason, she had to tell herself that. She had to have something else to fight for.

Margaret appeared by her side, and she gave Andromeda a

comforting nod. Margaret's icy aura washed over Andromeda, but she ignored it. Her thoughts were elsewhere. She remembered the prison, remembered the merciless precision with which Ashyla had slaughtered the undead hordes and the terrifying power as she leaped upon the dreadknight. Andromeda glanced at her companions, then locked her sharp gaze on Ashyla. She knew they couldn't win the fight.

Around her, the other companions shared similar thoughts. Ro's mouth curled into a nervous frown, and Margaret seemed hesitant. Even SmibSmob and Nalgene seemed uncertain about the situation. Fasto was just confused. But Captain Osann remained immovable, a towering mountain among the barren lands.

"What say you?" he repeated for the final time, his patience wearing thin.

"Please, tell us," Ro pleaded with Ashyla, his voice shaky. "Why are you here? You saved us, and yet ..." He trailed off, yet his gaze held firm, boring into Ashyla. He wanted answers, needed them, but they seemed as distant as when they first spoke to Mariah.

"Why?" Andromeda finished for Ro, stepping forward. She studied Ashyla, trying to find any clue or weakness. There were none. The woman was flawless, a dazzling specter of beauty, and an endless well of power ...

Andromeda shook her head in a vain attempt to clear her thoughts, but her gnawing lust for power tore at the back of her mind, and it was only magnified when she gazed upon Ashyla.

She looked back to her companions, who stood as if on the razor edge of a knife. She had to have something to fight for. No. She *had* something to fight for.

"Why?" Andromeda repeated.

Ashyla shook her head, chuckling. "Pray tell, why indeed?" she echoed, her voice a melodious charm. She released her hair and glanced down at the wondrous sword still held in her hand. She sighed, and after a brief pause, she continued, her voice a faint murmur. "Because of my children ..."

Her visage grew twisted with mania, and a dangerous, cutting edge seeped into her voice.

"I mean only to avenge what you children and that pathetic man ..." Ashyla paused, and a tranquil calm washed over her expression, replacing the harsh cruelty that was there. Her body visibly relaxed, and she smiled — not a deriding smirk, but a warm, open smile. A gentle aura of light seemed to radiate from her, giving her pale skin a delightful glow. Ashyla shook her head, as if shaking away the vile darkness from her enchanting purity.

"You see, my dears," she said, her voice a soft caress. "It is quite simple. I am not here to mock you or scorn you for your ignorance."

"No?" Captain Osann questioned, a weary edge to his voice. "Because that seems to be the only thing you have done."

Ashyla shot the Captain a wry smile.

"No. I am here because of you, wretched Osann" she said, her voice growing into a thin hiss. Her eyes slashed across the companions, cutting down their morale with reckless abandon, before driving back into the Captain. Her soft face once more grew harsh under the clutches of mania. "You think you understand, child? You think you can slink around in the shadows?"

Captain Osann reeled back under the weight of Ashyla's words. He stammered for a moment, before an iron mask fell over his face. "Why you," he growled, locking his wrathful gaze upon Ashyla. "I abandoned the darkness. No longer can it hold any sway over me. I gave my vow, and I will see through with it."

Andromeda stared, her eyes wide with horror. Her heart wrenched, torn by the Captain's sudden confession. So, it was true. All this time, Nalgene was right.

She felt helpless, as if she were being tossed about in a furious storm. She wanted to let out a cry, wanted to strike him down, but something held her back. It didn't matter what he did, for now he had something else to fight for: them.

An iron determination settled over her tormented mind,

filling her with an eerie sense of calm. She had something to fight for. Her eyes locked on Ashyla, and she began to fade into the shadows, her halberd appearing in her hand.

Ashyla chuckled, her gaze still focused on the Captain. "Is that so, child? Is that truly what you think?" she asked, her voice solemn. "You are a fool. I know who you swore your allegiance to: my little puppet."

Her voice softened, and she glanced down at her sword. "It is not so easy to abandon your sins."

The Captain took a step forward, his mighty greatsword held firm in his grasp. "You know nothing," he hissed.

Ashyla shrugged, unconvinced. "Perhaps not."

She raised her hand, and with a casual flick of her wrist, a torrent of black butterflies erupted from her palm, swirling on the ground in front of her. But as quickly as they had come, the butterflies retreated into the surrounding shadows, leaving behind the huddled form of a woman protecting her child.

The woman was dirty and worn, yet a subtle beauty still shone through the grime. Her hair was wavy and brown, and her skin was olive. The woman would have been considered attractive, but next to Ashyla, she seemed nothing more than common. The small child had not yet reached his fifth year, and he too was dirtied and ragged. But shining out through the filth shadowing his face were two, deep brown eyes, looking on with a knowledge well past his age.

The Captain froze and fell to his knees. It was his family. A surge of relief washed over his face, but it was quickly covered by a tide of despair. "Elizabeth," he gasped. "Kyle. It can't be …"

He shook his head, as if trying to clear the illusion, but still his family remained. He narrowed his eyes, and he stood up, his voice deep and threatening. "They are dead, killed by the Shadow." He shook his head again in a vain attempt to wash away the lie, but there his family still lay, looking up at him with wide eyes.

Ashyla laughed.

"Is that so?" she mocked, striding forward to stand over Elizabeth. "First you forget your history, and now you forget your own family?"

Ashyla reached down and brushed her hand through the woman's hair. Elizabeth glanced up, a mask of terror twisting her face. She tried to scramble away, tried to escape, but she was bound in place, frozen by the will of the Goddess.

"And what convinced you of their death, child?" Ashyla continued, still running Elizabeth's dirty hair through her hand. A murderous gleam shot across Ashyla's face. "I assure you; they appear most alive and well."

Falling into another fit of madness, the Goddess began to close her hand, digging her slender fingers into the poor woman's head like a thorny vice. Elizabeth struggled violently under the pressure, and her mouth opened wide in a silent scream of pain. Trickles of blood began to seep down the woman's head, and her eyes rolled back into her head.

"Stop!" the Captain howled; his face torn with despair. His eyes darted between his family and their oppressor, anguish filling their brown depths.

At the sound of the Captain's voice, Ashyla's madness passed and her collected calm returned, washing away her violent rage. Her slender hand loosened, and Elizabeth fell to the ground, moaning and squirming.

"How dare you," Captain Osann hissed, taking another step forward.

Ashyla pursed her lips as if she were a child caught pulling a prank.

Still groaning, Elizabeth managed to straighten herself from the cold ground, blood still trickling down her head like crimson rain drops. Her body trembled, but she attempted to appear in control of her terror. She had to remain strong for Kirk, and for Kyle.

The Captain's eyes locked onto his wife's, and a connecting spark could be felt between them, linking their eternal love. Captain

Osann gave Elizabeth a faint nod, a weary smile appearing on his face. A tear welled up in the corner of his eye, but he shook it away, his face growing harsh. His gaze raised, and his deep eyes seared into Ashyla, accusing her of her deception.

"Release them," he growled. No longer was there any doubt in his mind. He had to save his family.

Ashyla smirked.

"As you command, my dear Captain." Ashyla held out her hand, and two inky butterflies appeared on her palm. With a flap of their wings the butterflies soared over to the Captain's family, landing on their shoulders. The butterflies took a step forward, their heads morphing into dreadful needles of death.

Before anyone could react, the needles plunged.

Elizabeth's head shot back, her face open in a silent scream of horror. She fell back, releasing Kyle from her grasp. As the companions watched, the Captain's family began to flake away, disappearing into a horde of butterflies. The Captain let out a desperate cry, and he tried to rush forward to embrace his family, but a cutting glare from Ashyla bound him in place. Kyle fell back against the ground, crying uncontrollably. He tried to reach for his mother, tried to reach for her protection, but as his arms extended, they fell away into the shadowy insects.

Andromeda watched in dread, a hollow void clawing at her stomach. The power was — NO! She was a monster!

She tried to rush forward to save the family, but the crushing weight fell atop her shoulders, freezing her in place once more. Another butterfly landed upon her back. Or so it seemed. She tried to escape, tried to deny what she saw, but it was useless. A furious cry escaped her lips, but Ashyla ignored her. She was helpless. All she could hope to do was watch in horror as the Captain's family vanished.

Her eyes locked onto Kyle's, and all his emotions came crashing over her. His terror, his anguish, his endless despair. It overwhelmed her mind like a raging typhoon, washing away any other thought. The last thing Andromeda saw of him was his brown eyes, pleading for a savior.

The companions watched in shocked horror. Rage billowed inside of them, yet they were bound in place, unable to help the broken Captain. Captain Osann fell to his knees, tears streaming down his face. He tried to grasp the butterflies of his family, but as he grabbed them, they vanished into nothing in his hand. After a moment of mourning, the Captain slowly rose to his feet. An aura of fiery fury radiated from him. His greatsword burst into a more furious inferno than ever, and he raised it in front of him, determined to strike Ashyla down. How dare she mock him? How dare she desecrate his family? His eyes burned holes in Ashyla, driving her back under the heat of his glare.

"You will pay, fiend," he hissed.

Ashyla appeared unconcerned, her open smile taunting the Captain.

"My dear Osann, be reasonable," she sneered. "They were already dead; you said it yourself." The Captain gave no response, only taking a step forward. Ashyla sighed, and she glanced down at her shining sword.

"How ungrateful. And I call myself generous …" Her eyes shot up, locking onto the advancing Captain. This time he did not falter under her glare. "So be it," she shrugged, casually waving her hand. "Have your fun."

From behind Ashyla the butterflies reappeared, once again circling in front of her. The shadowy insects fused together forming two vile zombies that stood ready. Their hollow eyes mocked any sense of life, and their rotting flesh hung in tatters over their nightmarish bodies. A wide jaw hung open, displaying rows of vicious teeth, ready to rend the flesh from the Captain's body. One of the zombies was shorter than the other, and it seemed to cling to the other, as if desperately seeking its protection.

The crushing weight still bound Andromeda to the ground, forcing her to watch the pitiful charade play out in front of her. Rage crashed against her mind, and she desperately tried to free herself.

The two zombies charged at the Captain, their maws open, and their arms held out wide in front of them. The Captain shifted his weight back, and a burst of flame appeared under his feet. Suddenly he was gone, only to appear behind the larger zombie. With a fiery slash, he cut the monstrosity down. With an eerie despairing wail, the vile creature crashed to the ground, its lifeblood pooling out around it. It felt pain.

Ashyla smiled.

Whipping about, the Captain turned on the smaller zombie, his face a merciless mask of revenge. The pitiful creature tried to swing at the Captain, but it was heartless, and the fearsome Captain effortlessly dodged the pathetic excuse for an attack. His eyes seared into the vile zombie, and it cowered in terror.

Ashyla glanced behind her, to some unseen observer in the shadows, her eyes twinkling with glee.

Mercilessly, the Captain backhanded the pitiful zombie, sending it staggering back, blood splattering out of its torn face. A ball of fire appeared in the Captain's hand, and he threw it at the creature, showering it in a burst of searing flames. The bitter stench of burning flesh filled the air. The zombie fell back, raising its rotting arms in a vain attempt at protection. The Captain was unwavering. With nothing more than a step, he disappeared again, only to reappear behind the pathetic undead, his blazing greatsword targeted on the creature's exposed back.

Ashyla laughed.

The sword plunged.

With a burst of flames, the sword erupted through the zombie's chest, and the Captain raised it above his head in a triumphant victory. He turned to Ashyla, his gaze burning with hate. Ashyla laughed ever harder. Calming herself, she gave a dejected sigh, shaking her head. She turned to the Captain, a sly smile appearing on her rosy lips.

Black butterflies fluttered off the two zombies. The illusion lifted.

Andromeda gave a horrified gasp, despair washing over her thoughts. It couldn't be … How could one be so cruel? She was a monster — a true monster. There was no redemption to be had.

Hanging limply from the Captain's sword was the charred body of Kyle, a pitiful scream of anguish twisting his young face. The boy's blood ran down the length of the sword, covering the Captain's hand in a red coat. And lying upon the ground was the cleaved body of Elizabeth, a massive slash searing through her shattered back, and her thick, red blood pooling about in a scarlet lake.

The Captain glanced up in shock, a desperate cry erupting from his lips. His mighty greatsword fell from his hand, clattering to the ground. He fell to his knees, clutching at his tainted hand. Tears streamed down his face, and his back lurched with sobs.

Ashyla laughed, a dull, hollow taunt that broke the Captain's will.

Crawling across the ground, Captain Osann reached for his slaughtered wife, but he could not bring himself to touch the limp corpse. He looked up to Ashyla, his eyes dull and devoid of their former light. He was a broken man.

The weight lifted from Andromeda. With a furious scream, she charged at Ashyla, her halberd appearing in her hand. Hissing wildly, she swung her halberd at the target's head in a wild attempt at vengeance. No one deserved such a horrible fate.

Ashyla jerked back, avoiding the deadly strike. As the halberd passed, Ashyla reached out and caught the halberd in her grasp. Andromeda tried to rip her weapon free, but it was futile. She hissed at her target, her eyes two simmering flames of hatred, and she began to fade into the shadows. But a thundering voice inside her head froze her in place.

You think you can escape, my dear Andromeda? Deny it as you might, you know the truth. Your struggle is meaningless. No matter what you do, you will never be able to save them all. No matter how powerful you become, sometimes you will only be able to watch as the ones you love perish before your eyes. There is no resisting it, child. The poison has already set.

Andromeda tried to argue, but her thoughts were dominated by the taunting voice. Two emerald fires appeared in her mind, incinerating any thoughts of resistance. The voice grew harsher, a low hiss that cut through her very being.

Accept the truth, child. There is no fighting it. Your lust for power can only result in one outcome. Despair. And not just for you, but also for the very ones you wish to protect. But ...

An image appeared of Andromeda looming atop a bloody mountain of corpses, her halberd raised to the shadowy sky, and a black flicker of light shining behind her eyes. The corpses were not undead. But before Andromeda could comprehend the shadowy image, it was gone, leaving her desperately trying to retrieve it. Instinctively she licked her lips. She couldn't help it. Because of the power ... the might ... the freedom ...

The voice inside her head applauded her, and it grew lighter, and more soothing.

You see, my dear Andromeda, there is a place for all ...

The green fires within Andromeda's mind flickered away, and the gentle voice faded out, leaving her alone with her torn thoughts. She did not know what to think — what to feel — anymore. Ashyla released her halberd, and Andromeda stumbled back, lost her in mind.

Andromeda violently shook her head, her emotions a ravaged jumble. No. It was all a lie. The woman lied ... right?

Ashyla smiled, and she turned away, her black skirt flowing about her like an inky orchid. She strode away, her cascading braid waving behind her. Andromeda gazed after her, her mind swirling with turmoil. Andromeda shook her head, desperately attempting to regain her clarity.

Suddenly, a furious cry thundered from behind her. Whipping around, she saw the companions grimly stalking towards

Ashyla, the broken Captain at the lead. His greatsword drug in the ground behind him, yet his eyes shone for only one thing. Revenge.

Brushing her doubts away, Andromeda rushed over to them. Ro looked down at her, worry shadowing his face. Margaret gave her an encouraging nod. Andromeda did not meet their gazes.

The others marched behind Captain Osann, their faces ruthless. They would strike down the dark Goddess. Fasto's bow was held out, and the two gnomes marched side-by-side, blue and purple alike, their hands raised and ready to unleash a devastating torrent of spells.

"Halt," the Captain growled at Ashyla, his determined stride unwavering. His voice grew stronger with every passing step. "Halt," he repeated, his glare burning into Ashyla's back.

Ashyla paused, and she turned back, her glare matching the Captain's. She sighed. "My dear Osann, you never do learn. All this macho and bravado must be exhausting."

The Captain did not answer. He merely continued his determined march forward.

Ashyla shook her head in disappointment. "It is a shame, really. She thought you had so much potential." She shrugged, apparently unconcerned. "So be it. Just another rotten egg."

Ashyla waved her hand, and the forsaken ground in front of her began to crack and quake. This time there were no butterflies.

A massive, armored hand burst through the cold earth, its black armor adorned with jutting spikes and symbols of death. With terrifying strength, the hulking being ripped itself up, effortlessly breaking through its earthy tomb. The dust settled, revealing a mighty dreadknight now standing upon the forsaken ground. Its black cape flowed behind its bulky shoulders like a waterfall of darkness, and its inky greatsword radiated in an aura of deathly frost. Yet the dreadful gaze bound the companions in place, two icy chasms of death billowing out from underneath the crowned helmet of shadow. Even the unflappable Captain faltered under the dreadknight's vile glare.

A sharp sense of terror cut through Andromeda's mind, and her thoughts were thrown back to the fateful day at the prison. She shook her head in a vain attempt to clear the memories.

Ashyla laughed for one final time, and her glare turned harsh and unforgiving.

"Just remember, child, you made your decision," she said. As she spoke, her body began to crumble into butterflies and fly away in the still air. The last thing the companions saw was her two emerald eyes, gazing upon the unseen watcher in the shadows.

The Captain turned to the companions, his face tight with desperation. Behind him, the vile dreadknight began its solemn march, ready to smother any signs of life. He ignored it.

"Listen to me," he panted, his breath coming in short gasps. "Run! You have to run. I'll try to hold off this dark monstrosity for as long as I can." His voice trailed off, but he shook his head, regaining his composure. "Listen. Cross the river, and head south through the mountain pass. There you will come across the shores of a great lake; I will try to meet you there. Now go!"

Not waiting for their response, he turned to meet the oncoming dreadknight. He raised his greatsword out before him. Its blade shone pure and clean, without a sign of his family's blood. But before the companions could ponder at the blade, it erupted into a furious flame. Andromeda watched with horror. She wanted to rush after him, wanted to strike back against the Shadow, but she knew she could not.

No matter how powerful you become, sometimes you will only be able to watch as the ones you love perish before your eyes.

A surging rage filled her stomach, and her heart felt as if it were made of lead. Yet it was this weakness that gave her strength. No, she could not save them all. But she could damn well fight for the ones she had. Yes, there was a place for all, but hers was not at the side of that monster. She had a place. She had something to fight for. But the pain …

It was never easy.

The Captain gave one final glance over his shoulder, his eyes shining with life. The dreadknight towered over him, its icy greatsword clashing against the Captain's fire. The Flame against the Shadow. There could only be one victor.

"Run!" the Captain commanded, turning back to the dreadknight, his flaming sword held high like a shining beacon of hope.

And so, they ran.

Chapter 8

The two Shadowfriends marched through the forsaken land. One was frail and thin and wore light armor. The other, the fresher of the two, was still bulky and strong, and donned a heavy plate mail. Around them, night hung thick like a shadowy blanket. They hardly noticed, as the night was all they knew now. Ahead of them, there was a ruined village hidden among the surrounding hills, out of sight. Yet they knew it was there. They had traveled this path many times before.

They were summoned not hours ago. For what, they could only guess. To ask too many questions is a quick route to an early death in the Shadow, especially for Shadowfriends — the lowest of the low in the rungs of undeath.

The thin Shadowfriend sighed. How he yearned to gaze upon the purifying light of the sun once more. How he dreamed of basking in the warm embrace of the Light, away from the endless abyss of the Shadow. How he wished to hear the musical sound of his name being spoken once again. The Shadow cared little for names. They were worthless, mere objects that were to be discarded like filthy waste. And he had made his choice. He was a traitor, ridiculed even by the groveling cultists. He had long ago forsaken his Inner Fire, and his name, to the glory of the night, and there was no turning back.

Better this than to be dead. So be it. He had made his choice.

The robust Shadowfriend at his side had only recently succumbed to the Shadow and was still optimistic about his situation. He would trot along merrily, his mind filled with the promises the Deathspeakers had given. Promises of power and wealth. They were all empty. The only fulfilled promise was survival. Even so, that could all too easily be broken.

What a fool.

The thin Shadowfriend snickered under his breath. Many a time had he been witness to a Shadowfriend falling to the wicked blade of a cultist, or the flanged mace of a Deathspeaker. Yet still he survived — hardly.

He was nothing more than a loose tatter of skin and bone. The Shadow had not been kind, and there were many nights where he would go hungry or was beaten by a mob of cultists. Yet his promise still held true.

But, it was better this than to be dead.

The two Shadowfriends marched on, not daring to say a word to each other. Making friends was never wise, as sooner or later, they would become nothing more than another rotting corpse in this land of decay. Their mission had brought them together, and that was enough.

As the night wore on, they finally stumbled across the ruined village. It was nothing more than piles of destruction strewn about the rolling hills. Any signs of life that once lived there had long been scrubbed away with the relentless comb of death.

Entering the devastation, the thin Shadowfriend studied the surrounding shadows. They were not alone. Cloaked cultists emerged from among the fallen buildings, their hollow eyes mocking the pitiful Shadowfriends. The thin Shadowfriend paid them no mind. He had long been hardened to their contempt. His burly companion, however, eyed the cultists with a wary gaze. His hand kept reaching for the longsword that hung at his side — but he dared not draw it.

The thin Shadowfriend pushed forward with iron determination. His business was not with the cultists. He had a mission; he was summoned here. Reaching out, he tugged on his companion's shoulder, urging him forward. To fight was to die. Only fools thought differently.

Not caring whether the other heeded his call, he continued his steady march.

The center of the forsaken village opened around him like the sprawling bones of a broken rib cage. Dust and debris cluttered the ground in a cold graveyard of destruction. The ruined buildings hung over the square, limp and lifeless. At one point, this had been the center of trade in Anland. Those days had long passed, leaving not even a trace of their grandeur.

At the center of the fallen square was a large boulder. The frail Shadowfriend trudged toward it, his companion following cautiously behind. That was the designated rendezvous location. Yet no one was there. Typical.

The Shadow cared little for promises. Sighing, he unstrapped his worn blade and laid it to rest on the boulder. He would wait, for to do anything else would be to die. Crossing his arms, he leaned upon the rock in a silent vigil.

He could not tell how long he rested upon the boulder. There was no way to read the passage of time in the hollow night sky. No stars. No moon. Just an empty void. Countless cultists darted past, their sneering comments melding into one senseless blur. The thin Shadowfriend gazed out into the darkness, lost in his own thoughts. His burly companion shuffled about at his side, impatiently awaiting their orders. Soon he would learn, or he would die. Either way, he wouldn't mourn. He cared less for the fate of fools, and even less for fools he didn't know.

As the thin Shadowfriend's thoughts were dancing amid the shadows, two purple flames opened before him, tearing him back to reality.

At last, the Deathspeaker had arrived.

The Deathspeaker was a shadowy cloaked figure. Skulls and other symbols of death swirled around the inky robe in gray rivers of thread. Its face was hidden under the drooping hood, yet two, vile purple eyes burned out from the darkness, searing any who were unfortunate enough to gaze upon them.

The frail Shadowfriend stood up, respectfully not meeting the Deathspeaker's raging glare. To do so would be to chance death. The other Shadowfriend grumbled under his breath, but he settled as the Deathspeaker turned to him.

"There has been a slight … disturbance in our plan," the Deathspeaker hissed in a thin, snake-like voice that cut deep into the Shadowfriends' living flesh. The thin Shadowfriend strained his ears, for the screech of two metal blades would be more pleasant to hear. He didn't know what plan the Deathspeaker spoke of, but he did not care. "The one known as Captain Kirk Osann has failed, and you must take his place."

"Captain Kirk Osann?" the built Shadowfriend started, but he was silenced by a harsh backhand from the Deathspeaker. Blood began to drizzle from a torn lip, and the Shadowfriend spat on the ground. He remained silent.

"It doesn't matter," the Deathspeaker continued, an irritated undertone seeping into its voice. It was never wise to anger minions of the Shadow.

"There is a group of companions, a group of Sparks, that must be removed." The Deathspeaker paused, and its voice grew low and harsh. "The Sister has placed utmost importance on this task."

The thin Shadowfriend flinched, and his eyes opened wide with shock. The Sister. No Shadowfriend, or cultist, or even Deathspeaker had ever spoken with the Sister. Rumors hold her to be a most beautiful woman with ebony hair and rosy lips, whose very glance can steal even the heartiest of souls. Her sword cut deep, yet her words cut deeper, twisting you about until you could not tell friend from foe. Yet those were only rumors. None knew the true power of the Sister of Sin. And the frail Shadowfriend cared little to discover it.

All blood drained from his face at the thought, and his right hand trembled unsteadily by his side. There would be no failing in this task. His burly companions stiffened at the mention of the Sister, and suddenly the Deathspeaker's mission seemed most interesting.

"Head north along the road, beyond the mountain range. Search the west, there you will find the group," the Deathspeaker hissed. "Kill them all. Use the name of the Captain. The Shadow will guide you."

The thin Shadowfriend nodded slowly, his eyes still respectfully dodging the flaming, purple gaze. "Of course."

But his companion was unsettled. "Kill them?" he mumbled quietly to himself.

No doubt this was the first time he had been tasked with killing a Spark. The burly Shadowfriend glanced up to the Deathspeaker, defiance plastered over his face.

"But why, can't we just —"

Before he could finish, the Deathspeaker's pale hand shot up to his chest. With a crack of power, a dark lance of shadow burst forth from the outstretched hand, piercing the obstinate Shadowfriend. The thin hand closed, and the shadowy lance grew and darkened into a razor abyss. The Shadowfriend tried to scream, tried to call out, but he died before the breath left his lungs. The vile lance disappeared, and the Deathspeaker lowered its hand, its eyes seething with rage.

The body collapsed to the ground with a hollow *thud.*

The Deathspeaker turned to the remaining Shadowfriend, its voice a burning screech. "Do I make myself clear?"

"Of course," the thin Shadowfriend repeated. He dared not show any sign of nervousness.

Satisfied, the Deathspeaker turned away, and disappeared into the forsaken shadows, its black cloak billowing out behind it like a mournful river in the night.

The frail Shadowfriend sighed and glanced down at the body at his feet. It was never wise to make friends, as sooner or later, they would become nothing more than another rotting corpse in this land of decay.

Perhaps they were all fools.

Reaching out, he grabbed his sword and strapped it across his hip. He turned to the north, and with steady determination he began his trek across the desolate land.

He was never comfortable with killing Sparks, but he had long ago made his choice. To fail would be to die. He had abandoned the Flame, and he must live with the consequences, even if it meant slaughtering his fellow brothers. He had made his choice.

Better this than to be dead.

So be it.

◆　　◆　　◆

Fasto's feet thundered against the hard ground. His breath crashed hard against his lungs, each pant a desperate struggle for air. He had long since lost track of how long they had been running. He did not know where they were or where they were going. All he knew was that he had to keep running, and fast.

The other companions ran along beside him, unwilling to look back at the horror they had just escaped. How could they? Their entire world had just been thrown into an inky abyss. They could not know who to trust. They could not know who was right. They could not even trust what they were seeing, for without warning it could disappear into a swarm of infernal butterflies. And so, they kept running, with nowhere to go.

The land flashed past them, desolate fields and shriveled shrubs all blended together into a dull, gray tapestry of death. The bleak sun was falling to the west, and the black blanket of night was starting to cover the land.

The companions had lost the road they were traveling on, and only the Captain's final orders gave them any sense of direction — south. While they were yet unable to see the wispy peaks of the mountains through the darkness, they knew they were there. They had to be.

While Fasto ran beside the others, his thoughts were still far behind them. Why did the butterfly lady attack them? She wasn't evil. Fasto knew. She was even their friend before. But now, she attacked them.

Memories of her from the prison returned with pure clarity. She came down in a rain of white light, sending brilliant lances of light to decimate the undead horde. A mighty bow appeared in her hand, and with a marvelous grandeur, a chromatic arrow streaked from the bow like a shot from the cosmos, cutting deep into the dark dreadknight. But then the butterflies came, and he awoke to Andromeda perched on top of him. Even still, Fasto rejected his thoughts, as if the very idea of Ashyla not being a tyrannical murderer sickened him. It was as if some lurking hatred from a lost memory was burrowing into his consciousness. When he had raised his white bow against the goddess, it had felt so … right.

Fasto shook his head. It was all too confusing. Yet amid his jumbled thoughts, one shown through like a clear beacon: she tried to hurt Fasto's friends.

That was enough of a reason for him to despise her.

The companions continued running to the south well into the night, until their exhaustion forced them to stop. And so, they collapsed, lost in some forsaken field in the land of Shadow.

◆　　◆　　◆

Fasto awoke to the pale sun high in the cold sky, shining down upon him like the face of an angel. Slowly, he rose from the shriveled grass, scratching his head. His whole body ached; it was as if searing lightning crackled through his worn muscles. His legs burned, and his head throbbed with a monotonous ringing. He glanced around, hoping to find some end to the desolate meadow. He wanted a forest, needed a forest. The trees gave him a sense of life and purpose, and his thoughts always cleared among the wooded guardians. But there were no trees, no end to the grave meadow. No mountains could be seen to the south.

The other companions were still sleeping around him, so Fasto let them rest. He would not dare disturb his friends. They may still need their energy for later. It was fine. Fasto could be alone. Fasto could let his friends sleep and become strong.

Shrugging, Fasto turned back to the hard earth, his gaze steady and determined. Fasto would be helpful. Savagely, he began to tear the dead grass from the grasp of the earth, creating a barren patch of gray dust and broken earth. Fasto smiled. Perfect. He reached behind him and pulled a white arrow from his quiver. His mighty bow and quiver were still anomalies to the orc. No matter how many arrows he shot from the white arms of his bow, there was always another waiting patiently in the quiver. Fasto did not know how it worked, but he did not care. It let him protect his friends.

Blinking back to reality, Fasto gripped the arrow tightly in his grasp. With a steady motion, he began to etch marks and shapes into the patch of earth. Fasto would be useful. Fasto would help his friends. The arrow dug furiously through the ground, tearing up chunks and sending a cloud of dust into the still air. Fasto's brow furrowed and sweat began to bead upon his wrinkled forehead. He drew a sharp wave, and a small "X". He added some more various shapes, adding onto the masterpiece before him. A dotted line followed by a hollowed-out circle. Perfect. Fasto would help his friends.

Fasto paused for a moment to study his work. Before he could continue, a rough hand clasped him on the shoulder. Fasto flinched in terror, caught by surprise.

"What in the bloody hell are ye doin', ye damn orc?" Nalgene asked, quite concerned. He released the orc, and stood dumbfounded, studying the mangled earth in front of Fasto. "Wha ... Are ye feelin' alright? Or did the ground look at ye funny or somethin'?"

Fasto glanced up to the gnome, a proud and beaming smile wide upon his face. Nalgene's sarcasm passed right over his head.

"Fasto help friends," Fasto replied merrily. "Fasto draw map, so Fasto know the way."

Nalgene could only stare.

"What in the bloody hell," he mumbled. "Yer daft!" The gnome squinted and peered closer at the supposed map.

"Bwahahahaha!" Nalgene burst out in laughter, and patted Fasto on the shoulder again. "Yer bloody daft! I'd say yer face is more o' a map than this mess!"

With that, Nalgene turned away. "C'mon, ye damn orc, let's wake the others."

Fasto smiled. Fasto's face was a map?

A brilliant idea popped into the orc's mind, but before he could act on it, another cry from Nalgene broke his thoughts.

"Get off yer arse, ye damn orc!"

Shaking his head, Fasto rose to his feet and marched over to wake the others. Nalgene had already been to SmibSmob and Andromeda, and was heading to the slumbering Ro, so Fasto moved over to Margaret.

Upon reaching her, he studied her for a moment, running his eyes across her body to her demonic arm. Fasto shivered. He was wary of Margaret's strange powers — even scared. Even though he felt some sense of kinship with the fellow orc, he knew that her demonic side would always tear them apart.

He nudged her gently on her shoulder, trying to softly wake the troubled orc. Immediately, Margaret's eyes shot open, and an icy chill washed over Fasto. Their eyes locked. Margaret narrowed her gaze, and with a snort of disgust, she pushed Fasto away and rose from the hard ground.

Fasto studied her for another moment, his mouth agape. He scratched his head. Margaret must be tired. Or hungry. She must be. What other explanation could there be? Why else would she push Fasto away? Shrugging, Fasto followed her to the others.

A heavy exhaustion and ache were apparent on all the companions, especially SmibSmob, who had not taken well to the long night of running. The gnome's face was drawn and pale, looking more ghost-like than fleshy. Nalgene stood beside his brother, protecting the frail gnome. Both Ro and Margaret were still weak with exhaustion, but their eyes shone bright with energy. But it was Andromeda who caught Fasto's attention.

The feline stood separated from the others, a gloomy aura surrounding her. Andromeda's tail slashed violently behind her, and her claws clenched at her side. Blood dripped from her closed fists. A sense of sorrow washed over Fasto, and he marched over to her, determined to soothe her turmoil; however, a sharp glare from her toxic gaze froze him in place. A quiet whimper escaped his lips. He wanted to help, but Andromeda made it clear she wanted no part of him.

The companions stood in a grim silence for some time, not daring, or wanting, to break the vigil. They all knew what they had seen. There was no need to speak of it. A slight breeze brushed across the land, and Fasto glanced back at his map in the earth. He had to help his friends. He took a deep breath and mustered all the confidence he had.

"Fasto think go south. Captain friend said to. Fasto want to help Captain friend. So Fasto go south." Fasto paused, his profound statement complete. Forget what Ashyla had done, forget the overbearing threat of the dreadknight. Fasto knew the Captain would see them again.

The others stared at him for a moment, their faces blank. Slowly, Ro nodded in agreement. "To the south, beyond the mountain pass," he said. "That is where Captain Osann told us to go."

"Bloody hell — he's dead," Nalgene grunted. "Ye saw what them armored horrors can do. Ye were at the prison. There will be no one to meet us at the lake."

Ro turned to lock his gaze upon Nalgene. "No. He gave us his word."

"He friend," Fasto piped in, but the others ignored him. Fasto sighed. He just wanted to help.

"Much good Osann's word was," Nalgene spat, the fires of distrust reigniting within the gnome. "He's bloody dead, ain't nothin' gonna —"

"I agree with Ro," SmibSmob interrupted, turning to face his brother. The gnome's strength was returning, and he stood with an air of authority that was never seen before. Yet Fasto knew the gnome was still haunted. "I don't mean to be the obvious one, but we have nowhere else to go. It might as well be to the south, to where the Captain told us. I don't know what earlier was about, but …" SmibSmob's voice trailed off, and he turned away from Nalgene, his drawn appearance returning.

"But she wanted to kill us," Margaret jumped in, her voice harsh. "Much good this little 'adventure' is doing." Her black fist clenched at her side. "She wanted to kill us," she repeated, her tone offering little room for arguing.

"No, I don't think she did," a fierce hiss cut across the forsaken field. The companions paused, their eyes shooting over to Andromeda. The feline would not meet their gazes. She turned away, shaking her head, mumbling to herself. Fasto watched her with a solemn stare. How he wanted to help his friend, but he was afraid that she was going to have to help herself first.

"Damn cat, figure out yer bloody emotions already," Nalgene grunted. "Are ye a pretty, happy kitty, or are ye some skulkin' panther?" The gnome threw his hands in the air with exasperation. "Bloody hell!"

Ro glared at the gnome, and he opened his maw to protest. "Nalgene! How dare —"

"Please!" SmibSmob cried, a hint of pain undercutting his voice. "We can't do this right now. We have to move. I don't know where we are, but I reckon the Shadow does. Sooner or later more undead will find us."

"Pffft, bloody undead me arse," Nalgene growled, his eyes still boring into Ro. "Nothin' we haven't fought before, eh?"

Margaret rubbed the gruesome scar across the back of her neck, her face shadowed. "And look how well fighting the undead has got us ... or at least me," she mumbled.

Fasto flinched at this. He should have been there to protect her. He shook his head. Fasto would do better next time. He promised himself.

"Nalgene —" SmibSmob started, his voice unsteady, but Nalgene surprisingly cut him off.

"Ah, just a minute, me brother. Damn dragon's tryin' to start somethin'. Again."

"I'm trying to protect us," Ro countered, his voice a harsh growl, and he pointed to Andromeda. "She is one —"

"What, ye can't let the damn cat speak fer herself, eh?" Nalgene roared, his fists rising in front of him. "Do ye have to try to fight other's battles? Do ye think they need the help? Ye can't fight fer everyone. Or is it that ye feel like too much o' a failure if someone —"

"Nalgene, please!" SmibSmob gasped in a strained voice, placing a hand upon his brother's burly shoulder. "That's enough. Let us travel to the south. It is the only way we have."

Nalgene lowered his fists but still spat at Ro. "Damn

dragon."

SmibSmob's fist came crashing into the side of Nalgene's jaw, rocking the rough gnome back. Nalgene glanced up in shock, his hand moving to rub the welt on his face.

"What in the bloody hell!"

SmibSmob stood glaring at Nalgene, his pale hands raised and opened in front of him. Shadowy tendrils swirled about the gnome in a threatening vortex, and an aura of darkness grew from his feet, casting dark hands reaching across the cold ground. The gnome's eyes were an unholy purple.

SmibSmob raised his hand, a mighty orb of shadow forming within his grasp. An evil smirk widened across the gnome's face.

"Just another annoyance," he hissed in a snake-like tone. But before anyone could react, SmibSmob collapsed to the ground, all the dark power disappearing back into the safety of his mind. His eyes returned to their natural shining blue.

Nalgene stood in shock, his mouth wide. Shaking himself back to reality, he rushed over to his brother, embracing him in an apologetic hug. "I'm sorry, me brother," he mumbled.

The companions stood in horror, not knowing how to react. Fasto's mouth was agape. What had just happened? The two, loving brothers … His mind could not even comprehend. Everything was too confusing for the poor orc.

Ro took a step toward the two gnomes but stopped as Nalgene glanced up to him. The gnome's face was twisted with fear. This had never happened before. SmibSmob's power had overcome the gnome.

"Aye," Nalgene said, his voice soft. "I be thinkin' we go to the south."

Regrouping, the companions began their trek to the south. Nalgene kept by SmibSmob's side, aiding his weakened brother in the rough journey. Fasto and Ro led the march, while Margaret and Andromeda trailed at the rear. Margaret tried to speak with the feline, with little success.

As the first day passed, there was no end to the forsaken plains. Only a steady dread kept the companions at a determined pace. Fasto had the sense that they were being followed, or watched, but nothing appeared. Even still, his wary gaze never ceased its watchful scan across the fallen lands. As the next day's sun was casting its pale rays across the lands, the peaks of mountains could be seen far to the south, rising high into the grim sky. Their hope rekindled, the companions redoubled their efforts, eager to finally be out of the vast plains of death and despair. But Fasto's sense of a watcher had only grown stronger. Sure enough, as the second sun was falling to the west, a lone, thin figure crested the horizon in front of the companions.

The companions slowed as the newcomer approached and warily eyed his thin frame. He did not appear threatening, with his hollow face and frail build, yet still they were cautious. Everything was dangerous in the Shadow. Fasto's eyes ran across the man's light armor, only to rest upon the man's face.

Fasto flinched.

The man was a shallow husk of life, the harsh beatings of starvation apparent on his sunken face. A well of sympathy pooled inside Fasto, and he urged to rush over and aid the skeleton of a man. But something held him back. Fasto frowned.

The man beckoned to them with his sword in a salutary wave, a thin smile spreading across his face. The companions halted, still wary of the thin stranger. Beside Fasto, Ro waved his sword back in response.

Satisfied, the man sheathed his sword and continued his solemn march toward the companions. Fasto studied the man's uneven steps, and the unsettling quiver in the man's right hand. The man needed help. Fasto's help. The orc took a step forward, his sympathy overcoming his doubts, but an outstretched hand from Ro held him back.

"No. Let him come to us," Ro said, suspicious of the lone man. Grunting, Fasto reluctantly obliged.

As the man drew nearer, he rose his empty hands out in front of him in a gesture of peace. "Good to see fellow Sparks still burning bright," he called in a weary voice. The companions flinched. This man was not the first person to greet them in such a way.

"Oh good, now all we're missing is the great ball of fire," Margaret mumbled from behind, but no one acknowledged her comment.

"May your light pierce the Shadow," Ro replied to the newcomer, in what he assumed was the proper response. The man nodded, and he lowered his hands. His right hand still quivered by his side. "Who do you be?"

The man smiled. He had long ago perfected this charade. "Erus, Erus Atrat."

"Bah," Nalgene spat, walking forward with SmibSmob by his side. "I'm ain't buyin' yer filth."

Erus's smile disappeared, and he turned to the distrustful gnome, his eyebrow raised. "Pray tell, my good gnome."

"Ignore him," Ro said, moving to stand in front of Nalgene. "He can be quite … temperamental."

"Aye, ye damn dragon, I can bloody well show him what I am," Nalgene grunted, pushing past Ro and leaving SmibSmob to stand alone. The gnome's hands raised, and he marched towards Erus, each step a thunder stroke across the ground.

"I ain't buyin' yer filth," he repeated dangerously. "How in the bloody hell did ye even find us?"

Erus stepped back, his hands raised in surrender. "Please, my good gnome," he stammered. "I was sent here."

"Sent here me arse," Nalgene growled, unrelenting in his march. "I ain't be trustin' ye, Shadowfriend."

Erus steeled, and his gaze turned harsh and cold. "My good gnome —"

"Bah!" Nalgene shouted before the man could finish. "Last time I trusted one o' yer ilk —"

"Nalgene!" Ro interrupted, shooting forward and clasping

his strong hand across the gnome's shoulder. "Let him speak."

Fasto studied the exchange with open wonder. So many twisting lines, he could only dream of keeping up. Not for the last time, he felt the urge to find a forest. His thoughts were always clear among the leafed guardians. Scratching his head, he studied Erus with a squinted eye. The man's hand had gone eerily still. For some unknown reason, this deeply unsettled the orc. But before Fasto could ponder too much, Erus began to speak.

"I was sent here," he repeated, his gaze growing softer. "I was told you would be coming this way, by the man known as Captain Osann."

Fasto gasped. That was their friend!

Behind him, Andromeda flinched, her gaze fixated on Erus. Margaret's face was skeptical, yet a spark of hope burned deep within her eyes. Both Ro and Nalgene grew somber at the mention of the name, the gnome even lowering his hands. SmibSmob had no reaction.

"Could it be?" Ro wondered; his voice saturated with hope. They had seen the Captain charge the vile dreadknight. They all knew the havoc that hulking abomination could wreak. Was it possible for him to survive such overwhelming odds?

"Fasto happy friend alive!" Fasto exclaimed, rushing forward to embrace Erus. But the man's empty gaze stopped him in his tracks. Even still, Fasto's joy just spilled from his mouth in a tide of relief. "Fasto want to see Captain friend! He save Fasto! Fasto must repay friend!"

Erus stared at him for a long moment, not quite sure how to handle the ecstatic orc.

"Indeed," he finally said. "You will see him, in good time."

"Eh, that bloody Osann's alive, ye say?" Nalgene questioned, still stubbornly holding onto his distrust.

"But he is very injured," Erus whispered, his gaze turning to the ground in a mock expression of sorrow. "He his hidden just beyond the mountain pass to the south. We must make haste, for I fear how long he can last in such a tattered state."

Ro nodded in agreement. The draconian was completely swayed by the thin man's story. Fasto, too, was eager to journey to the Captain.

Nalgene grunted, but he did not argue. He merely moved to stand by his brother, who was still weak and pale, and said not a word. Andromeda stalked about, her tail slashing wildly.

"How can we trust you?" Margaret said, stepping forward. "Trouble always seems to come with trust around here."

Erus studied her for a moment, before reaching into a pouch at his side. His gaze still locked upon the skeptical orc, he pulled his hand out and threw something on the ground in front of her. It was a small, golden locket. One eyebrow raised, Margaret reached down to collect the trinket and opened its worn case.

Margaret gasped. Imprinted into the heart of the locket was an unmistakable etching of the Captain's son, Kyle.

"He said you would know him by this," Erus stated flatly, before turning away, a thin smile on his face.

Of course, the locket was fake, but the companions did not know that. He had acquired it as a "gift" for his mission. His right hand began its steady quiver. The bait was set. He knew how to play the game.

"Let us make haste," Erus called behind him, already marching away at a steady pace. "Let us find your friend, Captain Osann."

Victim to the Shadowfriend's woven lies, the companions set off after Erus.

Throughout the first three days, Erus kept them at a brisk pace to the south, the mountains rising ever steadier into the still air. The companions still had many questions for the thin man, and he was more than happy to oblige to their requests.

Brilliant stories about the Captain and how he had survived poured from Erus's mouth. He gave them just enough to keep them deceived and never dove too deeply into the details. It was all a lie, of course. The frail Shadowfriend had never met the Captain before, had never even heard his name until the Deathspeaker had issued his orders. But he had had plenty of time to masterfully craft his story as he ventured forth from the ruined village. He spent this time gauging the companions, measuring their strengths and their weaknesses. He knew how to play the game.

The companions began to open to Erus, even the distrustful Nalgene and the skeptical Margaret. Only Andromeda shied from him. Even SmibSmob regained some life and was occasionally joining the banter. Fasto welcomed it all with open arms. At every chance he got the orc was asking about his "Captain friend" and how he wanted to "help friend". Erus tried to ignore Fasto, but the orc was unrelenting. He had to help his friends.

On the third night after the meeting with Erus, the companions stopped to rest their weary muscles for the night. They finally trusted Erus enough to sleep while he stood watch. The southern mountains climbed high in the near distance. It would only be another day before they reached the foothills of the great range. Fasto's thoughts were still overwhelmed with the urge to help his friends. So, while the others lay down to sleep, Fasto began to tear at the earth once more. He would be useful. He grabbed another arrow and began to score the hard earth with an even more disorienting array of lines and marks. Another map — or so he called it. The lonely night drug on, and still Fasto tirelessly worked on the barren patch of earth, creating his greatest work yet. He would be useful.

The sharp cry of the wind whistled past Fasto, catching a patch of gray dust and casting it into the unforgiving air.

Fasto paused. He looked back at the others, still slumbering peacefully in the inky night. He frowned. Slowly, he counted. Ro. Margaret. Andromeda. Nalgene. SmibSmob. Five. He smiled. All was as it should be.

Turning back to his supposed map, he resumed his relentless scoring and marking.

Another whistle cut across the barren fields, and a rustling echoed from the shriveled grass behind him. Fasto paused again, and he turned back around, his wide, red eyes scanning across the land. He wished he was in a forest. Right now, he didn't feel so good ... Something was off.

But there was nothing, just the desolate plains and his slumbering companions. Shrugging, Fasto turned back to his work.

Before he could continue, a thin hand clasped over his mouth in an iron grip, holding his mouth shut and muffling any sound that he could have made. Suddenly, Fasto remembered. He should have counted six.

Erus's longsword appeared by Fasto's throat, ready to make the finishing slash. Quick. Silent. Lethal. Erus did not like killing Sparks, but it would be enjoyable to rid himself of this annoying orc. He smirked. It would be another mission completed.

Fasto's mind reeled. This man wasn't a friend!

Then another thought appeared in his mind: Fasto needed to protect his other friends.

That was all the encouragement he needed.

Fasto bit down hard, his fangs burying into the Shadowfriend's hand. Dropping his arrow, Fasto's hand shot up, and he tore Erus's sword away from his throat.

With surprising strength, Fasto jumped to his feet and grabbed the frail man's shoulder. Grunting with effort, the furious orc flung Erus over his hip, tossing him to the hard ground like a limp corpse.

The air rushed from Erus's lungs, and he landed with a shocked gasp. This dull orc could fight! But Erus would not have survived this long if he could not adapt.

Fasto pounded on the stunned man, his hands outstretched and ready to strangle the weak Shadowfriend. But Erus rolled away, dodging the obvious attack. Still sucking for breath, Erus rose to his feet and braced his sword out in front of him. His hollow eyes gleamed.

His sword in his right hand, Erus darted forward, but the dull quiver misguided the stab, and the sword caught harmlessly in the straps of Fasto's leather armor.

A feral growl escaped Fasto's lips, and he scrambled away from the Shadowfriend. Reaching behind him, Fasto grabbed another arrow from his quiver, and brought it out to bear on his attacker. With a twitch of his muscled legs, Fasto shot forward, the shining arrow plunging towards Erus's neck.

Frustrated, Erus released his sword and rolled away from the oncoming blow. He would have to get creative. As he tumbled to his feet, he scooped a fistful of gray dust in his hand, ready to blind the orc with it.

But he had underestimated Fasto one too many times. As Fasto darted forward, his other hand reached around and grabbed his majestic white bow, pulling it out in front of him. Fasto nocked the arrow.

A flash of white light.

The arrow streaked from the bow in a brilliant ray of sunlight. Fasto never missed his mark. Before Erus could move, Fasto fired another, and another mighty arrow into the Shadowfriend.

Erus glanced down at the three smoldering holes in his chest. He glanced up to Fasto, blood bubbling from his lips. He had made his choice. So be it. He had lost the game.

Panting like a wild bear, Fasto watched Erus collapse to the ground, dead. Fasto had to protect his friends, and Erus was no friend. That was enough reason to kill. Fasto studied the limp body for another moment before shrugging and turning away, satisfied that he had been useful this night.

Fasto sat back at his map, and once again began to tear into the cold earth, but exhaustion quickly overwhelmed him, dragging him into slumber.

◆　　◆　　◆

Fasto awoke to the harsh shouts of Nalgene, who was roughly shaking the orc awake.

"Another one o' yer maps, eh?" Nalgene grunted, turning and walking away from Fasto. "Never mind that, ye damn orc," the gnome cried. "What in the bloody hell is this?"

Shaking himself awake, Fasto rose to his feet, and found the gnome gesturing to the fallen body of Erus. Fasto smiled. Both Ro and SmibSmob studied the corpse with worried expression, and their sharp gazes turned up to the beaming orc.

"Thin man no friend," Fasto stated proudly. He pointed to himself, then to the rest of his companions. "Fasto protect friends."

Ro sighed, and he rose to his feet, a look of disappointment shadowing his gentle face. "So, I suppose that means Captain Osann is …"

"Bah, that bloody traitor's dead," Nalgene finished, throwing his rough hands into the air. Ro could only nod somberly.

"I reckon you're right," SmibSmob agreed quietly. "We saw what those hulking horrors could do."

A soft tail brushed against Fasto, and he turned to find Andromeda striding past him, a mischievous gleam in her eyes. She smiled at the orc, before joining the others.

"Mmmm, enough of your sad talk," she purred, her first words in days. "To the south, shall we?" Surprised, the other companions wholeheartedly agreed. Andromeda had returned to them. Or so they hoped.

Fasto smiled. A spark of connection had jolted between the two.

He had protected his friends.

Daniel Whitman

Chapter 9

Margaret glanced down at the smoldering body of Erus, the Shadowfriend, then up to Fasto, a faint twinkle of respect in her eyes. The dimwitted orc was busy musing over his questionable map, nodding in approval. Margaret wanted to berate the other orc, but she glanced down to the corpse of Erus once more. There was no denying the skill with which Fasto had brutalized his attacker. Perhaps he was not as dull as they all thought. Margaret almost laughed aloud at the absurd thought.

Shaking her head in amusement, Margaret turned away. Just another danger in this treacherous world. No doubt there would be many more.

"Aye, are we bloody goin'?" Nalgene called, already heading south toward the mountains. SmibSmob, Ro and Andromeda strode by his side, eager to reach the looming mountains at last. Margaret studied the cryptic feline for a moment. She could not understand Andromeda. One moment she's secluded and alone, but the next, well … she could not be more alive. As if reading her thoughts, Andromeda glanced back and gave Margaret a playful wink.

Margaret sighed. There was so much more than meets the eye, and Margaret was not sure if she wanted to explore the possibilities. Shaking her head, Margaret glanced down to her black arm, her prison. She hated it, but she knew she could not escape it, or its dreadful pulsing. Yet strangely, it lay dormant, and so Margaret was filled with optimism and energy. Perhaps it would never start again.

Margaret snorted. She knew it to be a fleeting hope. But there was always the chance.

Her brooding thoughts were interrupted as Fasto skipped past her, urging on to follow the others who were already well in the distance. Margaret gave one final look at the dead Shadowfriend, before moving off after her fellow orc. And when Fasto tried to talk to her, she was not so quick to ignore him.

The companions moved at a brisk pace toward the approaching mountains, determined to reach the pass by nightfall, even though they had no idea of knowing where to find the pass. Margaret mentioned this more than once, but her remarks were only met with a hearty laugh from Nalgene, and an unconcerned shrug from Andromeda. Only Ro and SmibSmob seemed remotely concerned that they may never find the Captain's elusive pass. Fasto was just lost, as usual. Much good his maps were doing. Even still, as the companions continued south, the mountain peaks reached high into the air above them like the teeth of a gargantuan dragon. No snow capped the mighty peaks, and the mountains' bare, gray stone was perfectly matched by the decay of the surrounding land.

As the cold sun fell well past its zenith, and was sinking deep to the west, the companions had at last reached the foothills of the towering mountains.

"Wow," Fasto gaped at the overbearing masses of stone. "Fasto think very big."

"Another one of your brilliant remarks," Margaret snickered.

Fasto glanced over at her, nodding in agreement.

"Bwahahaha," Nalgene roared in laughter. "Damn orcs. O' course they're big, they're bloody mountains! Haven't ye ever seen 'em?"

Fasto merely shrugged, and Margaret glared at the gnome. But try as she might, she could not disprove the annoying gnome. She had never stood so close to the majesty of a mountain, at least not that she could remember.

"Never mind the mountains," Ro said with authority. "Where is the mountain pass?"

Nalgene grunted and stamped his feet upon the ground. "Ah, forget the damn pass," he growled, raising his fist. "We can make our own bloody pass!" Water began swirling in his fist, and with a roar of triumph, he hurled the mighty orb at the face of the mountain, only for it to splash harmlessly against the gray stone.

Margaret laughed aloud, with Andromeda quickly joining. Even SmibSmob could not resist a little chuckle at his brother's futile attempt.

What an idiot.

Ro was too troubled by the missing pass to join in the levity, while Fasto stood confused, as always.

"My, my," Margaret shot at the frustrated gnome, not bothering to hide her amusement. "I can practically see through the mountains after that."

Nalgene snarled, and he turned to Margaret, his face hot. "Ah yeah, ye bloody orc, let's see ye do better," he challenged, his fists clenched by his side.

Margaret glanced down to her demonic arm, a sly smile on her face. She may hate her power, but she may as well use it to benefit her. She clenched her fist, feeling the rippling muscles twist in her arm. But before she could try anything, Andromeda stepped forward as the voice of reason.

"Mmmm, as much as I would enjoy seeing this little... contest," Andromeda said between fits of laughter. "Let's find the *actual* mountain pass, shall we?"

Nalgene growled, but his good sense — what little of it he had — won out, and he nodded in agreement. "Damn cat," he muttered.

Margaret smirked, and she gave another look across her demonic arm. She was sure she could have done more damage than the annoying gnome. She remembered the devastating blow she had inflicted upon the dreadknight at the prison. But then again, that was only after she had already slaughtered a handful of undead ...

Shaking her head, she glanced up to Ro, who still stood perplexed. Despite all his bluster and attempts at leadership, the others still did not see him as anything more than equal. Ro's gaze locked onto Margaret, and he gave her a smile. Margaret shot him a sly wink in return, before turning away from the draconian.

What a leader.

Suddenly, a sharp cry from Fasto drew all their attention. "Fasto see fire!" the orc exclaimed, pointing to the west.

Sure enough, when the companions turned to see where he was pointing, a small, orange fire was burning some distance to the west along the foot of the mountain. Margaret narrowed her eyes at the billowing flame. The everlasting night had already begun creeping in, but even in the growing darkness, Margaret could make out the figure of a woman with flowing, red hair.

"It can't be," Ro whispered, studying the strange fire. He too had recognized Mariah.

"Pretty fire lady!" Fasto shouted, and immediately began to skip over to the fire, a wide smile beaming across his face.

"So now she decides to show up, eh?" Nalgene chuckled, running after Fasto with his hand clasped around his crystalline bottle.

Without a moment of hesitation, the others followed quickly behind.

Reaching the fire, the companions gathered about, eager to see what insights the long-missing Mariah had in store for them. But she did not seem ready to give any. Nay, Mariah seemed worn and tired, as if she had had one too many sleepless nights. And she may very well have.

The Flame was not as she remembered, or as she had left it. Personal motives ran supreme, rather than the combined effort of survival. She had not been able to make the reappearance she had hoped for as darkness now surrounded the once-bright Flame. But that was not her only trouble. Her search for *him* had been all but unsuccessful, and so she travelled now to the companions, desperately trying to see a bright future. Even so, she managed to have a positive outlook and dared not reveal any of her troubles to the companions.

"You seemed lost," Mariah quipped in her melodious voice, a shining smile on her face. "I said I would always be watching over you, and so now here I am. Your guide."

Behind her was the mountain pass, which meandered through jagged canyons and sheer ravines.

"Ah, ye should've seen some o' our other guides," Nalgene started. "From bloody traitors to shady Shadowfriends, ye be the …" The annoying gnome quieted as Mariah brought her cool gaze over to him, a sorrowful shadow in her orange eyes.

"Ah yes," she sighed mournfully. "It seems that even the purest hearts can fall to darkness."

From the corner of her eye, Margaret saw Andromeda flinch, and she shook her head in amusement. More than meets the eye, that's for sure.

The companions sat in silence for a long moment, their eyes lost in the flickering flame before them. It felt an eternity before SmibSmob finally dared break the overbearing vigil.

"So, what … ah … brings you here?" the frail gnome stammered, still unsure how to speak with the majestic woman before him. "I reckon that you mean to do more than just point us along the path."

Margaret nodded her head in agreement. At least one of the gnome brothers had some sense in him. This was only the second time Mariah had come to them. Last time she had bestowed upon them great gifts. Margaret glanced down to the shining breastplate she wore, a sly smirk on her face. What else could the fiery woman give to them? She clenched her black fist by her side. Unfortunately, the dreadful pulsing had renewed and was shooting waves of agony thundering through her body. She hated it, wished she could escape it. Of course, there was a simple solution to free herself of the vile power, but she wouldn't be much use if she only had one arm, and she wasn't sure if she was ready to sacrifice it ...

Shaking the dark thoughts away, Margaret glanced back up to the fiery woman before her.

Mariah scanned the companions. Margaret noted the hesitance in the woman's demeanor. So much for the all-powerful facade. Margaret smirked.

At last, Mariah began to speak, and when she did, the fire grew dim and ominous. "You are correct, my good gnome, for there is a matter of great importance I have come to discuss," she said. "I have come to warn you about the Flame."

Margaret's ears perked up. The Flame. The lone force standing against the unrelenting tide of the Shadow. The only source of hope for the Light — other than the Beacon, of course. Margaret shrugged. She could only guess what Mariah hinted at.

"The Flame?" Ro jumped in, a hint of desperation in his voice. "What of it? Kraalek already told us —"

"Bah, that bastard Kraalek?" Nalgene snorted, interrupting the draconian. The gnome threw his hands in the air. "That bloody snake didn't tell us nothin'. Just talked in circles and threw his damn die like a bloody madman. Pulled us like we be nothin' but bloody puppets!" Nalgene pounded his fists on the ground in frustration, a scowl shadowing his face.

Margaret chuckled softly to herself. For once she actually

agreed with the obnoxious gnome. Kraalek hardly told them anything.

Mariah sighed, and her crystal gaze burned into Nalgene. "Now, now," she chided. "Take care with your words, for he has his own reasons for what he does. You would do well to tread carefully around that man."

Nalgene snorted, but said nothing, for once not willing to jump into an argument.

"So, the Flame?" Ro prompted, eager to regain control of the conversation. Margaret studied the draconian. Always wanting to be in control, regardless of how the others felt. Not the greatest way to lead, in her opinion.

"Fasto go to Flame," Fasto piped in, wanting to become relevant.

Mariah studied the dull orc for a moment.

"Indeed," she said, sweeping her eyes across the companions, her voice nothing more than a soft whisper. "The Flame is corrupted. You must take care, for the Shadow has already cast its reach, even into the Light. You are the Beacon, and there are those who would see you killed, or worse. Beware Sab —"

Suddenly Mariah yelped in pain and looked behind her frantically, as if seeing some specter of death. When she turned back, her soft face was saturated with fear.

"Go, cross the mountain pass, I will find you —" Her voice caught in her throat as an iron shackle materialized behind her and clamped across her neck. The chain on the clasp pulled taut, and she was jerked back. Before the companions could react, she disappeared into a brilliant column of flame, leaving not a trace.

The companions sat shocked for a moment, not quite sure how to react. The Flame was corrupted? Sab? They could only guess. The only thing they knew for certain was the absolute terror in Mariah's eyes before she disappeared into the blazing inferno.

"Well, let us be hopin' that she actually shows up," Nalgene grunted while staring at his crystalline bottle, and running it through his rough hands. "Unlike the other who be tellin' us that."

The companions did not have the heart to argue. And so, they stared at the smoldering fire long into the black night, until they each succumbed to the gentle caress of exhaustion.

◆　　◆　　◆

Margaret awoke to the cold light of the dim sun shining from the far eastern horizon. Scratching the back of her neck, and the ghastly scar that was branded across it, she sat up. She was not proud of the scar. It had meant she had failed. She had lost the fight. Ro had to save her, and that just did not sit well with her. She strove for independence. Any help she received clashed against her naive morals. Growling to herself, she gazed at the others.

The rest of the companions were still sound asleep by the cold ashes left by the fire. Shrugging, Margaret stood up, stretching her aching muscles. Sleeping on the hard stone did little good to any of them. But that was the least of her worries. Her arm pulsed like strokes of thunder, and Margaret was surprised she had even been able to fall asleep.

She clenched her fist, gritted her teeth, and tried to force the horrible pulsing away, with no effect. Her thoughts drifted back to Mariah the night before, and the warning she was trying to impart to them. Margaret chuckled to herself. If only the fiery woman had cut straight to the point, instead of droning on about how lost they were.

What a guide.

Even still, she could not so easily dismiss the vague warning. The Flame was no longer safe, of that Margaret was sure. But was it ever safe? From Osann to Erus, where would it end?

Margaret growled, warning away the uncomfortable thoughts. She looked back to the others, who were still sound asleep at the mouth of the mountain pass. Many days ago, she would rush at this chance in her grand quest for freedom, abandoning the others and braving the dark world on her own. But the more she traveled alongside the others, the more she realized that was not an option. There was no freedom in this barren world. Just the flitting ghosts of her imagination.

Margaret growled again, deeper this time, and she took a step away from the others, wanting to prove her own thoughts wrong. But before she could take her second step, a gentle hand grasped her shoulder, stealing her resolve and holding her in place. Frustrated, Margaret whipped around, only to find the smiling face of Fasto before her.

"Fasto help friend," the dim orc stated proudly, still holding her shoulder.

Margaret wanted to shoot something back, but she hesitated, and the biting words fell flat in her mouth.

... friend ...

Now that was a thought. For the over two years she had been with the companions not once did she ever think of them as friends — merely others in her life. She thought back to her hesitancy to abandon them, but shook her head frantically, desperately trying to rid herself of the thought. No. Monsters can't be friends.

She glanced back at her demonic arm, a dark scowl on her face. She would never have friends — they made sure to tell her that. She shuddered at the memory, and she wished that it was one of the ones that had been forgotten.

But still Fasto held her, a beaming smile spread wide across his face. He would help his friend. Margaret pushed his arm away, and stalked back to the camp, where the others were finally waking. Clearly, he was an idiot.

Gathering their wits and their thoughts from the tragedy of the previous night, the companions began their long and treacherous trek through the winding mountain pass. At some points the passage was wide and comfortable, with protective walls rising high on both sides. At other times it was narrow and dangerous — even a slight misstep would lead to a quick and fatal plummet into a jagged ravine. And all around them there was no end to the mighty mountains — the vast range stretched endlessly in every direction. The companions' feet ached from the hard stone, yet still they pushed ever onward, wishing to be free of the claustrophobic mountain pass.

As the sun was setting on the first day in the pass, the companions noticed a strange, bird-like creature flying high in the cold, gray sky. As they watched the creature soar across the sky, it opened its sharp beak and released a horrible, hammer-like sound that echoed off the mountain faces and cut deep into the companions, driving them down in a vain attempt to escape the dreadful drumming noise.

"What twisted mind created that bloody creature, eh?" Nalgene grumbled to himself, still cowering from the thunderous hammer noises.

Yet as quickly as it had come, the strange bird-creature was gone, leaving behind a gnawing silence. Margaret stared at the sky for a moment, trying to make sense of what she had just seen. But before she could ponder too deeply, her demonic arm flared to life so intensely that Margaret wished to smash it against the sheer rock face of the mountain. But the pulsing held her in check, imprisoning her in its dreadful beat.

Suddenly, a mighty quake rocked the mountain range, shaking the very cores of the towering mountains, as if answering the hammering noises. The companions scrambled about, desperately trying not to be thrown from the treacherous pass. But then it was gone. The mountains sat still. Yet Margaret's arm still pulsed, and she knew it would not be the last earth-shattering quake.

As the next couple days passed, the companions trudged along the pass, weary of the endless gray labyrinth about them. No more quakes threatened to tear the very ground from beneath them, but that gave them little comfort. They wanted to reach the end of this winding pass, and soon.

On the fourth day of their precarious journey through the mountains, the companions found themselves against the sheer face of a rising mountain to the east side of the pass, and a sharp cliff falling far to the west. The path was cracked and worn, and it seemed that it would crumble and fall into the opening abyss at any moment. But the companions had to cross it, and so they braved along the path. Fortunately, it was quite wide, so there was no real threat of plummeting to their deaths, but even still, the companions eyed the chasm with wary trepidation. As they were crossing, a second quake hit, shaking the mountain and sending crumbling bits of the pass falling far below.

The companions cowered against the rock wall for protection, praying for their safety. Yet as the mighty quake was quieting, a massive boulder came soaring from the far end of the pass, crashing into the ground behind them. A deafening *crack* echoed through the mountains, and the path behind them collapsed into the darkness below, blocking any chance of retreat.

Still recovering from the second quake, Margaret stumbled to her feet, searching for the source of the boulder. Her eyes locked on the far end of the pass and opened wide with panic.

Standing like a hulking reaper of death was a zombie giant, its dead eyes thirsting for fresh blood. Twisting muscles and tendons hung in tatters around its body, yet strength rippled through the monstrosity. It took a stride forward, its very step sending another quake thundering through the mountains.

A sickening roar echoing from its gaping maw, the giant began to charge the companions, eager to feast upon their flesh.

Her arm raging wildly at her side, Margaret clenched her black fist. Her power had some uses. Roaring in return, she charged at the giant, a shard of ice already forming within her grasp.

Behind her, the others readied themselves for the oncoming juggernaut. Ro had unsheathed his sword and was quickly following behind Margaret. Andromeda had already disappeared, no doubt seeking to flank the rotting monster. Nalgene and Fasto remained at the back, with spells of water and white arrows already streaking toward the zombie. SmibSmob had not turned to his darkness, fearing another wild outburst. Instead, he turned to his pointed hat and was busy digging through its expansive folds.

Margaret did not notice anything that was happening behind her. Her focus was solely on the charging giant. A feral battle-cry escaping her lips, she met the hulking beast head on, her black fist jabbing the icy shard into its rotting leg.

The giant did not even notice. Its hand came crashing down, sending another small quake through the crumbling pass, but Margaret was long gone. Sprinting behind the giant, the raging orc brought her fists to bear and unleashed a mighty barrage of punches into the giant's left knee. Bits of gray flesh and tendon were torn from the zombie's knee, and a spray of black blood washed over Margaret.

Oh, how she loved that.

A wild look in her eye, she spun in a tight circle, an icy hammer forming within her grasp. With a sickening *crunch*, the hammer slammed into the weakened knee, and the rotting hulk buckled under the impact, falling to one knee.

But it was hardly out of the fight. Indeed, it seemed more enraged than injured. So, with terrifying strength, the zombie balled its fist and punched the very mountain face at its side. It had more luck than Nalgene against the mountains.

A mighty shock wave thundered through the cold stone, and bits of loose rock and debris began crumbling down the mountain side, leading to a barrage of boulders that quickly followed.

Caught off guard, Margaret could barely dodge the hail of falling stones. By the time the rockslide had ceased, the zombie giant had reclaimed its footing and was towering over the other companions, ready to crush them into oblivion.

Fasto unleashed a hail of streaking arrows, but it had little effect on the hulking creature. Nalgene's water fared slightly better, with every swirling orb or streaming spray tearing chunks of flesh from the rotting abomination.

Yet still it continued its relentless attack.

Andromeda had managed to scale the undead giant and was tearing at its mighty shoulders and neck with her halberd, a wild gleam in her fierce eyes. Ro darted between the legs, and was slashing away at the beast's ankles, desperately trying to fell the vile giant. And then there was SmibSmob, whose foul luck had only produced a coiled rope from his pointed hat.

Margaret growled. She would decimate this beast. Charging back into the fray, she raised her black fist, another shard of ice forming in her grasp. With a flick of her wrist, the shard went soaring at the giant, sinking deep into its rotting back.

Again, it did not even notice. Undead cared little for pain.

But before Margaret could conjure another shard, the giant reached down with surprising speed and grabbed Ro in its iron grasp. The draconian tried to escape, but the rotting fingers held him as surely as a massive vice. With a guttural roar, the giant turned and hurled the draconian at Margaret!

Acting purely on instinct, Margaret just managed to duck the oncoming projectile. Ro crashed into the ground with a bone-crunching *thud*, and rolled another twenty strides down the pass, where he lay quite still. But Margaret was so lost in her demonic pulsing, she did not even turn to see if Ro was alive.

Unconcerned, Margaret scrambled back to her feet and rushed at the giant. She darted between the stomping legs, and whipped about, an icy axe in her grasp. The frozen blade buried itself into the giant's shin, releasing yet another spray of black blood across the crazed orc.

She licked her lips. Delicious.

She was about to call upon another icy axe, but at that

moment, one of Nalgene's orbs came soaring above her, crashing into the giant and sending it stumbling back a step. Margaret pondered for a moment, a brilliant strategy forming in her mind.

She turned, seeing the gnome raising another swirling orb high above his head. Perfect. The moment Nalgene released his mighty spell, Margaret called upon her devilish arm, casting its vile power out to the oncoming orb.

The mighty sphere froze, and crashed into the giant, causing severe damage with its frozen edges. Another rain of black blood poured forth from the giant, and its eyes shot down at Margaret, eager to be rid of the small pest.

Margaret smiled. It would not be that easy. She turned back to Nalgene, and she found him staring at her with a look of genuine respect. He glanced down to his gnarled hands, then back up to the frenzied orc. Perhaps they were on to something. He smiled.

Raising his hands, Nalgene unleashed a streaming jet of swirling water at the giant. Margaret did not hesitate. Her demonic power reached out, freezing the oncoming spear of water. The giant did not stand a chance. The massive spear crashed into the undead creature — nay, *through* the beast, and shot far beyond, crashing into the distant mountain face with a brilliant shower of ice.

But it would take more than that to fell the rotting gargantuan. Reaching up, it tore Andromeda from its shredded shoulders and slammed her onto the ground like a limp rag doll. Margaret could only watch as the feline thudded into the ground, no doubt shattering her bones. The giant turned, its hollow eyes seeking vengeance. Margaret was next.

She did not run. For that was weak. She would fight. She formed another icy axe with her demonic arm, but it was too late. The giant shot forward, ripping her into the air. Margaret felt the crushing grip of the hulking monster. Her ribs screamed in protest, and her head grew faint. Even the pulsing of her arm seemed distant to her.

Before she could hope to escape, she went soaring into the

air. She felt alive. She felt free. Yet she knew she was about to die.

Margaret turned in the air, desperately trying to orient herself. The whole world was spinning. And so, she fell, off the sheer cliff and into the vast chasm below.

Suddenly, a rush of water surrounded her, and instinctively, her demonic arm shot out, an icy nova freezing all the surrounding water and creating a frosty platform for her to stand upon. Shaking her head, and trying to regain her senses, Margaret was able to make out the small form of Nalgene high up on the pass, a relieved look on his face.

But the giant towered behind him. Margaret called out a warning, but she knew it was too late. The giant reached down, eager to slaughter the defenseless gnome. But as the rotting hand reached down, a twisting beam of shadow crashed into it, knocking it away from Nalgene.

SmibSmob had finally joined the fight.

Tendrils of shadow wrapped about the undead giant like the mighty tentacles of a kraken, and swirling orbs of darkness rained down upon it, driving it back and away from Nalgene. The area grew dark, as if the very light was being devoured by a shadowy god. The very mountains shook under the brilliant, and terrible, display of power. Margaret could only imagine the horrible display of dark power, which mocked even her demonic arm.

Still, she stared up at the form of Nalgene, who now held something in his hands: a coiled rope. The one that SmibSmob had pulled from his hat. She shook her head, at a loss.

Trying to ignore the chaos behind him, Nalgene tossed the rope down to Margaret, urging her to climb back up, and quickly. For the darkness was already diminishing. Growling, Margaret rushed up the rope, scaling the cliff face with reckless abandon. She had to get up to the fray.

Her arm pulsed.

All thoughts fled from her mind. She only had one focus.

The giant.

She reached the pass, a frenzied look twisting her face into a barbaric mask of rage. Her fists raised before her; Margaret rushed at the hulking creature. She did not notice that the overwhelming shadow had disappeared, and that SmibSmob now lay helplessly upon the ground, with Nalgene desperately trying to protect his frail brother. She did not notice that Fasto sat crumpled against the face of the mountain, blood dripping from his shattered face. She only had one focus.

The giant.

She darted between the undead giant's legs, dodging its futile attempts to grab at her.

The giant.

Her black arm crashed into the giant's already weakened knee, shattering it and sending vile gore raining upon the ground.

The giant.

She unleashed a barrage of rapid punches at the giant, not caring where she hit. She only wanted to hit and feel the thick blood upon her fists. But the giant swatted her aside. Margaret went soaring back, only to crash into the rock face behind her. Her head cracked against the hard stone, and she felt blood pouring down her body. Not the giant's blood. Her blood. And it only enraged her more.

The giant.

Shrugging off her injuries, she shot forward, a bloodthirsty gleam burning in her eyes. And Nalgene was beside her, charging at the giant in a final assault. This was it. There would be no other chances. The gnome raised his hands, and a mighty tsunami surged forward, washing over the giant.

Not missing a beat, Margaret's demonic arm shot forward, freezing the powerful wave of water into an impenetrable wall of ice. The undead abomination desperately tried to hold back the oncoming surge, but a layer of ice had frozen beneath it. All it could do was roar as the mighty wall of ice washed it from the pass and into the jagged ravine below.

With one final roar, the giant plummeted into the dark ravine and crashed into the hard stone far below.

The giant was dead.

Margaret collapsed from exhaustion, her injuries overcoming her blood lust. Her vision went black, and she knew no more.

◆   ◆   ◆

Margaret awoke to the warm caress of water rushing across her body. The back of her skull fit itself back together, and her torn hands regenerated with iron knuckles. Her eyes shot open, finding Nalgene crouched atop her, his face grim. Her energy rejuvenated, Margaret sat up and began to thank the gnome, but he was already gone, bolting over to SmibSmob.

Shaking her head, Margaret vaguely remembered the titanic display of shadowy energy, but she could not hope to fully appreciate its grandeur. She had only seen the mere edge of the darkness, and not the heart of the void. Even still, that was enough to make her somber.

She moved through the pass, collecting the bodies of the others and bringing them to Nalgene to heal. Her heart was heavy, and she thought back to Fasto, and the one, simple line he had said to her those few days ago:

Fasto help friend.

She glanced down at the limp orc in her arms, and she felt more than a stab of anguish.

Nalgene cast his healing tide of water across each of the companions, stitching their wounds back together and reigniting the fire within their eyes. Yet as Margaret watched, she could not help but think that one of these times the gnome's magic would not be enough.

As the companions were recovering from their injuries, Margaret moved over to the cliff on the west side of the path and peered down into the murky depths below, trying to spot the broken corpse of the giant. But the ravine was too deep, and so she saw only darkness. She held out her demonic arm, studying its twisting, black muscles, and her ruby eyes gleamed dangerously.

Her thoughts were interrupted by the talking of the others behind her, who had recovered and were more than eager to finally reach the end of the winding mountain pass. She turned to them, a devilish grin across her face. They tried to talk to her, but she ignored them, still lost in the rippling cords of her arm.

Perhaps her power did have its uses.

Chapter 10

Nalgene gazed upon Margaret, who was now healed. A small grin peaked on his rough lips, and a glimmer of newfound respect could be seen buried deep within his eyes. There was no doubt in his mind — it was the orc's creative use of her demonic powers that had allowed the companions to prevail against the mighty undead giant.

Margaret's black arm still brought chills to Nalgene, and not just because of the bone-piercing cold it emitted. The damn thing just wasn't natural.

But even still, as Margaret had proven, her powers did have their uses.

Nalgene shook his head, and turned away from Margaret, who was lost in the dark corruption of her arm. He had more important priorities to worry about, such as SmibSmob. Anxious, Nalgene rushed over to his brother, who looked more like a shriveled corpse than a living, breathing gnome.

"Are ye alright, me brother?" Nalgene grumbled, his voice dripping with worry.

Nalgene knew of the constant struggle SmibSmob faced against his dark powers, an endless battle over control of the poor gnome's mind. Yet Nalgene always told himself that his brother was winning that dreadful conflict, that SmibSmob was able to control the insatiable darkness within. But now Nalgene had to face the truth. In all his time with his brother, he had never once seen him this violated. Of course, there were times when SmibSmob had accepted his power in order to fight. But this was something entirely different. SmibSmob had lost. SmibSmob had succumbed to his demons, and it shook Nalgene to his core. Even the surge of emotion he felt when SmibSmob struck him paled in comparison to the utter horror that now consumed Nalgene.

SmibSmob looked up to him, his once-shining blue eyes now hollow sockets of exhaustion.

"I … yes," SmibSmob managed to say in a thin voice. "I … I don't know. It all just overwhelmed me."

Nalgene studied his brother for a long moment, before putting a reassuring hand on his shoulder. "As long as yer alright," he said gently. "I be here for ye, and as long as I be here, there ain't nothin' that can be stoppin' us."

The words sounded hollow in Nalgene's ears, but he did not know what else he could say. SmibSmob nodded and straightened himself up as best as he could. Nalgene believed in him, and SmibSmob would hate to disappoint.

Nalgene smiled. He would keep telling himself his lie. SmibSmob could triumph over his dark power. He had to. Yet even as Nalgene's hope rekindled, he could not shake the image of a corrupted SmibSmob floating high above the mountain pass amid a swirling void of shadow. The very sun seemed to retreat as his brother's unholy fury unleashed itself upon the rotting giant. Nalgene remembered the agonizing gnawing at his mind and soul, as if his brother was actively devouring all life around him. And SmibSmob's eyes — two shadowy abysses that had lost every fragment of the gnome deep within.

Bloody hell. He didn't want his brother losing himself on them yet. SmibSmob was all he had. They started the journey together, and he meant to ensure that they would finish it together, too.

Nalgene turned away from his brother, eager to distract his mind. Around him, the other companions were more than ready to finish their trek through the mountain pass. Fasto rushed up to Margaret, and was desperately trying to talk to her, and, surprisingly, she was listening. Andromeda paced back-and-forth, her tail slashing like a vicious whip, and her eyes flaring with impatience. Ro merely studied the gnome brothers, a blended mix of sympathy and empathy swirling across his face.

"What do ye say, ye damn dragon," Nalgene called out to Ro. "I think we best be leavin' these bloody mountains."

"Mmmm, I like the sound of that," Andromeda purred while stalking up to stand next to Ro, her tail still twitching vigorously.

Ro shook his head, Andromeda's voice snapping him out of his trance, and he nodded to the gnome. "I couldn't agree more," he said.

"Then lead the way, will ye?" Nalgene said. "That's what ye like doin', eh?"

Ro chuckled softly, and without hesitation, he started down the mountain pass, Andromeda following closely behind.

Nalgene turned to the two orcs. "Are ye two dolts comin'?" he shouted. "By leavin', I be meanin' now."

Fasto nodded his head with excitement, while Margaret sent him a cold glare.

Nalgene turned back to SmibSmob, a gentleness returning to his gruff voice. "C'mon, me brother, let's be gettin' outta here."

SmibSmob looked at him, his face beaming with true appreciation and his dark eyes twinkling with newfound hope. It was a face that Nalgene vowed never to forget.

The companions continued their journey through the treacherous mountain pass. The sheer, gray faces of the mountains passed by like grim bystanders to a solemn funeral. The cold sun rose overhead, and plummeted far to the west, swallowed by the jagged peaks far before it reached the distant horizon. As they finished their trek through the mountains, the surrounding world seemed to rest in an eerie silence. There were no other thunderous quakes, or towering giants. Everything was still and the companions could not be more grateful for it. On the morning of their fifth day in the pass, the companions finally reached the end.

As they exited the mountain pass, it was as if a weight had been lifted from their shoulders. Eyes sparkled with rekindled hope, and feet stepped lighter upon the bleak ground. Nalgene was more than grateful for the change in scenery.

Rolling foothills stretched in front of the companions, a vast lake waiting at the end. A dark mist clung to the surface of the water, creating an impenetrable wall of fog that even the blusteriest weather would have trouble dislodging. Nalgene shivered at the sight of the great lake, yet he did not know why. Behind them the mountains reached high into the sky, looming over the backs of the companions like shadowy assassins, ready to pounce at a moment's notice. Far to the east rested a great darkness, and it seemed as if the entirety of the Shadow was flowing forth from that great void.

"Do you think that's the lake?" Ro asked quietly. It seemed wrong to disturb the unnatural silence enveloping them.

"Eh?" Nalgene grunted, not catching the draconian's meaning. The more he studied the misty lake, the more certain he felt that they should not go anywhere near it. It just seemed … wrong. "That definitely be a lake, no arguin' that."

"Oh, another brilliant observation," Margaret shot. Yet her insult was undercut by a gentle intrigue in her voice.

"Through the mountain pass and to the shores of a great lake," Ro mumbled to no one in particular. "That's what he said, right?"

"What in the bloody hell are ye talkin' about?" Nalgene asked. Of course, now he knew what the annoying draconian was talking about. He just did not want to accept it. Damn dragon … No. Damn Osann. He wanted nothing to do with that man again.

"Mmmm, what are we waiting for?" Andromeda said, stepping forward, her gaze lost in deep thoughts. "This is where the Captain said to meet, at the shore of a great lake." She turned to them. "Let's go, shall we?"

Nalgene's rage flickered to life at the mention of the Captain. He did not care what kind of heroic sacrifice he underwent. That did not stop Nalgene from seeing the truth. He was a liar, a traitor.

"Nah, I don't be thinkin' this is the lake," Nalgene growled, unable to keep his simmering fury out of his voice.

No one else seemed to hear him, or care.

"Fasto go see friend!" Fasto exclaimed, stepping forward to match Andromeda. Nalgene wished he could sink a punch into the orc's annoying face.

"Do you think he will be waiting?" Ro wondered aloud.

"Eh, did ye all lose yer bloody minds?" Nalgene shouted, exploding at their continued blind faith in the Captain. His gnarled fists clenched at his side. "Ye all saw what he was facin'. Ye all know what it can do. That bloody traitor be dead, and we be better off fer it. So, I be sayin' it's the wrong lake, and I be sayin' we be goin' elsewhere."

The companions stared at him for a long moment, but Nalgene stood firm against their hard gazes.

"How many times have we discussed this?" Ro asked, breaking the tense silence.

"Way too many times," Margaret snorted.

"We have to try," Ro continued, ignoring the orc's snarky remark. "He's the only hope we have. We are lost in this grim land."

"Well, I don't be needin' his bloody hope," Nalgene growled. He felt like he was talking in circles. The draconian was right — how many times had they argued over the Captain? Why were they so blind to his side? He knew what he saw.

There was only sympathy in Ro's eyes, and Nalgene felt as if he were a scolded child.

"That be the wrong lake," Nalgene repeated, his voice as steadfast as the mighty mountains behind them.

Ro started to argue, but he was cut off by the frail voice of SmibSmob. "Brother, please, there is no point in arguing," he said. "We are wasting time."

"Eh?" Nalgene turned. But no matter how deep his rage burned, he could not bring himself to argue with his dear brother.

"We are going to the lake," SmibSmob said, leaving little room for argument in his stern voice.

Nalgene opened his mouth to protest, but no words came forth. One look at his frail brother, and the memories of the dark devastation upon the mountain pass, were enough to silence him.

"Fine, we be goin' to the bloody lake," Nalgene grunted. "And if some damn creature of the deep swallows us up, then that be the last time ye all listen to that hairy arse of a traitor." The disgruntled gnome turned to Ro. "Don't be thinkin' this is yer victory, ye damn dragon," he shouted, before stomping down the foothills.

Sighing, the companions started off after him.

The companions wove their way through the rolling foothills, not a single sign of movement disturbing their travels. Shriveled bushes and the decayed corpses of once-proud trees dotted the land about them, but none of the companions took any notice. They had seen too much darkness and atrophy to be concerned about the loss of a few trees. The gray sky above them began rolling with black clouds, and a heavy mist began seeping from the land, much like the dreadful blanket covering the lake. As they approached, Nalgene could not shake the feeling that they should not go near those black waters. Some prick at the back of his mind, some forgotten memory, warned him away, yet still he stomped towards the barren shores, much to his displeasure.

Bloody hell.

A Land in Shadow

As darkness began to claw its way up into the wasteland, the companions searched for a place to brave the endless night. Yet there was no shelter — just empty hills and shriveled shrubs. There would be no hiding from the Shadow this night. And so, the companions pushed on, until their legs would carry them no more. They would reach the shore in the morning, and there, hopefully, they would reunite with the Captain.

As Nalgene lay upon the cold and unforgiving ground, he studied the boiling blackness above him. This was the wrong lake. This lake was wrong. They should not go.

But what could they do? The stubborn dragon had his blind faith. Nalgene knew it was nonsense. Pretty words didn't necessitate belief. He knew what he saw. And his conviction was only reinforced with that dolt that Fasto killed. But, apparently that was not enough to open his companion's eyes.

Nalgene wanted to lash out, to strike something. But he kept it inside. This dark world cared little for the problems of a single, lost gnome. Frustrated, Nalgene felt as if he were a pawn in a great game of chess, and there was nothing he could do about it.

"Pullin' us like puppets ..." Nalgene muttered. But no one heard, and no one cared. Not even his dear brother stirred from his sleep. Defeated, Nalgene finally succumbed to the determined clutches of exhaustion.

◆　　◆　　◆

The gnome looked around. Nothing. Pure emptiness. He tried to move, but his body would not obey his commands. He wanted to call out, but his mouth had been sealed shut. Nothing. Around him, the empty void began to swirl, and flickers of movement darted about at the edges of the gnome's vision. Something. But as quickly as the disturbances had come, they disappeared, leaving the gnome stranded in the eternal blackness.

And then he was falling.

With a booming thud, the gnome landed upon the hard ground, in an impact that surely would have shattered his legs — yet he felt no pain. He was in a desolate forest, surrounded by vile, clawing trees. A menacing, red orb floated in the black sky, casting a bloody light across the lands. The gnome looked around. He seemed alone. Yet he knew he was not. Something tugged at the back of his blue cloak, and he whipped around, his hands clenched in front of him.

Nothing.

And still the red orb shone, its damning light relentless upon the shriveled land below.

Eerie whispers began to surround the gnome, teasing him with their silent calls. Another shadow clawed at the back of his flowing cloak, and the gnome whipped around, only to be met with the same barren forest. He was not alone. Before he could stop, the gnome was running, but what from he could only imagine. The skeletal trees darted past, raking at him with their bloody branches. The gnome felt the branches slice into his body, felt the sharp sticks tear into his flesh. Yet still he ran. Thick blood ran down his face, its deep color only matched by the infernal orb floating above.

Roaring in denial, the gnome braved a glance behind him, anxious to get a glimpse of his mysterious pursuer. Another gnome, draped in a robe of shadow, bolted after him, a desperate plea for help plastered on his frail face. A sudden, heart-wrenching pain tore through the gnome, and he felt as if his very soul was being torn from his body. Yet still he ran, for that was all he could do. Blood oozed from his many gruesome gashes, weighing him down in a thickening pool of blood. A gray root burst from the ground. The gnome tried to dodge it, but it was too late. The blood was too heavy.

And so, he tripped and fell into ... nothing.

The void boiled around him. Something.

A Land in Shadow

The gnome plunged into a dark lake and sank deep below the churning waves. He looked up, and desperately tried to swim for the distant surface, but still he kept falling, sinking into the murky abyss. He should have been able to swim. Water was his to command, yet this liquid shadow paid little heed to the gnome's wishes. And so, he sank. No matter how vigorously the gnome kicked out, the thick water pressed in, suffocating him. The gnome closed his eyes, defeated. The black water rushed into his body, filling his lungs like tar. His body pounded in pain, desperately trying to push out the invading water. But it was no use. He was drowning. The light at the surface was long gone. Only the darkness remained. Nothing.

The gnome opened his eyes, only to find himself sprawled at the shore of a great lake. He coughed, and a surge of black blood spewed from his mouth. The gnome shivered violently, an icy chill penetrating his soaked body. He coughed again, and more black blood was expelled from the depths of his lungs. The gnome looked at the waves of the lake, trying to find some solace in their gentle rhythm. He coughed yet again, releasing another round of blood. He tried to sit up, but his body would not obey, he was too weak, too cold. As he watched the crashing waves of the lake, two piercing red eyes appeared in the murky depths. A harrowing horror filled the gnome, and he desperately clawed at the bloody sand beneath him, anxious to escape the ominous eyes. But he could not escape the terror of the tides. The sand gripped at him, pulling him down, filling his lungs, and smothering any hope the gnome may have had. And still the two eyes drove into him.

And then he was falling through the empty void once more. Nothing.

But then something appeared. Another gnome, who was cloaked in shadow. The one he had seen before. The one who was hounding him in the forsaken forest. His brother. The gnome tried to call out, but once again, his mouth was sealed shut. He could not move, could not escape. A beautiful woman appeared, her emerald eyes sparkling with a devious light. The gnome knew he should recognize her, but he could not. His mind was blank.

As the gnome watched, the mysterious woman approached his brother, her graceful stride like that of a stalking lion. Her lips moved, yet he could not hear what she was saying. At first, his brother seemed to cower from the wondrous woman, yet as she wove her words, he began to relax and become vulnerable to her silver charm. The gnome wanted to call out, but his body would not answer. He knew this was wrong. His brother should be running away. This woman was dangerous. Of this he was certain.

As he watched, the shadows surrounding his brother grew thicker, weaving about in a curtain of darkness. The woman smiled, and reached out to his brother, her slender hand radiating with a shining light.

A beacon in the dark.

A gripping terror overwhelmed the gnome. This was not right. This was wrong. He was certain of it. Yet all he could do was watch as his brother accepted the woman's hand. It was too late. The radiant light from the woman's hand turned harsh and cold, like the light from the simmering eyes of a demon. It cut deep into his brother, rending his shadowy barrier apart and searing into his pale flesh. The woman turned to the gnome, and smiled, her piercing eyes burning holes in his soul. But as he watched, his body writhing in agony, her eyes turned a deep black, two endless pits in her delicate face.

And then the butterflies appeared, rushing forth from the woman in a terrible swarm.

They surrounded the gnome, jabbing at him in a storm of a thousand infernal needles. Each prick seemed to last an eternity, yet only a heartbeat passed.

His vision blurred.

He was back in the forsaken forest, with the menacing red orb floating high in the night sky. The trees reached out to him, clawing at his flesh. Shadows darted about, tugging at his blue cloak. *Paralyzing agony filled his rough body, and he collapsed. But as blood pooled from his body, another butterfly appeared and landed upon his arm.*

Another prick seared into his mind.

The black water washed over him, smothering him in its inky waves. The thick water rushed into his lungs, driving out any air. Yet this time the gnome did not struggle. He had done this before. He knew it was hopeless. But then the butterfly appeared.

Another prick incinerating his soul.

The black blood surged from his lungs, and the gnome lay sprawling on the shore of the lake. The icy chill drove into him, but he did not struggle. He was living a hopeless cycle of despair. The two red eyes appeared in the murky depths, a threatening menace just beneath the waves. But then came the gentle flapping of the wings.

Another butterfly, another prick, and another endless torrent of burning pain.

The gnome opened his eyes. He was back in the desolate emptiness. Yet it was not as empty as he had hoped. The storm of butterflies swarmed around him, their sleek, obsidian wings dancing about in a tantalizing routine of death.

Another prick.

His brother appeared in front of him, battered, broken, and covered with water.

Another prick.

A shattered, crystalline bottle.

Another prick.

A decrepit gravestone, with writing that had long ago worn away.

Another prick.

Two emerald eyes.

Another prick.

A furious storm, washing away a small, huddled group of companions.

Another prick.

All the gnome knew was the pain. It consumed him, yet at the same time, everything seemed distant, as if he was merely an observer of this dastardly cycle. There was only the pain.

Another prick.

The pawn moved across the chess board.

Another prick.

A marvelous hammer, raised high to the sky ...

◆　　◆　　◆

Nalgene awoke, the cryptic dream already fading from his memory. Ro carried the gnome upon his back and was desperately trying to run through the solemn foothills. Nalgene shook his head vigorously, his senses returning. This was not another dream. He glanced around, his eyes straining in the murky darkness. It was not yet dawn.

The other companions ran alongside Ro, their frantic footsteps being weighed down in the thick mud.

It had been raining.

"What in the bloody hell is goin' on?" Nalgene grumbled from Ro's back. The draconian was not exactly a comfortable mount, and Nalgene so wished to let go and run along with his own two legs. Yet he held on.

"We were attacked," Ro gasped between heavy breaths. "More undead."

"Eh?" Nalgene grunted. "Why didn't ye wake me? We coulda fought them."

"You don't think we tried?" Ro panted, his legs growing heavy in the unrelenting mud. "We're headed to the lake — there we can hold back the undead."

Nalgene snorted but said nothing. He still could not shake

the sinking feeling he had about the lake. Some memory, some pang, told him not to go, yet here they were, running to lake as if it were their holy salvation.

The companions continued running for a short while, their heavy pants drowning out any conversation. Occasionally Fasto turned around to unleash a hail of streaking arrows into the darkness. There was no doubt he found his mark. The unearthly sounds of the pursuing undead trailed behind them like the insatiable growls of a furious bloodhound. As the cold sun began to rise in the east, the companions finally made it to the shore of the great, misty lake.

Exhausted, Ro placed Nalgene down upon the sandy shore, and turned about, his mighty greatsword drawn and ready. The others also prepared for the onslaught, creating a defensive formation behind Ro. Margaret stood by the draconian's side, a sly smirk on her lips. Fasto had an arrow nocked in his white bow, and his laser eyes were eagerly seeking their first target. Andromeda had already disappeared into the stretching shadows. SmibSmob rushed over to his brother's side, a concerned look twisting his already frail face.

"Nalgene; are you alright?" he gasped. Running long-distances was never a strong suit of gnomes, and the battered condition of SmibSmob only made the ordeal worse. "We tried to wake you, but you wouldn't stir. And then the undead attacked, so we ran."

"Ah, me brother, I be fine," Nalgene said reassuringly, staring up into his brother's gentle eyes. Where would he be without him? "What do ye say we kill us some undead, eh?"

SmibSmob smiled, and nodded, yet Nalgene did not miss the hint of nervousness on his face. Reaching up, the pale gnome took his pointed hat from his head, and turned around, ready to meet the onslaught with the others.

Nalgene smiled. As much as he loved decimating undead with his devastating spells of water, the gnawing feeling of dread remained. This sand seemed all too familiar to the shores of his dream.

Shaking the thoughts away, Nalgene stood, brushed the wet sand from his blue cloak, and readied his hands, water already swirling around his clenched fists.

"Let them come," he growled.

The undead washed upon the shore like a raging tsunami. Hordes of rotting zombies and shambling skeletons charged the companions, their hollow eyes eager for the taste of blood. Yet the companions held strong. They had faced many such undead before. Surely this would be no different.

A mighty roar thundering from Ro, the draconian rushed into the fray, his shining greatsword cleaving through the surrounding undead like a farmer would to wheat. Streaking bolts of lightning burst from his maw, arcing between the undead with a brilliant shower of sparks.

A delightful grin wide upon Margaret's face, the orc rushed in after Ro. Her demonic arm pulsed with an icy chill, and her devastating punches shattered bones and crushed empty skulls. A massive axe of ice appeared in her hand, and she swung it about like a mad lumberjack, cutting down anything that dared step too close.

Fasto remained at the shore, his white bow raining an endless torrent of arrows into the throng of undead. Almost every time an undead would be about to strike one of the companions, Fasto's arrow was there, obliterating the rotting filth. There was little shortage of shambling undead, so Fasto's arrows pierced through the rotting ranks with ease.

SmibSmob stood by his brother's side, digging around in his pointed hat. His blue eyes lit with excitement, and he pulled forth a twisted black sword. Perhaps this hat could be useful. SmibSmob was certainly no sword master, but this black sword seemed to move the gnome about with its own free will, slicing through any undead that wandered too close.

Nalgene smiled and turned to the swarm of atrophy. A massive orb of water formed above his head, and with a feral growl, he hurled it into the horde. Without missing a beat, he opened his hands, and two steaming streams of water jetting forth, cutting deep into the rotting flesh of the undead. He formed another orb of water, this time aiming it at Margaret.

"Aye, ye bloody orc!" Nalgene shouted, releasing the mighty spell.

Margaret turned, and her demonic arm shot out, freezing the ball of water into a devastating sphere of ice.

The horde did not stand a chance.

And so, the fight wore on, the companions desperately defending against the endless swarm. Yet for every undead they cut down, two more took their place. Undead cared little for pain, or exhaustion, yet the run, and the ongoing battle, sapped the companions' strength. Dozens of cuts and bruises appeared on the companions, and blood covered the fighters — and not just from the rotting undead.

Nalgene growled. He could see no end to the oncoming onslaught, and he feared they would not be able to hold off for much longer. Yet still he fought on, unleashing torrents of powerful spells into the vile mass of decay.

Suddenly, razor shards of ice whistled at Nalgene, thudding into the ground around him and piercing deep into the sand.

"What in the bloody hell is that damn orc doin'?" Nalgene gasped, startled.

Yet when he looked up, he found it was not Margaret, as she was occupied by the undead around her. His eyes wandered across the bloody battlefield, only to rest upon a group of cloaked skeletons. Icy missiles formed within their bony grasp, and with a wave of their hands, were sent soaring at the companions.

Nalgene growled. That would not do. He had to end the skeleton mages, and fast. Yet even as he raised his hands to obliterate the mages, Andromeda streaked out of the shadows, landing amid them. Her mighty halberd ripped through the mages' weak spines, sending shards of bone in every direction. She darted about, avoiding their piercing spears of ice and lashing out with her own devastating barrage of claw and halberd. The skeleton mages lasted only a few seconds. Andromeda looked up, meeting Nalgene's wide eyes, and she gave him a curt nod, before disappearing back into the foggy shadows.

Nalgene grunted. She did have her uses.

The battle raged on as more undead fodder and skeleton mages rushed towards the companions, their unholy growls and moans drowning out all other sounds in a gruesome symphony of death. Yet as much as Nalgene was focused on the battle in front of him, he could not shake his nagging terror of the lake behind him. It was nothing, he kept telling himself. But the pang persisted.

Shaking his head, he braved a quick look at the misty lake behind him, hoping to quell his harrowing fear.

He knew instantly they had made a mistake by running to the shores of this vast lake.

The black water boiled and bubbled, as if something were about to break the murky surface. As Nalgene peered closer, two, hollow eyes filled with hatred and death appeared just below the surface. His head jerked back. He remembered this part of the dream.

Before he could warn the others, the water exploded, and out burst a mighty, undead serpent. Its long, snaking body curled above the water like the patient coil of a viper. Long strips of rotting flesh were hanging from its body, and the once-shining scales were now black and decrepit. Massive brown ribs could be seen through the worn skin of the serpent, and the inner organs had long ago decayed and been washed away by the dark water. Its head was that of a mighty dragon, with a gaping maw filled with rows of spear-like teeth. It seemed the decay had not taken all the serpent's dangerous assets. Torn fins and rotting gills hung just behind the serpent's jaw, and a slender row of spines jutted out of the serpent's back, running down the length of the serpentine body. The two, hollow eyes of death locked onto Nalgene, boring into the gnome and driving him back across the sandy shore. The serpent's gaze was a cold certainty. There would be nothing left alive on this shore.

All would be devoured.

Nalgene scrambled back, falling to the sandy shore. He wanted to call out, to warn the others, but he was paralyzed by the demonic being before him, and his words caught in his throat. His mind raced. He knew they should not have come to this lake. He told them, yet they did not listen — not even his brother. They trusted that filth Osann, and now here they were, about to be devoured by this ghastly serpent of hell.

It was all his fault — that bloody traitor, Osann. This was where he told them to come, and look at what good came of it. If that bastard wasn't dead yet, Nalgene vowed he would be killing him himself.

The serpent glared at Nalgene. No doubt the gnome looked like a mere insect to the towering abomination. Its maw opened, displaying the rows of razor teeth, and a terrifying roar thundered from deep within the serpent. The unholy sound echoed across the landscape, sounding like a challenge to the gods themselves. It cut into the companions and drove back even the emotionless legions of undead.

Terrified, the companions turned about, their eyes gaping in horror. They had barely managed to survive the titanic, rotting giant in the pass. What hope did they have against this monstrosity?

"What … what is that?" Ro gasped, his face pale with dread.

Beside him, Fasto visibly trembled in the wake of the undead serpent. "Fasto scared," the orc whimpered, tears beginning to stream from his face. "Fasto want friends."

Margaret paled. Even her demonic arm seemed like a child's toy compared to the towering serpent. "Oh good, this is just what we needed," she muttered.

Andromeda appeared next to Ro, her gaze wide with awe and terror. "What power …" she whispered to herself.

"What did I tell ye, eh?" Nalgene snarled. It was Osann's

fault they were in this bloody mess. "But no, what do I know?"

Ro glared at him and was about to argue, but at that moment the serpent let out another thunderous roar that drowned out the draconian's words.

Nalgene shook his head. This was no time to argue. They could bicker later, if they survived. The gnome stood up, and readied his hands, water swirling around his fists. "Come 'ere, beastie," he growled.

Just as he was about to unleash upon the serpent, a small stone whistled by and bounced harmlessly off its black scales. Nalgene looked; his brother now held a small, wooden slingshot. Silly hat. If only it were useful.

The serpent's hollow eyes narrowed. That was all the excuse it needed to attack. With one final growl, the serpent coiled up, and lashed out at the companions, its head whipping forward with tremendous speed.

It was all the companions could do to dodge the lethal strike.

The serpent's maw crashed into the sandy shore, sending sand and dirt spraying in all directions. Its teeth cut massive gashes into the cold ground. Nalgene could only image what those fangs would do to them. Not even his wondrous healing would be able to stitch together those terrible wounds.

The serpent reared up, once again preparing to strike. Its eyes locked on SmibSmob. This time it would not miss.

Behind the companions, the undead horde once again continued its pursuit, mindless fodder and skeleton mages alike.

And so, the battle continued. It was all the companions could do to hope to survive.

The serpent lunged, but Nalgene was ready. With a roar of fury, he launched a swirling orb of water at the serpent. With a mighty splash, the powerful spell crashed into the serpent's head, driving the abomination's fatal strike sideways and into the cold earth. SmibSmob looked petrified.

"C'mon, me brother," Nalgene roared. "Now is a bloody

good time to use yer powers!'"

But SmibSmob shook his head. As much as he wanted to help, he had overexerted himself in the pass. His power would be of no help.

They were on their own.

The serpent pulled its maw from the earth, quite uninjured. Fasto rained arrows at it, piercing its hide and cutting through its rotting tissue with burning holes of light. It did not even notice. Ro and Margaret had turned and were desperately trying to hold off the oncoming undead, but without the concentrated might of all the companions, there was little hope for them. Nalgene continued to pelt the serpent with mighty spells, some of which would have caused the very mountains quake. Yet the most he managed to do was distract the unholy beast from his other companions. Andromeda appeared out of the shadows, and leaped upon the serpent, scaling its rotting neck with graceful agility. Her halberd plunged again and again, drawing black blood and raining decaying gore down into the lake below.

The serpent did not even notice.

It lunged again, this time at Nalgene. With a cry of terror, Nalgene tensed his legs, and leaped to the side, praying that he would survive. He felt the rush of air as the serpent plunged into the ground where he stood. But he was not quick enough. The side of the serpent's head caught the gnome with a glancing blow, sending him flying across the shore to crash hard into the wet sand. His lungs seared in pain, and his shoulder screamed as if a hot iron was being plunged into his shoulder blade. All Nalgene could do was try to regain his breath.

His vision blurry, he could barely make out the forms of his companions. Or were they undead? He could not be sure. The serpent pulled its head back, and with a violent shake, threw Andromeda off itself. The feline went soaring through the air, gracefully flipping and managing to land upon her feet. Her toxic eyes burned into the serpent. Fasto turned between firing arrows at the towering serpent and supporting those fighting against the other undead hordes. SmibSmob had regained his black, twisting sword, and was carving up any vile zombie or dreadful skeleton that dared approach him.

Ro and Margaret fought back-to-back, lightning and ice alike streaking through the army of decay. Yet still the undead came on, replacing any that the companions cut down. A row of skeleton mages stood in the background, hailing down sharp shards of ice down upon them. At one point, a skeleton mage raised his hand, and a block of ice burst from the ground beneath Ro, trapping his foot in a glacial prison.

Nalgene looked on with horror. They could not hope to win this battle, let alone survive.

He staggered to his feet, his body howling in protest. Growling, he placed his hand over his chest and let the cool water wash across him, mending his dislocated shoulder.

The serpent lunged at Fasto, eager to be rid of the pesky annoyance. The orc screamed, tears running down his face. But at the last moment, Andromeda streaked out of the shadows, tackling Fasto and driving him away from the devastating maw of the serpent.

Dozens of wounds covered Ro and Margaret, and Nalgene knew it would not be long before the two succumbed to the relentless tide of rot. Ro had blasted his lightning upon his sword, and was swinging the crackling weapon through the undead, each slice releasing a small, arcing bolt of electricity. Margaret was mounted upon a hulking zombie and was busy pummeling its shattered skull into a pool of black blood and gore.

Nalgene watched his brother, who was frantically running across the shore, trying to find something good in his pointed hat. Nalgene looked at the hat for a moment. It was his brother's gift from Mariah. Unconsciously, Nalgene reached into his robes and pulled forth his crystalline bottle. It was a miracle that it had not broken. He stared deep into its clear, shining water, and then looked up to the undead serpent, which was once again trying to devour Fasto.

Nalgene's dark blue eyes glittered. Yes. It'll do.

Brimming with a new hope, Nalgene stomped over to the others, his crystal bottle held firmly in his hand.

"Leave this abomination to me, will ye?" Nalgene shouted, his gruff voice ringing out loud and clear in the surrounding fray. "Ye hold of the undead swarm, this bloody serpent be for me."

The companions glanced at him, confused. What could he possibly do to this tyrant of the sea, especially alone? But, for the first time it seemed, the companions nodded in agreement. They would trust Nalgene.

He smiled and opened the bottle.

Immediately, Nalgene felt a spiritual connection with the clear water within, as if it was forged from his very life force. A warm embrace enveloped the gnome, and he felt at peace in a world of destruction.

The water swirled out of the bottle, dancing above Nalgene's head in a tantalizing vortex. It seemed to grow and shrink, as if volume was never a construct of the miraculous liquid. It ebbed and flowed, listening to Nalgene's every thought and will. It was part of him. It *was* him. The old him. But there was no time to marvel. He looked up to the undead serpent, and with a wave of his hand, sent the shimmering water at the rotting abomination.

The sparkling water soared through the air, but instead of crushing the decaying beast with some terrifying power, it simply covered the serpent, swirling about it in its marvelous dance. Without warning, the water plunged, flowing into the serpent's very being, through the rotting holes and across the exposed ribs, saturating everything with its own will — the will of Nalgene.

Immediately, Nalgene felt a connection, a bonding, with the serpent. He was seeing the world from two perspectives: one of his, and the other of the serpent's. He felt the unholy strength of the serpent, its rippling muscles twisting and pulling with terrifying power. The misty lake lapped against his serpentine body, and he looked down at the shore, the swarm of undead and his companions looking like mere insects to be crushed underfoot. Yet at the same time, he was still the gnome, able to move and breathe with his other body. He was both — together, but still separate.

Nalgene smiled. This bottle was a wondrous gift indeed.

The serpent opened its mighty maw, releasing another thunderous roar. It coiled up, and like a viper, it plunged into the horde. Its sword-like teeth cut through the undead, and Nalgene felt the rush of black blood cover his mouth and heard the sickly *crunch* of bones as he crushed the vile creatures. His companions darted back in surprise, expressions of terror upon their faces. But as they looked up to the serpent, their mouths fell in awe. Instead of the two hollow eyes that they were expecting, they instead found two, deep blue eyes. The eyes of Nalgene. The serpent nodded its head and tried to give the best smile it could manage before plunging back at the undead and devastating another mouthful.

Meanwhile, the gnome continued his barrage of powerful spells, raining water down upon the battlefield. Litters of undead bodies piled up around the companions. Still more came. The gnome peered up at the foothills, where more skeleton mages were gathering, matching his torrents of water with their own display of ice. Yet there was something else coming, something bigger.

"Undead giant," Ro gasped, looking up to the foothills. "We can't keep going like this."

Margaret's face spun to see the hulking beast and she smiled; her demonic fist clenched at her side. "More fun for us," she snarled.

But Nalgene had other ideas.

"I can deal with that … er … I can," the gnome said, pointing up to the serpent. The companions shook their heads, at a loss, but they would not argue.

They had to trust Nalgene.

The undead giant stomped down the foothills, crushing

many undead under its hulking feet. Its bulky arms swung about, tearing up the earth and swatting away any unfortunate being in its path of destruction. Upon seeing the serpent, the undead giant roared, issuing a challenge.

Nalgene was more than happy to accept.

The serpent smiled and reared its slender head, ready for the fatal strike. It watched as the giant stormed down the shore. Even the once gargantuan beast seemed small in the presence of the serpent. With terrifying speed, the serpent snapped forward, its maw clamping down upon the giant. The teeth tore through the creature's rotting flesh, and another surge of putrid blood filled the serpent's mouth. The serpent whipped its head up, its decaying muscles straining to lift the giant high into the air. The serpent clenched its jaw, grinding down upon the bones of the great giant. Any normal creature would have been long dead, but undead do not feel pain, so the giant persisted.

Clenching its fists, the giant pummeled the head of the serpent, battering and tearing at the great skull. The serpent couldn't feel the pain, but Nalgene certainly could, and his head rocked in explosions of pain. Each strike felt like a hammer against an anvil. The serpent growled and bit harder, its teeth cleaving through bone and flesh. There was a *crunch*, a sickly tearing, and the serpent's jaw snapped shut. Blood and gore flowed down the serpent's maw, and the undead giant fell to the beach, severed in two.

The companions could only watch the spectacle in amazement. An undead giant, an abomination that they could barely defeat with their combined might, now lay severed upon the beach. Yet as much as Nalgene would like to celebrate, his head throbbed from the battering. He had no idea how long he could retain control of the serpent, and he would hate to unleash it back upon his companions.

The serpent scanned the mayhem, searching for its next meal. It was not disappointed. Four more undead giants approached the shore. The serpent smiled. It had made short work of the first.

Surely this would be no different.

Yet looking closer, the serpent saw it was not just more hulking giants approaching. No, there was a woman, an evil fragment of a Demigod who had long ago succumbed to the cause of the Shadow. She had gray skin and white hair. Two swirling wings of darkness sprouted from her back, and a mighty black greataxe was held comfortably in her small hand. She looked up, her two burning red eyes locking onto the serpent.

Nalgene reeled, a wave of pure, agonizing hatred washing through him. His mind pounded with pain; each heartbeat seemed like a knife stabbing into his ribs. He had to get out of here. His dream ... never before had Nalgene been so simply terrified.

He had to get the others out.

The serpent lowered its head, resting upon the sandy shore. The gnome rushed about, frantically waving his hands.

"Get on, will ye!" the gnome ordered, leaving no room for debate. They had to leave.

Nalgene already felt his grip on the serpent weakening, and a heavy exhaustion started gnawing at the edges of his mind.

The companions looked at the gnome, obviously confused.

"Get on the bloody serpent, ye dolts!" the gnome shouted. Just as the words left his mouth, a thunderous chorus of roars filled the air, and the four undead giants began their devastating charge down to the lake.

The woman had not yet arrived.

Nalgene watched the battle, his mind growing heavy and slow. This was the only way. They had to leave.

Frustrated, the gnome stomped over to the serpent, and climbed upon its head, using the jutting spines as handholds. The companions looked to the serpent, and then back to the oncoming giants. What other choice did they have? They were all worn, beaten by the endless tide of vile undead. Gashes and bruises covered their bodies, and a shard of ice protruded from Ro's sturdy shoulder.

"C'mon, will ye?" the gnome growled, beckoning. There

was no time. She was coming.

Nalgene hoped his hold on the serpent would last.

With no other option, the companions rushed to the serpent. Ro helped SmibSmob up, but he remained upon the shore until everyone else was already on. Fasto and Andromeda came next, following hastily by Margaret. Finally, Ro leaped up and found a place at the back of the serpent's head.

The serpent shot up, turning away from the shore.

"Take us across!" the gnome shouted, frantically looking behind him. There was no sign of the woman. Without hesitation, the serpent obliged, and snaked through the black waters of the lake, keeping its head just above the murky water. And so, the companions went into the thick mist of the lake, away from the undead. They would never know the horror that Nalgene saw approaching.

Nalgene felt his grip on the serpent slip and he returned, once again becoming wholly the gnome. Somehow, he knew that the serpent would continue its journey across the lake, but he doubted it would listen to him after that.

His whole body ached, and his head throbbed uncontrollably. He reached into his cloak and pulled out his crystalline bottle. It was dull, empty of its glittering contents. He felt somehow less, as if he had lost a part of himself with the use of the bottle, and yet somehow free. Nalgene glanced down to the undead serpent, then back to the bottle. What a wondrous gift indeed.

He lay back upon the serpent, exhaustion threatening to overcome him. As his eyes closed, he felt a soothing presence in his mind. It was a swirling, shaping water that coursed through his thoughts, washing everything away. The impenetrable walls within his mind crumbled, and some of the lost memories came rushing back.

Everything went black.

Daniel Whitman

Chapter 11

Fasto clutched onto the undead serpent with every ounce of willpower he could muster. His poor, dim-witted mind could barely comprehend what was happening. He knew they were fighting the massive swarm of undead, and they were losing — that was obvious even to him. And then when the massive serpent burst forth from the black depths of the misty lake, he knew it was all over. It would be the end, and he would go out protecting his friends. For that was what was important to him. Fasto protect friends. But right as he was willing to give his life, Nalgene conjured a magical, confusing, stream of water, and before Fasto could attempt to figure out what was happening, the rotting serpent began fighting on *their* side. Fasto was sure it had even smiled.

Fasto shook his head vigorously, his struggling brain working overtime to figure it all out. But it was beyond the scope of his simple thoughts.

And so, he held on to the undead serpent as it soared across the black lake, carrying the companions through the dense fog. Fasto looked at the others, who seemed similarly stunned at the miraculous turn of events. Ro and Margaret were on edge, their two heads swiveling about as if expecting another ghastly beast to attack them at any moment. Andromeda stared blankly into the cold fog. While her face was as hard as the serpent's iron scales, her eyes shone with a life such that Fasto had not seen since the prison so long ago. SmibSmob was next to his brother, a comforting hand on Nalgene's shoulder. Fasto stared at the unconscious gnome for a long moment. It was because of Nalgene that they survived the endless torrent of undead. The gnome's face was pale, and his hand was clenched around his marvelous, crystalline bottle. Fasto clenched his fist. Nalgene had protected Fasto, so Fasto would protect Nalgene.

Fasto protect friends.

The undead serpent kept its swift pace across the murky lake. It was hard to tell how far they had already traveled, or how much farther they still had to go, as the dense fog disoriented their sense of direction. All the companions could do was hold on and pray that the rotting behemoth beneath them would not have a sudden change of heart. After what seemed like an eternity, the serpent finally slowed and came to rest upon the opposite shore of the lake.

Like an obedient dog, the serpent lowered its head to the sandy beach and patiently waited for the companions to dismount. Without hesitation, the companions eagerly rushed off the serpent, casting wary gazes as they slowly backed away. Fasto waited until the others had climbed off the serpent's mighty crown, making sure that everyone reached the ground safely. As SmibSmob crawled down, the frail gnome tried to carry Nalgene upon his scrawny shoulders, with little success.

Without hesitation, Fasto swooped in and snatched the unconscious gnome from SmibSmob, easily hoisting him upon his own shoulders. SmibSmob's head whipped back, his eyes wide with alarm. But Fasto merely smiled, his ugly, toothy grin doing little to put the gnome at ease.

After a long pause, SmibSmob finally relented and climbed down the serpent. Proud of his friendly deed, Fasto was quick to follow.

As soon as Fasto placed his feet on the sandy ground, the serpent jerked up, its powerful head snapping back like the tip of a whip. Its terrifying maw opened wide, displaying the rows of spear-like teeth and the endless void of its throat. Its eyes cut across the companions, and they shrunk back from its dreadful gaze. But it did not attack. It clamped its maw shut, and without so much as a roar, it turned and disappeared into the black waves of the misty lake.

The companions stood petrified; their breaths caught in their throats. They had all seen the unparalleled power of the rotting abomination, and how it had so effortlessly dismantled the undead giant. They were less than eager to challenge it. So, they stood watch, their eyes scanning the suffocating fog, but the serpent did not return.

When their nerves settled, the rush of exhaustion from the battle overcame them like a churning tsunami, drowning them in fatigue. Without Nalgene, they had no real way to mend their many wounds. Every cut seared with fire and every bruise pulsed with pain. All they could do was hope Nalgene would wake from unconsciousness. Defeated, the companions were barely able to build a makeshift camp on the sandy shore before they collapsed into a deep slumber.

♦   ♦   ♦

Fasto awoke to the distant light from the cold sun. His entire body ached from the previous day's ordeals, but he managed to shake himself awake. He had been the first to rise. He scanned the surrounding landscape. Even though the gray sun was almost at its zenith, it seemed darker, and more forlorn, than it had before. It was as if a permeable darkness was covering the land, casting it into an even deeper pit of despair. To the north lay the misty lake, its fog lessened from the previous day. A wide river flowed from the lake not a hundred paces to the west, making barely a sound as it wound to the south, where the land grew even darker — as if the very Shadow was growing from that direction. As Fasto gazed to the south, his eyes rested upon a swirling black in the near distance, and an unnatural chill crawled across his body. A heart of darkness. An edifice of shadow.

A Dreadring.

Unsettled, Fasto turned away, unable to quite grasp the vile scope of darkness he was witnessing. But while he was not sure what the swirling blackness was, he was sure that he did not want to go anywhere near it. He shivered, and he had the sense that he would much rather been in a comforting forest, away from all the despair.

Fasto glanced back at the others, who were still fast asleep. Fasto smiled, this was his opportunity. There was no doubt in his mind that his companions were lost, and that they had little idea where they were. Fasto would fix that. Fasto would help his friends. And the sand made a perfect canvas. Determination burning within his eyes, Fasto removed an arrow from his endless quiver, and gripped it tightly in his hands.

With a feral growl, he plunged the arrow into the sandy earth, and immediately tore it across, creating a massive score in the cold ground. Smiling, he continued gashing and tearing with his white arrow, sending a cloud of gray sand into the still air. A slash here, a line there, and a swirl over there. This was truly his time to shine. This would be his masterpiece. Sweat began beading upon his forehead as he continued to create his grand map. His mind churned, desperately trying to remember the path that the companions had traveled on since their rescue from the prison. Another gash, and a sketchy drawing of an undead behemoth.

Fasto became so engrossed in his marvelous cartography that he did not notice the approach of the other companions, who had been awakened by the constant rain of sand. His hands reached high up to the sky, ready to make the final plunge to complete his map. He growled, but before he could finish the strike, a gentle hand rested on his shoulder, breaking him from his trance. Startled, Fasto dropped the white arrow and scrambled to his feet, scuffing some of the sand of his map.

Ro stared at Fasto, a concerned look on his face. Behind him stood Andromeda and a very disgruntled Margaret, who was brushing sand from her hair.

"Fasto," the draconian started. "What are you doing?"

Fasto smiled, a proud pillar of light illuminating his mind. Because of him, his friends would no longer be lost in this shadowy land. He would be their guide through the trenches of destruction.

"Fasto make map," he said proudly. "Fasto help friends!"

"You certainly helped us lose sleep, that's for sure," Margaret growled.

"Another map, huh?" Ro sighed.

"That is definitely not a map." Andromeda piped in, her tail twitching mischievously. She glanced down, and ran a paw through the map, wiping away some of Fasto's hard work.

Fasto scrambled over to stop the feline. He would not let anything destroy his work. It was his gift to his friends. Laughing, Andromeda skipped away, just out of reach. The poor orc glanced down to his handiwork, the mess of gashes, lines, and swirls looking like absolute madness scribbled into the sand. He nodded. Perfect.

"Uh, what is this supposed to be a map of, my friend?" Ro asked, trying to humor the dull orc. He tried to search for some kind of pattern, but it appeared to be utter nonsense.

"A map of his dull mind, that's what," Margaret spat, turning away with a scowl darkening her face.

Fasto was not quite sure what she meant by that. Looking back at Ro, he gestured around. "Everything Fasto see," he said.

Ro glanced around at the surrounding land, then back to the scribbles in the cold sand. "Ah, right," he stammered. "Obviously."

Before he could continue to entertain Fasto, a rustling sound caught his attention.

SmibSmob, now awake, approached from behind Ro, anxiety dragging his steps through the earth.

"Nalgene is still unconscious," he said, his voice low and grim. As he neared, his eyes were drawn to the tangle of gashes behind Fasto. "As much as your ... er ... map is a great help, I'm worried for my brother."

SmibSmob seemed small without the support of his brother. "I hope —"

Before the frail gnome could finish, a deafening screeching sound cut through the air, driving deep into the companion's minds and grinding against their bones. The sound was far from natural, like a knife sliding across a steel plate. Their heads whipped around, searching for the source of the infernal cry. Nothing. The land was barren.

Another diabolical screech, and the companions scrambled back, desperately trying to protect themselves from the horrendous sound. But the harsh noise burned into their minds, scrambling their thoughts and numbing their bodies.

Fasto's eyes cut across the black land. If only he were in a forest. He always felt safe, and at home, in the arms of the oaken trees. But this land was desolate, with no protection for Fasto.

With nowhere safe he could protect his friends.

"Looks like we have some company," Margaret managed to growl through the pain of the shriek, pointing to the south.

Appearing from the forsaken land like some ghastly specter of death was a large, horrifying wraith. A draping tattered black cloak covered the undead creature's skeletal figure, and a dark hood shadowed the pale face. An aura of cold surrounded the rotting ghoul, leaching and suffocating whatever life may have been left in the surrounding land. Reaching out were two claws, their razor ends glittering with an icy promise of finality. But shining out from underneath the hood, like two chasms of icy doom, were two blue eyes, driving a freezing fear deep into the companions.

Exactly like the dreadknight's.

The companions reeled back under the pressuring glare of the wraith. All thoughts of Fasto's map fled from their minds, and they scrambled to ready their weapons against the approaching menace. But their wounds were still not healed, and so their weapons felt slow and clumsy as they readied them.

Fasto unslung his brilliant bow and nocked a white arrow. Drawing the string, he took aim at the undead horror. It was a sure shot. Yet his arm was unsteady, and the dreadful gaze of the wraith cut deep into him, causing his once steadfast arm to shake.

Fasto growled under his breath, and he clenched his teeth in denial. Fasto *will* protect his friends.

He took aim once more, his eyes gleaming with a raging ferocity.

The arrow loosed, cutting through the air like a white beam of light.

Fasto watched with cool certainty. It was a sure shot.

The arrow thudded into the soft ground behind the wraith without so much as glancing the approaching terror. The arrow had missed its target. Fasto had missed!

The companions turned to Fasto, their eyes wide with shock. Through all their battles in the Shadow, they had never once seen Fasto miss a shot. Even amid raging battles where they were darting about in a desperate attempt to remain alive, Fasto always managed to weave the arrows through the mayhem to strike his targets. But now, with the shackles of exhaustion and terror heavy on his arms, Fasto had missed.

Fasto glanced down to his bow, his eyes burning with betrayal. No, he never missed. It must be the bow. The bow had betrayed him. No other explanation came to his dull mind. It must be the bow. It could not possibly be that he was worn from the previous battle. No. Fasto never missed.

But while Fasto was lost studying his bow, the wraith pounced upon the companions, its icy claws cutting frosty gashes through the air. Its deathly aura leached at the companions' life force, draining what little energy they had. Its cold blue eyes instilled a deep terror within them, sapping their very will to fight.

Ro raised his mighty greatsword and with a thunderous roar charged the wraith, his sword cutting across in a lethal arc. Shrieking, the wraith turned to the draconian, its dreadful gaze halting Ro's heroic attack. Its claws flashed, and four massive gashes appeared on the draconian's arm, drawing a spray of thick blood. Ro howled in pain, and he glanced down at his arm. A vile frost began seeping from the wounds, freezing his arm. His greatsword dropped to the ground. Snarling, he grabbed his shining longsword and strung his iron shield to his injured arm as best he could manage.

Andromeda appeared from the shadows behind the wraith and pounced upon its cloaked back, her claws tearing at the undead flesh beneath. Enraged, the wraith flailed about, its claws cutting across in a chilling slash. Just before the massive claws could rend Andromeda's face, Ro plowed into the wraith, driving it to the ground in a tangle of cloak and claw.

Shaken, Andromeda gently caressed her face, searching for any signs of frost or damage. That could have been her end. Finding none, she gave a ferocious hiss, and her halberd appeared in her slender hand.

Throwing Ro away like a limp rag doll, the wraith rose into the air, its two blue chasms blazing with an unholy fury. It would end these miserable specks of fire. It turned to Andromeda, eager to finish the deed. But before it could soar at the feline, a shard of ice crashed into it, driving hard into its rotting shoulder. Yet the shard was small and fragile — nothing like the mighty shards from before. Margaret stood next to Andromeda, her demonic arm pulsing weakly at her side, her eyes clouded by doubt.

The wraith barely noticed the pitiful attack, and with

another horrifying screech, it charged, its icy claws cutting in a whirlwind of death.

Fasto glanced up to the chaos. Ro lay on the ground, struggling to get to his feet, his arm frozen. Andromeda and Margaret danced away from the wraith, barely avoiding lethal strikes from the claws. SmibSmob cowered over his brother, ready to give his own life to protect Nalgene's. And what was Fasto doing? Was he protecting his friends? No. He shook his head, the scrambling sounds of the battle breaking through his jumbled thoughts. He had missed, yes. But that did not mean he had to sit by and watch as his friends were dismantled by the undead menace. A feral growl escaped Fasto's lips.

Fasto would protect his friends.

His eyes two red infernos, Fasto dropped his bow and scooped a few stones from the ground. Time seemed to move in slow-motion for the orc. Raising his arm, he took aim at the ghastly creature.

Fasto would protect his friends.

The stone whistled through the air. And another. Two holes appeared in the wraith's flowing cloak.

The wraith whipped around to face Fasto, its icy eyes boring into the orc. Yet Fasto held his ground. He would face the very Goddess for his friends, so what would this wraith be? He released his remaining stones, and they bounced on the ground by his side. He unstrung his quiver and raised his two fists up before him. He would protect his friends. He did not need some traitorous bow to help him with that.

The wraith's eyes burned, and its frosty claws flashed across. The companions watched on with utter horror. What was this dull orc doing? But Fasto had unwavering confidence. He would protect his friends. He would defeat this unholy beast.

He was delusional.

The icy claws slashed, cutting across Fasto's forearms with a wide spray of blood, and tossing the orc to the ground. The icy gashes burned like a touch from death, and the frost began to spread from the gruesome wounds, freezing Fasto's arms. Fasto glanced at his arms in shock. This was not how it was supposed to be. He was supposed to protect his friends. He tried to move his fingers, but they would not respond to his will.

The wraith reared up to finish the dumbfounded orc, but Ro barreled into it from behind, knocking it away from Fasto.

"We need to run!" the draconian shouted as he crashed into the wraith. "I'll keep it busy!"

They could not hope to win this fight. Ro's arm was frozen, and he was unable to effectively wield his weapons. Both Margaret and Andromeda panted heavily, even though the battle had barely just begun. SmibSmob refused to leave his brother's side and was watching with dismay.

Growling, Fasto rose to his feet and brushed off the sand. His arms were shaking, the frost enveloping his forearms. He turned to the wraith, which was leering down upon an unconscious Ro, its deadly claws about to rend the draconian's head. Ro was right. They had to run. There would be no winning this battle. Not now. But something kept Fasto from turning away, something else Ro had shouted:

I'll keep it busy.

Ro was protecting his friends. So Fasto would protect him.

Growling away his pain, Fasto rushed at the wraith, his boots thundering across the ground in a furious stampede. Fasto did not need his bow. He tried to bring his fists to bear, but his forearms were frozen, and his hands would no longer heed his commands. Fine. Fasto did not need his fists.

A feral snarl escaping his lips, Fasto crashed into the wraith, his shoulder barreling into the creature's rotting back. He did not slow. The deathly aura sapped at his strength, but he kept pushing, driving the undead away from his friend. The wraith shrieked and turned upon the orc.

But Andromeda was there, pouncing upon the wraith and

tearing it to the ground.

Fasto did not notice. His focus was on Ro, who was ready to give his life for the others. A true friend. Reaching down, he wrapped his frozen arms around the draconian's battered body, and with a strained growl, hoisted the mighty draconian onto his shoulder. Ro's shining sword and shield fell to the ground, but the orc did not notice. Fasto would protect his friends.

"Follow me!" SmibSmob called to Fasto, attempting to drag Nalgene toward the nearby river. Perhaps if they crossed the river, they would be safe from the terrifying wraith. It was futile endeavor, but it gave them hope. And that was what the companions needed.

Fasto glanced at the frail gnome and nodded. Growling with every breath, he marched to SmibSmob. His legs grew weary, but he could not stop until his friends were safe. He would not. He reached down with his free arm and cupped it around the unconscious gnome. His eyes burning with a roaring determination, he hoisted Nalgene onto his other shoulder and began his slow-yet-steady trek to the river. His legs ached under the added weight, and his body urged him to collapse into the soft sand. But he did not. Fasto would not. Fasto would protect his friends.

SmibSmob watched the orc with awe and respect. So what if the dull orc could not put together a coherent sentence? He did not need to. His actions spoke for him.

Fasto marched away. Behind him, Andromeda and Margaret still wrestled with the dreadful wraith in a failing attempt to buy the others time. He did not notice. His mind was solely focused on the river and the two he held upon his shoulders. He did not even notice when SmibSmob retrieved his bow and quiver from the ground.

Another step. Another step closer to safety. Every step was arduous for Fasto, yet still he pushed on. He would not stop.

Forty more strides.

His ruby eyes flared.

Thirty more strides.

The wraith unleashed another bone-cutting shriek, but Fasto did not turn. SmibSmob marched along beside him, his hands clutching the orc's weapons as if they were precious children. From behind, Andromeda came darting past, her breath coming in short, pained gasps, and her back covered with a frosty slash. Margaret followed soon after, and she looked no better off than the feline. They had fought against the wraith with every ounce of their strength, but it was not enough.

"We couldn't hold it," Margaret gasped, her voice barely audible. "It's coming."

Fasto nodded, but he did not slow and did not look back.

Twenty more strides.

The icy aura from the wraith washed over the companions, and another screech penetrated the still air. It was right behind them, its two eyes burning like funeral pyres. They would not escape it. The river would not help them, as it could easily float across the flowing water. Its icy claws flashed out, frosty flakes falling from their razor ends. They would not escape it.

The companions did not turn, for how could they? All they had left was the river. And so, they pushed forward.

Ten more strides.

SmibSmob cried out in pain and collapsed to the ground, an icy gash across his back. Fasto's bow and quiver fell to the ground by the orc's feet. The wraith had caught them. There was no more hope. The companions turned, their eyes wide with horror. They could not escape the wraith. As the solemn fact settled over them, the hope in their eyes sputtered out. Only Fasto remained strong in the face of such despair.

All they could do was watch as the wraith hovered above SmibSmob, its glinting claw ready to end the gnome's life. Its blue eyes seared with an infernal fire, and yet another diabolical shriek echoed forth from the wraith. Yet it did not strike.

The companions watched dumbfounded as the wraith stood frozen above the gnome. Its skeletal arm trembled, yearning to slash at the gnome. Yet it could not.

An obsidian butterfly rested upon the wraith's arm.

A gentle sound came from the river, as if a boat was coasting through the mild waves. The companions turned. Sure enough, there was Ashyla, sitting upon the bow of a beautiful, white boat. Swirls and engravings covered the hull of the boat in a decorative mosaic, and a large, twisting mast rose from the center. There was no sail.

The Goddess was draped in her silky, black dress, and her golden jewelry glittered even in the absence of light. She appeared distracted and was busy studying the marvelous sword she held in her hand. She was mumbling to herself, and she kept gently shaking her head. One could only wonder what preoccupied her fractured mind.

"Oh, look who it is again," Margaret sneered. "Back to taunt us some more."

Ashyla did not look up.

Fasto gazed at Ashyla, then back to the frozen wraith, and then to his bow upon the ground. He was as lost as ever in Ashyla's winding webs, yet one thing seemed obvious to him. The wraith was Ashyla's doing. She had once again tried to kill his friends. It was unacceptable. His eyes two raging infernos, and a rumbling growl escaping his lips, he gently set Ro and Nalgene down upon the ground and reached for his white bow. His hand would not close upon the sleek wood, as his forearm was still frozen. Undeterred, he brought his arm to bear in front of him. He just had to unfreeze it.

With a sickening *crunch*, he slammed his arm down upon his knee, shattering the ice. An explosion of pain bolted through the orc as his frozen muscles stretched and tore, and his bones cracked. But he growled through it. His gaze was locked upon the approaching Goddess. He brought his other arm up, and with the same grisly fortitude, shattered it upon his knee. Blood oozed from his mangled forearms, and they trembled violently under the severe wounds. But that would not stop Fasto.

He would face the very Goddess for his friends.

He grasped his white bow tightly in his hand, his arm roaring in protest. Fasto would give his bow this chance at redemption. His thick blood oozed down his hand and stained the once-brilliant wood a deep crimson. He grabbed an arrow with his other hand and nocked it in the bow. His body would only allow for one shot. He brought the bow to aim and drew the string. Everything shook violently, but his gaze was locked on Ashyla. Fasto only missed once.

The arrow loosed, rocketing forward in a blinding streak of light. The bow fell from Fasto's hands, and his arms fell limp by his side. He would protect his friends. The arrow spiraled through the air directly at the center of her chest. Fasto wouldn't miss again.

And he didn't. The arrow met the woman's chest, but rather than piercing and burning her twisted heart, it simply passed *through* her as if she were a ghost.

Fasto grunted in dismay. There was no damage. His bow had failed, not once, but twice. First it missed, and now it didn't even injure Ashyla. He couldn't understand.

Fasto would never trust his bow again.

Ashyla's frightening gaze shot up; her focus regained. She glanced down at her chest and erupted in a wild cackle. After regaining her composure, a smile appeared on her rosy lips.

"Is that how you greet your friend?" she said.

The companions watched Ashyla in shock. Fasto *did* hit her, right? SmibSmob had crawled out from underneath the frozen wraith and was crouching next to Nalgene. Both Andromeda and Margaret were ready to strike at a moment's notice, with Andromeda's tail slashing violently and Margaret's arm pulsing uncontrollably. Fasto merely glared.

The white boat came to a rest in front of the companions, stopping on the riverbed.

"I thought you would be happy to see me again," Ashyla chided playfully.

"What do you want?" Andromeda asked, her voice steady. She would not let another outburst happen again. She had had much time to think about their last encounter with the Goddess, and she refused to let Ashyla toy with her emotions.

Ashyla glanced down to the feline, noticing Andromeda's newfound resolve.

"My dear Andromeda, I did not strike you as so impatient. Did you think on my offer?" she teased. "Are you going to let it all slip away?"

Andromeda growled, but she did not falter. "Answer the question."

Ashyla shrugged, unconcerned, and gestured to the boat. "Is it not obvious?" she said. "I am here to save you. Again. You are making this quite the habit for me."

"Right," Margaret snorted. "Is that what you did to the Captain? *Save* him from the Shadow?"

Ashyla smiled. "I saved him from his mistakes, if not necessarily the Shadow. He deserved that much."

"You killed him. And you would have killed us," Andromeda hissed, her halberd appearing in her hand.

Ashyla appeared hurt, and she reeled back under Andromeda's harsh accusation, putting a hand over her mouth in feign shock.

"When have I ever tried to kill you?" she asked. Her soft voice grew colder. "Poor Osann was a most troubled man. He knew what he deserved. I can assure you; it had nothing to do with you."

"Nobody deserves death," SmibSmob piped in, his voice seeming feeble in the presence of the imposing Goddess.

"Oh, is that truly what you think?" Ashyla asked, her gaze turning to the small gnome. "What of traitors? Liars? Murderers? Should someone who slaughters innocent children be permitted to live? My dear, it is never so simple."

"The Captain was a good man," Andromeda growled through clenched teeth. Margaret nodded in agreement.

Ashyla shrugged.

"Is that what he told you?" she asked. "Perhaps he was. Or perhaps you should have listened to your poor gnome when you had the chance."

Andromeda prepared to launch a cold retort, but Margaret cut her off.

"Are you here to taunt us?" Margaret asked. "To play with us? Or can we return to being slaughtered by the wraith?"

Ashyla sighed. "Are you not listening? I am here to save you."

"Why?" Andromeda asked, not hiding her skepticism.

"Call it … generosity."

Margaret let out an exasperated sigh, throwing up her arms in defeat. "This is going nowhere," she snarled. "Time to wake up the wraith."

Just as she spoke the words, another howling screech cut through the air — but not from the frozen wraith. Two icy eyes ignited across the river, and another terrifying wraith appeared from the shadows, its dark cloak swirling about in an icy aura. Raising its vicious claws, it began its steady approach.

Alarmed, the companions turned back to Ashyla. If they could not defeat a single wraith, what hope did they have against two?

"Why should we trust you?" Andromeda asked, growing frantic. She was less than eager to battle with another wraith.

Ashyla smiled. "I am afraid you do not have a choice." She raised her hand, and the frozen wraith jerked forward before returning to its frozen state. She glanced down at her sword, then back up to the companions. "We have the same goal, so why not help each other?"

"No," Andromeda said unwavering. She glanced down to the unconscious Ro before looking upon Ashyla once more. "No," she repeated, her voice softer.

Ashyla shrugged again.

"Perhaps not," she said softly. "Perhaps you should not be permitted to live." Her eyes met the companions once more, and she disappeared into a swarm of black butterflies, soaring off into the still air.

Andromeda turned to the others.

"Let's go," she ordered, leaping aboard the white boat.

"Unbelievable," Margaret grumbled under her breath. Shaking her head, she glanced up to Andromeda. With a sigh, she boarded the boat.

Fasto watched the exchange with dull confusion. There was too much gray in this shadowy world, too much ambiguity. He needed black and white. Fasto needed his friends. Shrugging, and eager to escape the two wraiths, he reached down and hauled Nalgene and Ro back upon his strong shoulders. SmibSmob grabbed the orc's bow and quiver. Even if the orc was too dim-witted to keep them, the gnome knew how valuable these weapons could be.

The wraith across the river released another shriek, and the butterfly that was perched upon the frozen wraith fell off its arm, flapping away. It had completed its job.

Enraged, the wraith shot forward, its icy claw slashing through the air with a harsh whistle. Its eyes shot up, locking upon the companions. It would end what it started. Howling, it charged at Fasto, who was scrambling to board the boat.

Fasto watched the approaching wraith with steady resolve. He would be the last to board the boat. Fasto would protect his friends. With a strained grunt, he heaved Ro up to the deck, and Nalgene followed soon after.

The wraith's eyes bore into him, cutting into his mind, and bringing his nightmares to life.

"Faster you idiot!" Margaret cried. The other wraith was already futilely slashing at the side of the boat, but its claws just went right through it! Normally, this would give the companions pause, but they didn't have time to ponder the oddity.

Holding his broken arms out, Fasto grabbed SmibSmob,

and with a hiss of pain, launched him up to the deck. He would be the last to board. He would protect his friends.

The wraith lunged, its icy claws reaching forward like a fractured spear.

Fasto leaped up, just avoiding the deadly strike, and crawled up to the deck, both Andromeda and Margaret pulling him to safety. As soon as he lay on the deck, the boat lurched and pulled away from the shore, turning downstream. The wraiths screeched in rage, and followed in hot pursuit, but the white boat was too swift. There was no wind, and no sail, yet still it soared down the winding river in an eerily smooth ride.

Fasto glanced at the others. Ro lay unconscious next to him, the draconian's body covered with frosty gashes and frozen blood. Yet he was breathing. Fasto smiled. He had protected his friend. Nalgene was still unconscious and was clutching his crystalline bottle in a calloused hand. SmibSmob sat next to his brother, his breath ragged from the strain of the encounter. Both Andromeda and Margaret watched at the bow of the boat, their eyes searching the distant horizon. A tangible respect sparked between them, and they seemed closer than ever. Perhaps fighting side-by-side for each other's lives could create such bonds.

Satisfied, Fasto laid back, casting his gaze up to the cold, gray sky above. It was no forest canopy, but still it soothed him all the same. A warm sensation covered the boat, as if it were a safe haven, a sort of salvation. Exhausted, the orc was more than content with letting the white ship drift off to sea. The barren landscape trotted by, and desolate plains of murky shadow passed without any sign of movement. The massive storm of shadow, the Dreadring, that Fasto had seen to the south drifted by with the land, was soon to be forgotten. There was no indication of where the companions were going, or when they would finally stop, but Fasto did not care. He had protected his friends, even without his damned bow.

Fasto smiled.

Chapter 12

Ro opened his eyes. His entire body was bruised and battered from the scramble against the wraith, with gruesome gashes now scabbed over from the undead ghoul's vicious claws.

What happened?

He shook his head, his vision growing clear, and he glanced around. He was laying upon a bed of white sand, a cloak gently placed over him like a makeshift blanket. A salty breeze tickled his nose, and the faint crashes of the ocean waves murmured in the background.

Where was he?

Beside Ro lay Nalgene, who was still unconscious from his heroic efforts with the undead serpent, his crystalline bottle still clenched in his iron grip. SmibSmob's purple cloak lay across the sleeping gnome. Not ten paces away, the rest of the companions sat huddled around a dim, flickering fire, their eyes lost within the dancing flames. They all looked just as ragged and beaten as Ro. Both Andromeda and Margaret were covered with bruises and scratches, and Fasto's arms were mangled and shattered. Behind the companions, was the shore of the lonely beach. There was no sign of any boat, but of course, Ro didn't know there was supposed to be a boat.

The last thing Ro remembered was his final charge against the wraith in an attempt to save the others. He remembered the wraith's fearsome claws, and its terrifying blue eyes. And the pain … But after that, his mind was empty. So how did he get here?

As much as his mind yearned for the answers to these mysteries, a sudden realization captured his thoughts. The others were safe! Battered and bruised, yes, but alive and safe, nonetheless.

Shaking his head once more, and convincing himself this was not some dastardly illusion, Ro slowly rose to his feet, his muscles straining with the effort. As he rose, the companions looked up from the tantalizing fire, their expressions lighting with joy. A wide smile beamed on SmibSmob's face, and he began running toward Ro. While Margaret's face remained stoic, her eyes betrayed her happiness. Andromeda waited patiently behind the others, a genuine smile on her lips. Upon seeing Ro, Fasto howled with glee, and bolted over to the draconian, overtaking SmibSmob, and smothering Ro with a warm embrace — or as best an embrace as he could manage with his broken arms.

"Friend safe!" Fasto cried. Ro could have sworn the orc was sobbing. "Fasto protect friend!" The orc detached himself from Ro and proudly held up his shattered arms for Ro to see. "Fasto help dragon friend! Fasto break arms!"

Unsure of how to respond to Fasto, but not wanting to diminish the orc's overwhelming joy, Ro simply smiled and nodded, hoping the dull orc would accept his answer.

"Ah, don't mind him," SmibSmob chuckled, finally catching up to Fasto. "He … uh … well, he did protect you, that's for sure."

"He almost got himself killed, is more like it," Margaret teased Fasto. Of course, it went straight over the orc's head. Shaking her head, Margaret jogged over to Ro, a smile finally breaking through her stoicism.

"It's good to have you back," she said. "With both you and Nalgene gone, it was getting rather boring. Who knew I would actually miss your arguments?"

Ro chuckled and nodded his head. He was still quite overwhelmed by it all, but he figured it would work itself out eventually.

"Right," he stammered, finding it difficult to express his joy and relief. "I'm glad you are all alright. I figured, when I charged that wraith, that …"

He shook his head, unwilling to finish the thought.

"Mmmm, you had nothing to worry about," Andromeda purred, finally joining the merry gathering. She moved to stand beside Ro, her tail gently brushing against his back. She knew what he was going to say. They all knew what he was going to say.

"This hero had it all under control," she said, pointing to Fasto.

The orc beamed with pride, and he forcefully nodded his head. "Fasto protect friend! Fasto protect friends!" he began chanting, spittle flying from his mouth.

"Oh, now you've done it," Margaret sighed, rolling her eyes. Andromeda shot her a mischievous look.

"I'm sure he did," Ro chuckled. But his smile faded, and his voice grew serious. "But what happened? And where are we?"

It was time to get some answers.

"Ah, well," SmibSmob started, trying to speak over the chanting Fasto. "Fasto saved you from the wraith, and then … uh … well, the beautiful woman appeared on this boat, and, well, we climbed on and sailed away. After a couple days, we landed here. I reckon we're on some other continent, by the looks of it."

Ro studied the gnome for a moment, trying to wrap his mind around the story. "The beautiful woman?" he asked, his brow furrowing in thought. "As in the woman who killed the Captain?"

"The very same," Andromeda said.

Ro glanced over to the feline, expecting to see some hint of the turmoil that had once torn at her. There was none, and that pleased Ro.

The story was not piecing together in his mind, but he did not press the others. He still had no idea what boat they were referring to. He had no doubt they were speaking the truth, for why would they lie to him now?

"Well, it doesn't matter," Ro said, putting the matter behind him. Maybe the boat sailed away like the serpent. "What now?"

Fasto ceased his pointless chanting and fixed his gaze upon Ro. "Fasto follow dragon friend," he stated, giving his best attempt at a salute.

"Indeed," Andromeda purred, her sparkling eyes like two, swirling saucers. "Now, that you're finally awake, I was hoping you would tell us."

Ro paused at her words and scanned the companions. There they stood, awaiting his thoughts. Awaiting his lead. Even Margaret, although she would never admit to it. He opened his mouth, but closed it, and glanced around at the surrounding land. It was the same, barren wasteland of desolation. Not a single tree or shrub could be seen. There was only the churning ocean, and the vast expanse of forsaken plains.

What now indeed.

It was for him to decide. He opened his mouth once more, but before he could say anything, a loud coughing fit sounded by his feet.

"Bah!" Nalgene grunted, finally awaking from his unconsciousness. Grumbling, the rough gnome rose to his feet, dropped his miraculous bottle, and brushed the white sand from his blue cloak. He violently shook his head and looked around him. "What in the bloody hell?"

Before he could continue, he was smothered by an ecstatic SmibSmob, who wrapped his brother in a loving embrace, tears streaming down his thin face.

"Nalgene, my brother!" SmibSmob managed to say through his tears. "You're alright!"

Startled, Nalgene stumbled back a couple steps but quickly returned the embrace. "Ah, me brother, I never be better."

Ro watched the spectacle with a wide smile. There was true, brotherly love, and nothing would be able to break it.

"Well, isn't that nice," Margaret mumbled.

"Aye, ye damn orc," Nalgene growled, releasing his brother and stepping forward, a stubby finger pointed at Margaret. "I be hearin' that. So why don't ye be lettin' us have this moment, eh?"

Ro laughed. Somethings never change.

"Eh, did I be sayin' somethin' funny, ye damn dragon?" Nalgene shot, turning to face Ro, his face red with heated anger.

"Nalgene," SmibSmob whispered, placing a hand upon Nalgene's robust shoulder. But the frail gnome did not have to say anything else. Immediately, Nalgene's fuming facade fell away, and a brilliant smile appeared on the gnome's face.

"Bah! I be just messin' with ye, ye damn dragon!" Nalgene rushed forward and took the draconian's hand in a firm clasp. He turned to the others, his smile emitting an irresistible joy. "It be good to finally be back."

Ro glanced down to the gnome, stunned. Some things never change, right? Well, perhaps they do.

The others watched Nalgene with similar surprise. Even SmibSmob had not seen this turn coming.

"Ah, don't be lookin' too excited to be havin' me back," Nalgene joked. Grunting, he released Ro, and turned about, studying the surrounding land. "Now, where in the bloody hell are we? I be takin' it that the bloody serpent got us across the lake?"

SmibSmob chuckled. "We have a lot to tell you."

Ro smiled as the others filled Nalgene in on the recent events. He glanced down to his hand, still shocked by the gnome's behavior. For once, they had not burst into a raging argument. Nothing made sense to the draconian. From their arrival on another continent, to Nalgene's open friendliness, the pieces certainly did not fit in his mind. And Ro was content with that fact. He did not have to understand it. He just had to accept it.

"Eh, yer tellin' me we be on another bloody continent?" Nalgene roared, stamping his feet on the sandy ground.

Ro smiled. Some things never change.

"What in the bloody hell?" Nalgene continued, scratching his head in thought.

"It's true, look around you," Margaret said, gesturing to the desolate earth around them. "It looks completely different."

"Ah, I be seein' that, ye dolt," Nalgene snorted. "What I don't be seein' is some boat. Also, I be wonderin' why ye trusted that bloody butterfly witch."

"She didn't exactly give us much of a choice," Andromeda stated flatly, her tail twitching behind her. She glanced at the others in surprise. He couldn't see the boat?

"There always be a choice," Nalgene grumbled, shaking his head, apparently unconcerned with the missing vehicle. "Ah well, ye can't be changin' what ye did, ye can only be changin' what ye do."

"Aren't you the philosophical one?" Margaret shot at the gnome, a thin smile on her lips.

"Fasto friend wise," the orc said, his mouth agape in awe of Nalgene.

Nalgene snorted.

"Well, ye all be seemin' pretty beat up," he said, raising his hands. Water began to flow from his fingertips. "Let me see what I can be doin' to fix that."

One by one, Nalgene cast his healing magic across the companions, stitching together their many bloody gashes and mending their numerous swollen bruises. Energy coursed through them, and it became abundantly apparent how much they had taken Nalgene's soothing powers for granted. Without him, there was no doubt they would all be dead many times over. It was a fact they would not forget. As the gnome cast his swirling water over Ro, a humbling sense of gratitude filled the draconian. His blood washed away from him, and the frosty slices across his arm began to seal themselves shut. But as the slashes closed, Ro cut the gnome short, insisting that Nalgene allow the wound to fully heal by itself. After some persuasion, and a lot of being called a "beardless dwarf" and a "bloody dolt," Ro finally managed to convince Nalgene to end the healing. Ro hoped the gruesome gashes would scar to forever serve as a reminder of his arrogance.

When Nalgene reached Fasto, the gnome took Fasto's arms in a gentle grip.

"What in the bloody hell happened to ye, ye damn orc?" Nalgene murmured, studying the gruesome wounds. After a long moment, Nalgene began to heal the horrifying injuries, repairing the orc's arms and fusing bone back together.

But Fasto jerked his arms away from the gnome, a feral snarl appearing twisting his face. "No!" he screeched, retreating from the annoyed gnome. "Fasto protected friend!"

"Yeah, I get that, ye bloody dolt," Nalgene growled, staring down Fasto, his gaze shooting cold daggers of ice. "Now get yer arse over here so I can be healin' that mess."

Fasto planted his feet and stood steadfast against Nalgene's withering glare. "No," he repeated, shaking his head.

"Yer gonna get yerself killed," Nalgene callously stated. "We can't be protecting yer sorry arse out here."

Fasto matched the gnome's gaze, unwavering. "Then Fasto die." There was no questioning the orc's tone. He would not allow his arms to be completely healed.

Throwing his hands up in defeat, Nalgene turned away, shaking his head in disgust. "If ye die, that be on ye, ye bloody dolt."

After Nalgene had finished healing the other companions, they began to prepare to journey out into the ceaseless Shadow. They had no way of knowing where they were, or where they would be going, but that did not stop them. They had to move and hope that they would find some way out of the oppressive blackness. SmibSmob retrieved his purple cloak, which he had placed over Nalgene as a blanket. Andromeda and Margaret threw sand in the fire, smothering the remaining flames.

As Ro watched the others prepare, he noticed something — in fact three things — was missing. After a frantic glance around the makeshift camp, and much scuffing through the sand, he sighed in defeat.

Now he was defenseless.

Just for the sake of it, he scanned the beach one more time, but even with his heightened vision, he could not find his mighty weapons.

"Where are my weapons?" he asked SmibSmob, who stood nearby.

The gnome ran his eyes across Ro and then glanced around at the dismantled camp. He scratched his head, and then his blue eyes widened with realization.

"Ah, well … you see …" he stammered, obviously quite embarrassed. "When you were fighting with the wraith … ah … we left them on the other continent."

SmibSmob looked away from Ro and did not meet the draconian's steel gaze.

Ro studied the gnome for a minute, his mind flying back to his skirmish with the undead creature. He *had* dropped his greatsword, and he must have lost his sword and shield sometime while he was unconscious. Chuckling softly, he smiled and patted the gnome on the back.

"Worry not, my friend, all is forgiven."

Relieved, SmibSmob matched Ro's smile. "Ah, but I reckon I can give you something from my hat," he said.

Reaching up, he took his pointed hat from his head and plunged his hand into the void within. His brow furrowed, and his hand fumbled about while he waited for the spark. The gnome looked up to Ro, and his eyes brightened like two beacons on the shore of an ocean. With dramatic flair, he pulled his hand from his hat, clutching a small dagger. The dagger had a glimmering, golden blade, and a simple, leather-wrapped hilt. The pommel was decorated with a marvelous, faceted gemstone of the purest white, and it sparkled in the gray light with the majesty of a starry night. SmibSmob eyed the small dagger with disappointment. Sure, for the gnome it was a fine weapon, but it was nothing more than a whittling knife for the towering draconian.

"I don't mean to be the obvious one, but it's not exactly the greatsword you had," SmibSmob said softly, moving to return the dagger to his hat.

Reaching out, Ro placed his claw atop the gnome's thin hand, a gentle smile on his face.

"It will do just fine, my friend," Ro said reassuringly. "Thank you."

Taking the golden dagger from SmibSmob, Ro looked it over before tucking it away in his belt.

Glowing, SmibSmob placed his pointed hat back atop of his head and skipped away.

Ro smiled as he watched the gnome gallop away. It was hard to believe that there was a dark, horrible side to the friendly gnome. Ro had seen that side before, and he shivered at the thought. He did not want to see it again. For SmibSmob's sake, and Nalgene's, he prayed that the gnome would stray from his insidious power.

Shaking the black thoughts away, Ro turned to see Nalgene studying his crystalline bottle, turning it over in his rough hands. There was water swirling once more in the glass. Nalgene looked up, noticing Ro's inquisitive stare, and glanced down at his bottle, deep in thought. Ro could only wonder at the gnome's struggle. As far as he knew, the bottle was the reason they had survived the gargantuan, undead serpent. If Nalgene had not unleashed its shimmering contents, they would long be dead. Another life debt to the gnome.

Nalgene grumbled something to himself and looked to the ocean. Shrugging, he threw the bottle into the waves. It disappeared beneath the churning water, never to be seen again.

"Why did you do that?" Ro gasped. He wanted to dive into the ocean to retrieve the wondrous bottle, but he knew it would be impossible. It was gone, a victim to the ever-changing tides.

Nalgene eyed the shocked draconian and shrugged. His blue eyes were at peace.

"That thing be the old me," he said. He seemed more than content with letting the bottle drift away.

"What do you mean?" Ro asked. Yet more pieces to an ever-growing puzzle. A puzzle with no solution.

"I be seein' a lot o' things when I was out," Nalgene answered. "And I had a lot o' time to be thinkin' about it all. We ain't who we think. Why do ye think we can't be rememberin' before the prison?"

Ro had no answer.

"That bloody bottle be who I was, not who I be now," Nalgene finished, turning away to find his brother.

Ro was speechless. He could only wonder at what the gnome was talking about. True, he could not remember before the prison. None of them could. But what did that have to do with anything, let alone Nalgene's bottle? He had no answers.

"What do you mean?" Ro called after the gnome.

Nalgene shrugged but did not look back. "Don't matter now. We be here, not there."

The companions finished gathering their belongings and set off south into the unknown wasteland. Ro took the head, leading the others into the darkness. He could only guess where they were going, but still he pushed on, with every ounce of confidence he could muster. The barren landscape seemed endless, the shriveled grasslands crawling by with every step. It was difficult to tell how far they had traveled, for every direction was the same, gray earth. After a long, monotonous day of travel, they finally reached a slow, winding river. It was the first sign of movement they had seen, but it did little to raise their falling spirits. The weight of the void was pressing down upon them, sinking their feet in the forsaken dirt and dragging down every step they took. There was no life, no movement — not even a stray undead crossed their path.

The days dragged on, the pale, cold sun rising and setting for what seemed like an eternity. The companions' abundant optimism from before had long ago been devoured by the oppressive Shadow, and now they trudged along, hunger wracking their bodies with a continuous, grinding pain. A lake was visible in the distant east, but they were less than willing to travel near any more murky lakes. A faint, cool breeze could be felt trickling from the west, signifying that the ocean was nearby. But the landscape still ate away at their minds, a gray painting in a world devoid of color. On the fourth day of their harrowing journey, just as the pale sun was rising to the east, two Sparks crossed paths with the companions.

The two Sparks wore simple, light mail, with various plates and straps crossing over their athletic bodies, and a crimson tunic to accent their armor. One of the Sparks had a brown, shadowy beard that matched his tousled, brown hair, while the other was clean shaven and blonde. Their faces were cold and grizzled, and there was no doubt that they had seen the horrible throes of battle. As they approached, their hands rested upon their longswords, ready to draw them at a moment's notice and slice down any foes.

"Good to see a fellow Spark still burning bright," the Spark with the blonde hair hailed, his sharp eyes scrutinizing the companions. He halted, as did his fellow Spark, and they waited for the companions' reply, respectfully keeping their distance.

Ro studied the two Sparks. He was overwhelmed with hope at the presence of life, and he wanted to cry out in glee, but he held himself in check. He did not want to give them any reason to attack. If these two Sparks were even half as dangerous as the Captain, then the companions would be in great danger. And Ro did not have a proper weapon.

But it was fine. He just needed to relax. He was a leader now, after all. So now it was time for him to lead.

Smiling, Ro raised his hand in a salute and began to say the proper greeting.

The Sparks tensed, and their hands gripped their longswords.

But before Ro could speak, SmibSmob stepped forward, cutting Ro off with a sharp cough. "May your light pierce the Shadow," he said clearly, projecting his quiet voice with an unwavering confidence.

The two Sparks relaxed, but they still did not approach. Even Shadowfriends remembered the proper introduction.

"What brings you to these parts?" the bearded Spark called. "It is uncommon to find Sparks far from the Shadowfront — let alone a group of six."

Ro studied the Spark, his brow furrowing in thought. Shadowfront? Why was there so much Shadow?

More pieces to the puzzle. He began to speak, but SmibSmob, the clever gnome, once again beat him to it.

"If it is so unlikely," SmibSmob began, his voice remaining steady, "then why are you two out here alone?"

"Mighty fine noggin' ye got," Nalgene mumbled quietly from behind SmibSmob.

Ro nodded in agreement. He glanced down at the small gnome, his eyes sparkling with respect. It was not so long ago when the gnome would stammer and stumble under the heavy weight of pressure.

Smirking, the two Sparks released their swords, and shrugged to each other, obviously caught in their own logic.

"Fair enough, my good friend," the blonde Spark said, his voice friendly. "My name is Roan, and this is Dain."

"Hail," Dain called, placing his hand upon his chest in a salute. "And what brings you to these parts?"

While the two were visibly relaxed, they still did not

approach the companions. They may have been overly trusting, but they were certainly not naive, or dull. No one survived long in the Shadow by leaping ahead without carefully thinking first.

"Ah, well," SmibSmob started, his voice cracking. Sweat began to bead on the gnome's head, and he shot a quick, panicked look at his brother behind him.

Ro smiled.

"General's orders," he said, saving the uncomfortable gnome. "General Kraalek Cardmaster, if you must know." The General was enough to somber the gnarled Captain, so perhaps a mention would be enough to win the two Sparks over.

Roan laughed aloud, his barreling laughter echoing across the empty plains, but quickly quieted when Dain gave him a sharp jab in the arm.

"Ahem," he coughed as he tried to regain his composure. "You mean to tell me you were sent by that gambler? He spends most of his time wasted away in money, booze, and whor —"

Another sharp jab from Dain was enough to quiet Roan.

"Don't mind him," Dain said, annoyance flitting through his words. "He's just upset that General Cardmaster is more popular among the women than he is."

Roan's mouth shot open in shock, and he wheeled about on his companion, anger flickering in his eyes. "Oh, now don't pretend like you aren't envious either," he fired back at Dain. "He should be commanding legions, not fooling about with barmaids!"

Dain's eyes ignited at this, and whirled around to face Roan, bringing his fists up, ready to beat down on his companion for his insolence. "Oh, don't place me on the same level as you!" he roared, his face red with anger.

Ro watched the growing spectacle with rising amusement. Of course, the two Sparks were not actually infuriated with each other. It was merely some friendly banter, a way to remove the mind from the surrounding depression. It was refreshing to see, even within the dismal blanket of Shadow, that the eternal bonds of friendship still held strong. Even with the everlasting blackness quenching all signs of life, the smoldering ember of love would always find a way to ignite. Ro's heart soared, and he thought of his own companions, a quiet chuckle escaping his lips.

"Kraalek, eh? That bloody worm?" Nalgene remarked, a shallow hint of amusement obvious in his gruff voice. "Now ye've done it, ye damn dragon. Ye set them off."

"Bedding unsuspecting women?" Margaret jumped in. "That certainly sounds like something he would do."

Ro laughed but said nothing. It was refreshing indeed.

"Ah, anyway," Roan said, turning back to the companions. A red welt had appeared on the side of his face, and a satisfied Dain smirked smugly next to him. "I apologize for our ... erhm ... behavior. It's just relieving to finally see more Sparks in this horrible land."

"Indeed," Ro agreed, smiling. Life had to cling together under the oppressive weight of the Shadow. In a land where the decaying land stretched forever like a black ocean, and where the once-great cities now lay devastated like broken guardians of a fallen kingdom, a lone soul could easily succumb to the iron clutches of madness.

"Seems you're not Shadowfriends," Dain said, "or you would have killed us while we bantered."

Or tried to," Roan said, patting his friend on the back.

Ro's stomach lurched at the mention of Shadowfriends. Who would possibly want to side with the dark misery? What monster would betray his friends for the sake of death and destruction?

"Mmmm, we certainly are not friends of the Shadow," Andromeda declared, her voice a thin hiss cutting through the still air.

"Excellent," Roan said in relief. Raising his hand, he beckoned the companions to follow him.

Dain pulled a strange looking horn from his belt. He held it up to his mouth, then closed his eyes, as if focusing. Then he said something into it before replacing it on his belt.

"Come, I'd say we've done enough," Dain said, turning to them. "Let's return to the Flame, together."

Ro's heart raced at the mention of the Flame. At last, after endless nights in this desolate land, they were finally going to reunite with the Flame. It felt as if a burdensome weight had been lifted from his strong shoulders. He turned and nodded to his fellow companions, who looked similarly relieved to finally escape the black maw of Shadow.

"Let's go," he agreed. It was refreshing indeed.

Without hesitation, the companions started off after the two Sparks. Their bleak journey was finally coming to an end.

The Sparks lead the companions across the great plains of Shadow. Many exhausting days passed on their travels, each cold sunrise reminding them just how devastated the world had become. Yet even in the heart of depression, their spirits stayed strong. They would pass the dragging time with banter and by telling great stories. Roan and Dain would talk of their many perils with the Flame, and the companions would do their best to make up stories as they went — it was far easier to fabricate than truly explain their situation. Fortunately, Roan was a brilliant speaker and would drone on for hours about his grand quests and untimely mishaps, so the companions rarely had to tell a tale of their own.

As the days wore on, the Sparks lead the companions around the mighty lake to the east. One morning, Dain admitted to falling asleep while on watch. He mentioned a strange dream of a beautiful woman, but they brushed it off as him fantasizing. No undead ambush, no problem. Eventually, they came upon a barren, twisted forest, much like the black forest where the companions had begun their adventure. Rotten trees reached for the companions with vile claws, scratching and tearing at their clothes and flesh. The trees' branches intertwined to form an impenetrable barrier against the sun's pale rays, creating a blanket of unending darkness.

However, there was no sign of the vile legions of the Shadow, and no undead bear appeared to maul them. Fasto was comfortable, but the others were not. The orc even told some stories with surprising eloquence.

After many days of travel through the treacherous forest, the companions finally emerged from its woody grasp, escaping into the surrounding, gray world. The lake now lay to the north, and the snowy peaks of mountains could be seen far to the south. Yet just beyond the mountains, there was light. Not the cold, unforgiving haze of the Shadow, but the brilliant, pure illumination of the Light. It was the end of the enveloping Shadow. It was their source of hope and determination.

It was the Flame.

Revitalized at the sight of their salvation, the group redoubled their efforts, blazing across the lands. Nothing could damper their soaring spirits. Nothing could soothe their ecstatic hearts. And nothing could stop their triumphant march. Nothing, perhaps, except for the Shadowfront.

As the companions neared the approaching mountain range, the cold air grew quiet and still, and the land seemed to ooze and leak the essence of darkness. The Sparks grew somber, their outgoing friendliness giving way to a reserved caution.

"We are nearing the Shadowfront," Dain said, his voice soft and low. His eyes darted about, as if constantly trying to spot an approaching enemy. "Luckily, we're going to avoid that chaotic mess."

Roan nodded in agreement. "I would do anything to avoid going back there."

Ro studied the Sparks. There was no doubt about their absolute terror of the so-called Shadowfront. "Agreed," he stated. He had to at least pretend he knew what it was. He glanced back at his other companions and gave them a faint shrug. They were all equally lost.

"Come," Dain beckoned, turning back to the towering mountains. His face was pale and taut, and his hand rested on the hilt of his longsword. "We have to reach the foothills."

Nodding, but not quite understanding the Spark's reasoning, Ro obliged. They didn't have a choice. And with the first sight of a world beyond the endless void, he cared little to argue.

The companions followed the two Sparks to the feet of the great mountain. Their pace had slowed dramatically, and they crossed the barren plains, attempting to keep their profiles low. It would not do well to be seen. The two Sparks jumped at every gust of wind and every rustle of grass. Their hands never left their swords. After a long, quiet day of travel, the companions finally reached the base of the mountain range. While these scaling monoliths were noticeably smaller than the other mountains the companions had crossed, they were dense and created a jagged barrier that would be nigh impossible to traverse.

"And how do you suppose we make it through this?" Margaret began.

"We don't," Dain whispered, his rumbling voice barely more than the slight passing of the wind. "First time?"

He shot Margaret a quizzical look, but he did not press the question. It did not matter.

Rustling in his pouch, Dain pulled forth a small, orange gem, and held it gently in his hand. It was not dissimilar to the gem Kraalek had used those many moons ago in the ruined city of Calinad. However, upon closer inspection, the gemstone was dull.

Roan placed his hand on Dain's shoulder.

Dain, noticing that the companions hadn't moved, gestured for them to do the same. Maybe it was their first time.

Shrugging, the companions obliged.

Dain closed his eyes, holding out the gemstone. Roan stared at it intently, his jaw clenching and relaxing in a nervous fit.

The minutes dragged by — agonizing. The Spark opened his eyes, and his hand began quivering.

"C'mon," he mumbled, shaking his head.

"What's taking so long?" asked Roan, his voice high with distress.

The companions stood in grim silence. They could only begin to guess what was transpiring, but they had enough wits about them to know it was not going well.

The two Sparks were growing frantic. Dain's eyes began darting about in a frenzy, and his face was drawn tight. Roan was similarly distressed, and his teeth could be heard grinding in the still air.

More time crawled by, but still the companions waited, unsure of how to react to the growing tension.

"C'mon, c'mon, c'mon," Dain kept muttering to himself, staring at the gem. But there was no light.

At last, after what seemed an eternity, Dain closed his hand. His arm dropped limply to his side, and his sunken eyes bore into the companions. He looked like a shell of the man he had been just a few moments before. Ro could have sworn the man was about to break into tears.

"Something's wrong," Dain uttered, his voice cracking. He glanced down at his closed fist and numbly shook his head. "I don't understand."

"What?" Roan cried, his voice thundering through the silent air. Quickly realizing his mistake, his voice dropped to a low whisper. "What is it?"

"Something's wrong," Dain repeated.

"Try again," Roan demanded, but Dain shook his head in defeat.

"It's no use," the solemn Spark said. His arm quaking, he returned the orange gem to his pouch and reached for his longsword. "There was nothing — no connection."

Roan gawked at Dain; his shoulders slumped under the weight of the grave news. He opened his mouth but promptly closed it. Nothing he could say would change the situation.

"So, where does that leave us?" Ro asked, unsure of the exchange. He did not understand the purpose of the gem, or what Dain meant when he said he did not feel a "connection," but he certainly did understand the grim results. The once-bantering Sparks, who skipped through the bleak Shadow with an unquenchable life, now stood broken under the harsh weight of reality.

"At the Shadowfront," Roan answered. Without another word, the two Sparks turned to the northeast, and began their solemn march to the edge of oblivion.

Unnerved, the companions started after them, slowly fitting the pieces together in their mind. They would have to fight to reach the Flame.

They would have to fight through the Shadowfront.

◆　　◆　　◆

Ro glanced over the edge of the boulder he crouched behind. Before him lay the Shadowfront, the gargantuan clash between Shadow and Flame — the battlefield where the eternal darkness tried to wash into the pure land of Light. The endless, twisting mass of vile undead shambling before him utterly repulsed the draconian. Suddenly, it became quite apparent why there were no undead to be found on this new continent. They had amassed into a black swarm, a sea of rot and decay, and now crashed against the mighty dam of the Flame. The endless groans and dreadful screeches seared into his mind, threatening to send him into a bout of madness.

And the screams.

Not the guttural screams of the rotting mass of Shadow. Nay, the blood-curdling screams of the living. The bone-chilling screams of a Spark whose life was torn away in the fanged maw of an undead. The piercing screams of a Spark whose limbs were torn from his mangled body. The horrifying screams of a Spark who just watched his friend become devoured in the endless mass of atrophy.

Ro's stomach churned, and he had to resist the urge to vomit. There were living beings in that horrible swarm of rot. Living beings who were desperately trying to hold back the dreadful legion of darkness, sacrificing their lives for the sake of the Flame, for the sake of their friends and families. It was almost too much for the draconian to handle.

Almost.

While the agonizing deaths of the Sparks horrified the draconian, they also bolstered his resolve. A simmering fury boiled inside of him, and it was begging to burst free, begging to be unleashed on the mass of bile before him. A harsh growl escaped his lips, and he clenched the golden dagger that SmibSmob had gifted him. He would avenge their deaths.

Behind him crouched the other companions. Roan and Dain were pale, yet their eyes shone with a fierce rage. They hated the Shadow, and they would stop at nothing to devastate its vile ranks. The others readied their weapons, halberds and spells alike. Andromeda had already faded into the shadows and was awaiting Ro's command to rush into the fray. Margaret's arm pulsed wildly at her side, casting a harsh cold over the others. Water swirled over Nalgene's fists, ready to wash away the tide of decay. Fasto held a handful of stones in his hands, as he was still unable — and refused — to wield his mighty bow. SmibSmob clutched his pointed hat in one hand, and a thorned hammer in the other. He would fight.

Ro glanced out from behind the jagged boulder one final time. Beyond wasteland of death, and the writhing mass of rot, there was the purity of the Light. At the end of the valley, a great stone stronghold stood proudly like a towering knight. It was the sole barrier holding back the Shadow from the heart of the Flame, the lone guardian of a land shackled in chains. It was his goal — their goal — and he would do anything to ensure he and his companions reached the Flame. He turned to the others, his heart thundering in his chest. They had to reach the stronghold.

"Let's go," he commanded, his silver eyes shining like two iron daggers. "Let's reunite with the Flame. Together — er — side-by-side as friends, we can make it to the Light." It was truly inspiring for their morale.

Without waiting for their response, Ro bolted from behind the boulder, his golden dagger held before him, and charged into the surging horde of undead, a roaring battle-cry thundering from his maw.

Immediately, Ro was enveloped in the vile horde. Rotting bodies crawled about him, reaching and clawing at his flesh. The dreadful smell of undead corpses filled his mouth, threatening to drown him in its black abyss. He tried to move, tried to breathe, but the overwhelming legion of death pressed in. Zombies bit at his flesh, their razor fangs scraping against his plate mail. Skeletons slashed at him with their weapons, and it was all he could do to survive the onslaught.

His golden dagger flashed, and his lightning breath arced across the battlefield, but it was not enough. Rumbling howls filled the air, and the undead mass surged over him, dragging him to the ground. He tried to breathe, tried to move, but black blood washed over him, and the weight of the horde drove him into the cold earth below. He tried to unleash another blast of lightning, but the undead drove their rotting arms into his throat, strangling him. All he saw was the gray, peeling flesh of undead. All he felt was the relentless rending of the dark horde. All he smelled was the oppressive stench of decay. All he tasted was the bitter, toxic taste of death. He vomited, but he did not even notice. He was going to die. The rotting mass pressed in, biting at his flesh, tearing at his eyes. His shining plate mail had been stripped from his body, leaving him exposed to the whims of the undead. And still the horde pressed in, suffocating him.

He was going to die.

But then a surging wave of water washed over the draconian, dragging the undead away in a tide of freedom. Brown stones flew across his vision, followed by raging balls of fire and whistling shards of ice. Ro tried to stand, tried to rise to his feet, but his body would not let him. He was a fool. He had allowed his emotions to win him over. He had thrown caution into the wind, and now he would pay the price. His entire body pulsed with searing pain. Bloody gashes covered his body, and his vision was a hazed blur.

Andromeda appeared next to him, her eyes churning with sorrow. She whispered something to him, but he could not hear her. She pulled him to his feet, but his legs would not support him. He had failed.

He was going to die.

Suddenly, a cool water flowed over him, mending his wounds, and dragging him back to reality.

"Don't be thinkin' I'd let ye die so easily, Ro," Nalgene grumbled before charging into the fray, devastating spells of water washing away any unfortunate undead in his wake.

Ro shook his head, regaining his senses. Andromeda stood before him, horror in her face. She opened her mouth but clamped it shut as the undead horde returned. There would be no time for emotions here. In the Shadowfront, it was a battle of survival. There was no room for gray in this realm of black and white.

Ro took a quick glance around, absorbing the surrounding chaos. His eyes locked on Roan, who was being mauled by a pair of hulking zombies. Blood seeped down the poor man's face. His mouth opened wide to scream, but no sound came. Instead, his jaw was torn from his face by a rotting soldier. Dain tried to save his friend, but it was too late. The Shadow had already claimed another victim. Dain's mouth opened wide, a piercing howl of sorrow filling the battlefield. Tears streaming down his face, he rushed at the hulking undead, his longsword swinging wildly in front of him. Burning orbs of fire shot from his outstretched hand, incinerating any who stood before him. Black blood filled the air as he cut down undead after undead. But it was not enough. It was never enough. The horde surged forward, enveloping Dain in its iron grasp of decay. Skeletons slashed at him with their weapons, hacking his limbs from his body. Zombies tore at his flesh, ripping his organs from his bleeding chest. Dain's head rolled back, his face frozen in an eternal scream.

Horrified, Ro could only watch as the Sparks succumbed to the Shadow. Everything went numb. All the screams and all the howls — it all went quiet. He locked eyes with Andromeda, his silver eyes burning like two fiery swords. He would avenge them. He looked to the stronghold, and then to the writhing mass of undead. Clenching his golden dagger in his hand, Ro rushed forward, cutting into the vile ranks of darkness. He would avenge them.

His instincts took over.

A twisted zombie rushed at the draconian, but he deftly stepped to the side, driving his dagger deep into its skull. Tearing the weapon forth, he flipped it about and decapitated the sickly creature. Three more undead charged at him, but he opened his maw, devastating them with a crackling bolt of lightning. More and more devilish beings rushed at him, tearing at him with fangs and claws alike, but then Andromeda was there, at his side, carving a way through the Shadowfront.

She darted through the undead, her halberd making short work of the vile beings. Her claws shot out, rending at rotten flesh and tearing down the undead. Before the Shadow could grasp her, she disappeared, only to reappear at the draconian's side.

Together, they cut through the Shadowfront, making their way to the towering stronghold in the distance.

A pair of rotting stallions rushed at them, and skeleton archers rained down a hail of iron arrows, not caring if they struck friend or foe. The draconian leaped at the rushing stallion, barreling into the undead rider and driving it off its unholy mount. His dagger flashed, cutting into the rotting flesh and releasing a thick pool of black blood. An arrow thudded into his shoulder, and another zombie crashed into him, dragging him to the ground. Rotting claws slashed at him, and dreadful fangs drove into his shoulder, digging into tendons and bone. Twisting, the draconian rolled out from under the undead, and his dagger shot forward, plunging into the being's leg. Tearing his weapon out, he clamped his maw down upon the zombie's knee and crushed it with a sickening *crunch*. The zombie topped to the ground where Ro finished it with his dagger.

But the stallion was still there, and it reared over him, its iron hooves rushing down to obliterate him. This time, without heavy armor weighing him down, he easily rolled to the side and to his feet. No horse was going to stomp him this time.

Just then, he was tackled by another hulking undead. His head cracked against the unforgiving ground, and his vision went blurry once more.

But then the zombie was gone, torn away by an infuriated Andromeda. She would not let Ro die. Not while she still had breath in her lungs. Blood spraying in all direction, she dismembered the vile beast, and leaped to her feet, her halberd arcing around to slice another two undead.

Shaking his pain away, the draconian stumbled to his feet. Yet another undead stallion thundered at him, a skeleton warrior mounted on its rotting back. It never reached him. Small stones bounced off it, and a mighty shard of ice crashed into its flank, driving it to the ground. They had reunited with Fasto and Margaret. Without hesitation, the draconian darted forward, his dagger cutting and twisting, dismantling the fallen steed. The skeleton warrior tried to hack at him with its jagged axe, but its leg was pinned under the rotting carcass of the stallion. Growling, he made short work of the skeleton as well.

Andromeda rushed over to him, her black hide bruised and bloody. Margaret and Fasto followed behind her, their stones and ice damaging creatures in the surrounding horde. A massive, shambling mass of rotting flesh stomped towards them. Dozens of rotting arms reached from its bulbous body, and mighty spikes jutted out in all directions. Its gaping maw opened wide, revealing rows of dagger-like fangs.

Leading the charge, the draconian rushed at the hideous abomination, lightning arcing from his maw. Shards of ice whistled above his head, piercing into the creature's gruesome body. Undeterred, it brought its burly, trunk-like, arm up, and smashed it into the ground, sending dust and gore flying into the air. The draconian rolled to the side before leaping to his feet and bolting at the dreadful beast. His dagger weaved across, slashing at outstretched arms and cutting at black flesh. Andromeda appeared from the air, landing upon the unholy beast's shoulders and plunging down with her halberd. The rotting creature flailed about, its spiked arms slamming into the ground with reckless abandon. The draconian darted and weaved, gracefully swerving through the storm of attacks.

But there were still more undead.

A horde of shambling fiends aided the flailing abomination, many of them becoming crushed under its mighty arms. But still more tore at the companions. The draconian could only avoid the devastating attacks for so long. His body burned with exhaustion, and another arrow struck him, dropping him down to his knee. Andromeda was flung off the rotting beast and lay dazed upon the cold earth. Fasto was attempting to fend off a group of four skeletons, but he could do little with his stones and shattered arms. Margaret's face was twisted with blood lust, and she viciously beat upon a mangled pile of gore while the swarming legion clawed at her, tearing her armor from her body. She didn't notice.

But there were still more undead.

A triad of undead stallions stampeded at the companions, their ghastly riders slashing down with jagged weapons. Growling, Ro snapped the shaft of the protruding arrow and pushed himself back to his feet. He dove to the side, narrowly avoiding the swing of the rotting abomination. But as he rolled to his feet, he was clipped in the face by another rushing stallion. Blood flew from his maw, and he crashed back into the ground, his head aching from the impact.

Andromeda managed to regain her senses, but four undead were already on top of her, rending at her flesh with vicious claws. An anguished screech escaped her lips. Blood oozed from Fasto's head, and one of his eyes was swollen shut. He had somehow felled two of the pursuing skeletons, but three more rotting soldiers of death had taken their place. Margaret howled wildly and a nova of ice burst from her body, freezing any nearby undead in an icy prison. Her demonic power had spread and covered her entire body, transforming her into a devilish nightmare. Her black arm swung about, devastating the rotting legions with icy blows. An icy storm swirled around her, and with a ferocious roar, her dark arm shot forward, crashing into an undead stallion and unleashing a massive shock wave of icy destruction, washing away dozens of undead in a single, terrifying blow.

But there were still more undead.

For every undead the companions managed to defeat, five more were ready to take their place. There would be no escape. The Shadow would consume all. Sparks died all about, their blood pooling on the saturated ground. Rotting abominations thundered through the battlefield, crushing any unfortunate being that wandered too close. Undead giants stomped about, smothering any hope under their mighty feet. A constant barrage of jagged arrows filled the air, raining death upon the bloody frenzy. At the stronghold, barriers and reinforcements, manned by legions of Sparks, managed to keep the onslaught of Shadow at bay. Great spells of fire incinerated dozens of vile undead, and unparalleled warriors held strong against the black tide. But for how long? There would be no escape. The Shadow would consume all.

And there were still more undead.

It was all the battered companions could do to try to survive.

They were still far from the stronghold and the safety of the Flame. The situation seemed hopeless. Undead piled upon Ro, drowning him in a pool of rot. Andromeda crawled across the ground, desperately trying to escape the undead pursuers. Fasto had been driven to the ground, and he shielded his face with his mangled arms, tears streaming down his face. Even Margaret's devastating wave of ice had done nothing to reduce the staggering scope of the oncoming storm. She had returned to her normal appearance, and was surrounded by undead, her face twisted in a maniacal rage. There would be no escape. The Shadow would consume all.

Suddenly, Nalgene burst from the ranks of death, water swirling about him in a crackling storm of energy. A shield of water twisted about him, and wherever he beckoned great torrents of steaming water washed away the filth, and brilliant strikes of lightning thundered into the battlefield below.

"AYE, YE BLOODY DOLTS!" Nalgene hollered, his gruff voice cutting through the mayhem like a knife through paper. "DON'T YE BE DYIN'' ON ME NOW!"

He raised his hands, and jets of water cut through the undead, allowing the others a moment to escape. A primal shout escaped his mouth, and a mighty bolt of lightning thundered into the rotting abomination, devastating it in a nova of energy and gore. Nalgene rushed over to the companions, his godly aura disappearing as he neared. Scratches and bruises dotted his body, but he paid them no mind.

"C'mon, we gotta keep movin'," he said, healing water flowing from his outstretched hands to the others. "We don't have time to be sittin' here and healin'. Ye gotta be gettin' up and movin'!"

The water washed over the others, mending their major wounds. Pain racked their bodies, but they were back in the fight. They were still able to reach the stronghold. There was still hope. The draconian nodded to Nalgene in gratitude before rushing over to help Andromeda to her feet. The feline was badly injured, and limped on one leg, but there was a fire in her eyes. The draconian smiled. Margaret helped Fasto along. The poor orc was mangled beyond belief, and his broken arms quivered violently. But there was no time to celebrate their minor victory. The endless horde of undead was already closing in.

The draconian turned, his eyes fixed upon the mighty stronghold before them. They were growing near. Just one final push, and they would be free from the dark clutches of the Shadowfront.

"Let's go," he commanded, pointing his golden dagger at their salvation.

"Wait, where's me brother?" Nalgene asked, alarmed.

Well, shit.

Ro glanced about, desperately searching. He heard a scream somehow cutting through the chaos. There was no doubt who it was. Snarling, Ro charged in the direction of the sound. Without hesitation, the others bolted after him.

Together, in the heart of battle, they cut through the ranks of dreadful minions of Shadow. Ro weaved with his dagger, nimbly cutting away at the undead. Bolts of lightning thundered from his maw, carving a path through the wall of decay. Andromeda slashed with her halberd, hacking away limbs and pooling the ground with thick blood. Her body constantly faded in and out of the shadows, avoiding fatal strikes time and time again. Margaret stood with Fasto, unleashing icy shards to support the headliners. Fasto attempted to fight, kicking at any vile creature that managed to break through the others. Behind them was Nalgene, his tremendous power washing away legions of undead and rejuvenating the others whenever they fell victim to the weapons of the Shadow. As they pushed, other Sparks joined their crusade, creating a solitary spear plunging through the black hide of darkness. But they couldn't find the gnome.

Then, suddenly, as if the very heart of the void had materialized, the Shadowfront went black. Not the pale, shining black of a cloak, nor the thin, transparent darkness of the night. Nay, this black was thick, tangible. It devoured any remnants of light, and tore at the companion's souls, chewing them into oblivion. It was suffocating, oppressive. It was the Shadow. But as soon as it had appeared, it was gone, leaving the world stumbling in its absence.

A thin, frail gnome floated high in the air, his eyes two purple embers. Tentacles of shadow oozed from him, writhing about and slaughtering anything that was unfortunate enough to get caught within its inky grasp.

SmibSmob had succumbed to his unholy darkness.

Daniel Whitman

Chapter 13

SmibSmob hovered above the tumultuous battlefield, a black tempest of death swirling around him in a seething storm. Dozens of dreadful, shadowy tentacles reached forth from the frail gnome, unleashing a hail of devastation upon everything below. His vile aura gnawed at all life, tearing at others' life force and rejuvenating him. His eyes were emotionless pits. There was no sympathy, no empathy, no awareness. Only the desire to devour, and to decimate anything and everything.

Somewhere in the back of his mind, hidden behind a fortress of darkness, the gnome knew it was wrong. He had lost. His power had overwhelmed him and had taken a life of its own. He had to fight back, but it felt so good, so exhilarating. Perhaps he should just stop resisting. It was far easier to just annihilate everything in his path. But the lives, and the cost of such wanton destruction ... No, this was freedom. This was what he desired.

Crackling energy coursed through his veins, and his heart thundered in his chest like a beating war drum. Every sense was on edge, absorbing him in a world beyond any other. The grimy, dusty scent of thick blood filled his nostrils, driving him mad like a bloodhound. The bitter, vile taste of decay filled his mouth, threatening to suffocate him. The endless, droning sound of battle rang harshly in his ears. He could hear the cold wind, the clashing of steel, and the horrendous wails of the dying. He wanted to scream, to free himself from this overbearing world of death and destruction, but he could not. He was alive. This is what he lived for: the raw, shadowy power that rested deep within him.

Below him, the battle raged on. Countless undead ebbed and flowed like a singular wave of rot, constantly crashing against the mighty stronghold. But how long would it hold? The Shadow cared little for the loss of its twisted minions. They were cannon fodder, a mass sent to die in a billowing tower of flame. But every loss of the Flame was a harsh blow. Every death of a Spark struck like a searing iron. How long could they possibly hope to last?

The gnome snickered, a vile and twisted cackle. He did not care. It could all crumble and burn. He was alive. He had his power. That was all that mattered. Everything else was merely an illusion, a distraction from the true purpose of reality. To devastate everything under a blanket of shadow.

But one thought irked the gnome, a thought hidden deep within the dark abyss. Life was about loving, and caring for others, not slaughtering everything for the sake of entertainment. And yet, it felt so good. It was satisfying to watch everything flee in terror in the wake of his power. It was satisfying to crush everything under a swirling fist of darkness. Then a thought broke into his mind.

Why was he up here?

He chuckled, and an evil smirk twisted his lips. It was always more enjoyable up close. You can see the pain more clearly.

Without a second thought, the gnome leaped from the air, crashing into the broken ground below like a falling meteor. His head whipped up, the surrounding commotion barreling into his senses like a raging stampede. The shambling feet on the bloodied ground. The unholy groans of the undead legion. The stench of rot and decay. The brush of wind of the slashing blades. He smiled. This was where he belonged.

Roaring, a trio of hulking zombies charged at the seemingly unprotected gnome, their bulging muscles twisting with every stride. Their maws open wide, revealing rows of jagged teeth and long, snake-like tongues. Their claws flashed, and they lunged for the gnome's exposed body, their maws clamping shut with staggering force.

But the gnome was not there.

Deftly twisting about, the gnome avoided their attacks, each fanged mouth or slashing claw missing by a mere hairs-width. He smiled. Two black tentacles lunged forward, grasping two of the attacking zombies in a fatal clutch. The tendrils pulsed and shifted, never quite agreeing on a set size. A wave of dark energy coursed through the vile appendages, and with unrivaled strength, the tentacles squeezed, crushing the unfortunate zombies into a shower of blood and gore.

The third zombie slashed at the gnome, its yellow claws whistling by the gnome's head. Raising his hand, a mighty lance of darkness formed within the gnome's grasp. Turning about, he plunged it into the zombie's decaying chest. The lance pulsed, releasing a vile nova of energy into the zombie that devoured the creature's insides, leaving a gaping hole where the zombie's ribs once were. The rush of revitalizing energy coursed through the gnome, rekindling his eternal blackness. He smiled. It certainly was more enjoyable up close.

The ground quivered, and the gnome's empty eyes shot up, searching for the source of the commotion. Another mass of undead attempted to rush at the gnome, their maws open wide at the promise of flesh. The gnome paid them no mind. He had more important things to worry about. His wicked tendrils shot out, annihilating each one of the approaching undead, bending and breaking the pursuers with unholy strength and tossing their broken corpses about as a dog would a newborn rabbit.

The ground quaked once more, drawing the gnome's attention. A deafening roar washed over the battlefield and a gargantuan skeleton giant stomped toward the gnome, its feet crushing dozens of lesser undead. The gnome watched the approaching beast with cautious respect. He had not forgotten the last time he had attempted to best one of these towering behemoths. It had not ended well for him.

Now, it was time for some revenge.

The giant thundered closer, each footstep seeming like a powerful earthquake to the gnome. The giant reached down, grabbed an undead from the ground, and whipped it at the gnome. A black tendril shot up, swatting the projectile from the air. But the giant was already atop him, its skeletal foot plunging down to crush his thin body. Irritated, the gnome dove to the side, just managing to avoid his certain demise. A wave of dust and grime washed over him as the giant's foot crashed into the ground, blinding him to the surrounding battle.

As he struggled to get the dust from his eyes, his other senses took over, each ascending to a new heightened potential. The scuffs of the feet on the ground. The stench of death all around. The slight ripples in the air as an undead rushed at him from behind.

The gnome gasped in alarm, but it was too late. The bulging undead barreled into him, driving him into the cold ground. Yellow claws scratched at his flesh, and jagged teeth plunged into his shoulder, sending waves of agony through his thin frame.

How dare it!

It was unacceptable! He desperately struggled, attempting to crawl out from under his oppressor. While immensely powerful in the ways of devastating spells, he had little physical strength, and no hope of overpowering the bulking zombie.

Another ripple cut through the air. The skeleton giant had returned, its massive foot raised, ready to finish what it had started. The gnome had to move fast. His thin hand shot up, and he clutched at the zombie's arm, unleashing a devastating wave of shadowy energy into his transgressor. The zombie went soaring back, landing somewhere in the surrounding battle. The rush of revitalizing energy jolted through the gnome, stitching his wounds and cleansing his thoughts.

He felt the shift in the air, heard the rush of the wind. It was the giant. He had to move. Diving once more, he just managed to avoid the skeletal behemoth's crushing stomp. Dust clouded his vision again, and he was once more cast into a world of his other senses. His black tentacles lashed out, striking at the giant's leg without much success. Frustrated, the gnome leaped up into the air, desperately rubbing his empty eyes to clear the grime and dust. While it was certainly more enjoyable up close, he was hardly willing to risk his life for such a petty emotion as joy.

It was time to annihilate the pesky thorn. It was time to defeat the undead giant.

Rising higher into the air upon a cloud of shadow, the gnome scanned his eyes across the battlefield. The giant stood in front of him, its hollow eyes burning into him. A mass of writhing undead swarmed at the giant's feet, looking more like a sea of rotting arms and heads than a horde of individual enemies. Rows of skeletal archers rained rusty arrows at the gnome, but shadowy bolts of energy cut them from the air before they had any chance of injuring him. Not far from the gnome was a spearhead of mismatched soldiers, cutting through the Shadowfront in his direction. A silver draconian led the charge, his golden dagger and lightning breath piecing into the rotting ranks. A shadowy feline darted about behind him, slashing undead with a curious halberd. Two orcs manned the center of the formation, unleashing a barrage of icy shards and fearsome kicks at the surrounding fray. A handful of Sparks had joined in the charge, and supported the silver draconian to the sides, desperately cutting at the undead in a vain attempt to reach their beloved Flame.

Pathetic.

But at the heart of the spearhead was another gnome, mighty

torrents of swirling water surging from his gnarled fists. A pang of love sparked in the gnome's mind, and he had the fleeting thought that he should be with the others, fighting towards the promise of Light. They were all ragged and beaten, bloodied and exhausted, and would be hard-pressed to reach the Flame alone. No doubt he could be of great assistance to them.

His shadowy power wavered. But before he could regain control, it snapped shut, enveloping him in its unholy grasp. The gnome smirked wickedly. He had more important things to worry about. There was still the annoying pest of a giant.

The gnome turned to face the menacing giant, its cracked skull staring down at his frail form.

How insolent.

He raised his hands, and a mighty orb of twisting shadow formed above his head. Reaching forward, he cast the massive spell at the giant, watching as it crashed into the yellow skull with grim satisfaction. The giant lurched back, its head cracking back under the weight of the spell. The rush of energy pooled in, invigorating the gnome. He had changed his mind. It was plenty enjoyable to battle from the air.

Regaining its footing, the giant lunged forward, its skeletal hand reaching out to crush the soaring gnome. Shooting forward, the gnome barely passed between the large fingers, just avoiding being crushed into oblivion. He could say he got lucky, but that would undermine his power.

The white hand snapped shut behind him. Raising his hand, a powerful, black fist formed from the swirling shadows. Smirking, the gnome cut his hand down, causing the dark fist to slam into the giant's vulnerable elbow. A gruesome snap radiated through the air, and the giant's forearm was torn from the body at the elbow in a shower of jagged bone fragments. The forearm fell crashing to the dusty ground below, crushing a host of lesser undead under its staggering weight.

The giant reeled back from the blow. Of course, it did not

feel any pain at the loss of its arm. Nevertheless, it was not pleasant to have an arm severed. Roaring, it swung with its remaining arm, its iron fist rushing in the air to decimate the vile gnome. It would strike the annoying pest from the air like a fly.

The gnome felt the rush of air as the fist soared toward his head, heard the whoosh as it rapidly closed in. He growled in frustration. While being in the air provided him with unparalleled advantage over the battlefield below, his maneuverability was quite limited. It was quite difficult to nimbly jump through the air, as quite simply, the air did not provide much of a platform. He could not hope to dodge. So be it. His black eyes leering at the giant, he brought his thin arms up to cover his face. A wall of tendrils twisted together in front of him, creating a stone barrier. Nobody escapes a fight without taking a hit.

Even with his barricade of inky tentacles, the giant's punch struck like a battering ram, breaking through the dark wall and smashing into the gnome. He felt searing pain, and a flash of black. His ribs fractured, and his nose flattened to the side of his pale face. His arms crunched and cracked, breaking under the staggering power of the giant. Stunned, he went soaring back, blood pouring from his shattered face. It was all he could do to remain in the air. His mind wheeled about in frantic circles. Every ounce of his body pulsed with mind-numbing pain. His arms fell limply to his side, and his breath struggled to escape his caved-in chest. White dots danced across his vision, swimming in a blurry smear of gray.

The gnome had grown arrogant with his dark power. He had felt invincible, as every wound he took had been immediately healed when he absorbed the strength of those around him. Unfortunately, there was only so much his power could mend. A snake could not re-attach its severed head. He shook his jumbled head, desperately trying to regain some sense of his surroundings. All he could think of was the pain. All he felt was the pain. The pulsing, radiating pain. He heard the giant rushing toward him, its steps thundering across the bloody ground, and its remaining hand raised to finish the deed.

He had grown arrogant. He had felt alive with his terrible power, transcended to a realm above all others. Much good it had done him.

The shadow began to slip, retreating into the dark recesses of his mind. He was falling, plunging from the air into the surging fray below. There was no doubt in his mind that he would soon be dead, whether from the impact or the ravenous horde of undead, he did not care. Arrogance was the downfall of kings, and he was hardly a king. Blood oozed from his body, leaving a red trail following him through the air. There was only the pain. He would never see his companions, nay, his friends again. He was just another victim to the harsh bloodbath of the Shadowfront, just another nameless corpse in the mountain of decay. He would never see his brother again …

He would never see — no. He would see him again. They had all promised to reach the Flame, and he would do anything to uphold his end of the bargain. He would do anything to embrace his dear brother one final time.

Even if it meant allowing his power complete control over his body. Even when his power had overwhelmed him, there was still a small fraction of SmibSmob that remained, battling to surface in the endless abyss. But what if he just … let it win? What if he completely succumbed to his twisted side? He was repulsed by the thought. This is what Ashyla had shown him, and he had been terrified ever since. He hated his vile power, but what choice did he have? At any moment he would crash into the unforgiving ground. He would never see Nalgene again.

Tearing down his mental barriers, SmibSmob invited his power in. This was for his dear brother.

The darkness was more than happy to oblige.

The Shadow rushed in, devouring any remaining scrap of the pathetic gnome host. The gnome was gone. The darkness thrived. There would no longer be any pestering emotions, no longer be any irritating pangs of regret or remorse. The Shadow cared little for such pathetic feelings. All would be consumed by the Shadow. The dark being opened its eyes.

Two emotionless voids looked upon the world.

A nova of darkness burst from the creature, cutting into anything that was caught in the dreadful blast. It did not matter if it was living or undead. The Shadow devoured all. An influx of revitalizing energy crackled through the creature. Broken ribs bound back together. Shattered arms wove themselves back together. Perfect. It would not do to have a damaged host.

Twisting about on the earth, the creature managed to get its feet underneath it and leaped up into the cold air. It did not leap far, but it was far enough to leave the stone ground below. It raised its hands, and razor beams of darkness arced forth, cutting down everything with reckless abandon. Shadowy tendrils writhed about the being, decimating all that wandered too nearby. The skeletal giant lunged at the dark being, but the being remained in place. It was far above such insignificant pests.

It raised its hand, and a spiraling beam of power arced from its fingertips, surging towards the skeletal annoyance and piercing into its massive skull. The beam twisted and turned, looping around to strike the undead abomination again and again. The giant desperately tried to fend itself against the darting beam of vile energy, but it was all for nothing. Its remaining arm was severed at the shoulder, and one of its legs was broken at the knee. Roaring, the giant toppled to the ground like a felled tree, crushing many under its massive body. And still the beam continued its relentless barrage. Weaving through the giant like a black python, cutting through bone as if it were made of butter. Satisfied, the dark being lowered his hand. The giant was nothing more than a mound of shattered bone.

A hulking abomination appeared before the dark being, its many bulking arms flailing about to crush the being. A host of mighty zombies and undead skeletons accompanied the bulbous monster, and they charged at the vulnerable being.

Or so they thought it was vulnerable.

Unconcerned with the massive swarm of approaching enemies, the creature raised its hand once more, and a beam of pure darkness shot out, disintegrating dozens of the lesser undead. Spiked arms came crashing down all about the being, but it deftly wove through the flurry of attacks, casting more dark beams as it wove across the battlefield.

Another hulking behemoth appeared, and it charged at the frail being, its arms mauling anything that dared come too close. There was no possible way for the dark being to escape.

The creature snorted. This was child's play.

Raising both hands, it conjured a mighty vortex of black between the two abominations. The dark hole of nothingness swirled and pulsed with an otherworldly life, and with terrifying power, it pulled the two rotting behemoths into its endless abyss, ending their wretched existence. The decaying masses tried to resist, tried to strike back at the shadowy being, but nothing could escape the grasp of a black hole. The Shadow would consume all.

Turning, the vile being looked at the towering stronghold of stone at the end of the valley, an evil grin wide on its face. While devouring endless insects of rot was certainly fulfilling, there was a much more ... scrumptious option. The Shadow would consume all. And what better meal than the Light? Legions of battle-hardened Sparks manned impervious barricades, raining down formidable spells of fire upon the unsuspecting legions of undead far below. Great columns of fire burst from the ground, and a steady rain of flaming arrows arced into the writhing fray. There were the unfortunate Sparks who found themselves within the throng of the Shadowfront, but they were usually heavily supported by the warriors of the Flame high above. The spearhead that the being had seen earlier had reached the base of the great wall and was being escorted in by a host of Sparks. The dark being laughed. It did not care how many supposed "soldiers" there were. He would devour them all. The Shadow consumed all.

Cackling hysterically, the vile being soared toward the mighty stronghold, devastating spells of darkness forming within his hands. How long could the stone guardian withstand his terrifying barrage of power? There was only one way to find out.

But before the being could unleash its destructive barrage, a woman appeared in the air before it. Two amber eyes sparkled on her scarred face, and her hair was like a dancing flame. Blood was trickling from the side of her head, but the being had little time to ponder the curious fact. Who was this insect, and how dare she interrupt its grand march of triumph? Its two, inky voids locked upon the woman, and its clenched fist shot out, a swirling orb of black forming over the knuckles. So be it. She would be devoured too. But the woman held her ground, and her olive hands darted forward to rest upon the being's chest.

Immediately, an incinerating pain coursed through the being, wracking its mind. Growling wildly, the being grasped the woman's wrists and attempted to tear her fiery touch away. The woman's arms quivered with effort, but she did not relent. She had no other choice. She had to save SmibSmob.

Another fiery burst coursed through the dark beings, tearing away some of the corrupting darkness.

YOU SHALL NOT PERISH TODAY!

A commanding voice cut into the being's thoughts, but it was quickly lost under the churning of the darkness. A hiss escaped the being's mouth. It would play her game. Without warning, the being ceased attempting to push the woman away, and instead jerked on her wrists, pulling her towards itself. The woman stumbled forward, caught off balance by the sudden shift in force. The being's head snapped forward, cracking into the woman's face with a satisfying *crack*.

Blood splattered across Mariah's face, and a sharp pain cut deep into her. There was no doubt her nose was broken. But she did not relent. She had to save SmibSmob. Shaking her head, she wrapped her arms about the poor gnome in a warming embrace. As Ashyla had showed her: "There is nothing to fear anymore."

And so, she had escaped the dreadful clutches of Calitha to rescue him, and there was nothing she would stop at to succeed. He did not deserve his dark powers. He did not deserve to be constantly hounded by a black wolf. He did not have to succumb to his unholy abyss. Yet he did anyway. All for a promise. All for love. It took a great person to make such a sacrifice. It took the Beacon. So, she had to save SmibSmob, even if it meant breaking her nose.

Another burning flame exploded within the dark being, searing away another fraction of its wicked abyss. It had to get the woman off it, but it could not move. She bound him in place. Every time it thought to strike the woman, another traumatizing blast coursed through its body, rendering it helpless to the irritating woman.

The thundering voice returned in its head, nay, SmibSmob's head, commanding away the vile corruption.

THIS IS NOT YOUR DESTINY!

What did the voice know? The Shadow would devour all.

YOU ARE A BEING OF LIGHT!

A feral growl escaped the being's lips. It opened its mouth wide and clamped it down upon the woman's shoulder. Thick blood filled the being's mouth, enraging it even more. It bit down harder, digging into the woman's soft flesh with animal-like ferocity.

Mariah whimpered in pain, but she did not relent. She had to save SmibSmob. She was slowly driving away the eternal blackness, decimating it with a barrage of blazing attacks. There was no doubt that the shadowy power greatly aided SmibSmob in combat, but at what cost? Was it worth all the sorrow it brought? No. It was not a difficult question for her to answer.

Still biting down upon the woman's flesh, the dark being drove his knee up, connecting with her groin with staggering force. It felt the woman grow weak under the impact.

Perfect.

It drove its knee up, again and again, smashing into the woman's groin with more and more force.

Buckling under the constant blows, Mariah's vision grew hazy. Her stomach churned, and she had to resist the urge to vomit. Blood began trickling down her leg as the frail gnome pounded yet another knee into her. Her head was swimming with a dull pain. She wanted to let go, but she knew she could not. She had to save SmibSmob. She would endure whatever pain it took to decimate the roiling shadow within him. No matter her physical torment, it paled in comparison to the horror the gnome had suffered. Growling with determination, she embraced SmibSmob even tighter, casting her powers back into his thin frame.

Another smoldering explosion rocked the dark being, cutting away more of the darkness within.

CAST AWAY THE SHADOW!

It growled menacingly, and bit down harder, its teeth grinding on bone. It was the Shadow. No, it was a gnome.

YOU ARE NO LONGER BOUND BY THE CHAINS OF DARKNESS!

It was SmibSmob. It ceased its ruthless barrage of knees, and its vicious bite loosened. SmibSmob spat thick blood from his mouth, his mind whirling about in confusion.

What was happening?

He tried to make sense of his surroundings, but the darkness rushed back in with a renewed fury, washing him away under a tide of black. The dark being reached with its hands and clawed at the woman's hair, tearing away fiery chunks of scalp. The woman gasped with anguish, which only served to redouble the being's efforts.

CAST AWAY THE VOID!

The being's body quivered violently. He, nay, it had to stop this woman. It would not relent its control.

YOU ARE NOT A MINION OF DARKNESS!

The being's head whipped up; its mouth opened in a silent scream of horror. It had to stop the woman. It had to keep its control. It would devour her. The Shadow consumed all.

Below them on the walls of the keep, the Sparks were chanting and pointing at the spectacle in the air. "Can it be? Is it her? It's Mariah! She has returned!"

But the being didn't hear them. Gods didn't listen to the chittering of rats. Its only focus was to remove itself from the grasp of the wretched woman. All else was inconsequential.

It tried to move, but its body would not respond to its will. This was all wrong. There was nothing that could survive the unforgiving tide of Shadow. There was nothing that could fend off the black army. Except for this woman, apparently. This vile, damned woman. Insects were not supposed to be able to crush a man.

YOU ARE SMIBSMOB!

The being wanted to deny it, but it was hopeless. The woman had won. The woman had neutralized the great beast of Shadow. The two black eyes burst into flame, incinerating the darkness within.

COME TO THE LIGHT, MY BEACON!

The darkness was torn away from SmibSmob, each remaining remnant being smitten down by a brilliant ray of fire. SmibSmob's eyes returned to their gentle blue, and a rush of air filled his lungs. He was free. His dark powers were no more, obliterated by Mariah. His mind swayed with exhaustion, but he was free. Even still, he felt empty, as if a great part of himself were missing. Indeed, a great part of him *was* missing, but SmibSmob would be ever thankful for that. He glanced down to the beautiful woman who now held him suspended in the air. Blood streaked down her face, and her fiery hair was ragged, with patches having been torn out by his very hands. She was shaking, and with every breath came a soft whimper. But her eyes beamed with triumph.

"Thank you," SmibSmob whispered, his voice shaky. He

was forever in her debt. Because of her, he could still see Nalgene. He leaned forward and returned her embrace.

"Come, let us find your friends," Mariah finally said after a long moment. Her whole body ached, but she ignored her problems for the sake of SmibSmob. She knew it would not be long before Calitha found her and roped her back into her winding labyrinth. Saber did not want her to interfere with her grand scheme, and who better to imprison her than the Daughter of Despair? Sighing, Mariah led SmibSmob out of the Shadowfront, gently carrying him over the mighty wall and into the realm of the Flame.

As SmibSmob crossed out of the Shadowfront, his eyes were blessed with a holy sight. The sun. And not the cold, distant sun of the Shadow. Nay, this was the warm, inviting sun of the light. A bright, blue sky glowed above him, and it was all he could do to stare in wonder. A gentle breeze caressed his skin, enveloping him in a peaceful blanket. It was beautiful. After countless days of barren gray, it was hard to imagine the wondrous world of Light. A tear trickled down his pale cheek.

The battling Sparks watched the pair soar over the wall, but they did not attack. They had been given strict orders to hold their fire. Strict orders from a General.

Landing on the ground behind the wall, Mariah gently released SmibSmob. Tears beaded in her eyes, but she held them in check.

"Thank you," SmibSmob repeated, a wide smile glowing on his face. "And I apologize. I don't mean to be the obvious one, but I injured you quite badly."

Mariah chuckled, her white teeth sparkling under the warm sun.

"Ah, don't worry about me," she said, her melodious voice sounding like songbirds in the cool air. She nodded and pointed behind SmibSmob. "I think they would be happy to see you."

Before SmibSmob could guess at who she meant, a loud, barreling voice cut through the air.

"SmibSmob!" Nalgene cried, sprinting over to SmibSmob. Without thinking if SmibSmob was injured, Nalgene wrapped his arms around him, squeezing with a brotherly embrace.

"I be so glad yer alright," Nalgene mumbled, tears streaming down his face. "We be just about to go back out and get you. I be seein' ye all dark ... and ..." he tried to say more, but he choked on his words.

Radiating with joy, SmibSmob returned the embrace, tears flowing down his face. He did not need to say anything. He had felt empty in the absence of his dark power, but right now, holding his dear brother, he had found his remedy. SmibSmob glanced behind him, wanting to say one final thanks to Mariah. But the fiery woman was already gone. Shaking his head, SmibSmob turned back to his brother. It did not matter. He had *far* more important things to worry about.

The other companions rushed over to the pair of gnomes, smiles wide upon their beaming faces. They were all injured and covered in blood, but they had survived the horrors of the Shadowfront. It did not matter what terrible things they had witnessed. What mattered was the now, with them all together at last.

SmibSmob felt a strong hand upon his shoulder, and he turned to see Ro standing next to him. Blood caked the draconian's scales, and he was curiously missing his shining plate mail, but he was alive and thriving.

"Good to have you back, my friend," Ro said.

Before SmibSmob could reply, another set of strong, yet still injured, arms wrapped him in a loving embrace.

"Friend alive!" Fasto cried in glee, torrents of tears raining down his face. "Gnome friend alive!" Fasto's arms were damaged, but that would never stop him from celebrating with his friends.

"Good observation, Fasto" Margaret teased. There was no heavy sarcasm in her voice. It was simply a friend teasing another.

The orc turned to SmibSmob, a genuine smile on her face. "I'm glad you're alright."

She too was missing her armor. But her demonic arm was dormant at her side. It had seen enough bloodshed this day.

"Mmmm, I second that," Andromeda said, stepping up to stand next to Ro. Her soft tail reached out and brushed against SmibSmob's back. She appeared the most ragged out of the companions. Her black fur was matted in bloody patches, and she leaned heavily on one leg. Even so, her eyes sparkled with joy. She had found something to fight for.

"I'm glad you are all safe," SmibSmob said, choking on his emotions. It was all so overwhelming for the little gnome. Before he could continue, he spotted another person approaching them.

"Oh, fantastic," Margaret chuckled, shaking her head. This time sarcasm was oozing through her words. "Just who I wanted to see."

"Bloody hell," Nalgene grumbled, finally releasing his brother and turning to see the newcomer.

General Kraalek skipped towards the companions, his billowing cloak flowing out behind him like a crimson wave. His hood draped over his pale face, and his two eyes gleamed mischievously. He was running his strange, metallic cards nimbly through his fingers. Noticing their gazes, he gave them an exaggerated bow with a crooked smirk on his face. Standing up, he threw his arms out wide, gesturing to the surrounding area.

"What do you think?" He asked. His metallic cards had disappeared.

SmibSmob stared at the sly man for a long moment. He remembered how the two Sparks, Roan and Dain, had spoken about this man, and he could not bring himself to argue with them. There was no doubt in his mind that Kraalek spent more than a few nights in the beds of barmaids.

That man was definitely no amateur.

"I be thinkin': What in the bloody hell are ye doin' here,

Kraalek?" Nalgene replied, his voice gruff. Nalgene had never come to trust the sly man, and SmibSmob could not really blame him. This man was a trickster, but an undeniably clever trickster.

"Why, isn't it obvious?" Kraalek chuckled. "I have come to welcome you to the Flame!" He dipped into another dramatized bow, the cowl of his hood brushing against the ground. Before the companions could reply, he shot back up.

"Oh, I almost forgot." He reached into one of his many pouches, his nimble fingers digging through its contents. His face lit up, and he pulled out a strange, wooden die. None of the faces were marked. It was the same one from the great Ruins of Calinad. He ran the mysterious object through his fingers, allowing the companions to observe its blank faces. He was always the showman. Smirking, he released the die, and it tumbled across the stony ground to land at SmibSmob's feet.

The gnome glanced down at the wondrous object and then back up to Kraalek. As far as he could tell, the face-up side was no different from the others.

Kraalek chuckled, and his eyes twinkled with mischief.

"You've won. Isn't that right?"

*E*pilogue

Saber trekked through the shadowy forest. Black trees loomed all about her, blocking the gray sky in an interwoven canopy. Branches reached for her with razor claws, but they did not touch her. They would not dare. A thick mist seeped from the ground, covering the tangled brush in an opaque blanket. Skulking undead watched her through the dark trees, their hollow eyes feeding upon her pale skin. They followed her everywhere, a pack of wolves hunting its prey, but they dared not attack. They could not. The Mistresses held them on a tight leash, reigning them in whenever their insatiable hunger dared get the best of them. And for as long as Saber remained on their merciful side, she was in no danger — she hoped. In truth, they terrified her. For whom they were and what they are now. For what their hollow existence *meant*.

She would never forgive Ashyla for it.

As she stomped through the murky woods, an uneasy miasma settled over her. This was not her domain. She spent most of her time managing the Flame, carefully manipulating the Torch to think they had hope against the oppressive Shadow, even though she worked against their cause. She had become quite fond of the radiance of the sun and the warmth of the air. It was a shame it would not last for much longer.

A boiling rage simmered deep within her. Her black sword flashed, cutting through the surrounding bracken as she walked. She could not understand why Ashyla had not yet slaughtered the miserable band of misfit companions. They were destined to strike her down, so what good was there in keeping them alive? They could be the doom of everything they — *she* — worked for. The thoughts burned deep in Saber's mind. She had attempted to deal with the companions herself, but there was only so much she could do without directly opposing Ashyla. Just what was the Goddess's plan?

Saber had thought herself quite clever by using the Captain to decimate the companions. Oh, how he groveled and begged at her feet at the mention of his poor family. Pathetic. There was no room for love in the winding abyss of the Shadow. But, for some unknown reason, the Captain failed. Even with the threat of his family looming over his miserable head, he faltered in his one moment of triumph.

Saber lashed out with her sword, cutting it deep into a nearby tree. A feral growl escaped her rosy lips, and she wrenched her sword free, only to slash it back into the black trunk.

What a pathetic excuse of a man.

But that was not the worst part. Somehow, Ashyla caught wind of her devious plan and had cut it short in an all too extravagant manner. Saber smirked. As frustrating as it was, it did give her great satisfaction to watch.

But her moment of pleasure soon passed, washed away under her seething rage. No matter what she attempted, no matter how cunning or devious her plan, it always seemed to crumble. From the slimy Shadowfriend to the legion of rotting warriors she managed to convince a Mistress to send their way, the damned companions always managed to escape. She even forced them to battle through the unforgiving Shadowfront, yet still, they were alive and well. It was infuriating.

Fucking Ashyla.

Saber's black sword lashed out again, this time cutting clean through the mighty trunk of another tree. The twisted tree fell crashing to the ground, splinters and dust clouding the cool air. She did not understand the Goddess's apparent lack of concern. Another growl escaped her lips, and her eyes gleamed with a murderous light. No more backstabbing plans, it was time to take the matter into her own hands.

Saber continued her furious rampage deep into the dark woods, slashing wildly at anything that dared come too nearby. She knew that she would infuriate Ashyla with her actions, but she did not care. It had to be done. Either the bitch would come to her senses or be distracted long enough for Saber to devise an alternate, more permanent, solution.

After some time — more time than she would have liked — she came upon an open clearing. The black, empty sky swirled about like the gateway to the abyss. Towering mountain peaks could be seen over the trees to the west, watching Saber with stony gazes. The grass was shriveled and gray, but it seemed to shift in and out of focus, as if it were never quite there. It was always frustrating to find the barren clearing, as it never stayed in the same spot. Rather it shifted about, appearing and disappearing at the whims of its creator. And it seemed that its creator had not wished for Saber to find it.

Fucking Calitha, as well.

It didn't matter. Saber would play her childish game.

Floating at the center of the clearing was a thin, ghostly woman. She seemed more like a skeleton than a living being. A simple, gray dress draped over her frail form in a wave of silk. The woman had short, silver hair and a gruesome, oozing gash cut across the front her chest in the shape of a T. Thick blood trickled from the wound, creating red rivers running down the woman's white body.

Her eyes were sewn shut, and blood trickled down from her eyelids and over her hollow cheeks. Calitha did not need eyes to view the bleak world around her — not that there was much to see.

Saber shivered as she glared at Calitha. It was always unsettling dealing with the ghostly woman, but there was no other choice. It had to be done.

"How nice to keep me waiting, Calitha. You know I enjoy the walk," Saber called out to the tranquil woman. Oh, how she wished she could just cut down this floating specter. But wise judgment held her back. She did not wish to be trapped in Calitha's nightmarish labyrinth. "Do you have her?"

Calitha turned in the air to face Saber. Even though the ghastly woman's eyes were forever shut, Saber could not shake the feeling that Calitha was gazing straight through her, unraveling all her thoughts and emotions. It was always unsettling dealing with the ghostly woman. Calitha smiled, her white lips curling unnaturally, and her head tilted to the side, jutting her neck at a painful angle.

"Greetings, Sister," Calitha said, her voice nothing more than a thin wisp floating through the air. "I ever do enjoy your growing company."

Saber stared blankly at the floating woman. It was impossible to have a straightforward conversation with her. It was like talking to an infant — a rather grown, sickly infant.

"Do you have her?" Saber repeated. The sooner she finished this business, the better.

"Who do I have, Sister?" Calitha answered cryptically. "Many are lost within their own fears."

Saber sighed. It was never straightforward with her.

"You know what I want. Where is Mariah?" Saber hissed, growing impatient. She began to pace back and forth, her knee-high boots clicking on the soft ground below. Clicking? No, that didn't make any sense.

She did not ponder thought. She had to focus on far more important matters.

"Where is Mariah?" Calitha echoed. "Many are trapped in a place known only to themselves."

Saber growled. She did not have time for this annoying little game.

"Don't waste my time with these childish games. I know she escaped you," she pressed. Not for the first time, she wondered if she could indeed defeat this skeletal woman. How she wished to cut her down.

Calitha flinched slightly, straightened her legs, and gently lowered herself to the ground. The game was up. It was time for business.

"And what of it, Sister?" she whispered, striding towards Saber. "There are those who can fight beyond their fears."

Saber did not respond, instead choosing to glare at the approaching woman.

Calitha's voice grew high pitched, and it seemed the whole clearing was speaking for her. "Do you accuse me of releasing her, Sister?" Her pale feet seemed to phase in and out of the ground, as if she was never quite where she seemed. "To lie is to be lost within your darkest fears …"

Saber took a step back as sweat flushed over her body. It was hardly an empty threat, and she had little desire to be forever lost in Calitha's ever-changing labyrinth. She raised her hands before her defensively and eyed the gruesome wound on Calitha's chest with trepidation. Oh, how she wished to cut down this insolent woman. Her bubbling rage still burned, but fear reminded her not to draw her black sword.

"I'm not here to fight," Saber said, her voice shaky and gentle. "I am here for Mariah. Nothing more. So, the sooner you hand her over, the sooner I can take leave of your … humble abode."

Calitha laughed an unnatural sound that grated against Saber's ears. "Is it a humble abode, Sister? Is it a lie that you are bestowing upon me?"

Saber did not answer, but her eyes darted around in panic.

It was never straightforward dealing with this woman.

Calitha halted her steady advance, and her head tilted to the side once more.

"Mother is not going to be pleased," she warned, her voice growing soft once more. Her silver hair waved behind her, even though there was no wind. She was nervous.

Saber raised an eyebrow. Good, maybe Calitha will stop acting like a child.

"Ashyla's not going to know," she replied to soothe the pale woman. In truth, Saber was nervous as well. It was just that her anxiety was buried deep under a red storm of rage. It had to be done. There was no other way. "I entrusted you with her, so now all I am asking is for you to return her. Ashyla's not going to know."

Calitha nodded but remained silent. This was no time for games. The Mother never took kindly to such open acts of disobedience, but Calitha agreed with Saber, at least partially. She did not understand Ashyla's apparent lack of concern for the recent events. It had to be done.

Raising her hands, the clearing suddenly grew dark and ominous. Not a single disturbance could be heard in the clearing. Even if Saber tried to speak, no sound would come forth. The black sky above the clearing roiled and bubbled, churning like a boiling pot of water. The laceration across Calitha's chest began to fold open, revealing the terror underneath, and Saber averted her gaze from the ghastly sight.

But as quickly as it started, the oppressive silence disappeared, along with the growing darkness. The inky sky returned to its tranquil calm, as if nothing had happened. Satisfied, Calitha curled her pale legs, and returned to her floating perch in the cold air. She did not care to know what Saber wanted Mariah for. The less she knew, the better.

"Mother must not know, Sister." Calitha said, her voice wavering under the stress. Unlike Saber, she would, for the moment, remain loyal to Ashyla, even after the strange turn of events. It was never wise to play Mother's game.

Saber smiled and glanced up.

"Don't worry, Daughter. She will never know." Satisfied, she turned about, only to find a beaten and bloody Mariah laying upon the soft ground. It was always unsettling dealing with the ghostly woman, but it did have its uses. She had to open Ashyla's eyes. And drastic times called for drastic measures. It had to be done. A smirk twisting her rosy lips, Saber stood over the bloodied Mariah as a lion would its prey. Her eyes drove into the fiery woman.

"So nice to finally see you again," Saber sneered. "Wouldn't you agree?"

Mariah said nothing, and tried to rise to her feet, but a brutal kick from Saber kept her in the dirt. Tears welled up in her eyes, but she held them back, she would not give Saber the satisfaction of seeing her broken. Oh, how she wanted to retreat into her despair, but she did not. She had saved the companions. There was still hope, and that twinkling spark is what she clung onto. For what else could she do?

Chuckling maniacally, Saber thrust another kick into Mariah's ribs. She was going to enjoy this. It was not that she hated Mariah; nay, she did not hold anything against the fiery woman. Rather, she was just another victim to Saber's seething fury. Saber's thoughts flashed with visions of Ashyla, and the smug look she bore as she summoned a dreadknight to slaughter the poor Captain.

"You bitch," Saber growled, jabbing a third kick into Mariah. As she roiled in her frustrating thoughts, she lashed out with a fourth kick, and then a fifth. With each blow came a sickening *thud* and a delicious whimper.

The companions had to die, and Saber had to take matters into her own hands. So be it. It had to be done. There was no other way. She had to guarantee her salvation.

Pathetic moans of pain trickled from Mariah, but the proud woman still refused to cry. No matter the cost, or the pain, she had rekindled Ansalon's hope. The Beacon had come; may the Shadow quake in his presence. No amount of darkness could last forever. There was always a Light that would bring back the shining dawn. At least that is what she told herself. Right now, while being beaten by Saber, it seemed a feeble thought indeed.

Howling with pleasure, Saber hounded over the pathetic woman. Gashes and bruises marred Mariah's olive skin, and blood trickled down her alluring figure. Reaching out, Saber grasped the woman's orange hair and pulled her to her feet. Mariah's scalp was scabbed, and chunks of her hair were missing, but Saber did not care why. Just a consequence of Calitha's labyrinth, she supposed. Saber glared at the miserable woman, her eyes shooting raging lances of flame. Mariah struggled to break free of Saber's iron grip. But there would be no escape for her now. There would be no one to set her free.

Saber pulled the woman close and inhaled her pleasant scent. She smelled of a cool, autumn day, tainted by the heavy scent of iron from her blood. Saber smiled, the wicked, devious smile of a tormentor.

"I hope they remember you when you're gone," Saber whispered in Mariah's ear, her voice cutting like a frozen dagger. She pulled away from Mariah and looked deep into her amber eyes.

Mariah's look of pure, uncontrollable terror was one that Saber would not forget.

She would most certainly enjoy this.

◆   ◆   ◆

Ashyla studied the mangled corpse of Mariah. She wasn't revolted or disgusted by the gruesome scene; she wasn't even angry about it. Rather, she was disappointed. The Sister was pulling her leash taut.

Sword gashes covered Mariah's body, and patches of skin were torn from various places, leaving dark splotches of dried blood and raw flesh. The fiery woman's luxurious red dress had been stripped away, leaving Mariah battered and naked on the cold stone ground. Her limbs were spread in unnatural directions — the torturer certainly took their time breaking them, letting Mariah agonize over each mutilated limb — and a gruesome cut ran across the right side of her face, leaving a bloody socket where her eye had once been. Most disturbingly, a flaming cross had been deliberately etched into Mariah's chest. The symbol of the Flame.

The symbol of the Beacon.

Ashyla had little doubt as to who had done this dastardly deed. There was only one person she knew who would mutilate such a kind woman in this way. It was a shame, surely, for Ashyla was quite fond of the fiery woman. As she said, Mariah always had a safe place in her withering heart.

But it did not matter now, Mariah was gone, and there would be no bringing her back from the cold clutches of death. Only one was capable of such a feat and it wasn't her. She sighed and drew her marvelous sword, turning it over in front of her. Saber was always so blindly angry. And always so blindly stupid. Just another child regretfully fixated on the lovely companions.

Sighing again, Ashyla sheathed her sword, and reached down, straightening the brutalized corpse as best she could. It was not Mariah's time to die, but what could she do? Ashyla had no power over people's fate. Ashyla narrowed her eyes.

She had little power at all.

Ashyla scanned the gruesome corpse of Mariah once more, only to rest upon the hollow eye socket. Her thoughts danced in her fractured mind. Who knew it would be so difficult? Everybody pranced about like worthless sheep in a meadow, chanting that their cause was just and that they deserved the world. Everyone thought they were the "good" and the righteous.

But what of *her* cause? Was it not just? *They* killed all her beautiful children; *they* stole everything from her, and she just wanted it back. She needed it back.

Was that not a noble cause?

A lone tear fell from her eye and wove down her face. Why was it so painful? She never asked for this; her garden was blissful. How many deaths would haunt her before she could know peace?

With a sudden screech Ashyla stomped on Mariah's face, caving in her skull with a *crunch.* Blood splattered up her leg, but she didn't notice.

As quickly as it came, her fury passed, buried once more. Ashyla straightened herself, wiped the tear from her face, and turned away from Mariah.

Ashyla was never fond of traitors, and this was most surely an act of defiance. So be it. Her patience could only be worn so thin before it violently snapped. Insolent, arrogant child. Saber never did learn. Such a shame. Ashyla always did think of her as the more … interesting sister.

Ashyla strutted out of the barren, stone room, leaving a bloody trail as she walked. She didn't look back. Mariah's corpse would no doubt rot away into oblivion, forever lost in the room. She did not care. Just another carcass in the annals of time. Eventually, they all blend into one.

Ashyla's eyes shone with a green fire. *Her* cause was just. She would break that damning seal. She would undo what was done. She would repair the damage that miserable cretin had inflicted. She would avenge her children that they horrifically slaughtered. She would regain what they stole from her. And if that meant she had to rend it from this broken world with the vile claw of the Shadow, she wouldn't hesitate. Any who dared stand against her would be devoured by the ever-ravenous darkness.

So be it. They insisted on dying.

How … tragic.

About the Author

Daniel Whitman is an engineer who, on the side, loves to dabble in the realm of fantasy. He grew up reading fantasy books and playing games such as Dungeons & Dragons, Magic: The Gathering, and Diablo. Now, he is taking this childhood passion and crafting his own stories.

Daniel's passion is for dark fantasy, with a special interest in morally complex characters and heart-wrenching moments. He wrote his first book, *A Land in Shadow*, while he was still in high school. Now, in graduate school, he is continuing the adventures of both engineering and writing!